Elaine Doll

Christmas 2015
Joe + Debbie gave me
Beth Moore "to live to
Christ"

I traded for this
"The blessed Christian
Life" + $8 cash
already had Beth Moore

Whispers from the Soul

Elaine Doll

abbott press®
A DIVISION OF WRITER'S DIGEST

Whispers from the Soul

ISBN: 978-1-4582-0362-5 (sc)
ISBN: 978-1-4582-0363-2 (e)
ISBN: 978-1-4582-0364-9 (hc)

Library of Congress Control Number: 2012907958

Abbott Press books may be ordered through booksellers or by contacting:

Abbott Press
1663 Liberty Drive
Bloomington, IN 47403
www.abbottpress.com
Phone: 1-866-697-5310

Printed in the United States of America

Abbott Press rev. date: 05/25/12

For my loving husband, Charles, who has given me the support and encouragement I needed to write this book. His unconditional love and sweet spirit has made me a better woman.

Acknowledgements

To my dear cousin, Sandra Anderson, my deepest thanks and gratitude for your loyal support, your hours of proof reading, your prayers, and for holding me accountable to my writing schedule in a positive and uplifting way. You kept me from giving up when I was discouraged, and I can't thank you enough for that.

Many thanks to my very dearest life-long friend, Gladys Adams, for always believing in me, and for giving me your vote of confidence. Your friendship has been an inspiration and a blessing to me.

And thank you to Abbott Press and all who helped me make this long awaited dream come true.

Chapter 1

Oklahoma Territory 1893

LEOMA'S BREASTS WERE HARD, a painful reminder that she would never again nurse Elizabeth. Soggy earth soaked through her long wool skirt, and icy dampness numbed her knees from kneeling so long. The sight of the tiny pine casket was blurred through hot, salty tears. Leoma pulled her woolen cape more snugly around her shoulders and shivered between choking sobs.

"First my husband; now my only child! How much more will you take from me, God? How much more?" First Jeremy had been shot and killed, and then her baby had died. All that remained for Leoma was an empty house and dashed dreams.

Without her beloved Jeremy, the idea of going on alone in this desolate town seemed futile. And with baby Elizabeth gone, her house was a hollow shell that echoed with sorrow. Would it ever again be filled with happiness and laughter? She didn't expect life to be always fun or easy, but this was more than she could bear.

Wondering if God had deserted her, Leoma lingered at the open grave alone. Moments earlier, Reverend Gilroy and his young wife had driven away in their surrey, and soon after, her neighbors, George and Anna Jo Langley, had drifted toward home on foot. Oh, how she longed for the loving arms of her father and mother, but they lived far away.

Light mist shrouded the town. A frigid chill caused her teeth to chatter, but Leoma couldn't pull herself away from the gaping hole. For the briefest moment, she let her eyes stray through the gray haze. Across the cemetery, a tall, hunched man leaned like a giant question

1

mark on his shovel, waiting to fill her daughter's grave. The thought of him throwing piles of dirt over the box that held her tiny infant brought another agonizing sob from the pit of Leoma's being. Her head dropped forward; her chin rested on her chest. What was it her father had said so many times over the years? God would not give a person more pain or suffering than he could bear. But Leoma's heart was so heavy she couldn't comprehend that teaching right now. How could it be true? *God, if what my father said is true, I desperately need your help—if you hear me. I want to believe Daddy's words, Lord. I can't endure another day, unless you give me the strength.*

A ray of sunshine pierced the gray clouds. Still kneeling, Leoma straightened her back to relieve the burning ache in her spine and welcomed the heavenly warmth on her shoulders. She lifted her face for a moment, soaking in the gentle heat. Perhaps this was God's promise of brighter days ahead. *Oh, let it be so, Lord.*

A deep male voice interrupted her solitude. She flinched. "Excuse me, ma'am. Are you Mrs. Fisk?"

Leoma stole a sideways glance at the man. A pair of muddy work boots filled the space beside her. Rising from the worn boots were log-like legs covered in rain-soaked denim overalls. Her eyes continued upward, beyond the expansive trunk and broad shoulders, into the face of anguish. Eyes as forlorn as the gray winter sky gazed down at her. She hadn't heard him approach and didn't appreciate him imposing on her last moments with her baby. Leoma looked away from the stranger and dabbed her nose with a soggy, crumpled handkerchief.

"I know this is a bad time, ma'am, but Doctor Rhodes said I should talk to you right away. He said maybe you'd, well, my baby boy is starving."

Unable to conceal her frown and numb from exhaustion, Leoma craned her neck to look up at the man again. The physician hadn't been able to save Elizabeth. Now he apparently couldn't save this man's child, either. What kind of doctor did this town have, and why would he send a stranger to her at a time like this? It seemed the entire population of this forsaken dust-hole was void of proper manners or empathy. Couldn't the man see she was burying her child? She wanted to be left alone.

Several moments passed before Leoma quelled the uncharacteristic contentiousness that had welled up within her. The man appeared as grief-stricken as she was. She said softly, "I don't understand what you want from me."

She stood slowly, her legs stiff from kneeling in the wet snow-crusted dirt. Her body shook, and for a moment, her legs almost failed to support her. Several weeks had passed since she'd slept soundly, and her stomach was empty. Eating and sleeping had held little importance these days.

Back on that lovely summer morning when Leoma had learned she was carrying her first child, she'd been elated. The world and everything in it was perfect. She had a wonderful husband and a lovely home, and she carried a child in her womb. Now, next to her husband's grave, their daughter lay in a wooden casket. Everything good and wonderful was gone in a flash. *A lot of good your prayers did, Mama.* Mama was always praying about something.

Immediately ashamed of her disparaging thoughts, Leoma cupped her hands against her face and tried to squelch her anger. She sucked in a deep breath and exhaled the warmth onto her cold hands.

"Ma'am." It was the deep voice of the stranger standing beside her. Leoma started, shaken from her meandering thoughts and intermittent outbursts. Through burning eyes she turned to face him and cringed. The smell of sour alcohol and cigarette smoke mixed with foul body odor accosted her senses, causing her to step back.

"Excuse me." Leoma's voice was distant, cold. "I don't know why Doctor Rhodes sent you to me. I can't possibly help you."

Leoma didn't want to talk to this repulsive man or anyone else. How rude that he approached her here. "Go away!" she wanted to scream, but she bit her lips together. Arms crossed tightly across her chest, she shivered. Her gaze dropped to the ground.

"I'm sorry for your loss, ma'am. But you see, the doctor told me you are the only hope for saving my boy from starving to death."

"What about his mother?" Leoma's words were cold, almost harsh, and she winced at the sound of her raised voice. She didn't mean to be ungracious, but she knew nothing about this person or his family,

3

and she didn't know why he expected her to help him. She was in no condition to help herself, much less anyone else.

The man's head lowered until his bearded chin rubbed the bib of his stained overalls. After a moment, he lifted his head. His eyes glazed as he spoke in choked words. "My wife's buried over yonder." His head jerked toward the other side of the cemetery, where the gravedigger stood. "She died last week, just hours after birthing our son, Dyer."

Leoma's voice dropped to a near-whisper. "I'm sorry. But what do you want from me?"

The man bobbed his head several times, looking into the distance, as if searching for words. When he finally looked at her again, his face, what she could see of it beneath the scraggly whiskers and beard, flushed red. He cleared his throat and stammered. "I'm sorry for my bad manners, ma'am. I'm Welby Soderlund." He hesitated and began again. "Doctor Rhodes said since you just gave birth a few days ago, you could maybe wet nurse my son. He won't take cow's milk in one of those glass feeders, and we've tried everything else. The boy is withering away. Doc said maybe you'd be willing to nurse him until he's stronger and old enough to eat regular food."

Brighter crimson peeked through patches of Welby Soderlund's thick, reddish-brown whiskers all the way down his neck, where the V of his dirty collar met. His gaze lowered again, and after a long pause, he glanced left and then right as if lost.

The pain in her full breasts reminded Leoma she would never again nurse her baby girl. But how could she be expected to feed a stranger's child? How could she put this man's son to her breast without her heart being ripped into a million pieces? *It doesn't seem fair, God, to put me in this position. How can I do this? I can't. I can't!* Leoma pressed the tips of her fingers to her tightly shut lips, trying to focus her scattered and confused thoughts. She shook her head. It was impossible. Impossible!

"I can't help you, Mr. Soderlund. Please excuse me." Leoma turned away from the man, away from the grave, and ran to her house, the mud-soaked hem of her wool skirt nearly tripping her along the way.

Once inside, she slammed the front door to shut out the bitter cold. Feet numb, she stood there for a moment, ready to collapse in the gray dimness of her foyer, gasping for breath, unable to move any farther. Sad memories whirled through her mind. The clock on the mantle ticked louder than usual. She wanted to run far, far away, yet she had no other place to go, no place to escape her grief. The momentary thought of returning to Boston was overshadowed by her desire to remain in this house, where she and Jeremy had planned to raise a family and live out their future. In spite of its emptiness, this was her home now, and she couldn't bear the thought of leaving it. Jeremy was everywhere; in the walls he'd built, in the fine woodwork he'd fashioned and polished with his own hands, in the elegant furnishings he'd provided. No, she couldn't leave no matter how painful it was to stay.

After several moments, Leoma forced her feet, one labored step at a time, up the stairs toward her bedroom. She dropped facedown across the bed she had once shared with the love of her heart; her beloved Jeremy. Oh how she needed his arms to comfort her and his kind words to console her. Though she would always grieve the loss of Elizabeth, at least if Jeremy hadn't been killed, she might have another child—perhaps several, as they'd planned. But that was impossible now. She rolled to her side and drew her knees to her chin, allowing her cries to fill the room. With the agony that squeezed the air from her lungs, she couldn't imagine living another day, let alone the rest of her life.

Gusts of wind beat against the house. A cold draft sifted through the windowsill. Still in damp clothes and cape, Leoma shivered. She wrapped her arms tighter around her bent knees. As evening fell, darkness shrouded the room. Losing all concept of time, her mind replayed the nightmarish events of the past weeks. She had no idea how long she'd been on the bed, until she heard the mantle clock in the front room downstairs begin to chime. She counted seven bongs. Only seven? It seemed time dragged by in slow motion, but what did it matter? Nothing demanded her attention, no one needed her.

No one?

She tried to ignore the question. Her stomach cramped in need of food, and she welcomed the gnawing pain. Bitter cold enveloped her, and for a while she submitted to it. The room grew dark and colder. She shuddered and crawled beneath the comforter, but sleep evaded her.

Suddenly, Welby Soderlund's words echoed in her ears, as if he stood beside the bed pleading with her. "My boy is starving. Doctor Rhodes said you're his only hope."

You must have mercy. Leoma jolted upright, wondering where the words had come from. Did she hear the faint whisper, or had she imagined it? Perhaps it was the wind playing tricks on her mind. Or was it? She was wide awake. Could it be God trying to get her attention? Maybe he hadn't abandoned her after all. She gazed into the darkness and listened.

Where is your compassion? Is your grief so great, you have no mercy for a dying child? This time the gentle whispers were very real, unlike anything she'd ever heard. Leoma trembled, certain now they were whispers from deep within God's soul. Her mind reeled as she tried to comprehend what was happening.

What if the Soderlund child died because she'd refused to reach beyond her selfishness to nurse him? Couldn't she step beyond her own feelings to spare the life of another? God would expect better of her, would he not?

Leoma covered her breast with the palms of her hands, acknowledging the discomfort there, and the longing to nurse her baby. She had within her life-saving nourishment. Maybe, maybe she could nurse Mr. Soderlund's son, at least until he became stronger. Unable to shake the image of another dying baby, another tiny casket being swallowed up by cold, dark, earth, she shuddered. Still she wondered how she could possibly carry out such a heart wrenching a task.

I will give you strength. Open your heart and your arms. Obey me, and your joy will be restored. Your reward will be great and your blessings many.

Never having had such divine promises impressed upon her heart, Leoma's entire body quaked. God was speaking to her. She sensed his presence and wanted to obey him. No matter how difficult it might be, she would nurse the Soderlund baby. She must try to keep him alive.

Leoma didn't know anything about Mr. Soderlund or where he lived, other than he dressed like a farmer. Most likely, he lived out of town, on one of the many farms that had cropped up in recent months. First thing in the morning she would ride into town and ask the doctor where to find the man.

Leoma's thoughts returned to the starving baby. She squeezed her eyes shut and prayed. "God, forgive my weakness and self-pity. I'm sorry for my bitterness and selfishness. Please, Lord, keep the Soderlund child breathing until morning, and help me find him. Give me extra strength to do your will, for I know now you have chosen me for this task. Please let the baby survive and thrive under my care."

It seemed she'd only dozed for a few minutes before she was awakened by howling wind as it beat against the windows. For several minutes, she lay listening, alert to the sounds in the night, wishing dawn would come. Unable to fall asleep again, Leoma sat up on the edge of the bed. A shiver almost sent her dashing back beneath the warm comforter, but she no longer wanted to sleep. She wondered if the Soderlund baby was still alive. Shivering violently, she stood in the cold darkness, and peeled off the damp clothes and shoes as fast as she could. She slipped into a long, flannel nightgown and dry stockings.

Even through the heavy woolen stockings the floor was icy cold, but she didn't care. Leoma put on a thick robe and tied it snugly at her waist. Eyes adjusting to her black surroundings, she made her way through the dim shadows, down the stairs and into the parlor. She lit the kerosene lamp on her writing desk and turned up the wick for brighter light. Her surroundings were illuminated by the yellow torch-like glow as she searched through several shelves of books, scanning the large collection for something to set her mind at ease. She ignored her favorites such as Nathaniel Hawthorn, passing over her coveted collection of poetry, included among the many, Keats and Browning. These were a mere fraction of the volumes she had planned to offer some day in her bookshop. Another dream dashed. A tired sigh escaped.

Words her father had frequently spoken echoed through the room. "If you keep your eyes on the goal you will succeed," he'd insisted. She wanted to believe her father's words, for he was a wise man, but it was impossible to focus on a dream right now, with so much loss and turmoil in her life.

Her hand touched the small, leather-bound Bible her parents had given her as a wedding gift. Leoma lifted it from the shelf and clutched it to her heart as she sat down in the Boston rocker; another treasured present from her mother and father.

Longing for the comfort of her mother's arms, Leoma thought about the letter she must write to her parents, to tell them of baby Elizabeth's death. How could she put into words the grief she felt, and the sorrow of losing their first grandchild? They would be broken-hearted. She wondered what advice her mother would give her about nursing Mr. Soderlund's starving infant.

Unable to read or write through tired, glazed eyes, Leoma continued to clutch the Bible, rocking back and forth, silently praying she would be able to save the Soderlund boy's life.

Chapter 2

STILL GROGGY FROM TOO much brandy the night before, Welby Soderlund shook himself awake at the sound of a crying baby. The break of dawn barely lit the room with gray haze. He pressed his hands to the sides of his throbbing head and groaned. After a moment he rubbed his eyes, attempting to focus on the girl standing beside his bed. Five-year-old Kristina watched him, her eyes droopy and red.

"Go make your brother stop that crying," he barked, wishing the pain in his skull would disappear. Kristina shook her head.

"He's hungry, papa. I'm hungry too."

Welby sat up holding his head, and tried to remember if he'd fed Kristina anything the day before. The girl knew how to help herself to fresh milk and what bread was left, and he was pretty sure there were crackers left in the jar on the kitchen table. He wasn't much of a cook. Other than bacon, which he usually burned to a crisp, about the only thing he knew how to fix were scrambled eggs. His flapjacks always ended up in the pig-slop pail. And the oatmeal he'd attempted to cook was so lumpy, the hogs refused to eat it. If the old sow and her young ones turned their noses up at the horrible mess, he could hardly expect Kristina to eat it, so he just quit trying to cook much of anything. Instead, he'd opened jars of vegetables or fruit Louise had canned. How would he ever make it without Louise and her good cooking?

Welby shooed his daughter from the room with a sweeping motion of his hand. "Go on now. Let me get my overalls on and I'll see what I can do."

Kristina shuffled out of the room, her head bowed and her bare feet taking tiny steps across the wooden floor. Welby could hardly watch her without falling to pieces. The girl was a miniature image of her mother. He shook his head and pulled on a dirty denim shirt and the same overalls he'd worn all week. His mind shifted back to his deceased wife. If Louise were alive she'd have Dyer nursed to contentment. The coffee would be brewed, and a hot breakfast would be waiting for him and Kristina on the kitchen table. He wouldn't be listening to that crying, and wondering how to feed two little ones.

Without looking in on his son, Welby pulled on his jacket and hurried straight to the barn. It wasn't as if he didn't care about the baby, he just didn't know what to do. As soon as he finished the milking and gathered the eggs from the hen house, he'd feed Kristina something to fill her stomach. Then he'd bundle up the two children and go into town. He had to find that widow woman and plead with her to nurse his son. It was the only chance the boy had to survive. With Louise gone, it sure would've been a whole lot easier taking care of only one child, but he had to find a way to keep his son alive.

A short time later and chilled to the bone, Welby came back into the house and set the pail of fresh milk on the kitchen table. Some slopped over the top. He started to tell Kristina to go outside and bring in the basket of eggs he'd left on the step, but she was nowhere in sight. The house was silent; not a whimper. His heart pounded as he rushed into the children's bedroom. Kristina was leaning over the cradle. His daughter had stuffed something in Dyer's mouth. What on earth was the girl thinking? Gasping, Welby rushed in and grabbed his daughter away from the boy. Then he stopped short, amazed at what he saw.

Dyer was sucking on a rag Kristina had placed in his mouth. At first, Welby had thought she was suffocating his son to stop the crying, but the baby sucked eagerly on the wet rag, like a new calf taking to its mother's teats.

"What are you doing?" Welby said in a low voice, not wanting to startle the baby.

"It makes him stop crying," Kristina said. "See how he sucks the sugar and water out of the rag?"

"I see. That's good, Kristina. But your brother needs milk."

"But he spits the milk out, and it makes him cry real hard." Kristina spoke like a concerned mother, far too old for her years. She was barely more than a toddler. Welby's heart knotted like a tight fist, and it was all he could do to hold back a sob.

It was true, the boy couldn't hold down cow's milk. The doctor had said goat milk might work, but there wasn't a goat in the entire community. He'd searched high and low already. How could he explain to Kristina that Dyer needed a mother's breast milk? Welby patted his daughter's head, sad that she carried so much weight on her little shoulders. It wasn't right, being saddled with so much grief and responsibility at her age. Already she'd experienced more bad things than many children did in their lifetime.

Welby forgot about the milk and eggs he'd gathered, and he forgot about feeding his daughter. "Put on your coat and shoes, Kristina, and bring me a blanket for Dyer. We're going into town right now to find help."

Whatever it took, he'd pay the price. He'd beg on bended knee, if that's what he had to do to save his son's life.

Kristina rushed around the room doing as she'd been told. Welby bundled the baby in the wool blanket and ushered his daughter out the front door.

IT SEEMED LIKE MORNING would never dawn, but at last, pale light seeped in through the windows. Leoma stoked the fire in the living room fireplace to take the chill out of the house. She stood near the roaring flames, holding her hands close the fire to soak in the warmth. After a moment, she went into the kitchen to build a fire in the cook stove, being careful to follow the instructions Jeremy had given her. With shaky hands, she filled the coffee pot with water from the hand pump over the sink, and scooped coffee grounds into the pot. She set the pot on the front burner to boil while she went upstairs to change into fresh clothing.

Leoma pulled off the robe and nightgown and dressed quickly, all the while thinking about the starving infant. She wondered if he'd survived through the night. Deciding not to garb herself in black, she put on a long petticoat and gray wool skirt that fell to her ankles and her blue, long-sleeved blouse. She did a hasty job of taming her curls, and twisted the heavy length of hair into a knot at the back of her neck, securing it with two long hairpins.

Eager for a cup of the fresh coffee, she hurried back downstairs. For the first time in weeks she felt like eating. As soon as she ate a piece of buttered bread slathered with homemade jam and drank her coffee, she would go to Doctor Rhodes' office to inquire about Welby Soderlund. If the doctor was out of town, perhaps the preacher could tell her where to find the man, although, she didn't recall ever seeing him in the church.

Thinking about nursing a strange child while her baby lay in that cold, hateful grave filled Leoma with apprehension, but she knew she must do it. She closed her eyes and sucked in a deep breath, determined to keep the tears at bay. She would keep her promise to God, no matter how difficult it might be to put that boy to her breast.

The wind had stopped howling around the house, and hints of somber daylight grew brighter. Leoma drew back the curtain on the window above the sink hoping sunshine would soon fill the kitchen. Standing near the cast iron cook stove, she breathed in the smell of boiling coffee. If she were back in Boston now, she would be enjoying the comfort of a coal-heated house. Rumor was that within two or three years, Oklahoma City would have piped in gas, and houses in town would have gas cook stoves. There was even talk about electric lights, but that seemed awfully far fetched, since she lived so far from any real cities. But she supposed anything was possible, with all the new businesses and houses being built.

If Jeremy were alive he'd be in the middle of all that construction, and he'd explain how electricity and piped in gas would work. Leoma didn't have many conveniences, but she was one of the few women lucky enough to have a water pump in her kitchen sink and a water closet with one of those pull-chain flush toilets. Thinking about Jeremy, she clasped her hands to her heart and smiled.

Sudden pounding on the front door startled her. Who would be calling on her so early in the morning? She hurried through the living room to see who it might be. As she rushed toward the door she glanced at the mantel clock. It was only six o'clock in the morning.

WELBY BUNDLED HIS SON the best he knew how, keeping the baby's face covered as he carried him through the fancy, white gate, and nearly ran up the steps of the Fisk's big house. His daughter stayed close beside him, clinging to his coattail when he reached the door.

Maybe if Mrs. Fisk took a look at Dyer, she'd take pity on the child and agree to nurse him. It was a lot to ask of the young woman, Welby realized that, especially after burying her own baby just yesterday, but it was his only hope to see his boy survive. Even if the woman started nursing the child right away, the doctor had warned him it might be too late. The only thing in the boy's favor was his momma carried him the full nine months, and he weighed eight pounds at birth. His wife had coaxed the baby to suckle two or three times, but her milk hadn't come in and she was weak. She'd died peacefully with the boy in her arms.

Welby gulped back the hurt and waited impatiently for someone to answer his knock. Now wasn't the time to get all pitiful over his loss. The door eased back a few inches.

Struck dumb by Mrs. Fisk's hollow eyes and red puffy rims, Welby almost apologized and turned to leave. Her face was pale and splotchy, yet she wore a faint smile and seemed hospitable.

"Good morning," she said eyes wide and clearly surprised. Welby was shocked by the lift in her voice, almost as if she were happy to see him.

Welby nodded, unable to remove his hat with the baby in his arms. "I'm sorry to call so early, ma'am. This is my son Dyer." Then he directed his nod and his eyes downward to his daughter. "And that's my girl, Kristina."

"Mr. Soderlund, I—"

"Please ma'am, before you say anything, I beg you to look at my boy. If you send us away he's going to die for sure. Doc says he won't live another two days without a mother's milk."

"Yes, I understand. The Lord worked on my heart all night long; he hardly let me sleep a wink. I was preparing to go momentarily to see the doctor, hoping he'd tell me where you live."

"You were?" Well, if that didn't beat it all.

"Yes, I was." Mrs. Fisk opened the door wider.

"That means you'll take my boy in for feeding?"

Before the woman could answer, Welby smelled the odor of burnt coffee. Sizzling noises came from somewhere inside the house. Suddenly, smoke billowed through the front room and toward the door.

"Oh, my!" Mrs. Fisk threw her hands into the air. "The coffee is boiling over." She ran through the house calling over her shoulder, "Come in, Mr. Soderlund. Bring the children in by the fire and close the door."

The young woman disappeared into another room. A moment later she came back looking frazzled. "I forgot about the coffee pot. I fear most of it boiled all over stove, but if you'd like a cup I'm sure there's enough left."

"No thank you, ma'am. I'm sorry to bother you so early, but—" He thrust his son toward the woman, hoping she would take the boy from him right then. There was no time to waste.

LEOMA TOOK THE BABY into her arms and gently pulled the blanket away from his face. The child was pale, his skin almost blue. Fine white fuzz capped his head. He was thin, limp, and appeared to be asleep. She looked up at the baby's father. His eyes were filled with concern and desperation. Much to her amazement, a sudden surge of milk brought tingling sensations to her breasts. Flustered and embarrassed, she covered herself with the baby's blanket before wet spots appeared on her blouse. She cleared her throat and gazed around the room. Certainly she wasn't going to nurse the child in front of this stranger who stood looking at her with anxious expectation.

"Would you like to sit down at the kitchen table and have a cup of coffee while you wait? Or perhaps you could leave your son with me for an hour or two and come back. I'll try to feed him right now but I need time and privacy. If he nurses successfully we can discuss a proper arrangement."

"Yes, ma'am, I umm—" The baby's father looked away, heat tinting his neck deep crimson. He pulled a neatly folded diaper out of his pocket and handed it to her. "You might need this. How about if my daughter and I come back after we have some breakfast in town, and we'll talk then?"

Leoma took the cloth and thanked him, keeping her tone gentle and caring. The cotton rectangle appeared unused. It was soft and the edges had been neatly hand-stitched just like the gown the boy wore. Even though the tiny garment was badly soiled, the fine workmanship was apparent. The child's mother must have spent the whole nine months, lovingly preparing for the arrival of this baby. "Yes, an hour is fine," Leoma said. "I should know by then if your son will let me nurse him."

Welby Soderlund and his daughter walked down the porch steps. A bit dismayed, Leoma shook her head. How long it had been since the man had bathed and put on clean clothes, or had his unruly, straw-colored hair washed and cut? And the poor little girl probably hadn't had a bath in over a week, nor had her head of wild dark hair been brushed in days. Who knew how many days she'd worn the same soiled dress? *Lord, bless the dear child. It isn't her fault.* The baby stirred in her arms and Leoma looked down at him, almost feeling trapped. Her heart wasn't prepared to feed a stranger's child. *Why, God did you allow this baby to live and let mine die? Why did you choose me for this task?*

This should be her child, her sweet little daughter. She inwardly scolded herself for allowing resentment and bitterness to creep into her heart, and though she didn't want to acknowledge it, holding the warm infant in her arms felt good. Her heart wasn't in to nursing him, but it was the right thing to do. She had a promise to keep, whether she liked it or not. Attempting to quell her distress, she walked into the parlor and settled into the rocking chair.

At first when Leoma put the baby to her breast, he showed no interest. His eyes opened slightly then closed. Somewhat lethargic, his head rolled slowly from side to side. Leoma gently guided the source of milk to his small mouth. After a few frustrated tries he tasted, hesitated, and began to suckle.

Leoma flinched and held her breath, shocked by the sudden pain. She didn't recall how the few attempts at nursing Elizabeth had hurt. But then, her daughter had been very weak and tiny. Leoma took a deep breath and let it out slowly, trying to relax. After several moments the pain subsided.

Leoma rocked back and forth, the smooth cherry wood rockers softly creaking against the oak floor in a quiet lullaby. Minutes ticked past and the baby was still feeding. Something akin to contentment washed over Leoma, though she tried to deny any satisfaction in nursing this child. Her head resting against the back of the rocker, she closed her eyes and attempted to clear her mind of the grief and loneliness that dwelt there day and night.

Dyer made a faint grunting noise and Leoma opened her eyes. When she glanced down the baby's eyes were open and trying to focus on her. She attempted a smile but none came to her lips. She wanted to coo sweet words but her jaws tightened. The baby had stopped feeding. She covered herself and lifted him, positioning him on her shoulder the way she'd seen other mothers do after nursing. In no time her gentle pats on the tiny back produced a healthy burp. She nuzzled her cheek against the baby's head and continued rocking, almost drifting into a peaceful sleep.

A knock on the door roused her. According to the clock on her writing desk, an hour-and-a-half had passed. With the baby still snuggled securely against her shoulder she rose from the chair and walked to the front door, relieved the child's father had returned.

WELBY STOOD WITH HIS hat in hand and nodded when Leoma Fisk opened her door. He brushed back the hair from his forehead. As Kristina had done often since her mother died, his daughter clung to his leg. The way Mrs. Fisk held his son it appeared the boy was content.

Welby hoped she would say Dyer had nursed without trouble, and that she'd continue as his wet nurse.

"Come in Mr. Soderlund," the woman said in a whisper. She looked exhausted and weary, but there was something peaceful about the way she looked.

"Thank you." Welby stepped into the front room and gazed around at the elegant furnishings. Obviously, the lady had come from a wealthy family on the East Coast, judging by the fancy furniture and all the pretty do-dads on the mantle and tables. He'd never seen so many frilly doilies in one room in his life, and he didn't much care for all the clutter. But of course, that wasn't important.

"Please have a seat." Mrs. Fisk motioned him toward a chair with dark plush upholstery and polished wooden arms. "I haven't changed your son's diaper yet. If you don't mind waiting, I'll go upstairs and do that."

Welby nodded. The young woman carried his son up the stairs and disappeared. Curious, he peeked through an open door to his right. All he could see was a wall of shelves filled with books, and a fancy, ornate desk and chair. The desk was most likely cherry wood, he figured. His eyes went back to the books. There must have been five hundred or more. He grunted. She was an educated, uppity woman, he'd bet his farm on it. Then again, his Louise had liked books an awful lot, and had a fair collection of them. Nearly every time he came into the house, back when she was alive, he'd find her in a chair with Kristina curled up next to her while she read, sometimes silently to herself, sometimes out loud to their daughter.

His heart grew heavy thinking about Louise, and he wondered how he'd ever live without her. One thing for sure, he could barely read, and he shied away from reading to his girl. Another year and Kristina would start going to the new schoolhouse where she'd learn to read and write, and he was going to make sure she learned well. He shook the thoughts out of his head. Now wasn't the time to worry about such things.

At straight up eight o'clock, the mantle clock above the fireplace chimed eight sharp bongs. He couldn't imagine having a fancy timepiece like that in his house, chiming every hour to keep him awake all night.

Old Crank did his job just fine at the crack of dawn every morning, and that was enough reminder of the time.

Kristina tugged on his arm, and asked with a worried frown on her face, "Is that lady going to keep Dyer?"

"No." He didn't know how to explain what Mrs. Fisk was doing for him, especially if the woman was willing to continue feeding his boy. "She's changing his diaper."

It did seem to be taking Mrs. Fisk an awfully long time. He'd no more processed the thought, when she came down the stairs with his son in her arms.

"Thank you for waiting. I haven't had much practice at changing diapers," she said. "I fear I'm a bit slow."

The poor woman looked as if she might burst out crying. Maybe it was just because she was exhausted and still grieving. He'd never been in an awkward situation like this. There was no way to console her, no proper words. It seemed there was so much grief and loss in the world these days: people dying from influenza, people being shot and killed by men who still robbed banks, and babies like Mrs. Fisk's, dying because they were born too soon. That's what doc Rhodes had told him anyway. Her daughter had been born several weeks too early, probably because of all her grief after the baby's father had been killed. Doc Rhodes had tried real hard, but he couldn't save the premature baby girl. Sure was sad. Here he was strapped with two children, and Mrs. Fisk had lost her husband and her baby. It didn't make a bit of sense to Welby. He didn't understand how God worked. It was mighty hard to believe in God when he let so many terrible things happen. What Welby needed, more than a God who didn't care, was a good stiff drink.

Leoma Fisk held his son out to him. He took the boy and cradled him awkwardly in his arms. Handling the child still made Welby nervous. Taking care of a baby was a woman's job. In his big, clumsy hands, all rough from farming, his son felt fragile; he feared he'd hurt the lad.

The woman spoke in hushed tones. "Your son was reluctant at first, but he finally nursed. He seems content for now. Did Doctor Rhodes tell you how often I should nurse him?"

The young woman's eyes filled with uncertainty. Welby shrugged and shook his head. It seemed, as he recalled, Louise fed Kristina a dozen times a day when she was first born, but he couldn't be sure. He didn't know much about that kind of female stuff, and it was mighty uncomfortable discussing it with a woman he hardly knew. "Will you continue to feed my boy?"

"Yes." Welby saw doubt in the young woman's eyes, but her answer was firm.

"Thank you." He sighed. Now what? Welby didn't know how to approach making arrangements in such an awkward situation. He surely couldn't run in and out of town a dozen times a day so the woman could feed Dyer. "How should we go about this? It's at least four miles to my farm, so I can't run back and forth every time he needs to be fed."

"Perhaps you could bring him to me early in the morning, and pick him up before bedtime." It was clear by the dark circles under the woman's eyes she hadn't slept much lately, and Welby hoped he wasn't asking too much of her.

"What if the baby wakes up crying in the middle of the night? Babies do that, sometimes more than once," he said. Dyer wasn't a week old yet and Welby hadn't had more than three hours sleep at any one stretch. He couldn't very well haul the child into town at two in the morning. And he couldn't expect Mrs. Fisk to ride out to his farm at all hours of the day and night. He scratched his bearded chin and tried to think of a solution.

Leoma stood quietly, a thousand questions in her eyes. She paused in front of the fireplace, her hands clasped at her waist.

"I know it's asking a lot, ma'am," Welby finally said. "If I pay you a reasonable fee, would you keep my boy with you full time until he sleeps through the night?"

Leoma lifted her hands together and pressed them to her lips, as if in prayer. Her eyes were focused on the baby in his arms for a moment before she closed them. Her hesitance worried him. Welby knew he was asking a lot, with the woman's feelings still raw. He waited. The baby squirmed in his arms, a reminder of the fragile life he held, a life that depended on him.

Mrs. Fisk stepped across the room to another chair and eased down

19

into the cushion. Her sigh was deep and audible. After a long pause, she forced a polite half-smile. "I think leaving your son with me is the best solution, but you don't need to pay me."

"It's only right that I compensate you, Mrs. Fisk. If not with money, I could bring you eggs and milk, and vegetables from my garden later on in the summer." Judging by the hollow in the woman's cheeks and the pallor of her skin, he'd bet she wasn't eating well. "If you're going to nurse my son you need to eat better. At least allow me to bring food. We have more than enough stored up in the cellar, and my hens lay too many eggs for us to eat. Same with the cows; even with what I sell, there's more than enough milk."

"All right," Leoma Fisk said graciously. "And perhaps you could bring whatever diapers and clothing you have for your son. He can sleep in my da—" She looked away for several seconds before going on. "He can sleep in the cradle upstairs."

Welby nodded. "My Louise made sure the baby had a proper layette, I think she called it. She sewed gowns, caps, blankets and all kinds of things."

"With loving hands, I'm sure."

"I can bring everything later this afternoon, just as soon as I can pack it up and return to town. If you don't mind I'll see to the chores first."

"That's fine." Leoma stood and took the baby from him.

Anxious to get things done, Welby ushered Kristina out the door. Climbing into his buckboard without his son tore at his heart, but he knew it was best for the child. Maybe now the boy had a chance to survive.

Chapter 3

STANDING AT THE FRONT window somewhat dazed, Leoma pushed aside the lace curtain, and watched as Welby lifted his daughter into the buckboard and climbed up behind her. Leoma looked at the baby in her arms, wondering if the responsibility she'd accepted was more than she could handle. She didn't take her promise to God lightly, but after all, she spent most of her time crying or pining for Jeremy and baby Elizabeth, and she just didn't feel well. The heaviness on her chest was slowly crushing the life out of her. She stared at the bundle she held. He was a pitiful little thing, in desperate need of the love she could never give him. If only she felt better about caring for him. A heavy sigh escaped.

Where had the gentle love that she'd felt for Elizabeth gone, and the compassion Jeremy had so openly admired in her? Turning away from the window, she grimaced, allowing angry thoughts and bitterness to creep in. This was too much to ask, even from God. She shouldn't have made a promise that she couldn't keep, at least with any semblance of joy. A jagged sigh escaped from deep within as she swiped away a tear.

Oh, God, give me strength to keep my word. Take my doubt and bitter thoughts from me, I pray. I know this child was created by you, and born to loving parents. I'm sure you must have a plan for his life. Help me, Father God. Help me do my part in seeing that your will is done in his life.

Leoma carried Dyer up the stairs and into the room directly across from her bedroom. She lowered him into the wooden cradle Jeremy had made for Elizabeth. Soft white blankets covered the mattress she had fashioned from cotton filling and washed ticking. For a moment, she gazed down at the frail, limp infant. He certainly wasn't a pretty baby.

Even premature, she recalled proudly, Elizabeth had been beautiful and angelic. Leoma tried to imagine her daughter in the cradle instead of this ugly, half-starved son of a stranger. Born seven weeks early, her Elizabeth had wisps of raven hair like her father's, a perfectly formed face, and the sweetest little heart shaped mouth Leoma had ever seen. Seeing this sickly, gray child was nearly unbearable. She gently covered the baby with a soft, hand-made blanket, and turned away, hoping he would sleep for an hour or two.

You must have compassion. Remember, just as your daughter was my creation, so is this child. He is special. Care for him tenderly. Leoma stopped in her tracks and covered her ears, as if the words blared at her from every direction. Wasn't Elizabeth special enough to live a full life? Leoma would have given her daughter every thing she needed, and trained her up to love and worship the Lord. Elizabeth would have become a fine young lady, with impeccable manners and gracefulness. Imagining her daughter as a young woman, Leoma walked into her bedroom across the hallway, and plopped down on the edge of her bed, a million questions swirling through her mind. "It's so hard," she whispered as her head dropped into her hands. How could she have compassion when her heart was torn to pieces?

Distracted by a light knock on the front door Leoma jolted and jumped to her feet. Surely Mr. Soderlund wasn't back from his farm in such a short time. She hurried down the stairs on tip-toes and opened the door a crack, peeking out to see who was on her porch. She was surprised to find Anna Jo Langley smiling back at her, the plump young woman's cheeks bright red and dimpled. Leoma smiled. Perhaps a cheerful visitor is just what she needed to lift her spirits.

"Good morning, Leoma." Anna Jo held up a small wicker basket, its contents covered with a blue and white checkered cloth. "I hope you don't mind me paying you a visit so early, but I just baked some muffins, and I'd like to share them with you."

Leoma pulled open the door and welcomed her neighbor. The rich, sweet aroma wafted up from the basket, and Leoma touched her abdomen. Her stomach growled. "That's very kind of you. Please come in."

Anna Jo stepped inside, and Leoma closed the door behind her. She led her guest into the kitchen and set the basket of muffins on the table. It had been Anna Jo who brought a chicken casserole after Jeremy's funeral, and she'd stayed to clean up after all the town folk had gone home. And it had been Anna Jo who wrapped her arms around Leoma yesterday at Elizabeth's graveside. Unable to bear a house full of gabby people again, with their trite condolences, Leoma had insisted no one gather at her house after her daughter's funeral service, but several had left food anyway. She wondered if they believed she could eat all that food. Yesterday, before leaving her at the cemetery, Anna Jo had hugged her long and tenderly, sobbing as hard as Leoma herself. What a dear, sweet person her neighbor was.

"I ruined the pot of coffee earlier," Leoma admitted, grimacing. "May I fix you a cup of tea?" Leoma was happy to have another woman to talk to.

Anna Jo pulled out a wooden chair at the kitchen table and made herself at home. "Yes, thank you. I can't stay long, though. I promised George I'd only be a few minutes. He's good about watching our youngsters, but pretty soon he has to get to work over at that new church they're building."

"Not many men would agree to tend their young children," Leoma said while moving about the kitchen.

"I suppose I'm luckier than most."

If only Anna Jo knew how lucky she was, Leoma thought. A little older than Leoma, her neighbor was soft spoken, yet her words tumbled out like a chattering mocking bird. She had a confident air about her that Leoma liked. Anna Jo and George lived a short distance away in the house George had built of hand-cut cedar. He'd staked his claim during the first land rush and wasted no time building a house for his family. He'd come west with Jeremy and when the cannon fired signaling the opening of the land for homesteading, George had been right beside Jeremy at the front of the pack. They'd protected each other and the property they'd staked out, making sure their plot of dirt wasn't stolen right from under their noses.

Like Anna Jo, Leoma came later, after their husbands had prepared a secure place for them. Anna Jo already had an infant and a toddler when Leoma met her, but with getting settled and the constant influx of new people, the two women hadn't spent much time becoming better acquainted. Now, Leoma was especially thankful for her neighbor's show of concern and friendship. She was sure she could learn a great deal from Anna Jo about surviving in this uncultured, backward little town. And just maybe, Anna Jo might teach her a few things about cooking and taking care of Dyer.

"Have you sent a letter off to Boston to tell your mother and father about Jeremy and the baby?" Anna Jo was direct with her question, but tough as it was Leoma knew it was her friend's strength that would help her through this difficult time.

Leoma's insides twisted. The pain was still so fresh she could hardly speak without choking up. "I sent a short letter after Jeremy's burial but . . ." It took several seconds to compose herself before she could go on. "I don't have the heart to tell them their first grandchild died. I tried so hard to keep her alive. I—"

Anna Jo's eyes widened then she frowned. She reached out and grabbed Leoma's hand. Her doughy fingers wrapped tightly as she pulled Leoma closer. "Now you know that baby came into the world far too early, and you heard Doc say nothing else could be done. Why, the Lord knows with all your grief and strain, and after all those hours of struggling through her birth, you hardly had the strength yourself to survive."

It was true. Leoma nodded half-heartedly. The doctor had tried to stop the labor, but after thirty hours of unstoppable contractions the baby came anyway. She was blue and struggling for breath. Doctor Rhodes had done all he could, and for a few hours it seemed Elizabeth might live, but late during the second night she had stopped breathing.

Trying to forget the nightmare of those days, Leoma added a few small pieces of wood to the fire in the cook-stove and filled the teakettle with water. She took two china cups and saucers from the cupboard and set them on the table along with the sugar bowl and spoons. Suddenly, she was hungry and anxious to bite into one of Anna Jo's muffins. Leoma started to join her friend at the table when a cry halted her steps. It was faint at first then louder.

Anna Jo's mouth dropped open; the color in her face faded. "Am I hearing things? It sounds like a baby is crying upstairs." Anna Jo craned her neck and listened, a hint of fear in her eyes.

Leoma shook her head and smiled as she turned toward the stairs. "You're not hearing things. It's Welby Soderlund's son."

"What? How did you come about having his baby here? Why?" Anna Jo got out of the chair and followed Leoma, chattering every step of the way to the top floor. "Where's his—"

"The baby's mother died. Doctor Rhodes sent Mr. Soderlund to me suggesting I become the child's wet nurse. Otherwise the baby will starve to death."

"But they have those glass feeders now. I saw one in Todd's store."

"They tried that. The baby immediately throws up the milk."

"Still, my oh my, how can he ask such a thing of you right after losing your own precious child?"

"I'm the boy's only hope. Leoma picked up the infant from the cradle and placed him on the nearby bed to check his diaper. He didn't squirm or kick his legs, but his head turned and he puckered his face and mouth to let out another cry. That was an improvement from when he'd first arrived and a bit of relief. She couldn't bear the thought of him dying. With shaking, inexperienced hands, Leoma managed to change the infant's diaper while her neighbor looked on.

"He does look sickly," Anna Jo said. Her voice was full of compassion and tenderness. "Oh my, look how his little ribs stick out. And his arms and legs haven't an ounce of fat on them. How sad."

After the baby was changed and bundled into a warm blanket from Elizabeth's layette, Leoma picked him up. She cradled him in her arms as she headed back down to the kitchen. By now the tea was probably too strong but she'd serve it anyway.

"Oh please. Let me pour the tea," Anna Jo said rushing to the stove and grabbing the teapot. "You sit down and I'll do this."

"Thank you."

Anna Jo filled both their cups, and placed a split muffin slathered with a layer of homemade strawberry jam on a plate in front of Leoma. "Eat. You can nibble a bit of muffin before you feed him. You look as if you haven't eaten a decent meal in days."

Leoma did as she was told, relishing the sweet jam laden with chunks of strawberries. With so little appetite lately, she had only nibbled a bite or two of the chicken casserole and apple pie neighbors had brought after Jeremy's funeral, and she couldn't recall what, if anything she'd eaten since Elizabeth's birth. The last few days were a blur and dishes of untouched food were wasting.

Anna Jo sipped from her cup. "How long are you going to nurse that child?"

"Until he's healthy and can be weaned."

"That could be months."

Leoma nodded. She hesitated, unsure if Anna Jo would think her daft. "Will you think I'm crazy if I tell you God spoke to me about this last night?"

Anna Jo's eyes twinkled as she lowered her cup from her mouth. "Not at all. God does amazing and wonderful things. Did you really hear him?"

"His voice was a gentle whisper, so real I'm sure I heard him. He promised to give me the strength I need to care for this baby."

"Is Mr. Soderlund expecting you to care for his son alone for all those months? Shouldn't he compensate you?"

"We made an agreement of sorts. The man can hardly run into town every time the baby needs to be fed, so I agreed to keep him here. He offered to pay me a fee but I refused. He'll return this evening with all the baby's dry goods, and he insists he bring me food: fresh eggs, milk, canned fruits and vegetables."

"I suppose that's all right. I don't reckon this is any easier for him, just losing his wife and all. A man like that doesn't know the first thing about taking care of an infant."

"That's true," Leoma said. "That little girl of his isn't getting the best of care, either. I guess she eats okay; I can't tell from the looks of her. But she sure needs a good bath and clean clothes. I'd bet she hasn't had her hair brushed since before her mother died."

Anna Jo wagged a scolding finger at Leoma. "You don't need to worry about that little girl. Caring for this baby is enough responsibility. Not only that, I hear tell their father's a stubborn brute and hits the bottle pretty heavy. Rumor was he wouldn't even take his wife and daughter to Sunday services."

"I don't doubt that. The alcohol was heavy on his breath when he approached me yesterday at the cemetery. And his clothing reeked of old tobacco. But this baby is innocent, and I promised to take care of him. I can't just turn my back and let the poor child die."

Leoma recalled the loving voice that pierced her conscience in the middle of the night, and again early this morning. No matter how difficult it was, she had to do what was right, even if it meant helping the little girl, too. Leoma glanced down at the baby. His dark eyes were trying to focus on her face. He squirmed and scrunched up his mouth, ready to cry. A strange sensation surged through her breast and she sucked in a quiet breath. She tried to remember what time it had been when she fed him earlier. Two hours ago perhaps. No matter, for the time being it seemed best to feed him as often as he needed. She'd heard a baby had to be on a regular schedule, but other women said a mother should feed a newborn whenever he acted hungry. Without Doctor Rhodes' advice or her mother here to help her, she would have to follow her instincts. Or perhaps Anna Jo would be of help since she already had two little ones of her own.

The child's wail burst out and filled the room, followed by another tingling surge in her breasts, like the one she'd experienced earlier. There was no need to ask Anna Jo. It was a sure sign it was time to nurse him again, no matter what the clock said.

Leoma took a sip of tea and smiled at her company. "Looks like my milk set okay with him and he's hungry again. I just hope he regains his strength and survives."

Chapter 4

BEFORE EVENING DARKENED THE rooms, Leoma lit the kerosene lanterns in the parlor and kitchen. She wished gaslights were available here, like those her parents had in their home in Boston. Of course that had changed since she'd left, and according to her mother's last letter shortly after Christmas, their entire house was now lit with electric light bulbs. Leoma could only imagine how wonderful it must be, to simply push a button or pull a chain and have light flood into a room. So far none of the houses in this settlement had electricity, though there was talk of it coming soon.

Dusky gray light, along with colder air, filtered into the house through the lace-curtained windows. It cast gray shadows on the walls. Leoma pulled her sweater tighter to ward off the chill. The days were still short and brisk. She gathered three pieces of wood from the pile outside the backdoor, and added them to the living room fireplace. After brushing her hands together to remove the dirt, she used the iron poker to jab the hot coals until new flames flared up, the way Jeremy had shown her when they moved into the house. She'd felt like quite the pioneer woman back then, but the fun and adventure had long worn off. Carrying splintered firewood and keeping fires going was no fun at all.

After she'd first arrived in Oklahoma, when she and Jeremy still lived in the tent, all they'd had for light was one lantern and a box of beeswax candles. For warmth they'd had plenty of comforters and woolen clothes, and many nights they snuggled and giggled beneath heavy layers of blankets. She could almost smell the candles burning and feel the scratching blankets against her neck and chin. The memory almost brought a smile to her lips, but her heart held it in check. Maybe someday she could laugh about those times with Jeremy, but not today. Not yet.

Before the next winter had set in, Jeremy had completed the house. He had been confident he could eventually put his education to better use and set up his own architectural firm. Meanwhile, he used his carpenter skills and the money he'd saved, along with the money his parents and Leoma's parents had given them, to build a magnificent two-story house for his bride. Though it wasn't as grand as their family homes in Boston, it was the finest and largest house in town. With four bedrooms upstairs and ample space downstairs, it was big enough for the family they'd planned to raise.

Leoma gazed around the spacious front room and recalled the many times she had watched through the large window, waiting for Jeremy to come home from work. She sighed and walked into the spacious kitchen with lots of built-in cupboards and work space. If only she knew how to cook; Jeremy had often teased her about that. Remembering his good-natured way with her, this time she couldn't stop the smile from escaping.

She scanned the kitchen. The lantern light cast a soft glow but left the corners dark. What would she do with all this space now that she was alone? Perhaps come summer she should sell the house, and return to Boston where she would be near her family. By then Dyer should be healthy enough to wean and stay with his father. But the thought of the long trip brought dread, and she couldn't bear the idea of leaving Jeremy and Elizabeth behind. Even though she felt lost rambling around in this big house, how could she leave the beautiful home Jeremy had put his heart and soul into? How could she return to her parents a childless widow? The very idea weighed heavily on her mind. And just thinking of the huge job it would be to move brought a shudder. What was she thinking? It was much too soon to make any decisions about the future. She flinched and tried to clear her head. Someone with a heavy hand knocked on the door.

Leoma walked back through the front room and drew open the door. As promised, Welby Soderlund had returned. In his arms was a big bundle tied in a plaid, wool blanket and his daughter carried a smaller bundle. The little girl smiled up at her, but she still looked shy and unsure of Leoma.

"Good evening." Leoma forced a polite smile and stood back motioning them inside.

WELBY REMOVED HIS HAT and stepped inside the wide entrance to Mrs. Fisk's living room. Two gas lamps cast a nice glow throughout the room. He examined the area more closely this time. The woman had a good blaze going in the fireplace, and he wondered if she'd had help cutting wood and building such an impressive fire. The space seemed cozier now, unlike the chill he'd felt that morning. He'd worried throughout the day about his frail son being kept warm enough. He felt awkward and at a loss for words. "Did my boy feed again?"

"Yes. I nursed him three more times today; it seemed agreeable with him." The woman clasped her hands at her waist and she fidgeted with her thumbs. "He's sleeping now."

Relieved that his son was taking nourishment, Welby nodded. "If you'll show me where to put these bundles, ma'am, I'll fetch the rest from the wagon."

Mrs. Fisk hesitated then turned. She motioned with one hand for him to follow her up the stairs. At the end of the hallway on the second floor, he stopped just inside the doorway and waited while Mrs. Fisk lit a candle atop a chest of drawers. A few feet from a full-sized bed with tall posters, he spotted his son fast asleep in a well-crafted cradle.

"Leave the baby's things on the bed," the woman whispered. "Would you like to peek at your son?"

Welby crept nearer the cradle and bent forward for a closer look. Dyer had a knitted cap on his head, and was covered with a fluffy, white blanket. Was it his imagination, or did his son have better color on his face already? He stood for a moment, his heart yearning for the boy's mother. Louise had been a good mother. Mrs. Fisk was a might younger than Louise and had lost her first baby, and he wondered if she'd have the common sense to care for his son.

Exhausted and worried, he let out a deep sigh. For now he had no choice in the matter. He had to trust the doctor's judgment and this young woman. At least Dyer was being fed; it was a start. After a few moments, Welby returned to his buckboard to retrieve the basket of food, and rushed back to the house as quickly as possible. A stiff breeze blew from the north bringing frigid temperatures with it.

Leoma Fisk drew open the front door for him to enter, and closed it quickly behind him. He held up the basket, hoping his offering would be good enough. "I brought you six eggs, a jar of fresh milk, and some canned vegetables from my cellar. Louise put up the canned goods last summer."

"Thank you," Mrs. Fisk said as he followed her into the kitchen.

As Welby set the food on the table, the woman examined each quart jar. Not knowing what she might like, he'd brought a variety: pickled beets, green beans, corn, and new potatoes. "If you like okra and black eyed peas, I'll bring some of those next time."

"I do. This is very kind of you. Thank you." The woman lowered her eyes to the bounty on the table. "I haven't learned how to can or preserve anything. I'm sorry I didn't get to know your wife; I'm sure I could have learned a great deal from her."

"More than likely." Welby didn't mean it in a hateful way. It was just that Louise had been a great cook, and she was a whiz in the kitchen. She could whip up fluffy biscuits and rich, creamy gravy in a flash, and she had a way with spices that made every meal down right tasty. Just thinking about it set him to craving one of her good pot roast dinners and a sweet apple pie.

The faint smell of burnt coffee lingered in Mrs. Fisk's kitchen, probably from earlier that morning. It made him wonder if the woman could fry an egg, or cook anything edible. It wouldn't surprise him one bit if she couldn't boil water without burning up the kettle. And her house was too citified for his liking, with all those high-falutin' drapes over the lace curtains, and those curvy chairs in the living room with carvings on the arms and legs. However, he had to admit, everything was tidy and clean.

He watched as Leoma Fisk touched the top of his daughter's head and bent to her level. "Would you like a ginger cookie—that is, if it's all right with your father?" The woman looked to him for his permission.

His daughter's eyes lit up as she glanced his way. He knew Kristina's favorite cookie was her momma's snicker doodles with extra cinnamon and sugar on top, but what child would turn down a cookie of any kind? He'd bet his prize heifer, though, Leoma Fisk didn't bake those cookies. Most likely she'd bought them at Todd's, or some other woman in town had baked them and brought them over after one of the funerals.

"Just one," he said to Kristina, holding up one forefinger.

Mrs. Fisk opened the door to a walk-in pantry. She picked up a large clear jar and set it on the table. As she unscrewed the red metal lid, the spicy aroma made his mouth water. Maybe they weren't Louise's homemade snicker doodles, but gingersnaps had always been one of his favorites. He wouldn't mind having two or three of them. Remembering his manners, he waited while his girl accepted the cookie Mrs. Fisk gave her, and hoped the woman would offer one to him.

"Mr. Soderlund, would you care for a cookie?" Leoma Fisk held the jar in his direction.

How could he resist? It was the next best thing to a good stiff drink. But that would have to wait until he headed home. He reached into the offered container and pulled out two nice round cookies. "Thank you."

"Mr. Soderlund, please sit down for a moment." The woman sounded a bit hesitant or shy as she spoke this time. "I don't mean to be forward, but if I am going to care for your son full time, and you're going to be stopping in to see him now and then, I wouldn't mind at all if you'd address me by my first name. I mean, that is, if you aren't uncomfortable calling me Leoma."

Her suggestion didn't seem forward or inappropriate to him. Welby realized he hadn't properly introduced himself with a handshake when he'd approached the woman at the graveyard yesterday. But then he'd been in a panic and nothing had been normal. "Seems fine by me, ma'am." Welby stood and moved around the wide table to the chair where Leoma was seated and offered his hand. "Call me Welby from now on if you want to."

Leoma's hand was soft and warm and her grip was firm for a woman. He'd bet those delicate hands had never seen an ounce of farm work. For certain they'd never grabbed on to no cow teats for milking, or gathered eggs from a hen house.

Leoma nodded without smiling. "Well, it appears your son is content enough to sleep the evening away. If you would like to return tomorrow afternoon, a little earlier perhaps, you're welcome to pay him a visit."

"Thank you." Welby was glad Leoma had suggested that he come back so soon. He didn't want to make a pest of himself, but he wanted to see with his own eyes how Dyer was doing. It was an inconvenience running into town so often, but he worried for his boy. He nudged his daughter out of the kitchen. "It's time we be going home, Kristina. Thank Mrs. Fisk for the cookie."

"Thank you for the cookie, Mrs. Fisk. Can I come back tomorrow?"

"Yes, you may," Leoma said, patting the girl on the shoulder as they walked toward the front door. "I'll see you and your father tomorrow. And maybe your little brother will be awake so you can see him. Would you like that?"

"Yes, ma'am," Kristina said, moving closer to Welby as she put her tiny hand in his.

Welby was pleased his daughter had remembered her manners. His own behavior wasn't always the best, but something about being in Leoma's home prompted him to make an effort. "I'll return around two o'clock, if that's agreeable. I won't be able to stay long with evening chores waiting."

"I understand. That's fine." Leoma stood behind a wooden chair holding the back as if the piece of furniture protected her. Or perhaps she was feeling weak and wobbly. She was terribly thin and pale.

Welby thanked Leoma again, and hat in hand he said goodbye. Before Welby reached the buckboard Kristina tugged at his jacket tail. "Papa?"

Puzzled, he looked down at her. "What?"

"Why did *you* get two cookies?" Welby just grinned and winked at his daughter.

RELIEVED THE FARMER WAS gone Leoma closed the door against the brisk evening air. She'd wanted to offer a few words of advice to Welby about brushing his daughter's hair and putting a clean dress on her, but hard as it was, she held her tongue. Still, there was no excuse for allowing one's child to be dirty and unkempt.

Growing up Leoma had been taught cleanliness was next to godliness, and it wasn't unusual for the women in her family to bathe two or three times a week. Hair was brushed thoroughly every morning and night, and washing it was a Saturday evening ritual in preparation for church on Sunday morning. Of course, she'd been fortunate to grow up in a big city where hot water came right out of the spigots. Here in this dusty little town in the middle of nowhere, the inconvenience of heating water and carrying the heavy bucket up the stairs to her bathing chamber hadn't changed her grooming habits, but sometimes it was a struggle.

She'd not meant to be critical of Welby Soderlund, or grumble, even in silence, about the things she must do without since coming to Oklahoma. But it was hard not to miss the conveniences and loveliness of her parents' home. Oh how she missed her mother and father and her younger sister.

Perhaps she should do as Anna Jo mentioned earlier in the day, and write to them and Jeremy's parents. She hadn't yet received a letter from her mother, answering her own short note informing them of Jeremy's death. She hated to herald more bad news so soon. And there was another letter she must write to her dearest friend, Glenda. Glenda would be devastated by the tragic news of Elizabeth's death.

Leoma tiptoed up the stairs and looked in on the baby, still sleeping on his side, his fists curled beneath his chin. She left the room, and moments later lit a lamp on her writing desk in the parlor. After sitting down, she pulled open the top drawer. She took out three sheets of the fine stationary her grandmother, Della, had given her as a farewell gift when she and Jeremy left Boston. Only a few pieces remained, so she would keep the letters short.

Thinking once again of her life-long friend, Leoma decided she would write to Glenda first. With pen in hand she pondered how to begin. Grief flowed over her like molten lead. Finally, with a heavy sigh, she put the pen to paper.

3 March 1893

My dear friend Glenda,

I miss you terribly, especially now when I could use your shoulder to cry upon, and your good listening ear. Perhaps you have heard by now from my parents that Jeremy was shot and died on February 20 of this year. The strain of his death was too much for me to bear in my advanced stages of pregnancy, and now I must add more bad news, which I have not sent to my mother and father as of yet. I will write to them as soon as I finish this letter to you.

On February 25, my darling baby daughter came into the world, weighing less than 5 pounds and struggling. She lived less than 48 hours, but during that time I held her close and loved her dearly. Though small, she was beautiful, with Jeremy's dark eyes and hair, and a perfectly formed little body. I named her Elizabeth Rose.

I cannot tell you what a heartbreak it was to lay Elizabeth in the casket, and see the tiny box swallowed up by the muddy earth. I can only trust she is in the loving arms of her daddy in Heaven, both of them perfect and happy. I have to believe they await my arrival, and we will someday be together for eternity.

I trust you are doing well, and are very happy in your new job and home. In this rustic, dusty, little town, I do not enjoy the same comforts available to you there, but I can't complain. I am fortunate and comfortable here in the lovely home Jeremy built for us.

I miss you and hope someday before too long I will see you again.

Take care and God bless you.

Leoma signed the note, slipped it into the envelope, and addressed it. A hard lump in her throat forced her to take a deep breath. She set the letter aside and began the missive to her mother and father. Before she could finish the salutation, a cry pierced the silence. Dyer. A quick glance at the clock surprised her. The baby had slept well into the evening, nearly four hours since she'd last nursed him.

Though weary, Leoma set her writing aside, climbed stairs, and entered the bedroom, carrying a lantern to guide the way. Another cry from Dyer, heftier this time, brought a tingling surge to her breast. Moisture seeped through the heavy fabric of her blouse.

For several moments she gazed down at the strange baby, nestled in her daughter's cradle, swaddled in the blankets that had been made for Elizabeth. Imagining her beautiful infant there, Leoma touched her fingers to her quivering lips. She reached down and smoothed her hand along the edge of the cradle Jeremy had crafted. He had turned raw wood into this beautiful work of love. He'd sanded and polished it to a satiny sheen before proudly presenting it to Leoma, unaware his child would never sleep there.

Dyer fussed louder, his little fists flailing, his cry demanding Leoma's attention. She reached down and picked him up. His movements stirred her heart, for it was a sure sign he'd already benefited from her milk. "There, there little fellow, I know you are hungry. Be patient with me. With God's help we'll get through this together."

As Leoma sat on the edge of the bed feeding Dyer, her back ached and she longed for sleep. What a long, busy day it had been. The baby's appetite was heartier this time, and after allowing him to nurse for ten minutes, she moved him to her other breast. His tiny mouth anxiously found the source of his nourishment and he suckled, smacking loudly at first, then he settled into a contented state as he fed. Leoma studied his frail body. His features were unlike his robust father, whose face was square with a prominent brow and wide-set eyes. She couldn't yet tell the color of the boy's eyes. They were dark as the sea on a moonless night. As she examined the child he focused his eyes on hers.

Wishing she could sing a lullaby, Leoma's heart twisted. The words stuck deep in her chest. She rubbed the back of her bent forefinger across Dyer's cheek. "Grow strong little one," she whispered as the baby's eyes dropped closed. For the first time, Leoma noticed the long dark lashes that rested on the baby's pale cheeks. She brushed her fingers across his head; the golden fuzz was softer than anything she'd ever felt.

Leoma touched the palm of Dyer's hand with her smallest finger. Though his grip was weak, he captured her finger and held on. She watched Dyer nurse for several minutes before she realized her back muscles no longer ached as she rocked back and forth, enjoying the feel of little Dyer Soderlund in her arms.

Chapter 5

Now that his vegetable garden was sprouting, and good sized bolls had formed on the cotton, Welby didn't mind his daily trips into town before the evening chores. In fact, it was a right nice ride now that the days were warmer and longer. It also gave him a chance to hold Dyer for a few minutes. He'd skipped going in to town three or four days since putting his son in the care of Leoma Fisk, and he didn't want to make a habit of missing his visits.

Though a far cry too persnickety for his liking, Leoma was doing a fine job of caring for Dyer. The child was bright-eyed and alert. He seemed to have grown a good bit the past several weeks. Doc said at the rate Dyer was gaining weight he'd catch up to his normal weight before long. Welby imagined his boy big and strong in a few years, working out in the cotton field and helping with chores around the farm.

Mindful of a deep rut in the road ahead, Welby pulled back on the reins and slowed the buckboard. Heavy rains in recent weeks had all the roads suffering from washouts and mud holes. The late afternoon air was still hot and sticky, and it appeared a storm was brewing. He was glad for the shade when he pulled beneath the oak tree in front of Leoma's house. Kristina clapped her hands and popped up off the seat.

Welby had barely drawn to a stop when Kristina jumped to the ground. Before he reached the porch steps, his daughter knocked on Leoma's front door. The child had nearly driven him to madness all day, asking when they would go see Dyer and Mrs. Fisk. He reckoned Kristina missed her mother and needed a woman's attention, and the assurance that her baby brother was all right. Truth be told, he needed those same assurances.

The door swung open immediately. With his son nestled in the crook of Leoma's left arm, the woman greeted them with a polite half-smile. Welby's heart knotted at the sight. That should be his Louise taking care of their son instead of this fancy filly. Burying his anger at God the best he could, Welby removed his hat and dipped his head in a brief nod. "Afternoon, Leoma," he said.

Strange, he'd never noticed the woman's fair skin and big brown eyes being so striking. Truth was he'd never paid much attention to her looks. All he cared about was making sure she kept his son alive by feeding him. He stepped a little closer to the opened door. Leoma wasn't half bad looking now that the dark circles were gone from beneath her eyes. Her face had a peaceable expression, though solemn. For certain, she seemed more relaxed these days. She was still awfully skinny, however, and her dress bagged some on her bony shoulders.

"Come in," Leoma said, cocking her head sideways, and glancing across the yard to the southwest. "It looks like a bad storm is coming our way." She stood aside and waited for him and his daughter to enter before she glanced again at the ugly, black wall of clouds.

"More rain's coming, for sure." On his way into town, Welby had watched the thunder clouds billowing higher and higher into the sky.

"Well, I suppose your farm could use the rain."

"Yes, it sure could." The clouds had grown black and menacing, and Welby didn't like the looks of them. He'd seen hail and tornados come out of clouds like that, but not wanting to alarm Leoma and Kristina, he dismissed his concern with a shrug. Hopefully the rain would hold off until he returned home, but the way the wind was beginning to whip around the house, he wasn't so sure about that.

Welby reached for his son. "How's my boy today?"

He took Dyer from Leoma and looked him over. It was a relief to see the child's rosy cheeks and a bit of plumpness to his flesh. Doc. Rhodes had examined Dyer a few days earlier when Welby was in town, and he'd declared the baby's response to Leoma's care and nourishment was miraculous. Had it not been for her, Welby wouldn't be holding his son.

"Your son is becoming an armful. I think he's gained another pound or two since the doctor checked him. He's quite the handsome little fellow, too." Leoma's words were gentle, caring.

"I see my young man is growing some hair." Holding Dyer in one arm Welby brushed the palm of his free hand across the baby's cap of pale fuzz. It was still short and fine, but he could see his son was going to have a head of thick hair like his own, golden brown and naturally wavy. When Welby brushed his hand across Dyer's head again, the baby smiled, bringing a big grin from Welby's heart to his lips. Welby let out a hearty laugh, perhaps the first laughter out of his mouth since before Louise's death.

"I think that's the first time he's smiled," Leoma said. "It's a good sign. He's growing stronger, and for sure he recognizes his father."

"I want to hold Dyer," Kristina said, tugging at the pant leg of Welby's overalls.

"Of course you may hold Dyer, sweetheart," Leoma said, as she brushed her hand down the back of his little girl's head. Leoma took Kristina by the hand and led her across the room. "Come sit on the settee and let your daddy put Dyer in your arms."

Welby waited while Leoma positioned Kristina on the velvet cushion of the couch and placed a throw pillow beneath the child's right arm. He bent forward and placed Dyer in his girl's arms. A wide smile spread across Kristina's face as she gazed down at her brother. The boy smiled back.

"See, Kristina," Leoma said, "your baby brother likes his big sister. Talk to him."

"Hi," Kristina said in a tiny voice. "Hi, Dyer."

"I wish your mama could see you two," Welby said, his throat constricting. He swallowed hard, determined to keep his composure. Louise's tanned skin and huge brown eyes were still vivid in his memory. Would the pain of losing her ever fade?

Leoma touched his upper arm so lightly he almost missed it. For a moment no one spoke. The howling wind almost drowned out the sweetness of the moment. Thunder rumbled nearby. A short time later a flash of lightning sent fierce brightness through the front room window followed by loud thunder. Another flash and a loud crack followed instantly. Leoma jumped and Dyer let out a sharp cry, as did Kristina. The next flash of lightning struck with deafening thunder that rattled the entire house. Welby rushed to the window and yanked the lace curtain aside. Rain, driven at a sharp angle by strong winds, pelted the window panes. The sky changed to eerie green, a look Welby recognized as danger. "We need to take shelter! Do you have a storm cellar, Leoma?" He didn't mean to startle the woman with his urgency. He saw immediate fear in her eyes as she grabbed Dyer up from Kristina's lap.

"Yes, out the back door." Leoma was already running through the kitchen, Dyer held tightly to her chest. "You best carry your daughter," she shouted without looking back.

Welby had already grabbed up Kristina. He followed on Leoma's heels as she dashed out the back door with his son sheltered in her arms. He was grateful to see the woman's husband had built a sturdy cellar just a few steps from the house. In two long strides he was in front of Leoma, lifting the wooden door that led to protection from the raging storm. He sent Leoma and the baby down first then lowered Kristina to her feet.

"Follow Mrs. Fisk, Kristina. Now!" A loud clap of thunder sent the child scurrying without hesitation, down the steep wooden steps and into the darkness.

Welby scurried down a few steps gripping the rope handle on the bottom side of the door and tugged hard, battling the wind for possession. The slab of heavy wood just slammed shut when a horrendous pounding of hail pelted the earth and cellar door above his head.

"Do you have a candle or lantern?" he called to Leoma as he slowly made his way down each step in the darkness, bracing himself on the narrow side walls of the stairwell. A pale glow led his last two steps at the bottom. "You were well prepared, I see."

"One of my greatest fears has been the storms." Leoma's voice quivered. "Jeremy made sure the cellar was near the back door. He kept the lamp filled and a good supply of candles and matches handy."

"A wise man." Welby explored the room as his eyes adjusted to the dim light. This was more than a storm cellar or a cold storage cellar, though he didn't see an abundance of food like the store of fruit and vegetables, and salted meat in his own cellar. But this cellar had two cots, wool blankets, a roughly crafted wooden table flanked by two slat-backed chairs, and several shelves along one wall. On the table were a box of matches, a wooden box of tall candles, and a lantern. At the top of one wall there was a crude window, perhaps two feet wide and ten inches high, just enough to see a hint of daylight and flashes of lightning.

His son had fallen asleep. Seeing the baby secured on one of the cots with a pillow to guard him from rolling over the outside edge, Welby gathered his daughter close to him and sat down on the same cot, while Leoma efficiently lit the kerosene lantern and replaced the glass mantle. She turned up the burning wick allowing more light to fill the space. Then she blew out the candle. Outside the wind howled. Hail pounded above them sounding like large stones being thrust at the ground. Something heavy banged overhead. Tree branches or flying debris slammed down above the cellar door and Welby hoped they weren't trapped.

I am your refuge, a shelter from the storm.

Where'd that thought come from? Welby wondered if it had come from the very God he'd scorned with his anger. But somewhere in the back of his mind it sounded like something his mother had read aloud from the Bible when he was young. He shrugged it off. In the sultry heat of the afternoon and the small airless space, a chill covered Welby's back and arms. He rubbed his hands up and down both forearms as Leoma sat calmly on one of the chairs, her head bowed as if she were praying. Dyer slept within Welby's reach. His girl was snuggled close at his side.

"I'm afraid," Kristina said, a frightful whimper following her words.

"Don't be afraid." He put his arm around his daughter and nuzzled her closer to him. "It's just a storm. In a few minutes it will be gone."

They waited.

LEOMA SAT QUIETLY AND prayed, the only way for her to remain somewhat calm. If only her heart would stop racing. Outside the wind roared like a ferocious beast and smashed things against the cellar door, as if an angry demon would slash through at any moment and snatch her from safety. Several minutes passed before the storm began to subside. At last, with God's peace filling her heart she opened her eyes and turned her attention to the Soderlunds. Dyer was still asleep. Kristina and her father were huddled close by. In the flickering lantern light Leoma could see the little girl shaking as she nuzzled against Welby's side but the child was no longer crying. No doubt she was as terrified as Leoma had been. Welby's eyes were fixed on the door above the steps.

"We are safe in God's hands." Leoma spoke with conviction though her stomach quivered. "He is our refuge and our protection."

Welby turned toward her, his hair wet, eyes filled with anger. "Then why didn't this God of yours spare my Louise instead of robbing my children of their mother?"

Shocked by Welby's angry outburst, Leoma couldn't answer his question, any more than she could explain why Jeremy and Elizabeth lay buried in the graveyard. Who understood the mysterious ways of God? She took a deep breath and tried to speak as patiently and calmly as possible. "We don't know the mind of God, except that he loves us and wants the best for us. Do—"

"The best?" Welby's voice boomed above the angry roar of the storm.

The man's shout woke Dyer and the boy let out a shrill cry. Leoma jumped up and took the infant into her arms, whispering words of comfort, swaying back and forth to calm him. What manner of man was Welby that he would lose his temper so easily, and at the mention of a loving God? Her own inside quaked. "Do you think I haven't asked those same questions?" Her words were almost a cry of anguish. "Every time I think of my husband and my child buried in that hideous cemetery I ask God why? But I know he has a reason for everything; some day I'll understand."

"Well, I will never understand. Never!"

Leoma wanted to scream and whack Welby over the head with the chair, but she clamped her mouth shut, determined to not say another word. Arguing was unseemly, useless, and it disturbed the children. She shuddered. How did she end up trapped in this hole in the ground with such an obstinate, godless man? Her own anger, though mild, brought heat to her face. If not for the children, she'd tell Welby Soderlund to leave immediately, storm or no storm. Perhaps he needed to be clubbed over the head with a branch from the oak tree to knock some sense into his thick skull.

I'm sorry, Lord. Forgive me for my unkind thoughts.

Still steeped in her own grief, Leoma understood Welby's sorrow, but not his anger against God, and certainly not at this moment. The man still had two beautiful children. Cradling Dyer close to her breast she sat down on the edge of the chair and rocked back and forth, patting his back. If it were not for her care, this baby would also be dead and buried with his mother. Did she not deserve at least a tiny bit of respect and appreciation from his bull-headed father?

Dyer stopped crying but fidgeted and fussed. She shushed him the best she could, realizing he was probably wet and hungry again. Suddenly, Leoma realized quiet had settled overhead. "I think the worst of the storm has passed over."

"Let me look out first." Welby seemed calmer and spoke with a kinder tone. "Stay down here with Mrs. Fisk," he said to Kristina.

Leoma waited with the children, anxious to get out of the close confines of the storm cellar, while Welby climbed toward the exit. He pushed up on the cellar door but it wouldn't move. Shoving with his shoulder, he grunted with each repeated push. After several tries the door lifted a tiny crack.

"Something heavy has fallen on the door," Welby said grunting in a deep voice.

Leoma's heart pounded. They were trapped. Dyer fussed and Kristina whimpered again. Leoma prayed, quietly asking for God's help.

"It's beginning to budge a little more," Welby called down. "Maybe if we both push it'll give."

Leoma lay Dyer on the cot and braced the pillow against him. She'd do anything right now to get out. "You stand here and watch over your brother," she instructed Kristina. "I'll see if I can help your papa lift the door."

She quickly mounted the steps, and pressed much too close to Welby in the narrow space, Leoma lent her strength, and together they pushed repeatedly. Leoma inwardly grumbled. If the man would bathe more often the task would be much easier. Finally, the debris that had them trapped slid off the door. One last push freed them.

Golden twilight filtered through the opening. After a deep breath of fresh air, Leoma went back down into the cellar and snuffed out the lantern's flame. She sent Kristina out to her father and carried Dyer up the stairs. When she stepped out of the cellar she expected to find her house in shambles, but so far as she could see, there was nothing more than minor damage to the back porch and shutters. Scattered across her yard were tree branches of all sizes and bits of wood and tin. Large sections of roof from someone's home rested against the carriage house; she hoped it wasn't hers. The air was cooler now and a light rain continued to fall. With Dyer bundled close to her she dashed into the house while Welby held open the back door.

Instead of coming inside with her and the children, Welby walked to the front of the house, obviously concerned about the condition of his horse and buckboard, but she needed to keep Kristina and Dyer inside where it was safe and dry. She could examine the exterior of her house later. She'd just stepped into the kitchen when someone pounded repeatedly on the front door. The frantic banging sent her rushing through the kitchen and into the front room. Anna Jo and her children were hovered together on the porch, their clothes soaked, and tears streaking all three faces.

"I'm glad you're okay," Anna Jo said.

"Oh, my dears, come in, come in." Without hesitation, Leoma rushed the neighbors into the living room. "What happened? Did you get caught out in the storm? Where is George?"

"The tornado took off most of our roof and one side of the house." Anna Jo's voice quivered as she spoke. "George went into town to see if anyone needs help. May we stay with you until he returns?"

"Of course you may. Let's get all of you dry." Leoma took Dyer up to the bedroom and laid him in the cradle, hoping he would wait a few minutes longer without too much fuss to be changed and fed. With an armful of clean towels Leoma rushed back down the stairs. Anna Jo rubbed her son's head dry while Leoma wrapped Doris and Kristina in towels and dried their faces, arms, and legs.

"Your Jeremy tried to convince George to dig us a storm cellar, and that stubborn man of mine just wouldn't listen. It's a wonder we weren't killed." Anna Jo was clearly shaken to the core.

"I'm thankful God protected you. Next time a storm approaches you run here as fast as you can. There's plenty of room for you in our cellar."

"Thank you. I think perhaps George will make us a shelter when he repairs our house, at least, if I have my say in the matter."

Another loud knock rattled the front door. Leoma rushed to open it and found Welby standing there looking disheveled and worried. "I know you have extra folks with you but—"

"For goodness sake, Welby, come inside." By now the man should know he's welcome no matter who's there.

Welby dipped his head then looked up. "Some of the folks in town said after the storm blew over here, they saw a big tornado funnel headed in the direction of my farm." He slapped his hat against his leg and put it back on his wet head. "I'd like to leave Kristina here with you, while I ride out home to see if I still have a house and barn. Would you mind?"

"Not at all, Kristina will be fine here. I'll see that she's fed and bathed, and she can sleep upstairs if you don't return tonight. It appears the Langleys will be staying over, too, so she'll have some playmates."

"It's a lot to ask of you, Leoma. I appreciate your kindness."

The Lord would expect her to be hospitable and to help those in need. "Think nothing of it," she said. "I hope your farm escaped any damage."

"Thank you." For the first time Leoma saw something more than anger and sorrow in Welby's eyes. Before he turned away she was sure she detected a small measure of honest appreciation in his eyes.

Welby strode down the porch steps and across the yard. He jumped the small fence that surrounded the littered yard, and climbed into his undamaged buckboard in one swift movement. Leoma watched as he turned toward home, hoping with all the hope she could muster, that he would find his house and farm intact.

Chapter 6

Vicious clouds roiled in the sky north of town, a reminder of the fury they contained as they passed over head a few minutes earlier. Welby had seen remnants of the tornado's destruction in town already. Roofs were missing from a few homes and businesses, several overturned wagons littered the streets and yards, and sides of houses were ripped open leaving the furnishings exposed to the rain. As far as he'd heard nobody had died, but he didn't stay in town long enough to talk with many of the men. Everyone was still a bit dazed.

Thankful his horse and buckboard were unharmed, he rode along as fast as he dare, worried about what disaster lay ahead. Somehow, all of Leoma's talk about God's protection just didn't set well with him right now, and he expected the worst. He could abide by some of what the Good Book said, but it was hard to believe God cared about things like his personal needs, his family, or his property. Too many things had gone wrong in his life. He'd seen too much trouble and grief to have faith in that kind of God.

Welby snapped the reins, pushing the worn out old mare to her limits. Nightfall dimmed his view ahead and he wanted to get home before total darkness. A flash of lightning pierced the sky in the distance ahead of him, followed by thunder. At least what was left of the storm was far ahead of him, and there was no chance of riding into it. The muddy road indicated heavy rain had fallen recently, but it was passable. Bits of hail still lay on the ground. Trees had been stripped of their foliage and snapped into little pieces, like matchsticks, and strewn across the land. The roadside was littered with debris. Now and then, Welby had to slow down and go around large branches, or stop and remove those that lay across his path. It seemed the farther north he went the worse the damage was, though he couldn't see far beyond the edge of the road.

Thinking he should have passed the Gallager family's farm by now, he slowed again, but he'd seen no sign of their house or barn in the increased darkness. Surely if his neighbors were home he'd see some evidence of lantern light, even though their farm was back off the road several hundred yards. But he'd seen nothing but darkness. Another five minutes and he should reach his place.

The old wagon wheel that marked his driveway was still propped against the large rock. He pulled back on the reins and steered Mabel— fondly named after his mother-in-law, and just about as old and rickety— through a wide mud puddle and up the narrow lane to his farm. The outline of his house wasn't visible against the night sky, but over to the left loomed the black silhouette of his barn, a welcome sight. As he drew closer the landscape changed. Trees were twisted and broken, and where his house once stood, was a pile of rubble. Pieces of wood and furniture were tossed around the yard and strewn as far as he could see. Too dazed to move for several seconds, he sat in the buckboard, too numbed by the sight to climb down.

"To the barn Mabel," he finally ordered, turning the mare to the left across the yard. The wagon bumped and jerked as the wheels ran over the broken remnants of his home.

At first glance, when Welby reached the barn, he could see that one side of the building was missing, and the hen house he'd built just a few months earlier, was no where to be seen. He'd put a lot of work into making that structure strong and sturdy enough to last for many years. It was a shock to see that one storm had wiped it completely away along with all the hens.

Welby cursed beneath his breath as he climbed down from the buckboard and led Mabel into what remained of the barn. The lantern that hung beside the door was still there and he lit it, hoping to survey his damaged property. First he unhitched Mabel, pumped a bucket of water, and filled a trough with grain for the mare.

Lantern in hand he walked through the barn first. A few stars and a sliver of moon broke through the clouds and shone above him in one corner where the roof had been ripped away. His plow was still where he'd left it, but the side of the barn where a supply of hay once stood in tall, straight stacks, gaped wide open to the night, and bales of hay were tumbled and strewn about.

Nearby a cow bellowed. At least one animal was alive. If any of the chickens survived they must have been scattered to the next state. There weren't any roaming around the yard, and he didn't hear a single one clucking.

Ignoring the sudden chill in the air, Welby wandered across the yard toward his house, letting the lantern light his way. A distant rumble reminded him that he'd been visited by a power greater than anything he could control. He stopped short before stumbling over a child's wooden wagon, toppled upside down and broken. Careful to avoid tripping on downed limbs, pieces of roof, and barn siding, he reached what should have been the back porch and entrance into the kitchen. He mounted the steps to a pile of twisted rubble. A few feet away he spotted a heap of lumber as if it had been arranged for a giant bonfire. He couldn't be sure, but it appeared the twister hadn't unearthed the cellar. To be safe, he'd wait until morning to check that out.

Welby stood on the wooden steps still in shock. He tried to quell his anger as he surveyed the destruction of all he'd worked so hard to build. He'd come to this new territory with promises of prosperity, wide open space to farm, and dreams of a good home for his family. This was to be everything New York City was not: clean air, acres of rich soil for crops, and a land of opportunity. A lump formed in his throat. The rims of his eyes burned. He turned and stomped down the steps, walking in determined strides back toward the barn. He kicked debris out of the way as he went. With each step he growled out a curse word. *Leoma and her god, ha! She can have him.* All he needed right now was a long swig of brandy. He'd emptied the bottle he kept stashed beneath the seat of the wagon before he'd gotten half way here, but he was pretty sure another pint was secure in its hiding place, since that side of the barn stood unharmed.

Inside the partitioned off shop where Welby did his woodworking and repairs, he held the lantern high and glanced around. It looked just as he'd left it that afternoon. A half-finished bookcase he'd been making for Louise leaned against one wall. In the far corner, undisturbed, was an old storage trunk full of his wife's possessions, books as he recalled, that he'd insisted they keep stored in the barn until the bookcase was finished. He wondered what else was in the trunk besides books, but he didn't much care to look right now.

He hung the lantern on a hook over his workbench. The worn Indian blanket on a bed of hay, where he sometimes stretched out for a short afternoon snooze, was wrinkled from his last nap. Welby jerked up the blanket and found the brandy. He breathed a sigh of relief. It was nearly full and the cap twisted off easily. Clutching the liquor in his right hand, he took three long gulps of the smooth liquid. Hopefully it would soothe his nerves and ease his anguish. How much was a man supposed to endure? His wife was dead, his son was starving to death, the house was blown away, and his farm was destroyed! It was too much to handle all at one time. He tossed his head back and chugged down several more swallows, hoping it would dull his thoughts and help him get some sleep.

Welby tossed back his head, drained the last drop from the bottle, and belched. As if it would comfort him, he clutched the bottle with both hands, and dropped back on the straw bed, hoping for relief from this miserable life. His mind blurred, the bottle slid to the floor. Slowly, his anger subsided as he drifted into a stupor and sank into blackness.

AFTER NURSING DYER, LEOMA tucked him into the cradle. She turned her attention to Kristina, Anna Jo, and her two little ones who were down stairs. She carried a stack of blankets into the living room. Still damp from dashing out into the rain earlier, she suddenly shivered, chilled by the night air, so she quickly built a fire in the living room fireplace. Huddled together on the thick Aubusson rug, Kristina, Doris, and Jody were wrapped in towels. Anna Jo had gone into the kitchen to put a kettle of water on the stove for tea.

Moments later, Leoma's friend came out of the kitchen and stood beside her. "I can't thank you enough for taking us in. I don't know what we'll do now that our house is half destroyed."

"Your family can stay with me as long as you need to. Goodness knows I have plenty of spare room." Leoma liked having a house full of people to keep her mind off of Jeremy and Elizabeth. It seemed four months hadn't erased her sorrow, and sometimes she hated being alone, just her and baby Dyer, with so much quiet space. And Dyer's father wasn't much company, not that she wanted the company of another man. Even if she did, it sure wouldn't be that ungrateful clod. His usual visits were only a half-hour or so and most of the time, she could hardly wait for him to leave, with his cigarette smoke-covered overalls and whisky breath—or whatever the foul smelling stuff was that made his breath and body reek. She shuddered.

The flame in the fireplace roared and crackled. Leoma held her hands close to the fire to warm them, trying to put Welby Soderlund out of her mind. She helped Anna Jo remove the wet towels and the children's clothing, and hung it all in front of the fireplace to dry. She quickly wrapped each child in a blanket. "Once we get these little ones warmed up and their heads are good and dry, we'll tuck them into the guest bed for the night." Leoma lined up the bundled children in front of the blaze, staying close beside them to make sure they were safe and warm.

Anna Jo frowned. "Do you suppose Welby will be back for his daughter tonight?"

"I don't think so. But it's fine with me. I'd just as soon he didn't come back till morning. And who knows what condition he'll find his farm in. It's a long ride out there and back. I suppose if he does show up here later he can sleep out in the carriage house. It still has a roof and there's no sense him dragging his daughter out in the cold in the middle of the night."

Night had fallen and it wasn't long before George Langley came to check on his family. He was soaked and bedraggled, hat in hand. Leoma stood aside as he stepped into the front room. Anna Jo rushed into his arms. "Come warm yourself by the fire," Leoma said, her hand on his back nudging the man toward the hearth. "Is the damage in town severe?"

"It's tore up some, but it ain't too bad. The bell tower is ripped off the new schoolhouse, window shutters and railings are thrown about, and a few houses got hit hard. Some of those poor folks still living in tents got pretty beat up."

"Is anyone badly injured?" Leoma would gladly help in any way she could. There was plenty of room in her house for more people. She had four bedrooms upstairs and the guestroom downstairs, and if they wanted to bunk on the floor or in the carriage house, they were welcome. The least she could do was provide shelter and something hot to drink.

George inched his way in between his children and hunched in front of the blazing fire, rubbing his hands together vigorously. "I don't know. The doc is over at his office doing what he can. There's none dead that I know of."

Leoma shuddered at the thought of more death and funerals. The Langley children nuzzled close to their father and Kristina stood to one side, still shivering, wide-eyed and confused. Leoma went to the girl and pulled her close to comfort and warm her. "Why don't I put the children to bed," she said her arms around Kristina's shoulders. She ran her fingers through the girl's hair to make sure it was dry.

"There's no need to bed down our two," George said. "The folks at the hotel are putting up anyone who can't sleep in their homes. Free of charge. I already made arrangements for us. I just came to collect Anna Jo and my youngsters."

"You're more than welcome to stay here. And water is hot if you'd like some tea."

"I appreciate it, but they're expecting us. The room is ready and waiting." George straightened and ushered his family toward the door, like a mother duck lining up her ducklings to cross a road.

Leoma quickly gathered the discarded clothing that belonged to Doris and Jody and handed them to Anna Jo. "Well, at least keep the children bundled in the blankets to keep them warm on the way to the hotel."

After hugging Anna Jo, she kissed Doris and Jody on their cheeks.

Each parent picked up a child and left, thanking Leoma on their way out. Leoma watched them walk into the darkness in quick long strides, each clutching a child close to their chest.

The night was calm now, moonless and cool. Leoma wished there was some way to know what Welby had found when he arrived home. With both of his children left here in her care, she wondered for a moment when Welby would return. She didn't mind, but still not up to par physically, she sighed, longing for a good night's sleep. However, she supposed few people in town would get much sleep tonight.

Kristina sat alone on the floor in front of the fireplace. With the Langley children there earlier to keep her company, the little girl had been somewhat entertained and distracted, but now she looked frightened and confused.

"Where's my papa?" Kristina said, almost inaudibly.

Leoma walked over to the child and took her hand, pulling upward until the girl stood to her feet. "Come sit on the chair with me." Leoma guided Kristina to the big comfortable chair nearest the fireplace. She tucked the blanket snugly around the child and wrapped her arms around her. "Your daddy rode out to your farm to see if it was spared from the storm. He wants you to sleep here tonight, with Dyer and me. Do you mind?"

Kristina shook her head barely able to keep her eyes open. Leoma snuggled her closer for a moment, suddenly realizing the child hadn't eaten supper. Nor had she complained or asked for anything. Perhaps it wasn't unusual to do without. The poor girl's world was turned upside down right now, but Leoma doubted Welby would send his daughter to bed without something to eat. Leoma certainly couldn't allow the child to go hungry. She thought for a moment about what was in the icebox and pantry. Looking down into Kristina's dark eyes Leoma smiled. "Let's go see what I can find for you to eat. I bet you're hungry aren't you?"

"Yes."

It was the saddest little "yes" Leoma had ever heard. Her heart ached for the child. It only took a few minutes for Leoma to settle Kristina at the kitchen table with a bowl of warmed, canned beans, and a leftover biscuit with thick butter and molasses dripping over the edges. She poured milk into a cup, and placed it before the girl who was already eagerly scooping the beans into her mouth. Before long the bowl was empty. "Well I think you need a piece of gingerbread for dessert. Would you like that?"

"Yes, ma'am." This time the girl's answer came with more enthusiasm as she smiled and bobbed her head several times.

Leoma set a generous square of gingerbread in front of Kristina then cut a piece for herself. She poured a cup of steaming tea and joined Kristina at the table, enjoying the company. Studying the thin, disheveled child across from her, Leoma wondered what Elizabeth would have looked like at that age. What would they talk about? Such fun it would have been, to sew pretty clothes for her daughter, to put ribbons in her hair, and to read stories to her. Clearly, beneath the neglect, Kristina was a pretty child with promise of great beauty.

"Why are you crying?" Kristina said.

Leoma swiped away the unexpected tears that dampened her cheeks. She bit her lips together, unsure how to tell a five-year-old about her baby's death, and how much she missed her daughter. She sucked in a long breath and thought about how to explain it. Speaking in terms she hoped a young child might understand, using the simplest words Leoma told her the truth.

"Well you see, Kristina, a few months ago I had a baby girl. It wasn't long after your little brother was born. Her name was Elizabeth, and she was very little and sweet. But she was born much too soon, and she couldn't breathe very well." Leoma's throat tightened but she forced herself to go on. "God took her to live with him so he could take care of her. She's in heaven now."

"Papa said that's where momma is." Kristina looked thoughtful then said, "Maybe my momma is helping God take care of your baby, like you take care of Dyer. Can you take care of me, too?"

Leoma gulped a breath of unexpected surprise. How perceptive for a five-year-old child. She had no intention of raising Kristina, yet she couldn't tell the child it was impossible. Several seconds passed as she attempted to compose a reasonable answer. "Whenever your daddy needs me to help him, like tonight, I will be very happy to take care of you." Leoma rose from her chair and wrapped her arms around Kristina. She didn't want to stop holding the child.

A short time later, in the same bedroom upstairs where Dyer slept in the cradle, Leoma tucked Kristina into bed. She sat on the edge of the mattress until Kristina was sound asleep.

Lantern in hand, Leoma tiptoed down the stairs and went into the parlor. She raised the wick for more light, and lit a second lantern on the desk to brighten the room. Dyer would probably be hungry and wet again soon, but until he awakened she would steal a few minutes for herself. With her Bible in hand, she settled into the chair, and wondered what tomorrow held for the town and her friends. She'd never experienced this kind of devastation, and couldn't imagine how awful it must be for families whose homes were destroyed. Before turning to the marked page in the book of Psalms, she said a quiet prayer for the people in town and Welby and his children.

Chapter 7

THE MORNING DAWNED WITH scorching sunshine, and syrupy humidity dripped from his skin. It wasn't yet seven o'clock and Welby's shirt clung to his back. He dug a handkerchief from his hip pocket and swiped it across his face and neck as he scanned the sky. Dark clouds billowed in the west, threatening another storm. If he didn't get busy, he wouldn't accomplish a thing before rain hit. Angry and feeling defeated, he stuffed the damp hanky back into his pocket and stomped across the yard.

Welby rummaged through splintered wood and shattered glass, setting aside anything he might salvage or repair. He tossed the rest into a larger pile to burn. The few things Welby unearthed from the destroyed house: an unbroken hand mirror, his deceased wife's Bible, the damp pages creased and rumpled but intact, a few pots and pans, and a handful of unbroken dishes, were carried to the barn and placed in the dry corner. The metal bed frame and oak dresser, though tossed on their sides, were in fair condition, except for the broken mirror. Maybe that could be replaced. Out in the edge of the cotton field, he'd found the mattress of the bed he and Louise had shared since their wedding night, but it was soaked and useless.

Welby doused the mound of debris with kerosene and struck a match on the sole of his boot. Watching the flames rise to the sky, he swiped his forearm across his forehead, and stepped back from the intense heat. He grabbed up another dead chicken, shook his head, and tossed the limp bird on the burning rubble. How many chickens was that? Eleven? Twelve? The remaining dozen were nowhere in sight.

He surveyed the property again, walking around what was left of the house's foundation, and came upon the rosebush Louise had planted last spring. The flowers were bright pink, if he remembered right, but now it was half crushed by debris and stripped nearly bare. Louise had loved those roses. What was left of the bush appeared to be alive, and had one bud on a broken stem. He let out a deep sigh of despair and turned away. It would take months to repair and replace everything. There was nothing more he could do here until he bought materials to rebuild. His stomach was empty, and it was time he head into town and check on his children and Leoma.

As soon as the trash fire died down, Welby climbed onto the buckboard. As Mabel prodded along the muddy road toward town, Welby struggled to rouse himself out of the nightmare. When he neared the Gallager's farm he wondered if they'd survived the storm. He pulled into their yard, glad to find the entire Gallager family unhurt. Mr. Gallager greeted him. "How'd you fare the storm, Mr. Soderlund?"

"Not good at all. My house is gone, but part of the barn is still standing."

"Guess you never know what one of those twisters will snatch up. We spent the night in the cellar."

The Gallager's barn was gone and the roof was torn off their house. It didn't appear they'd lost many animals, though. Two dogs roamed around the yard sniffing everything, and it looked as if all their pigs were in the pen undisturbed.

After promising to help them repair the house, Welby continued on his way toward town, gazing at downed trees and twisted debris along the way. It looked much worse in the mid-morning light than it had on his way out last night.

He hoped Leoma had fared okay overnight with both children. Sometimes Kristina cried for her momma during the night, and a bad storm like the one yesterday could have set her off and given her bad dreams. He supposed the child would eventually outgrow the problem.

Leoma's house came into view. It was a relief to see it hadn't suffered much damage. When he'd left the evening before, Welby was in such a hurry to check out his farm, he didn't bother to thoroughly survey the woman's property. Other than a few missing shutters and pieces of trim on the porch, the twister had left her house in pretty good shape. It was in one piece and it appeared the roof was fine, so it wouldn't take much to repair the damage.

A few minutes later Welby knocked on Leoma's front door. With his son in one arm, and his daughter huddled in the folds of the woman's skirt, she welcomed him. Leoma motioned him inside with a tilt of her head. "May I pour you a cup of coffee?"

"Yes, ma'am." Welby followed Leoma and his daughter into the kitchen, and watched as Leoma opened the cupboard and took down a large mug, the kind a man could get a good grip on. She cradled Dyer in one arm and managed the coffee pot and cup with the other, keeping the steaming brew away from the child. She set the filled mug on the table.

"Please sit down." Leoma pointed toward the place at the end of the table. "Would you care for cream or sugar?"

"No, thank you."

Welby pulled out the chair, sat down, and took a swig of the coffee. Not bad. It was good and strong, but not burnt. He hadn't eaten since yesterday noon, and the scalding brew hit his stomach like red hot coals.

"Help your self to a blueberry muffin," Leoma said, putting the plate of muffins directly in front of him.

The perfectly baked muffins were obviously a gift from a neighbor, he surmised. Leoma Fisk certainly couldn't have baked anything that enticing—if she could bake anything at all. He helped himself to one and took a bite. The moist sweet blueberries and cake like muffin melted in his mouth and invited a second bite without delay. After he swallowed another mouthful, he washed it down with more coffee. "I don't suppose you baked those, did you?"

"Excuse me?" Leoma's frown was scorching. "I certainly did."

"Sorry, I just figured, never mind. They're very good." Whew, he got himself out of that pickle. He didn't think Leoma had such spunk in her.

Moving to the other side of the wooden kitchen table, Leoma rocked from side-to-side, his son's head now nuzzled against her shoulder. The boy was growing. He had a strong back, and when he was awake he held his head up without bobbing about.

"Is everything all right at your farm?" Leoma said, her voice cool.

"No. As a matter of fact, it's mostly gone. My house is completely destroyed, and one side of my barn is ripped wide open."

Eyes wide, Leoma snuggled Dyer close to her heart and lay her cheek atop his head. "I'm so sorry. I hoped for better news."

Welby downed another swallow of coffee before going on, ignoring the burning heat that singed his throat. "That's not the worst of it. The hail pounded my garden and cotton crop into the ground, and slaughtered nearly all of my chickens. I found half of their carcasses scattered all over the property this morning, and who knows where the other half are. I knew when the old rooster didn't crow at the crack of dawn it was bad. One pig's dead, too. That'll mean less meat stored up for winter."

Leoma clamped her lips together and shook her head, clearly dismayed. Not sure why he'd blurted out all that information, Welby lifted the coffee mug to his mouth and took two long swallows. Even though the woman irritated him with her fancy ways and her talk about the Lord God this, and the Lord God that, Welby could see she'd come to care about his children, and the concern she expressed about his losses was genuine. But he didn't mean to ramble on about the dead animals, especially with Kristina listening.

"What will you do?" Concern filled Leoma's eyes.

Welby squared his shoulders and lifted his chin. What could he do? Half the town was as bad off as he, and so were several of the neighboring farms. Some were probably worse. "Like everyone else, I'll rebuild the house and start over. There's not much else a man can do."

Leoma refilled Welby's mug without asking and excused herself to put Dyer down for a nap. After she placed the baby in the cradle she rocked it for a few minutes, until his eyes were closed. Dyer was a good child, rarely fussy or difficult. She tiptoed out of the room with a special feeling in her heart she couldn't quite identify.

Moments later, back down in the kitchen, Leoma poured a cup of coffee for herself. Welby lifted the brown stoneware mug to his mouth, gripping the big handle the same way Jeremy had always done. Having Welby at her table in Jeremy's chair, and drinking coffee from her husband's favorite mug was awkward. It was the first time Welby had been at her table and she couldn't stop the nervous jitters in her stomach. None-the-less, after all he'd been through, and considering the situation, it seemed the polite and hospitable thing to do.

Leoma's heart ached with the heaviness of missing Jeremy, and the constant reminders of his absence. She had to tell herself repeatedly, her husband was gone to his eternal life in Heaven, and her life must continue on here, without him. As she thought about the situation with Welby's house, she had many things to consider, and she wanted to do what was right and proper. An idea had popped into her head earlier, and she pondered long and hard whether it would cause a scandal.

Leoma blew on the hot coffee and chewed on her lower lip for several seconds. Considering the condition of the town, it seemed right and acceptable to help Welby and his children through this difficult time. She sipped the still-scalding coffee. Her decision was made.

Turning to Welby she smiled. "Our carriage house has a small room with a bed. It isn't fancy, but you're welcome to bunk there until your house is rebuilt. There's plenty of room for Kristina to stay here in the house with me."

Welby scratched his wooly beard. "With this weather lately it might be a few months before I can move back to the farm."

"I understand."

With one forefinger Welby scratched his beard again. "Do you suppose it's the proper thing to do, staying in your home and all?"

Leoma couldn't think of any reason why it would be improper. "Sleeping in the carriage house is not as if you'd be living inside with me. You have to sleep someplace, and you're here to visit Dyer nearly every afternoon anyway. A lot of people will have to make do until things get back to normal. We're no different."

Normal. Would her life ever be normal? Leoma was no longer sure what that meant. Her mind flashed over the past three years: traveling half way across the country to live in an unknown place extremely different from Boston, living in a tent until her house was built, becoming a widow at the age of twenty-three, and watching her baby die a short time later, none of it was normal. Now this destructive storm. Nothing had been normal in her life since she'd left Boston to come west.

At least while Jeremy was alive, she had his love, his protection, his smiles, and laughter. They'd shared the excitement of building a home, and preparing for their first child, wondering if it would be a boy or a girl, and spending long hours into the night deciding on names. They'd agreed on Joshua Blaine if it was a boy and Elizabeth Rose if it was a girl. Sadly, Jeremy never had the chance to find out if he had a son or daughter.

Such a short time ago Leoma's life had settled into a pleasant routine. For a time it seemed to be normal, now that she thought back to those days. Her marriage was excellent, and she'd been so filled with happiness.

"I do appreciate the offer," Welby said, drawing her mind back to their conversation. His words were hesitant. She waited for him to say more but he didn't.

Maybe he wasn't comfortable with the idea of living in her carriage house, or perhaps it was her ineptness in the kitchen that made him undecided. She was the first to admit she was unskilled in that area and Welby had already made his opinion clear after she'd burned the coffee. Then again, maybe that had nothing to do with his hesitation. Perhaps he was concerned about paying rent. "I wouldn't expect payment, unless you think that would make the arrangement more acceptable."

"I'll think on it."

Whatever Welby's decision, at least she'd done the neighborly thing. In spite of the man's unholy habits, Leoma cared about the welfare of his children. She could put up with their father for a few weeks, or months if necessary, while he restored their home. God would give her the strength and patience.

Welby patted the pocket of his overalls as if searching for something, then pulled out a cigarette. Leoma had heard of machine-made cigarettes, but she'd never seen one until now. No one in her family smoked, and she didn't know anyone who had taken up the habit. One thing was certain.

She would not allow such a nasty, sinful thing to smell up her house. Before Welby could strike the match he'd taken from his overalls, Leoma extended her arm straight out, the palm of her hand nearly touching the end of his nose.

"I'll have no smoking in my house!" So much for her patience. She just couldn't stop her spontaneous reaction.

Welby grunted and stuffed the cigarette and match back into his pocket. "I suppose if I accept your offer to stay you'll tell me I can't take a swig of brandy now and then either."

"That's absolutely right! Not under my roof." She lowered her hand but stood firm with both hands planted on her hips. Perhaps it was a mistake after all, inviting Welby to live on her property, but she couldn't very well renege on the offer. "You're welcome to stay in the carriage house and share my meals here as long as necessary, but I won't have you disrespect my home with your foul cigarette smoke and liquor."

Welby grunted again and glared at her. She glared back, at a loss for further words. Well, if the man didn't like her rules he could go sleep in what was left of his barn, or pay for a room at the hotel. She'd keep Kristina and Dyer with her as long as they needed her.

Welby drained the coffee mug and plunked it down on the table with a loud thud. He pushed back the chair, the legs scraping loudly on the floor, and stood up. "I'm going to walk through town and see what can be done today about building supplies and helping out the others. You mind keeping my girl with you a little longer?"

"Not at all. But if you decide to accept my offer for the carriage house, you best let me know so I can make up the bed. And I'd appreciate knowing if I should prepare meals for you."

"Don't know," was all Welby grumbled as he stomped out of the kitchen and through the living room. The front door banged shut, causing Kristina to jump.

Hands still firmly planted on her hips, Leoma walked to the front room window, her heart pounding. Kristina followed close behind her. Leoma pulled aside the lace curtain, and side-by-side she and Kristina stared out the window. Welby stormed across the yard in long strides, letting the gate slam behind him.

"I think your daddy needs to learn some manners," Leoma said in a quiet tone. "How ever did your mother put up with the bull-headed brute?"

"Is my papa coming back?" Kristina's eyes were brimming with confusion and worry.

Sorry the little girl had witnessed the unpleasant exchange, Leoma drew Kristina close to her. "Oh, yes, sweetheart. Of course your father is coming back, after he helps some people in town. He would never leave you behind. He'll be here by dinner time, you'll see."

Thank goodness for dear, sweet Anna Jo. She and her children had knocked on Leoma's front door just minutes after Welby stormed out. Her friend explained that she needed a more suitable place to spend the day than in the confines of the hotel. Every room in the two-story establishment was filled, and the lobby was teeming with anxious wives and unruly children of all ages. Leoma was glad Anna Jo had come to her with her two little ones. Not only was Leoma happy for the company, it would be a good distraction for Kristina to have playmates.

The two women worked harmoniously, side-by-side in the kitchen, preparing the noon-time meal. Dyer was napping again in the cradle and the older children played quietly on the living room floor. Leoma watched Anna Jo closely, taking mental notes, as her friend showed her how to make fluffy biscuits using real baking powder she'd brought from home. First thing tomorrow Leoma would purchase a can of her own baking powder.

"And now for the gravy," Anna Jo said, working like a well-experienced cook.

"I never could figure out how to keep my gravy from getting lumpy." Leoma stirred the bubbling mixture in the cast iron skillet and grimaced at her poor cooking abilities. "Jeremy wouldn't eat it, but he was always sweet about it and encouraged me to keep trying."

Anna Jo smiled and admitted, "I couldn't boil water when I married George. I was running to my momma every day asking for her help. I was lucky to have her nearby when George and I got married."

"Did your family come west too?" Leoma hadn't met Anna Jo's parents and didn't know much about her new friend's mother and father.

But she envied her. Leoma had grown up in a house with a hired cook and a maid. Her mother had no interest in cooking and spent most of her time reading or doing needlework and charity projects.

For a moment Anna Jo looked as if she might cry. "No. Just after Doris was born, my mother died from some lung disease. My father still lives in Philadelphia."

"I'm sorry." Leoma couldn't imagine losing her mother, no matter how far away she lived. Life would just be dreadful without her mother's letters, and the hope that someday they would see each other again.

The two women didn't talk for several minutes. Kristina and her playmates had moved to the dining room to play. They sat on one corner of the Persian rug that stretched beneath the large cherry wood dining table. Content with the simple clapping game Doris had taught them, they played happily. Anna Jo dipped her finger into the gravy and tasted.

"It needs a dash more salt and pepper," Anna Jo said. She shook some of each from the metal shakers Leoma kept on the shelf above the stove. "It's none of my business, but do you think letting Welby stay here is a good idea?"

Leoma kept her eyes on the gravy, stirring in slow even strokes as she pondered the question. She didn't know how long Welby would have to sleep in the carriage house if he accepted her offer, or what he would expect of her. Most likely she'd do his laundry and make his meals. It was only right for her to invite him in to eat with his daughter. But she hadn't decided whether it was proper or not. "I don't know. He will sleep in the carriage house if he decides to stay."

"True; and I suppose he'd pay you weekly rent." Without missing a syllable, Anna Jo moved the cast iron skillet off the hot burner and stirred the simmering kettle of corn. "It's just his drinking liquor I worry about. He seems like such a temperamental clod, and you know yourself, liquor and hot tempers don't mix well. I'd sure worry about you."

Leoma thought about Anna Jo's concern as she laid a large ham steak in a hot skillet. She jumped back as it hissed and sizzled. "I told him right off there would be no drinking or smoking on my property. He wasn't too pleased with my rules and he stormed off in a huff. But I think he'll honor my wishes if he bunks in the carriage house."

"Well a woman can't be too careful. You never know what a man will try when he's boozed up." Anna Jo took over tending the ham, poking it with a fork, and lifting it to check the bottom side. "This will be ready soon. Those men better get here while the food's hot if they expect dinner."

Leoma set the dining room table for four adults, assuming Welby's hunger would bring him back. She placed smaller plates and cups on the kitchen table for the three older children. Just as George and Welby came through the back door and into the kitchen, Leoma filled a pitcher with fresh water and carried it into the dining room. The screen door slammed behind the men, causing Leoma to flinch.

In spite of the unpleasant circumstances, Leoma liked having the house filled with people. For the first time in many weeks, she was too busy and distracted to cry or mourn the loss of Jeremy and baby Elizabeth. It made the time pass more rapidly.

Just as quickly as she felt happy for the company, Leoma cringed. Welby patted his pocket, clearly going for his cigarettes. He wouldn't dare! Her mouth opened and her hand shot out, but before her warning burst out, Welby produced a white envelope.

Welby held the letter out to her. "Sol asked me to deliver this to you."

"Oh," she said in a weak whisper as she accepted it, and retreated to the other side of the kitchen. A quick glance at the envelope told her it was from her dearest friend, Glenda. She could always depend on Glenda for support and encouragement.

Leoma held the envelope to her heart for a moment before tearing it open. It had been two months since her last letter from her friend. News from Glenda always came on the wings of excitement. Leoma hungered for any small tidbit of information from home. She'd met Glenda when they were both four years old, and she couldn't remember a time in her life when they weren't best friends. Every day of grammar school they'd walked hand in hand to school. Later, they rode to school together on their bicycles, until the day they graduated from high school. To this day they remained close friends.

When Leoma had headed west with Jeremy, it was as difficult to say good bye to Glenda as it was to leave her parents. Leoma was barely unpacked and settled into their tent, when she wrote her first letter to Glenda telling her about the long trip and her first *horrible* impressions of Oklahoma.

Nothing had prepared Leoma for the hardships she would face, or the lack of conveniences. Moving from her parents' estate, where she had a large private bedroom suite, and an indoor toilet and bathtub, and into a tent with a nearby outhouse, was quite a shocking adjustment. If not for Jeremy's love and the devotion he showered upon her, she'd have been on the first train east.

What held her here now? The question tormented her daily, and the answer was always the same. She couldn't leave her beloved husband and daughter's burial place. She sensed Jeremy's presence within every room of this house. She felt close to them here.

Anxious to read the letter from Glenda, she nearly forgot her manners as she pulled the letter from the envelope. Just as quickly, realizing the others in the room were waiting on her for dinner, she slipped the letter and envelope into her apron pocket, and helped Anna Jo dish up the food and set the serving bowls and platters on the table. Conversation turned to the damage from the tornado and the work that needed to be done. The men ate quickly anxious to return to town.

"I suppose I'll take you up on your offer," Welby said to Leoma on his way to the back door.

Leoma followed him into the kitchen, a stack of dirty dishes in her hands. "I'll make up the bed this afternoon. Supper is served at six o'clock."

Nightfall brought a chorus of crickets and sounds Leoma still hadn't become accustomed to since being alone. The air was still warm and lazy. Welby had retired to the carriage house shortly after supper, and Anna Jo and George had returned to the hotel with their children to sleep in the room they'd rented on the second floor. Upstairs Dyer and Kristina were tucked snugly into bed. Leoma walked into the parlor, glad for a few minutes alone, and lit the lamp. She carefully unfolded the thin, white stationary and smiled at Glenda's salutation.

My dearest friend, Leoma,

I was thrilled to receive your letter, though I was terribly saddened by the tragic news it contained. Oh, how you must ache for your baby and husband. It just doesn't seem fair, but we know God is in control. I wish with all my heart I could be there to comfort you in your time of sorrow.

I'm glad the little boy you are caring for is growing healthier. It must gladden your heart to know you were instrumental in saving the child's life. I hope he thrives in your loving care.

It sounds as if the baby's father is an ogre. I fear he will cause you trouble and heartache if you aren't firm with him. I pray his visits with you while seeing his son will remain short and that you'll be safe.

I had a wonderful visit with your mother this week and she misses you so much, as we all do. I'm quite sure it won't be long until she ventures to Oklahoma for a visit with you, though I suppose it isn't my place to tell you that. I can safely tell you I plan to visit you in the near future, for I need your cheerful company, dear friend. I miss your laughter.

It is I who needs your cheerful company and laughter, Leoma thought. A visit from Glenda would do wonders to lift her spirits.

Please take care of yourself, and may God

*bless you with good health and everlasting
peace. Be assured that you are in my
thoughts and prayers every day. I look
forward to seeing you as soon as I can make
the arrangements to take off from work and
make travel plans. Until then . . .*

My love to you,

Glenda

Leoma held the letter to her breast and smiled, remembering the
many days she'd shared with Glenda over the years. The words she'd
read echoed in her head and filled her heart. She could hear her friend's
sweet voice as clearly as if Glenda stood beside her. Leoma longed for
those breezy mornings when the two of them sat on the front porch,
sipping tea and munching on snicker doodles fresh from the oven, or the
afternoons when they strolled through the commons, watching birds and
the myriad of people coming and going. And the laughter, oh my. How
long had it been since she'd laughed so freely?

Closing her eyes, Leoma pictured her home in Boston: the springtime
flowers and green grass, the sultry summer sunshine, the changing fall
colors of gold and yellow, and the glistening snow-covered landscape in
winter with city lights reflecting on the icy wonderland. It was an exciting
city, filled with history and beautiful architecture. She missed it.

Here, it seemed, everything turned gray in the winter, a dreary
picture with a few trees clumped here and there and muddy streets.
Springtime brought wild grasses and scattered redbud trees, but few
flowers colored the countryside or town until summer, when the wild
Indian Blanket dotted the road side here and there. It was hard for
Leoma to find the beauty in this crude little town. Rough buildings had
been thrown together to accommodate the growing throngs of people
who continued to flock to the area. Many families still lived in tents. If
Jeremy had lived, he would be designing beautiful buildings, fine multi-
story hotels, elegant restaurants, attractive store fronts, and lovely homes
with fenced yards. He'd had a vision, a dream, and a plan to help develop

this land that the government had opened up for new settlement. What Leoma saw springing up around her was nothing like what Jeremy had described. Perhaps in time it would become everything he'd said it would. She hoped so.

Still tucked away in the drawer of her desk, were Jeremy's drawings of a lovely building that would someday be her bookshop, along with other architectural plans for buildings he'd hoped to see built in the town. But the community was young yet, and she'd heard that the men in charge had big plans. They already called it Oklahoma City and it buzzed with activity and growth. Perhaps in time it would improve and qualify as a real city, but she was convinced it would never have the charm and beauty of Boston.

Her mind went back to Glenda's letter and she re-read the last paragraphs. Was it true that her mother might make a trip to Oklahoma? The idea lifted her spirits and brought a smile to her lips. She must ask her mother to bring along the trunk of books she'd left behind. It would be a grueling trip, but her mother was a spry, adventurous woman for her fifty-one years, and Leoma had no doubt she could weather such a trip. Oh, what fun it would be to have her momma come stay for a month or two.

Leoma folded Glenda's letter and slipped it into the top desk drawer. She would answer it soon, but first, she'd write to her parents and plead with her mother to come soon for a nice long stay. She'd love to see her father as well, but he was always extremely busy with his work and speaking engagements.

She pulled a delicate sheet of her best white stationery from the flowered box on her desk and sniffed the lightly scented paper. Careful to not drip black ink on the desk, she filled the tortoise shell fountain pen and began to write.

WELBY SETTLED BACK ON the narrow bed and rested his head on the feather pillow Leoma had provided. The thin mattress sagged half way to the floor beneath the weight of his body, and the springs squeaked with the smallest movement. It was too warm to cover himself with the blanket. His mind wandered to his farm—or what was left of it—and he composed a mental inventory of materials he would need to purchase in the morning to begin rebuilding. Several men in town had volunteered to help each other. With community effort, the damaged homes and businesses would be repaired in no time. The new lumber mill at the edge of town was already buzzing with work; getting wood for framing his house and chicken coop shouldn't be a problem. With the rapid growth of the community, building materials were being transported into town almost daily to keep up with the demands. If all went well he'd only have to sleep in Leoma's carriage house a month or two at most.

Wide awake, his mind fast at work, Welby was anxious for daybreak so he could ride out to his place and get busy. The less time he spent under Leoma Fisk's, roof the better he'd like it. He supposed he should be more grateful for the woman's hospitality and the way she cared for his children, but something about her put him on edge. However, the money he'd save by not renting a room in town would make it easier to buy the lumber for his house. All the tools he'd need were already in his workshop in the barn.

Eyes closed at last, he remembered the day he'd carried Louise across the threshold into their new farm house. It seemed like decades ago, yet it had only been a little over two years ago that he lifted his wife into his arms and walked into their new home. He'd been one of the first to claim a piece of land away from town when the government opened up the unassigned lands for the white folks to settle, and he'd been the first to build a permanent house and barn. Welby had wanted the best for his new family. The house wasn't fancy, but it was big enough to raise a passel of kids, and it had everything Louise asked for—except an indoor toilet.

Welby wasn't keen on having a toilet inside the house. He'd heard about some homes on the east coast that had toilets and bathtubs indoors, but he'd built one of the best outdoor toilets in the area, and he wasn't going to change a thing. A partition separated the two individual seats and two doors. The raised seat holes were sanded smooth and painted to prevent splintering. Why, he'd even covered the large air vents near the top with screen wire to help keep out the flies and bugs. He grinned into the dark room, remembering Louise's reaction when she saw the magazine holder and a lantern shelf on the wall of each section. The only disadvantage he could think of was the inconvenience of having to walk outdoors, especially during the winter months. The outhouse had withstood the tornado so he'd keep right on using it when the new house was built.

Turning on his side, he tried to remember seeing an outhouse on Leoma's property. Aside from the main house and this carriage house, there were no other buildings. He'd find out in the morning. Meantime there was adequate privacy behind the carriage house if he found it necessary to relieve himself during the night.

Flopping onto his other side and attempting to find a comfortable position, Welby punched the pillow on both ends to give his head more support. He had to get some sleep before sun up or he'd be useless tomorrow. There was no point wasting his thoughts on such minor dribble as the advantages or disadvantages of indoor plumbing. The quicker he rebuilt his house the better he'd like it.

Chapter 8

WELBY THRUMMED HIS BIG fingers on the table and glared at her. Leoma turned away from him and placed her hands firmly on her hips. Her jaws ached from clenching them together to prevent spewing out words she'd regret. If she didn't posses better manners she'd clobber the lout with her cast iron skillet, gravy and all. Not a day passed that he didn't have some hateful comment or complaint about her cooking. Every evening he came to the supper table impatient, smelling of liquor and cigarette smoke. She wanted to stomp her foot and scream. Instead, Leoma sucked in a long, slow breath and exhaled as she sent up a quiet prayer. *Lord, I am your servant. Please give me patience. Help me to be kind and gracious to this man, no matter how difficult it is. Show me, Father, what I must do to keep peace in my home.*

Somewhat calmer, Leoma sighed and dipped the mashed potatoes into a serving bowl, hoping they didn't have any big lumps. She placed the dish on the kitchen table. Since Anna Jo and George had moved back into their repaired home, Leoma didn't have her friend's frequent assistance with meals, and it seemed there was no end to her culinary disasters. Anna Jo still visited often and gave Leoma new recipes and advice, but it wasn't the same as having her here to show her. Sometimes the biscuits came out too hard and other times they crumbled. The gravy was either too runny or full of lumps, and more often than not the meat was overcooked and tough. If only her mother had allowed her in the kitchen when she was younger, perhaps she'd be able to set a presentable meal on the table. Still, she was doing the best she could.

As Leoma moved between the stove and table placing the evening meal within easy reach of Welby's place, she diverted her thoughts to little Dyer and the progress he had made during recent weeks. The tiny boy was getting plump rolls on his arms and legs, and just that morning when she bathed him, she coaxed several smiles and loud jabbering noises from him. His cheeks were full and rosy now, and when she nursed him he gazed up at her with clear, blue focused eyes before dozing into a contented sleep. He'd outgrown his sleeping gowns, so she left the bottom ribbon untied so his little feet could move freely. Soon Dyer's entire layette would need to be replaced with bigger things.

Time had eased Leoma's pain of losing Jeremy and Elizabeth, but she couldn't help wondering how her daughter would look now. Would she be smiling and laughing? Would her hair be long enough to tie a pretty bow in it? She tried to imagine Jeremy holding their daughter, but it was difficult to put them both in the same picture. Her husband had never seen Elizabeth. Leoma realized Elizabeth's features were growing vague. If only she had a photograph of her daughter to help her remember. She paused and smiled happy she had Dyer to fill the emptiness.

Leoma's initial resentment toward Dyer had faded. With each passing week her heart grew fonder of the baby. And oh, how she adored Kristina. The child was such a pleasure. Leoma poured a small glass of milk and placed it in front of Kristina.

"Thank you," Kristina said in a very lady-like voice.

"You're welcome, sweetheart."

The little girl was also thriving in her care. Leoma enjoyed dressing her in clean dresses Anna Jo had handed down from her daughter, Doris, and brushing the girl's long wavy hair. Today Leoma braided Kristina's hair into pigtails that hung half way down her back, and she tied yellow ribbons into a bow at the end of each braid.

Leoma took her place opposite the girl and bowed her head to say a short prayer. The moment she opened her eyes Welby piled a large helping of potatoes onto his plate. Leoma watched as he smothered them with gravy, added a slice of ham, and two heaping spoonfuls of green beans. Before serving herself, Leoma dipped Kristina's food and cut the child's meat into bite-sized pieces. She offered the basket of hot bread to Welby. "Would you like a biscuit?"

Welby glared at the golden brown biscuits with one raised brow, as if to expect stones, or perhaps chunks of coal, but he accepted the bread with a slight nod. Leoma split one open for herself and slathered fresh butter on each half. The biscuit seemed to be fluffy and light and it didn't crumble into a million pieces, like those she'd made the day before. She lifted one half to her mouth and took a bite. It was good. No, it was delicious! If Welby found fault with these biscuits she'd clobber him for sure. Leoma spooned a heaping dollop of blackberry jam on the rest of her biscuit and smiled as she savored another bite, just daring Welby to complain.

The meal proceeded in near silence. Kristina chattered briefly about the games she'd played with Doris after naptime. Her father smacked, slurped, and burped. Once or twice Leoma thought she heard a quiet moan of approval from him, but she wasn't sure.

Welby had devoured three biscuits without a complaint or a reproving look.

Leoma took that as a good sign and watched as he sopped up the gravy on his plate with the last bite of biscuit number four and stuffed it into his mouth.

"Not bad," Welby finally said, as he pushed back from the table. "Looks like you might learn to cook yet."

It wasn't the kind compliment she'd hoped to hear, but it was better than his usual disparaging remarks. She'd accept it. "I am trying."

Welby nodded, and a half-smile appeared on his otherwise somber face as he stood. "I'll be leaving at sun up in the morning. The days are getting shorter and I want to haul that wagon load of lumber out to the farm and get as much work done on my house during daylight as I can."

"How much longer until it's finished?" She was ready to reclaim her privacy.

"Days, a week maybe, till it's livable. I imagine you're anxious to be rid of me and my girl. But I don't suppose Dyer is old enough to wean and take home yet is he?"

She shook her head. "No, he isn't." Leoma was startled by the sadness she suddenly felt at the thought of no longer having Kristina, and eventually Dyer, with her. What would she do with her time? The little girl had been wonderful company, and they'd spent hours each day reading stories, drawing pictures, and having tea parties, like Leoma's mother had done with her when she was a little girl. It was a joy to rock Dyer and sing lullabies to him, a thrill when he grasped her fingers and looked at her with his bright, blue eyes. Admittedly, she wouldn't miss Welby's crude manners and criticism, but she was almost getting used to having the man around. He'd repaired the damage on her house and kept her yard looking nice. Perhaps her privacy wasn't what she really wanted after all.

"I don't want to leave Miss Leoma," Kristina said, her lower lip protruding in a pout. "I want to stay here."

"You know better than that, girl," Welby said. "When the house is done we're going home."

"What about Dyer?" Kristina said. "Will he go home too?"

"Not until he's a little bigger and stronger," the child's father said firmly.

"He's bigger already. He—"

Leoma was out of her chair in an instant and put her arm around Kristina's shoulders. "It's all right, sweetheart. When your daddy gets the house finished and it's time to go home, he wouldn't know what to do without you there. He'd be all alone, and he will need your help. But you'll come and visit me and Dyer as often as you want, just like before."

The little girl looked up, her sad eyes glistening with tears. "What about our tea parties and story time?"

Leoma hugged Kristina tightly and kissed the top of her head, trying to reassure the child once again, knowing how difficult it would be for her to go home to a house with no mother. Kristina would have a lot of responsibilities heaped on her little shoulders long before she should. It was impossible to imagine what it must be like for her.

"We will still read and have tea parties, I promise." Leoma glanced up and noticed the anguish in Welby's eyes. Did he dread taking his children back to his farm without having Louise there to care for them? She fixed her gaze on Welby. "That will be okay with you, I assume."

How would he take care of these children on his own and run a farm at the same time? The task seemed overwhelming, impossible to Leoma.

"I suppose it'll be okay," Welby said.

"Promise, papa, promise like Miss Leoma did."

Welby groaned. "I promise." Kristina wiped her eyes and smiled up at Leoma. Relief and joy transformed the little face, making Leoma's heart leap. When she'd thought God had taken everything away from her, he had filled her life with more than she could have ever imagined. How could it be that she was so blessed by these two children when she felt so unworthy? She still longed for the warmth and love of her husband and the sweetness of her daughter, but she had two adorable children who loved her and depended on her. Her days were filled with laughter and contentment that she'd thought she would never experience again.

Leoma straightened, pressing one hand to her heart. If only the children's father would turn from his wicked, stubborn ways, she would feel much better about sending Kristina and Dyer home with him when the time came. How would the man bring up his son and daughter in the ways of the Lord, or teach them to have hope for the future, and instill in them a faith in God who loves them, if he won't even take them to church or say a simple prayer of thanks at mealtime?

Welby's lack of interest in godly matters was her greatest worry when it came to him caring for his children. She doubted he was able to read a Bible story to Kristina, and certainly he wouldn't say a bedtime prayer with her. Leoma would have to do everything in her power to keep Kristina and Dyer close to her, to be an influential part of their lives. But how?

Chapter 9

Welby shouldered another load of roofing material and climbed the ladder. If he worked hard the roof on his house would be done before dark, but billowing clouds pushed closer by the minute, and that could be a problem. With his arms full of shingles, he braced himself, and pushed into the stiff wind. He hauled the heavy load halfway up to the peak, where he'd left off.

In a few short minutes the sky had become menacing. Another strong storm was definitely blowing his way. A string of curse words flooded out of his mouth. Ah, what freedom he enjoyed here, knowing miss hoity-toity Leoma couldn't hear him, or tell him to mind his tongue. This was his house, and he'd say what he pleased. In a few days he'd be out from under Leoma's roof, once and for all.

He dropped the pile of shingles and began to nail another row into place, working feverishly against nature. George Langley yelled up from the back porch. "That lightning out yonder is getting closer! You best come on down off the roof and help me inside."

Welby glanced up just as a gust of wind grabbed some of the loose shingles and scattered them across the roof. In his haste to finish, he'd ignored the storm too long. The clouds had grown darker, bigger. Streaks of lightning slashed across the angry, gray sky. After the next flash he waited, and counted the seconds for the rumble of thunder.

"There's time to nail a few more. I'll be down pretty quick," he yelled as he hammered another shingle into place.

A blinding bolt of lightning hit the ground nearby, and instantly, deafening thunder cracked. Welby felt the hair on his body stand up before big drops of rain pelted his back. Swearing under his breath, he shoved the hammer into his belt and scurried off the roof and down the ladder.

"That was too close, old boy," George said, standing just inside the doorway. The minute Welby jumped inside to escape the deluge, George slammed the door shut. "I know you're anxious to finish this place, but getting yourself killed won't do you or your kids any good."

Welby pushed his wet hair off his face with both hands and grinned. "I just want to get out from under that woman's roof."

"What's the big rush?"

"I'm tired of her uppity ways, and her talk about the Lord this and God that. Since her mother got there two days ago, it's even worse. You'd think the old woman was a preacher the way she's always quoting the Bible." Welby shook his head several times. Nope, he couldn't get away from those two women fast enough.

"So, are you familiar with what the good book says?" George knelt down to lay another piece of hardwood flooring. "I haven't seen you at the church services."

"Why would I sit in a hard pew, and listen to some preacher tell me what a bad person I am, and carry on about how I'm going to some fiery pit when I die. I heard enough of that condemnation back when I was a kid. My mother and grandfather dragged me to church every Sunday."

George laughed. "Apparently it didn't scare you into repenting. When I heard the salvation message, why, I rushed right down to that alter. I got on my knees and begged God to forgive me right quick."

"You believe all that stuff?" Welby knelt down level with George and helped nail another plank in place. He glanced sideways at his new friend, waiting for an answer. He'd known George for a couple of years but never on a personal level. As two distant neighbors, they'd been busy settling in the community and raising families, so they'd spent little time talking until after the tornado had ripped their homes apart.

"Sure do."

"I just don't understand why." Welby shoved a wet strand of hair off his face, and looked sideways at George. "I mean, I can understand why old people get sick and die, or sometimes why careless accidents happen, and people get hurt or killed. What I don't understand, is how a caring God can let a young, healthy woman like my Louise die, or why he allowed that innocent little baby girl of Leoma's to die. Then you expect me to believe in him."

George's heavy hand landed on Welby's shoulder. "I don't know all the answers, my friend. I'm not much good at quoting a lot of verses from the good book. Why, I can't even read worth beans compared to the preacher, but I do my best. I know there's a purpose in everything that happens. God is real, and I know he cares about you and me."

"How do you know for sure?" Welby stopped hammering. He never did understand how a person could believe such a thing, but he had to admit, sometimes he did wonder about it. When Louise had tried to talk to him about what she'd read in her Bible, he'd refused to listen. Sometimes, the guilt he felt for turning his back on her when she spoke about the things she believed, ate at his gut.

George squeezed his shoulder and grabbed for another eight-foot strip of pine. "I just take what I read in the Bible on faith. I've always been taught the Bible is the divine words of God, given to us so we will know the truth of his great love for us. I feel that love deep down in my soul as much as I feel Anna Jo's love."

Without saying anything else for several minutes, Welby thought on George's words as they worked side-by-side. He wasn't sure he could go along with the man's way of thinking, but he wouldn't mind having the peace of mind George seemed to have. It almost seemed George was favored by the fates, or whatever it was that made him happy and successful. His family was healthy and cheerful, and George was a good man, a prosperous man.

LEOMA PULLED THE CURTAIN aside and looked out the front window, wondering if Welby and George would arrive soon. An hour earlier she'd fled to the cellar with the children and her mother, fearing this new storm would rip her house apart. Fortunately, the storm didn't last long, and it wasn't as fierce as the one that had torn the town apart earlier in the month. When she'd come up out of the cellar there were a few leaves scattered in the yard, and the ground was soaked but that was all. The thunder still rumbled north of town, but the rain had stopped. Dark, ugly clouds still roiled in the sky as if more rain might be on the way, but the wind had died down. It appeared the worst of the storm was over.

It would be dark soon. Dinner was ready to be dipped and put on the table. Earlier in the day, Anna Jo had come and helped Leoma bake a peach cobbler. Its fragrance still lingered throughout the house. A kettle of soup simmered on one burner, and a pan of cornbread, covered with a dish towel to keep it warm, waited on the side of the stove.

"When is my papa coming?" Kristina asked, for the forth or fifth time, as she came along side Leoma and tugged on her long skirt.

Leoma took a deep breath and smiled down at the child. "I'm sure he'll be along soon. He's working hard to get your house finished, but now that it's getting dark, I'm sure he's on the way here."

Uncertainty filled Kristina's eyes. What could Leoma say to reassure the child? Every time Welby went out the door, his daughter seemed worried that he wouldn't return. Too young to understand, no doubt, Kristina probably feared her father would go away and never come back, like her mother had done. Leoma knelt to Kristina's level and rested her hands on the girl's shoulders. She looked into the child's eyes and smiled. "What would your daddy do without you?"

Kristina moved one tiny shoulder slightly and lowered her eyes.

"Your papa needs you, and he loves you very much. He won't go away and leave you behind."

Kristina lifted her head and gazed into Leoma's eyes without blinking, without tears this time. It wouldn't be easy sending the child home with Welby when he finished the house. Knowing the girl would be in the house all alone, while her father worked his farm, concerned Leoma. Thank goodness it would be several months yet before Dyer could be weaned and go home to stay with Welby. She'd already decided she would not attempt to feed Dyer from one of those glass feeders, even though he was stronger now. Leoma worried about how Welby would take care of two young children without full time help, but that wasn't her problem. She was sure he'd figure out what to do. Meanwhile,

Kristina would have to go with her father when he said it was time to return home. Again, she hugged Kristina tightly then smiled at her. The child needed all the reassurance she could get.

"Your papa will be very hungry from all his hard work. I bet he'll come through the door any minute. And when you go back to your house to live, he will bring you to visit me and Dyer. Remember how you came to visit before you came to stay every day? Well, you may come any time your papa will bring you. And maybe, if it's all right with him, I can ride out to see you now and then, too. Would you like that?"

Kristina's eyes grew wide; a smile burst on her little face as she nodded repeatedly.

Leoma hadn't driven her buggy since long before Jeremy died. He wouldn't allow her to drive alone during her pregnancy. She felt much stronger these days and Dyer didn't demand quite as much close attention. He only nursed four times a day now and slept through most of the night. As long as the weather was nice, she could bundle him up and drive out to Welby's farm. That is, if Welby didn't mind. If he hired someone to help with Kristina, however, he might not want Leoma to visit. The thought was unbearable.

She looked down at Kristina. The girl was healthy now, and such a pretty little girl, with large brown eyes and dark brown ringlets around her chubby face. A pang of sadness filled Leoma at the thought of not spending every day with her. Surely Welby wouldn't be so cruel as to deny Leoma the right to visit at will. But then again, it was no secret that Welby didn't like her. Leoma didn't know if it was her looks, her lifestyle, or what. Most likely it was her faith. Any mention of her religious beliefs or God made him bristle.

Just then, Leoma's mother came down the stairs and joined her and Kristina in the front room. "I hear horses," her mother said to Kristina with animated excitement in her voice. "I think your papa and Mr. Langley are coming right now."

"Come Kristina!" Leoma sprang to her feet and rushed to the front door, pulling it open for Kristina to look out.

Welby jumped down from his buckboard and headed for the porch. George waved as he went on down the street toward his house.

"Papa!" Kristina raced across the porch, and into her father's arms, just as he mounted the top step.

Leoma stood aside and let Welby carry his daughter into the living room, wishing with all her heart that she was looking at Jeremy and Elizabeth. She closed the door behind them, and swallowed her envy and grief. "Supper will be on the table right away."

While Welby washed up on the back porch, Leoma set the large soup tureen filled with hearty potato soup on the table. Her mother followed behind with a plate of corn pone. "I've never seen bread made from coarse corn meal like this," Lillian said sniffing the hot pieces of yellow bread.

Leoma couldn't hold back her smile when she saw the puzzled look on her mother's face. "That's another thing Anna Jo taught me to bake. It's especially good slathered with apple butter. You really must try it."

"Well, dear, I surely am proud of the way you've taken to the kitchen. You are becoming quite a good cook."

"Thank you, Mother." Leoma leaned close and spoke softly, hoping Welby wasn't within hearing distance. "Welby Soderlund certainly doesn't think so."

"Pshaw! Don't listen to that man, sweetheart. He's lucky you gave him a place to stay and allow him to sit at your table for meals. If he doesn't like what you serve, he can go eat in that hotel restaurant or that new cafe."

"Remember, Mother, those who are kind to the needy honor God."

Leoma's mother raised a brow. "You consider *him* needy?

The last syllable no more left her mother's mouth when Welby walked into the dining room with Kristina right beside him. He helped his daughter onto her chair and eased it up to the table, then seated himself.

"Good evening Lillian, Leoma," Welby said.

Leoma and her mother replied in unison. "Good evening."

Not answering her mother's earlier question, Leoma filled each bowl with soup then took her seat. Welby reached for the plate of corn pone and quickly buttered the large square of the bread. He slurped a spoonful of soup. Leoma cleared her throat loudly and glared at Welby. Hands folded in her lap, Leoma waited. Welby glanced from one woman to the other, a question in his stare.

"We didn't thank God for providing this meal, and already you're gobbling your supper down like you're half starved," Lillian said. "What must the good Lord think?"

Welby slapped his napkin down on the table. "If I'm not mistaken, I provided the potatoes for that soup, poor as it is."

Leoma's mother huffed and drew in a long breath. "And just who do you think created the seeds for those potatoes, and brought the rain and sunshine to make them grow? We should always thank God for our provisions, no matter what stubborn, bull-headed farmer plants them."

Leoma winced. The snappy tone in her mother's voice was uncharacteristic for her. What on earth had gotten in to her? Contrary as Welby could be, Leoma understood him a little better since he'd been sleeping in her carriage house and dining at her table. She saw firsthand how much he cared about his children, and he was gentle with them. But like her, Welby's losses had been great, and this, no doubt, was a difficult time for him.

Welby still grieved for his wife, a vicious tornado had nearly destroyed his entire farm, and a woman he wasn't particularly fond of, was caring for his children. The difference between Leoma and Welby was that she relied upon her faith in God to help her through each day. Welby relied upon his liquor, or so it appeared. Obvious by the smell on his breath he'd already had a drink or two this evening. She didn't know when or where, but the foul smell was strong. Still, she held her tongue, knowing harsh words would only stir up his wrath.

Leoma sighed and forced a tight smile. "I'm sorry if the soup isn't to your liking, Welby, and I appreciate all you have provided for us. However . . ." She mustered enough courage to speak her mind and went on in a gentle tone. "In my home, as you already know, we always say grace before our meals."

Welby dropped the buttered piece of corn pone onto his plate. He clamped his mouth shut and waited. Leoma bowed her head and said a short prayer. "Amen" was immediately followed by a loud slurp from

Welby. He wasted no time shoving a spoonful of soup into his mouth. *Forgive him Lord and help me to remain patient and kind.*

Except for the clatter of spoons and Welby's slurping, quiet fell over the room for several minutes. Welby ate the soup and bread as if he hadn't had a bite of food all day. Apparently the meal wasn't too bad, for he didn't make any more sarcastic remarks as he devoured everything in front of him. When he finished his second bowl of soup, Leoma brought the peach cobbler and four small china bowls to the table. She began to serve the dessert, making sure Welby's serving was considerably larger than the others.

"Reverend Gilroy and his wife stopped me in the new department store this morning," Leoma's mother said as she dabbed her mouth with a linen napkin. "They invited me to attend church Sunday."

"How kind of them to personally invite you," Leoma said. She took a small bite of the cobbler and swallowed before speaking again. "I hope you accepted their invitation."

"Oh, yes, of course, dear. I assume you attend the service every week, and you will go with me, will you not?"

Leoma smiled, and bowed her head for a moment. "Actually, I haven't been to church since Elizabeth's funeral."

"Oh! Why not?"

"I've been nursing Dyer back to health and helping care for Kristina." Leoma knew that was only a half-truth, an excuse. Even though she read her Bible and prayed almost every morning, she just couldn't face stepping into the church without Jeremy. Not yet. After he died she was devastated. She still couldn't believe he was gone, and on several occasions, she'd thought Jeremy would walk through the door of their home at the end of the day. Then she was angry for weeks. She'd lashed out at God for taking her husband away from her, crying throughout the day and night. Before she had overcome the anger and sorrow, she went into premature labor and gave birth to Elizabeth. The labor had spanned two agonizing days. During the brief hours when she'd held her tiny daughter in her arms, she'd almost forgotten the grief. Then in less than forty-eight hours the baby died. This time the grief was far worse. Leoma had wanted to die, too, and escape this cruel world.

"Do you mean to tell me Welby doesn't allow you time enough to attend church?" Glaring at Welby, Leoma's mother was clearly perplexed.

"Life is different here," Leoma said. "We don't have the luxury of nannies and maids, or cooks. When Welby came to me for help I did what I knew was right. Dyer needed all my attention for several weeks. He was much too frail to take outdoors, and I was too exhausted to think of going to church, or anyplace else."

"My poor dear. You haven't even had time to grieve or recover from your own losses." Her mother turned to Welby, her brows raised. "And the way you speak to my daughter at times is shameful, young man, as if she isn't doing enough to help you and your children."

"Mother, please." Leoma touched her mother's arm hoping to quiet her.

"You shouldn't allow him to belittle you the way he does."

"I know, Mother," Leoma said, her voice barely above a whisper.

It was true. The slights and insults were sometimes more than Leoma could bear. It took all her strength to bite her tongue and maintain some form of dignity, especially during those times when Welby had been drinking and was angry. But she didn't want to provoke him by returning angry words she would regret. What was it the Bible said? A gentle answer turns away wrath?

Welby tossed his napkin on the table. "You don't need to worry. I'll be out of your hair very soon."

"But my daughter will still have your son." Then turning to Leoma her mother said, "You must take some time for yourself, Leoma. Beginning this Sunday morning I insist you attend church with me. I'll help you with the children."

Leoma held her breath and looked at Welby. How would he feel about her taking his children to church? She brushed one hand through Kristina's hair and smiled down at the child.

"Would you like to go to church with us Sunday morning, sweetheart? They have a special story time for children, and I'm sure Doris and Jody will be there."

Kristina's eyes lit up and her smile broadened. "Yes."

"Now wait just a minute," Welby said. "You have no business dragging my daughter to church and filling her head with your religious jargon."

Her eyes downcast, Kristina's smile withered.

Lillian glared at Welby. "It's not a bunch of jargon, *Mr.* Soderlund. And we certainly would not *drag* you children anywhere."

Leoma directed a smile at Welby in an effort to smooth over her mother's curtness. "I thought, perhaps, you and Kristina might come along with us," she said.

"Well, you thought wrong!" Welby jumped up, thrusting his chair back from the table, and nearly causing it to topple backwards. Then he stormed out of the house. The door slammed behind him and rattled the windows.

"THE NERVE OF THAT woman," Welby grumbled, and climbed into his buckboard. He yanked the reins and turned Mabel onto the road, guiding the horse away from town. Ignoring the rain that had begun to fall again, and the pitch black night, he snapped the reins several times, and pushed the old horse into a trot.

He was doing just fine with Leoma until Lillian came marching in like some royal queen. Living in Leoma's carriage house wasn't a perfect situation, but now that Leoma's mother was there it was downright unbearable. He'd had about all he could take of Leoma's lousy cooking and her busy-body mother's harping. "Who does that old woman think she is, Mabel?"

Welby's throat was dry. He reached down to retrieve the pint of brandy from the small box beneath the seat. Without slowing the buckboard, he managed to twist off the lid and guzzle a long swig. Welcome heat warmed his insides as it went down. Controlling Mabel with one hand, he gulped down a couple more long swallows and drove the horse into a faster run. "Move it, Mabel! Get the lead out."

Streaks of lightning arched and danced across the sky up the road in front of him, followed by long rolling thunder. The rain became a downpour and stung his face as he sped into it. He'd had about all the storms he could stand. If it wasn't storming outside, it was storming words from those blasted women.

Jaws clenched, Welby couldn't recall the last time he was this spitting mad. It was wrong to let his temper get the best him, but that woman and her fancy-talking mother had no business pushing their religion on him or his girl. And who was Lillian to carry on about how he treated Leoma? She made it sound as if he'd been a vile tyrant taking advantage of her daughter. Blast it all! The sooner he finished his house and moved out from under Leoma's roof, the better. All he needed was a few days without rain and he'd have his place done.

He'd have to figure out a way to get beds and some furniture, but he'd make do. If he had to, he would sleep on the floor. It wouldn't be the first time. When it came to furniture, there wasn't much to choose from in town, but he had money in the bank and good credit. His word and handshake was trusted. What he couldn't buy on the spot, he'd build, or order from the Montgomery Ward catalog. Certainly someone in town would have a copy of the mail order book that didn't get blown away in the tornado. He tossed his head back and downed another swig of brandy and let it sink into his veins.

Jagged fingers of lightning struck nearby. The sky lit up with eerie, blue light, and made the hair on his arms and neck stand on end. Thunder cracked almost instantly, causing Mabel to whinny and throw her head back and forth. "Whoa! Settle down girl!"

Welby dropped the bottle of brandy and tried to regain control of the horse, but it was too late. Mabel jerked sideways, away from the repeated flashes of lightning, and bolted off the road. The buckboard splashed through a gully full of water and flipped over, taking Mabel down with it. For several seconds Welby wasn't sure what had happened. The world around him was spinning out of control and everything was blurry. Fierce pain like a hot steel blade throbbed in his head. He tried to crawl out from beneath the wagon but he couldn't move. Something heavy pinned his legs to the ground. "Mabel! Mabel!" His voice was weak and all he heard was pounding rain and thunder. "Mabel!"

Nothing. Then blackness oozed around him until there was only cold darkness

Chapter 10

BRIGHT LIGHT SENT PAIN to his head when Welby tried to open his eyes. He tried to lift his shoulders but he was weighted down by some unknown force. He made another weak attempt to get up. Every inch of his body ached. He groaned and willed his eyes to focus.

"Welcome back." The familiar female voice was a mere whisper, almost angelic.

"What—" The effort to speak was too much. Welby groaned again.

"You had an accident with your buckboard. Lie still now," Leoma said. This time her voice was firm and he knew by the piercing pain in his legs and head, he wasn't going anywhere soon. "You're lucky Doctor Rhodes was on his way to visit the Gallagers Saturday morning. He found you along side the road. I have strict instructions to keep you in bed until he returns and says otherwise. I'll send word to him that you're awake."

Without moving his head Welby glanced around the unfamiliar room. Sharp pain exploded in his head. Grimacing, he slowly raised one hand to examine the bandages around the top of his skull. Unsure where he was, he struggled to speak, and finally forced out a few words. "Where am I? How long have I been here?"

"You're in my guest room," Leoma said. "Mother gave up the bed and moved upstairs two days ago, so you could recover here."

"Two days?" He'd rather hear that Lillian had gone back to Boston, but he kept his thoughts to himself. It was quite a surprise to hear the woman had given up her room for him.

"You cracked your skull on a rock when you crashed your buckboard, and you've lost a lot of blood. You also broke your right leg. You're lucky the doctor found you when he did."

"Where's my horse?"

"I'll let Doctor Rhodes explain everything." Leoma padded quietly across the floor and paused in the doorway. "I'll send for him now. You just be still and try to rest."

Soft female voices drifted from another room but the words were muffled, and Welby couldn't understand what was being said. He waited, hoping Leoma would return soon. He had more questions. Where was his daughter? He wanted to see his daughter. Were his children all right? How long would he have to stay in this bed? He wanted to get back to work on his house right away. A swig of brandy sure would be good right now . . . sure could use a smoke.

As he tried to remember what had happened Welby couldn't keep his eyes opened. Then, like a crack on the head, it came back to him. It was Lillian's remarks about religion, and his anger as he drove his horse and wagon like a crazy man. He'd pushed Mabel too hard. He remembered the lightning spooking her, then nothing but pain.

Something akin to shame overcame him. This accident was no one's fault but his. He knew better than to go off half cocked in a raging fit like a foolish boy. When he was a kid, he'd been spanked with a switch from the walnut tree for his temper fits. Louise had taught him the value of patience, with a few whacks to his head with the palm of her hand. He supposed he should have learned his lesson by now. Truth was, though, he hadn't acted like this in years, until recently.

There was a light knock on his door, and before he could respond Kristina approached his bed. "Hi, papa," she said, her voice cracking slightly. His daughter's eyes were dark with worry and fear.

He smiled and patted the edge of the bed, drawing her closer. "Are you being good for Mrs. Fisk?"

"Yes." Kristina answered and nodded.

"I'm going to be out of this bed real soon." Welby kept his voice calm, trying hard to reassure his daughter. "How's your brother?"

"Okay. He smiled at me." Some of the worry in his daughter's eyes vanished when a pretty smile lit her face. "Mrs. Fisk let me help give him a bath today."

"She did? I reckon you're a good helper." His little girl nodded again. Welby remembered when she gave Dyer a rag dipped in sugar water to suck on. She was a smart child.

Somewhere in the house a door opened and closed, and heavy footsteps came in his direction. Doctor Rhodes entered the room carrying his black medical satchel, a grim scowl on his face. Leoma stepped into the room and ushered Kristina out.

"Well, Mister Soderlund that was a downright foolish thing you did. I'm glad to see you're going to survive." The doctor removed his hat, and hung it on a poster at the foot of the bed. "How do you feel?"

"I hurt like the dickens." Each word made Welby's head throb, and keeping his eyes opened was a struggle. "Why'd you bring me here, of all places?"

Without answering the question, the doctor listened to Welby's heart with his stethoscope then lifted his eye lids. He shined a bright light into each eye. Doctor Rhodes moved his forefinger back and forth, up and down, instructing Welby to follow it with his eyes. He checked for fever and seemed satisfied that there was none. Finally, the doctor pulled the cover back and exposed Welby's legs. Wondering what the doc was looking for, Welby tried to look down, but it was too painful to lift his head. He groaned when the doctor lifted his right leg slightly. Pain shot from his thigh to his ankle.

"Leoma said it's broken. Is that true, Doc?"

"You mangled your right kneecap pretty badly, and broke the left femur."

"Femur? Speak English, Doc."

"Your thighbone. It'll heal, but you'll be off your feet for a while. I tried to patch up your knee, but it might give you trouble for years to come. Your legs will be fine in time."

Welby flinched and groaned wishing for a strong drink when the doctor changed the bandage on his knee. He didn't know which was worse, the pain from his broken thigh or the doctor changing the bandage.

"Now, let's take a closer look at your head." Doctor Rhodes pulled up the covers over Welby's legs and moved to the head of the bed. You have a nice line of sutures on your skull. You're going to feel quite a bit of pain for a few more days, but I think the rock you whacked your head against got the worst end of the deal."

"How soon can I get back to work on my house?"

The doctor laughed and shook his head. "You aren't getting out of this bed for several more days; maybe a couple of weeks and you won't be working on your house for a while yet."

Welby grunted and grumbled. "I have to get my house done so we can move back in, Doc." Time was wasting. He wanted out of Leoma's house. Much more of her and her mother's high-hat ways and holier-than-thou attitudes would drive him crazy.

Of course, as Welby thought about it, he realized he'd have to leave Dyer here with Leoma again, and he didn't like that idea. He'd become used to seeing his son every morning and evening, and he was growing attached to the boy. Kristina seemed to be getting awfully fond of Leoma, so it wouldn't be easy taking his girl back to the farm with no one there to tend to her needs. Goodness knows he'd been a miserable excuse for a father since Louise passed on. He closed his eyes, and for a moment, he wished he could sink back into that black oblivion until he was healed.

"First you have to get well, my friend, and that's not going to be tomorrow. So relax." The doctor was adamant, no bones about it.

"What about my horse?" He'd almost forgotten to ask the doctor if he'd brought Mabel back. "And my buckboard?"

The doctor's gaze fell to the floor for several seconds. After a moment Doctor Rhodes lifted his chin, his lips tight. He looked at Welby and put a hand on his shoulder. "Mabel is dead. My guess is the old mare had a heart attack when she ran off the road." Welby remembered how frightened and skittish the mare had been with the violent storm. Doc was probably right.

The doctor went on. "I'm afraid your buckboard is nothing more than a pile of firewood out in that ditch. You might salvage a wheel or two, but they're about the only things left in one piece. Now, be still so I can clean your head wound and get a fresh bandage on it."

"I sure could use a swig of bandy, Doc. You know, to help the pain."

"That's not going to happen, so forget it."

"I don't suppose I can have a cigarette either." Welby glanced at the doctor, knowing full well what the answer was.

The doctor grinned and shook his head. "Nope. I can't allow that either."

As long as he was laid up in Leoma Fisk's house, Welby could forget about enjoying a smoke or drink.

"Your drinking is what nearly killed you and put you here in the first place." What the doctor said was true, much as Welby hated to admit it.

If he hadn't gone off half cocked and started guzzling the brandy, this would have never happened. No one had to tell him that, especially those two women. He hoped now that he was awake Lillian wouldn't start preaching at him. He felt guilty enough on his own, and he didn't want to hear about his *sins* from that woman. Maybe seeing Dyer would cheer him. That shouldn't be a problem. "I'd like to see my son."

"I'll have Mrs. Fisk bring him in for a short visit. Then you need to take this medicine and rest. No more excitement for today."

Doctor Rhodes held up a bottle of liquid and gave him instructions. Welby could only imagine what vile concoction the doctor was making him take. He'd heard of some real quacks passing off useless medications as healing potions, but he had a pretty good feeling this doctor was legitimate. Welby had seen his certificate from some medical school in Philadelphia and a license to practice, both hanging on the wall of the doctor's office. Whatever it took to get better, Welby was willing to follow orders. He wanted to get well fast so he could get out of this bed and out of Leoma's house.

Chapter 11

THE SUN WARMED THE air the moment it crested the eastern horizon. Leoma gazed out the opened door a moment longer before starting breakfast, breathing in what little cool, fresh air remained in the early morning. She'd already nursed Dyer and put a dry diaper and gown on him. He was content now, awake in the cradle. Soon Kristina would come pattering into the kitchen, looking for Leoma and breakfast. The busyness of another day would begin, and she wondered; was this how her life with Jeremy and Elizabeth would have been, had they been alive? No. She was quite sure it would have been more pleasant. Jeremy was nothing like Welby.

Leoma sighed, wishing she had more patience and strength. Even though she loved Dyer and Kristina, how did she end up caring for a stranger's children and their surly, injured father? She hardly knew Welby well enough to have him living in her house. To this day, she couldn't figure out why the man was so angry and adamantly against church. She'd never known anyone who was that unyielding and temperamental. What had happened in his youth that had made him so opposed to God's word? She sighed, resolved to stop worrying about it. It wasn't likely he'd ever share his reasons with her, so she may as well leave it alone. Too tired to spend her energy fretting over Welby Soderlund, she determined, with God's help, to simply do her best each day.

Since Doctor Rhodes had hauled Welby into the house unconscious four days ago, Leoma had hardly a spare minute to read one page in a book, let alone a chapter or two in her Bible. If only she could enjoy an hour in her parlor with a good novel and a cup of tea, or enjoy a long soak in the tub. But the only way she could take a leisurely bath was late at night, when Welby and the children were asleep, and by then she was too exhausted to heat the water and haul it up to the bathing chamber.

Leoma's mother wasn't much help when it came to caring for Kristina or Dyer, and she was nearly useless in the kitchen. Oh, she did little things to help, such as setting the table, but Lillian had plenty of leisure time to relax, read, socialize, and—irritate Welby.

Leoma breathed in the wonderful aroma of freshly brewed coffee. She went to the cupboard and took out three coffee mugs and dishes for the oatmeal she would cook for breakfast. She poured herself a cup of coffee, wondering how many sips she'd enjoy before Welby's brass bell rang signaling he needed her, or Kristina's little feet pitter-pattered into the kitchen. One? Two?

None.

The dinner bell Leoma had placed on Welby's bedside table rang several times with clashing, nerve-rattling clangs. Leoma let out a quiet groan and set her coffee cup on the kitchen table before taking the first sip. She hurried through the dining room and living room to Welby's temporary infirmary, trying to muster up a pleasant smile. "Good morning," she said entering the room. "You must have smelled the coffee."

"Yes."

Leoma thought for the briefest moment, she detected a slight smile on Welby's face.

"Would you like a cup right now? Breakfast won't be ready for a few minutes. Or would you like me to bring the bowl of water so you can brush your teeth and wash the sleep out of your eyes?"

"A cup of coffee, please."

Please? Oh my. Welby said please. Maybe the crack on his head had knocked some niceness or good manners into him. This was the first day Welby had awakened early, and he was sitting up in bed when she entered the room. It was definitely the first sign of civility from him in a long while.

Funny, the man wasn't bad looking when he didn't have a scowl on his face. And it was the first time she'd noticed Welby had a mouthful of white, straight teeth, and a nice smile. Leoma smiled, pleased to see the color had returned to Welby's cheeks, what little she could see above his whiskers, and his attitude was considerably more pleasant than it had been since she'd met him. "I'll bring you a cup of coffee right away," Leoma said, adding another polite smile as she departed.

Well, she thought, as she walked to the kitchen with a lighter step than she'd felt in weeks, *the man isn't too awful, if only he'd smile and say please more often.* She wondered if he might even be handsome beneath all that wild, scraggly beard and hair. Leoma filled the brown mug that had become Welby's favorite with steaming coffee.

When she returned to Welby's bedside and handed him the mug, Leoma explained that Doctor Rhodes was seeing patients in another town this morning, and he wouldn't be checking in on him today. "However, he instructed me to change your bandages, and he also suggested you sit up on the edge of the bed and allow me to exercise your unbroken leg for one minute."

"I suppose if the doctor told you what to do, I best follow his orders," Welby said with another smile.

Surprised by Welby's quick compliance, Leoma responded with a nod. He hadn't been an easy patient the first few days, and more than once, she wanted to administer her rolling pin to his already injured head. Generally, he was most tolerable when he was unconscious or asleep.

Welby put the mug to his lips, slurping in the hot coffee. "That's good coffee this morning. Thank you."

Leoma did a double take and wondered if Welby's injury had done some brain damage. She almost stammered when she spoke. "You're welcome."

There was a knock at the front door. Leoma excused herself to go see who was there, all the while wondering what had gotten into Welby. Why was he suddenly acting so nice and polite? She opened the door hoping perhaps the doctor had changed his plans and decided to call on Welby before going out of town. She didn't doubt her ability to carry out Doctor Rhodes' instructions, but tending Welby's bandages was the last thing she wanted to do. "Good morning, Leoma." George greeted her with a broad smile and held out a covered basket with a familiar blue checked cloth.

"Come in." She accepted the offered gift and sniffed the sweet fragrance that escaped the covering. "What's this?"

"You know Anna Jo; the woman loves to bake. She sent over a few blueberry muffins. Said she thought you might like them for breakfast."

"Thank you. Your wife is so kind." Leoma breathed in another deep whiff of the muffins. Now she wouldn't need to cook oatmeal. "Umm, they smell wonderful."

Leoma led George into Welby's sickroom and hurried to the kitchen for another mug of coffee for her neighbor. She took a small plate from the cupboard, removed four of the muffins from the basket, and placed them on the dish. With the freshly poured mug of coffee in one hand, and the muffins in the other, Leoma carried them to the men. She placed the bread on the table beside Welby's bed and handed George his coffee.

Before she turned to leave the men alone so they could visit and enjoy their coffee, George said to Welby, "The preacher and I are headed out to your farm this morning with a couple of other men from church. We figure we can finish the roof on your house in a few hours. Is there anything else we can do for you?"

Welby seemed to be at a loss for words. He gazed at George for several seconds before he spoke. "Why would the preacher and those Bible thumpers want to work on my place?"

It was clear to Leoma that Welby didn't understand that's what the church members did for each other and for their neighbors, but she minded her tongue.

"We consider it part of loving one another and being good Samaritans," George said. "It's the way Jesus taught his disciples. We're just family caring for family."

Leoma was pleased to hear George's news, not because it meant Welby would be out from under her roof earlier, although she'd thought about that for a fleeting second, but it demonstrated Christian brotherhood, and perhaps, since the words came from a man Welby seemed to like, it would soften Welby's heart toward the church and other believers.

She was eager to attend the service next Sunday with her mother, and she hoped she could take Kristina along, but as long as she was nursing Dyer, and Welby refused to let his daughter step foot inside the church, it seemed hopeless.

Leoma knew she should leave the men to their conversation, but she couldn't help overhearing them talk as she meandered out of the room. She paused in the living room for several seconds, curious about what else George might say.

Standing just beyond the door, Leoma watched as George sat down in a chair near Welby's bed. He took a drink of coffee, and he narrowed his gaze on Welby. "Would you question why the men are doing this if they weren't church folks?"

"I don't suppose I would," Welby said after a long hesitation. "But what's in it for them? I can't pay them much for their work."

"No one expects a single nickel's worth of pay. We're following what God has put in our hearts—to love our neighbors as ourselves. It's simply friends helping friends, like you helped me, and we helped some of the other folks in town."

Leoma smiled to herself, recalling the long Bible discussions George and Jeremy had enjoyed. She hoped George would have some positive influence on Welby. George knew his Bible inside and out, even though Anna Jo had said her husband wasn't a very good reader. It certainly appeared he comprehended and remembered what he read. Leoma was convinced, if anyone could persuade Welby to believe in God, it was George Langley, not by quoting the Bible and preaching at him, but by his example of kindness. Before Welby could respond to George's comment someone else arrived. Leoma rushed to open the door. She recognized Benny Schmitts from the church, but she'd never seen the other man standing next to Benny.

"G'mornin', Mrs. Fisk," Benny Schmitts said tipping his worn and tattered hat. It looked as old as Benny himself. "This here fella is our new neighbor, Jason Alder."

The younger man removed his fine looking hat and dipped his head in a polite bow, holding her attention with eyes bluer than the clearest summer sky. "I'm pleased to meet you, ma'am."

Leoma offered her hand. "Likewise, Mr. Alder."

"Please, ma'am, just call me Jason." His voice was deep and mellow, with a musical quality, and his smile was playful. Leoma couldn't help but wonder when he had come to town and where he'd come from.

"Well then, I'm pleased to meet you, Jason."

"We came to meet up with George and the preacher," Benny Schmits said. "Then we'll be on our way out to the Soderlund place."

Leoma stood aside and invited the men to enter. "Reverend Gilroy isn't here yet. Would you care to go in and visit Mr. Soderlund until the minister arrives? George is with him now." With an open hand she motioned toward the room, and she stayed behind, allowing George to make the introductions.

In less than a minute Reverend Gilroy arrived, and Leoma led him to the other men, hoping Welby wouldn't embarrass everyone with some unpleasant remark. She held her breath when the preacher told Welby he'd been praying for him. Welby remained silent, and almost immediately, all the guests came out of the room. They each bid Leoma a polite good day as they departed. Waiting at the door, Leoma wondered when Welby would explode.

Silence.

Relieved, Leoma sighed. The day had begun so nicely she hoped it wouldn't change.

Just as she closed the front door Kristina came down the stairs, still in her nightgown and rubbing her eyes. Leoma went to the little girl. "Good morning, Kristina." She bent and gave the child a hug. "Would you like to say good morning to your father before you eat breakfast?"

"Yes." Without hesitation Kristina ran to her father's bedside. Leoma followed, making sure the girl didn't jump upon the bed or make too much noise.

After a few moments, Leoma touched Kristina's shoulder affectionately. "It's time to eat breakfast, sweetheart. Anna Jo sent over some fresh, homemade blueberry muffins. Would you like one?" The child scampered out of the room. Leoma smiled at Welby. "Would you like more coffee?"

Welby nodded then grimaced, apparently jarring his head a little too hard. "Yes, please."

While Kristina ate her muffin and drank a small glass of milk, Leoma fried two eggs for Welby. He needed more than sweet bread if he was going to heal properly. She took extra care not to burn the whites around the edges, and she made sure they were cooked all the way through. Early on she'd learned Welby didn't like any half-cooked whites in his eggs. They had to be thoroughly done or he'd let her know about it without hesitation. She scooped them onto a plate with a small slice of fried ham. Using a wooden serving tray, she carried the plate of food, silverware, napkin, salt and pepper shakers, and a fresh cup of hot coffee into Welby's room. With every step she breathed a silent prayer that the food would be satisfactory.

Welby adjusted himself on the bed and let Leoma place the tray across his lap. She made sure it was level and secure, then removed her hands and straightened her body at the side of the bed. When Leoma looked at Welby he was staring at her, a strange half-smile on his mouth.

Strange indeed. Leoma stepped back and folded her hands in front of her. "I hope this will be all right," she said, praying the breakfast was done to Welby's liking. "If you need anything else I'll be in the kitchen with Kristina."

Welby poked at the eggs with the tip of his fork, and acknowledged with a genuine, full smile. "Thank you."

"Ring the bell when you're finished, and I'll come take the tray away. Then we must get your bandages changed. And if you don't mind, we'll do those exercises Doctor Rhodes ordered. Maybe we can get all done before Dyer fusses for his next feeding."

"Yes, ma'am."

Leoma turned and left the room, a strange quiver in her stomach. What had gotten into Welby all of a sudden? He acted as docile as a lamb.

And smiles?

Thank you?

A polite yes, ma'am?

For certain, something had jolted the man's brain during the accident.

She'd thought for sure the moment George and the other men left earlier, Welby would return to his usual grumpy self—especially after having Reverend Gilroy show up. She expected him to begin complaining about the men from church and their motives. He was far too skeptical and hard headed—under normal circumstances.

Maybe she was wrong. Perhaps the men's kindness had made Welby think about his life. For his children's sake, Leoma sincerely hoped so. Kristina and Dyer needed a good father who would bring them up with some Christian standards, someone to take them to church and teach them about God. Oh how she prayed that would happen. Kristina and Dyer weren't supposed to be her concern or responsibility, but each day they'd become more precious to her, and she wanted them to know the kind of happiness she'd had as a child.

Some of Leoma's earliest and best childhood memories were of those Sunday mornings when she sat between her father and mother, on the third church pew from the front. Her mother always wore her best dress and hat and shoes. It was the one day of the week her mother fixed Leoma's hair extra special, with her prettiest ribbons, and let her wear her fanciest dress and newest shiny shoes. In his brown suit, a clean white shirt, and tan striped necktie, her father was the handsomest man in church. His shoes were polished and shined, and his brown, felt hat sat on the pew next to him until the service was over, and they went back outdoors. Father was a righteous man, a respected deacon in the church, admired and loved by members of the community. Most of all, Leoma loved and respected him because he was a caring, kindhearted father.

Even though Leoma's father had hoped for many sons, as her mother told her when she was fifteen-years-old, he'd been blessed with only two daughters. He loved Leoma and her younger sister unconditionally, and he treated them with the same respect and admiration he would have a son. Her father was kind and loving toward both of them, always stressing the importance of education. He'd instilled in Leoma great confidence and a strong self esteem. Most of all, he emphasized that God and his son, Jesus, must come first in one's life. Leoma didn't recall ever missing a Sunday church service with her parents.

Leoma had liked going to church for as long as she could remember.

She loved the stories the preacher told, and the angelic sound when the huge congregation sang to the music of the pipe organ. Her parents sang in strong, beautiful voices, her father's a deep, clear baritone, and her mother's a crisp soprano. In time, Leoma had learned all the songs, and she'd loved to sing standing with her sister between their parents.

Also, Sundays meant spending the afternoon with relatives. After the church service, there was always a big dinner with her grandparents, aunts, uncles, and cousins. There were no chores, except to help clear the table. The rest of the day the children were free to play with their cousins. They played tag and hide-and-seek among the gardens and trees in the large, shady back yard. In the winter the children played hide-and-seek in the house, sneaking into dark corners of closets and cubbyholes beneath the stairs, and in the basement. As Leoma and her cousins became older, the entertainment advanced to board games, cards, and reading. Those times were a wonderful part of her life.

After she and Jeremy were married, the family gatherings had become part of their lives together. One summer on a Sunday afternoon, they had gone out into the yard with three of her married cousins and their spouses, and they played hide-and-seek. Reminiscing about the silly laughter and fun brought a smile to her lips as she joined Kristina at the kitchen table.

Kristina picked the blueberries out of her muffin one-by-one before popping them into her mouth. Her little fingertips were stained blue. Leoma sipped coffee, savoring each swallow, needing a short break before she went on to the daily tasks. Hopefully Dyer wouldn't cry demanding to be nursed for at least another hour. Kristina finished eating the entire muffin and drank her milk. She sat quietly swinging her legs back and forth. When Leoma swallowed the last of her coffee she asked, "Would you like to hear a short story before I tend to your father?"

Kristina bobbed her head up and down several times sending her curls flying. "I like your stories."

"You do?" Most of Leoma's attention went to Dyer, and now his father, and she worried that Kristina might feel left out, even though the girl never complained or acted badly to gain attention.

"Yes," Kristina said with a huge, blue smile.

Leoma removed the dishes from the table and wiped the crumbs from Kristina's place. "Well then, let's wash your pretty blue mouth and fingers and go sit in my big rocking chair for a few minutes, shall we? I have to change your papa's bandages and do as the doctor instructed very soon, and your brother will probably wake again shortly, but we will take time for a short story."

Leoma took Kristina by the hand and led her to the rocker in the west parlor. She lifted her Bible from the shelf and opened it to the book of Matthew. Using her most expressive tone, in her own simplified rendition, she began to read the story of the birth of Jesus.

"One night a long, long time ago, a young lady found out she was going to have a special baby . . ." Kristina listened intently as Leoma went on.

HIS SON'S SHRILL WAIL woke Welby. He'd dozed after eating his breakfast and the tray with empty dishes still straddled his legs. Why hadn't Leoma returned to take the tray and change his bandages like she'd said? He listened as the cry grew louder. Where was that woman? Suddenly the child's crying stopped and Welby relaxed. The short silence was followed by singing. Two sweet female voices drifted down from upstairs. Welby couldn't understand the words at that distance and the tune was unfamiliar, but the sound of Leoma and Kristina singing was nice.

Welby had never heard Kristina or her mother sing a single note. Louise had been shy about expressing herself in front of others, and he didn't know if she could so much as hum a simple song. The singing upstairs went on for a few minutes. Leoma must have taught his daughter the song.

It was a sure sign, Welby believed, that the young woman's grief was letting up. He knew the last few months couldn't have been easy for Leoma. Not a day went by that his heart didn't ache for his Louise. If his son had died too—he let out a huge shudder—Welby couldn't imagine the heartache that would add to his anguish. After losing her husband

and baby, Leoma Fisk was nursing a stranger's son—his son—back to health and caring for Welby and his daughter, too. And she was singing. He couldn't help but wonder where the woman found her strength, or the inner joy she seemed to possess.

How long had it been since Louise passed on? Welby tried to count the weeks—or was it months? Nearly six months, give or take a week, best he could count. Shortly before his wife had died, he'd heard talk in town about the killing at the bank. It had taken Jeremy Fisk's life. He didn't know the man, but he'd heard how his death had left a young, pregnant wife to survive on her own. Those events all seemed a lifetime ago. Now, here he was in her home. So many things had changed in Welby's life, and it had left him with more uncertainty than he cared to face. As if he'd just awakened from a long sleep, Welby suddenly acknowledged the realization that he wasn't alone in his grief.

Welby turned his thoughts to his farm and more pressing things. He was tired of this bed, and he was ready to get back to work on his house. Thanks to George and those church men, his roof would be done, but there was still a lot of work to do before he could move back into his place: the floors, painting, furniture, and a million small details. Also, the problem of how he'd take care of his daughter out there alone, still weighed on his mind. It wouldn't be long, maybe three months tops, before Dyer would be weaned and ready to live at home with Welby; then what? He'd have two little young ones to take care of, one just an infant. On top of that, he'd have a farm to run. Welby's father and mother were dead, and his sister had a family of her own in Minnesota. His brother and sister-in-law had talked about moving out West, and wrote that they might consider the Oklahoma Territory, but in the end, Rita, his sister-in-law, didn't like the idea of having to begin all over in a small settlement. She didn't want to give up her conveniences and comforts for the unknown. They were in New York to stay.

Welby was mulling the dilemma over in his mind when he heard the patter of feet coming down the stairs. Kristina skipped into the bedroom ahead of Leoma, who had Dyer braced on one hip, an arm securely around his body. The boy, his back straight and strong, was wide-eyed and looking around the room.

"I'm sorry it took me so long to get back," Leoma said. She shifted Dyer to her other hip. "My mother went into town to visit Reverend Gilroy's wife, and she hasn't returned, so I have no help. Would you mind holding Dyer beside you while I clear your breakfast tray?"

Welby lifted the tray out of the way. Leoma took the wooden serving piece with one hand and traded it for the baby. Welby settled his son next to him, and held him with one arm wrapped around the boy's middle. As Leoma took the breakfast remains out of the room, Welby couldn't help but notice that her body had filled out some in the last month. She looked healthier. Her slender, but curvaceous, hips moved gracefully beneath the skirt of her dress. The dress was one he'd never seen, and the flowery fabric and white ruffles around the neck was down right pretty on her. He didn't usually notice women's clothing, but something about the way Leoma looked today in that pink and blue dress caught his attention, and shamefully, his imagination. Thank goodness his daughter quickly distracted him from allowing his eyes or mind to linger any longer on the backside of Leoma.

"Papa," Kristina said jumping up and down, clapping her hands. "Miss Leoma taught me to sing a song."

"I heard you ladies singing upstairs. You sounded like angels."

"We did?" Kristina came closer to the side of the bed and reached for Dyer's hand. The baby wrapped his fist around her finger. "Dyer likes to hear us sing. It makes him smile."

"That's nice. You'll have to sing for me sometime." Welby had missed so much lately. During the long hours he had worked to rebuild his house, he'd been gone every day from sun up until dark. Half the time, his son was napping when he came to Leoma's for dinner, and sometimes, several days went by when he didn't see Dyer at all. Clearly, Leoma was doing a good job caring for his children. She'd taken on a huge responsibility, and she was certainly going above and beyond what had been expected of her. Now she also had him laid up in her house with extra work expected of her. As soon as the doctor allowed him get out of bed and on his feet, he would get back to work on his house so he wouldn't continue to be a burden here. He didn't know how he would ever repay Leoma for all she'd already done for him and his children, and he was anxious to resume responsibility for his family.

Leoma returned to the room, a genuine smile spread across her face, her eyes beaming with light. Welby could swear her eyes shone with new life. "Your daughter is quite a good singer. She learns quickly, and she carries a tune very well."

"I heard the two of you upstairs. Maybe you ladies would like to sing me a song. I could use a little entertainment."

Leoma stammered before speaking clearly. Apparently his request caught her off guard. "Let's get your bandages taken care of first. And Dyer needs to be fed very soon." Leoma suggested Kristina sing the song she'd just taught her while she prepared warm soapy water and clean bandages.

Kristina looked at Leoma then at Welby. "All by myself?"

"Sure." Leoma hugged his daughter's shoulders, coaxing the child. "You can do it."

After a long hesitation, Kristina nodded and opened her mouth. His girl began to sing, her voice sweet and clear. "Jesus loves me . . ."

Welby clenched his jaw, letting Kristina sing the words about Jesus and the Bible. Not wanting to discourage his daughter, he let her finish the song, but the words irritated him. Leoma and Lillian knew how he felt about putting their religious hog-wash into his daughter's head. Teaching Kristina songs like this was just another way to sneak their beliefs into her head. He would put a stop to it once and for all. When Kristina finished the song, Welby said, "You sing real good, sweetheart." Then he yelled at the top of his voice. "Leoma!"

Kristina flinched. Dyer jumped and let out a loud squeal. Welby had forgotten the baby was tucked beneath his arm. Not meaning to frighten his children, he spoke in a lower but firm voice. "Go fetch Miss Leoma," he told Kristina as he picked up Dyer and cuddled him against his shoulder. "I'm sorry little guy. Hush now. Shhh."

Dyer quieted, and before Kristina left the room Leoma rushed in, her eyes wide and filled with distress. "What's wrong? Why did you bellow like that?"

Welby nearly cowered at Leoma's scolding tone. He was in deep trouble. "I didn't mean to frighten him. I forgot Dyer was next to me when I shouted."

"You forgot? How could you forget you were holding your son?" Fire shot from Leoma's eyes, and he was glad she didn't have a big stick in her hand, or for sure, she'd use it on him.

Welby tried to keep his voice even and low, but he wanted to explode. He admitted he shouldn't be angry and shouting, but he was tired of other people pushing their religion on him and his children. "What excuse do you have for teaching my daughter to sing about that Jesus stuff, especially after I told you I didn't want you putting ideas into her head?"

"We will discuss this when the children aren't present," Leoma said taking control. "As long as you're in my house you'll keep your voice down, and you *won't* tell me what I can or cannot sing in my own home." Leoma took the baby from his arms, cuddled him close to her breast, and she promptly showed Welby her backside—which he didn't rightly mind. She ushered Kristina out of the room without looking back.

A door opened and closed and he heard Lillian's voice. The women's words were muffled, but the gist of Leoma's anger came through loud and clear. A moment later Leoma came back into Welby's room alone, the children nowhere in sight. With a firm thud she shut the door. The look on her face was stern, but at least she wasn't carrying a rolling pin or cast iron skillet.

"Mother will watch the children while I change your dressings," Leoma said. The look in her eyes was one Welby had never seen before, one that warned him to keep his mouth shut, unless he wanted to suffer more pain. Now that Leoma was stronger she certainly had spunk. He rather liked it, but he bit his tongue and stifled a grin.

Welby sat without speaking while Leoma removed the bandage from his head. He flinched, expecting it to hurt when she cleaned the wound, but he found her touch to be gentle, her ministrations painless. She applied some kind of cold salve to the injury and put a fresh bandage in place, wrapping it securely, just comfortably snug. Leoma worked without hesitation, in a manner that suggested experience in nursing. He wondered if she'd gone to one of those medical schools in the east to be a trained nurse. He'd heard some women were even becoming genuine, licensed doctors. What was the world coming to?

Without warning Leoma whipped back the blanket to expose his bare legs. Just in the nick of time he tugged his nightshirt down to cover himself as much as possible. The heavy wrapping and splint on one thigh went from an inch above his knee to his groin. His knee on the other leg was bandaged. He looked at Leoma and frowned, not accustomed to having a woman care for his injuries. In fact, since he'd grown up, no female other than Louise had seen him in this half-dressed condition. Leoma, however, didn't seem the least bit disturbed by his white hairy legs, or anything else that might have been exposed. Nor did she seem interested. She went about removing the bandage from his knee without a blink.

"You're fortunate you didn't lose your entire leg," Leoma said without looking up. "Doctor Rhodes said if everything looks good when he returns the day after tomorrow, he will remove the stitches from your head and your knee." Leoma carefully cleansed his knee with warm water and soap, gently dabbing the area and patting it dry. In a matter of seconds she applied some yellowish salve and expertly wrapped his knee with a fresh bandage.

"What about my thighbone?"

"I don't know. That's broken, so I suppose you'll have to wear that splint and wrap for several weeks. I'm sure you'll be off your feet for quite some time, but Doctor Rhodes will have to answer your questions about that."

Welby remained in a reclined position in the bed, while Leoma stood at the washstand and scrubbed her hands with fresh water and soap. She dried them on a clean white towel. When she finished she returned to the side of the bed. With one hand placed beneath his ankle, and the other beneath the injured knee, she lifted his left leg ever so slightly, perhaps an inch or two, then lowered it. She repeated the movement several times, moving it a little higher each time. Then she bent it very slowly. What was the doctor thinking telling Leoma to move his leg? The pain was almost unbearable. He grunted and froze, gritting his teeth. "Ouch! Are you sure about this? Doc didn't tell me anything about you making me get out of bed."

"Stop being a baby. A big man like you should be tough. And I assure you, I am just following Doctor Rhodes' instructions. You're not getting out of the bed. We simply need to exercise a little. Easy now."

Leoma's hands were cool as she lifted his broken leg and bent it at the knee five times. He flinched and groaned as she worked. Little-by-little, Leoma bent and straightened his bandaged knee again. This time Welby sucked in a long breath and held it as long as he could without passing out. He held his tongue as long as he could before complaining. "Blast it all, woman. That hurts! I think you're just torturing me while the doctor is out of town."

Leoma smiled sweetly and continued moving his leg, then exercising his ankle by moving it in little circles. "I'm sure it hurts. But the doctor said if you don't begin moving, your legs will stiffen permanently. If you want to get out of this bed and return to working on your house, you will have to obey the doctor's orders."

Welby knew what Leoma said was true. And the pain wasn't really as bad as he expected. Clearly, using caution with each move, she had a tender way about her. Leoma's hands were soft and he liked her gentle touch. He hadn't felt the silkiness of a woman's skin since before Louise had died. Actually, truth be told, Louise's hands were rough from chores and working in the garden, and she was heavy handed—unlike Leoma's feather-light gentleness. Leoma's touch was a mighty pleasant feeling.

As suddenly as Welby thought the words, guilt flooded over him. Thinking on it for a moment brought anger. Maybe he shouldn't be having such betraying thoughts, but Louise was dead and gone. He was very much alive, and he suddenly realized, someday he might take an interest in another women, or he might even take another wife. His eyes closed, he let Leoma lift his leg and lower it several more times while he tried not to think about her soft hands on his body. The only thing that mattered right now was to get well and get out of this bed.

Chapter 12

Leoma woke with excitement brewing in her heart. Bright golden rays of sunshine already spilled through the window; the warmth was heavenly. She glanced at the clock, surprised it was already six-thirty. Across the hallway Dyer jabbered sweet baby sounds. He had slept through the entire night for the first time—eight full hours.

As quickly as Leoma tied her robe around her waist, she rushed to Dyer's room and picked him up from the cradle. He was getting big enough for a larger bed, and he was rolling over and trying to pull himself up. It was time she talk with Welby about getting a crib for the child, before he climbed over the edge of the cradle and fell to the floor. She kissed the boy's cheek. "My, my, you're a happy little fellow this morning."

Dyer's hands patted playfully against her shoulders. Snuggling and rocking from side to side, she cooed and spoke loving words, soothing him, so he'd be still when she changed him out of his wet night clothes. "How are you this morning, little man?" The baby smiled, his bright blue eyes focused on hers. She kissed the tip of his nose. "Today's a very special day. For the first time since your papa's accident, he is going for a ride outdoors. And just wait until he sees the surprise we have for him."

The last ten days had been warm and dry and the entire population of people had taken advantage of the good weather, building, repairing, painting, and moving donated furniture. George Langley headed up the group of men to finish the construction work on Welby's house. Reverend Gilroy and his wife, Mattie, had organized groups of parishioners to paint and furnish the inside of the house. Men, women, and several teen-aged boys and girls worked together. Even Leoma's mother had a hand in sewing curtains.

The project was a well kept secret, and Leoma was bursting with temptation to tell Welby about all the work, but she didn't want to ruin the surprise. The women had been careful not to talk about what they were doing within earshot of Kristina, for they were quite sure the little girl didn't know how to keep a secret at her young age. Besides, part of the surprise was for her, too.

Doctor Rhodes had said he'd arrive at ten o'clock. Leoma promised she'd be ready for the big event, and she'd have most of Welby and Kristina's belongings packed and ready to go. For two days Leoma had been secretly packing their laundered clothing into hidden baskets in her bedroom.

Welby wasn't supposed to put his full weight on the broken leg yet, but during the last three days he'd been allowed out of bed during meal times. Using his crutches he'd joined the family for dinner and supper at the dining room table, and today he came into the kitchen for breakfast.

Leoma noticed that Welby's attitude had improved greatly since he could get out of bed and move around the house, and after he got used to the idea that there was no way he could have his cigarettes or brandy during his recovery, he'd finally stopped complaining about it. She hoped he wouldn't begin the nasty habits again when he returned home. With exception of a few pleasant moments, the first few days after Welby had regained consciousness had been miserable for everyone in the house. He'd been desperate for a cigarette or a drink, and he made sure everyone was going to share in his misery.

Finally, though, Welby had calmed down and stopped asking for a swig to kill the pain. For several days after the accident, the doctor had given Welby doses of laudanum, but when he refused to continue administering the drug, Welby had done a lot of groaning and begging. Leoma felt a great deal of compassion for him, knowing he was still hurting, but she wasn't going to give in to his whining and needling. It

111

was for Welby's own good, and someday, hopefully, he'd thank her for it.

After nursing Dyer, Leoma rushed around in the kitchen and in no time she had biscuits in the oven and ham frying. As she broke eggs into the hot skillet, Welby maneuvered his way into the seat at the end of the table. Without asking, she poured a mug of coffee and set it in front of him.

When the eggs were done the way Welby liked them, Leoma asked her mother to pour milk for Kristina and help put the food on the table. Her mother was in a cheerful mood this morning, humming a lighthearted tune as she fluttered around the kitchen. Leoma hadn't seen the woman acting like this since she'd arrived in Oklahoma, and she wondered if perhaps her mother's exhilaration was because in a few days she'd return to her society friends in Boston, and to her husband who pampered and catered to her every need. Whatever the reason, Leoma enjoyed her mother's joyful humming. It reminded her of those childhood days in church when her mother sang hymns in her beautiful, clear voice.

"I can hardly wait to see the look on Welby's face when he sees the house," Leoma's mother whispered to her. Her mother had spent long hours, working with other women from the community, preparing Welby's house for his homecoming. Her attitude had softened considerably in recent days, and it seemed her grief over losing her first grandchild had lessened. She even seemed to enjoy sewing, cleaning, and helping to furnish Kristina's bedroom. It was unlike her mother to take on such tasks, although she had done quite a lot of charity work in the past, and she was quite good at sewing. But having a housekeeper, cook, and gardener at home, Leoma's mother had been very opinionated about the difference in life style here when she'd arrived three weeks ago.

Eventually, Leoma's mother had begun to do more and more around the house. The last several mornings, she'd brushed Kristina's hair, and she had seemed to enjoy giving the child her attention. It was especially good for Kristina, and since she had no mother or grandmother of her own, she was thriving on the loving care of two women

Leoma enjoyed her mother's company, and she appreciated all her recent help with Kristina and Dyer, especially since Welby had been placed in the guestroom to recuperate. At first, her mother had been reluctant, even haughty, when first asked to give up the large, sunny guestroom for the injured man, but at Doctor Rhodes request she'd done so graciously, even though she'd been against having him in Leoma's home. In time Leoma's mother relented and stopped mentioning the "*man in my room.*" It wasn't long before she seemed to take real joy in playing patty-cake with Dyer and reading to Kristina. One afternoon Leoma's mother had even tried her hand at baking a cake. Even though it turned out crumbly and the chocolate frosting was thin and sticky, it was quite tasty. Even Welby had enjoyed a large piece of it without complaining. Of course they'd given him the best piece with the thickest frosting. Leoma would miss her mother when she returned to Boston.

After the breakfast dishes were cleared from the table and washed, Leoma climbed up a small wooden kitchen ladder, and took her wicker picnic basket from the top of the cupboard. While her mother entertained Dyer and Kristina, Leoma began to assemble her contribution for the welcome home lunch that would be held at Welby's farm. Leoma knew she had a lot to learn about cooking, but her deviled eggs looked fine, and the potato casserole smelled delicious. Double checking the recipe Anna Jo had given her, she looked at the clock to make sure the dish had baked long enough. Oh, she'd die of embarrassment if the potatoes were still hard when her friends ate them. She opened the oven door and poked a fork into the bubbling casserole. Unsure, she closed the heavy door. She'd let the casserole cook another ten minutes and hope the potatoes wouldn't burn.

Leoma wrapped four plates in a dishtowel and set them in one corner of the basket along with knives, forks, and spoons. Next, she tucked a jar of pickles and a jar of beets into the basket. The canned food was some Welby had found after the tornado, still unharmed in his cellar. After the debris had been removed from his foundation, he'd discovered the cellar was intact, and all the canned foods were in perfect condition. He'd loaded up all that were left and brought them to Leoma's house.

Working quietly Leoma reflected on what she'd been told about Welby's new house. She hadn't been there yet and she was curious.

Mattie had measured the windows and dropped off the fabric she'd bought for curtains. Several other women, including Leoma's mother, had gone out to the house to clean and hang the curtains after they were finished, but Leoma had stayed home, sewing a dress for Kristina in her spare time and caring for Welby and his children.

From Leoma's impression of Welby and his attitude about her home, she pictured his house as a simple, little farmhouse and a rickety barn out in the country—certainly nothing grand or elegant. The change from Boston to this small undeveloped settlement was shock enough to Leoma, but thanks to Jeremy's fine building skills and the generosity of both his parents and hers, she had a lovely, grand home with exquisite furnishings. Leoma's house didn't have all the conveniences of her parents' Boston home, but it was comfortable and beautiful, and she felt extremely blessed. She couldn't imagine living in some plain, out-of-the-way little farm house, with pigs stinking up the property.

Still, Leoma was eager to see Welby's home and all the work that had been done there. She was equally eager to see Welby's reaction when he arrived home. She hoped and prayed he would be pleased with what the people had done, both inside and out.

Just as Leoma lifted the baking pan of potatoes out of the oven, there was a knock at the front door. Her mother called from the living room, offering to open the door for Doctor Rhodes. Leoma set the hot pan on top of the stove and removed her apron. She hurried into the living room to greet the doctor just as Welby hobbled in on the crutches the doctor had provided.

"I see you are doing well," Doctor Rhodes said to Welby. Welby had put the crutches aside the day before and used only a walking cane to help relieve some of the pressure from his broken leg, even though Leoma had warned him that the doctor expected him to stay off his feet most of the time, and to use the crutches when he was up and around in the house.

Welby nodded and smiled. "Yes, thanks to your good doctoring."

Leoma had watched as the doctor removed the stitches from Welby's head three weeks earlier, and his hair had already grown back where the doctor had shaved it away. He still complained that his knee hurt, but it had healed nicely. The stitches were also gone from that long incision, and he continued to do the exercises the doctor ordered. The tight wrap and splint was still on Welby's thigh, and he limped when he walked with the cane, but otherwise he moved around the house quite well, whether he used the crutches or walking cane. Of course, no doubt, there was a great deal of male pride at stake. Leoma had witnessed it often when Welby purposefully threw back his broad shoulders, and straightened his six-foot tall frame as he entered a room.

"More credit goes to the excellent care you've received from these two fine ladies." The doctor directed his eyes and compliment directly at Leoma and her mother.

Welby acknowledged the comment with a genuine smile. "Yes, yes. I can't complain about the care I've received. I don't know how I would have managed otherwise."

"Well, my friend, that's what good Christian neighbors are for." Doctor Rhodes clasped a hand on Welby's shoulder. "We were glad to help."

Welby didn't respond. In fact, Leoma thought perhaps she detected a change in Welby's posture, and tightening of his jaw when the doctor mentioned Christian neighbors. When it came to talk about religion or church, she'd been extra careful with her words, simply to avoid another disturbance in the house. She still prayed at meals, however, and tried to set a good example in her daily living. Clearly, Welby was softening in some ways, but it was obvious he still didn't want to hear anything about church, God, or religion. In fact, when she'd slipped out the previous Sunday and had gone to the church service while Mother watched the children, she hadn't mentioned a word about where she'd been, not that it was Welby's business. It wasn't necessary for her to answer to him for anything she did, and she certainly wasn't going to allow him to spoil the reverence she felt the moment she had stepped inside the church.

That Sunday had been the first time she attended a service since Elizabeth's funeral. Entering through the church door was difficult, and she'd almost backed out, but Anna Jo coaxed her forward and insisted Leoma sit with her family. Afterward, she was glad she'd gone. The reverend's sermon on joy in the Lord had lifted her spirits so much, she planned to return the following Sunday.

It had seemed as if a whole new world awaited her when she'd stepped outside the church doors and into the sunshine. In spite of her losses, the assurance that God would take care of her and fill her life with joy, overflowed from her heart. She walked home with a light step, and warmth in her soul made her want to sing, right out there on the main street in the middle of town.

When she reached the Langley's home Anna Jo hugged her long and hard. "God bless you, Leoma. I'm so happy you came along today. Isn't God good?"

"Oh, yes, he is." Nothing would keep Leoma from returning to church next Sunday morning. She, her mother, and Dyer would all go.

That same joy had bubbled and expanded in Leoma's heart all week. Prepared for the ride out to Welby's farm, she bundled Dyer and readied him to ride in the traveling box Welby had fashioned for her buggy. It might be a while before Welby would replace his wrecked buckboard and horse, so Leoma had insisted she loan hers to him until that time. Living in town, she hardly used it anyway, and after today Welby would need transportation.

Doctor Rhodes walked across the porch with Welby, his hand resting on his patient's shoulder. "You're doing very well, my friend. I just want you to keep using those crutches for a few more days. Then use the cane, and take it easy for another week or two. We should have that splint off by then. And no kneeling on that knee or climbing ladders for a while."

"How am I supposed to get my place done if I can't do any work?" Welby bellowed for all to hear. Everyone knew how eager the man was to get back to work on his house, and it wasn't easy for Leoma to hide her grin.

"It'll get done in due time," the doctor said. "I'm riding out to the Gallagers. Perhaps I'll go on out to your place afterwards to see the house. Do you mind?"

"Nope. Not at all." Welby seemed pleased that the doctor was willing to take extra time out of his busy day to ride on out to his farm for no special reason. He didn't appear to suspect Doctor Rhodes was trifling with the truth. The physician wasn't planning to stop at the Gallager farm at all.

Kristina skipped across the front porch, eager to go for the ride and picnic. "We're going to see our house, we're going to have a picnic," she sang as she jumped down each step.

"Yes," Leoma said, following with Dyer in her arms. "Your papa is going to drive my buggy and we're all going to see your new house. You'll have your very own bedroom to sleep in and a nice big-girl's bed. Won't that be nice?"

Kristina shrugged up both shoulders. Apparently Kristina didn't understand that she and her father wouldn't be returning to Leoma's home this evening. Rather than confuse the child she simply smiled. It was best to let Welby explain everything to his daughter after the gathering was over and the people were gone.

So far as Leoma knew, Welby believed that George and the small group of men had only finished the roof on the house and completed the repairs to the barn. Clearly, he had no idea about the surprise that lay in store for him, or he was an awfully good pretender if someone had spilled the secret. Leoma had convinced Welby the day before that she and Lillian should go along so Kristina could enjoy the outing. Leoma promised she and her mother would take care of the children. It hadn't been too difficult to convince Welby it would be a nice day to take along a picnic lunch since it was quite a long ride.

Leoma's mother set the food basket in the buggy and helped Kristina climb onto the front seat. Leoma and her mother climbed into the rear. With Welby's long legs it took little effort for him to hoist his body into the driver's place without hurting his injured leg. Leoma rode in silence except for the sound of hooves on the hard dirt road. She couldn't remember the last time she'd been for a ride in the country, and she'd never been out this direction beyond the last neighbor's house a quarter mile up the road.

While Jeremy was alive they'd spent most of their time in town, working on their new home, meeting new neighbors, and attending church. One time, before Leoma was pregnant, they'd ridden east of town for a picnic with George and Anna Jo. This area looked much the same with clumps of trees and green fields across the flat landscape.

Leoma's mind drifted back to Welby's farmhouse, and she wondered again what it would look like. She attempted to envision what the women had done with the curtains and furnishings she and the church members had donated. For the first time since Elizabeth had died, Leoma felt extremely good inside about helping someone else. She lifted her face to the clear, hyacinth-blue sky and took a deep breath. It was a wonderful feeling.

THE MORNING SUN WARMED his face and he'd never seen the sky so vividly blue. Welby sucked in a long breath of fresh air. It was good to be outdoors, and especially good to handle the reins of a healthy horse. He'd been allowed to sit on Leoma's front porch a few times in recent days, but the doctor had been strict with him about limiting his activities. Leoma made sure they followed Doc's instructions to the letter. Welby didn't like it, but he went along with it, hoping to gain his freedom as soon as possible.

He lifted the reins and guided the horse out of Leoma's yard and onto the road heading north. Anxious as he was to see his property, it was too nice a day to get in a rush. And besides, with the ladies and his young son on the back seat, he didn't want to jostle them around on the bumpy road. There was plenty of time to get to the farm, plenty of time to enjoy the ride.

George had told him some church folks had donated a double bed for him and a twin-sized bed for his daughter. Other than that Welby thought there would be a lot of work to do in order to make the house livable. But no matter. All he could think about was his privacy and being out from under the roof of Leoma Fisk. Not that he didn't appreciate all Leoma had done for him, he surely did, but it was high time he sleep under his own roof.

Doctor Rhodes was a short distance behind him, going at the same leisurely speed and would soon pull off at the Gallager farm. Kristina sat close beside him, quiet like she'd been after Louise had died. Welby was pleased to see the girl had brightened up over the last few months with Leoma, but he wondered now if she was afraid or worried. He looked down at her and winked. Kristina smiled up at him and snuggled her head against his arm.

It occurred to Welby that Kristina hadn't asked about her mother in several weeks. Or was it months? Now that they'd be back in their own home he hoped it wouldn't upset the child. At least in town, she'd had the care and attention of Leoma and Lillian, and she'd also had the Langley girl and boy to play with. Still unsure how he'd manage to take care of Kristina without help, his mind played with different ideas as the horse clopped along the road, taking him closer and closer to his farm.

It didn't take long before he turned up the lane toward his house. He squinted, trying to figure out what he was seeing. What was all that up ahead? As Welby neared the house several buggies and people came more clearly into view. He slowed and tried to count the buckboards and buggies in his yard. My goodness! There were at least a dozen or more. He could see the house had a full roof just as George had promised, and the entire house had been painted white. A spacious covered front porch that he hadn't built, stretched across the full span of the front of the house, and as he drew closer he began to recognize some of the people gathered on the porch.

There must have been at least thirty people there. When he pulled the buggy into the yard he spotted George and his wife in the middle of the group. Reverend Gilroy and his wife were there as well, and Welby saw Jason Alder who had come to Leoma's house two weeks earlier with George. Several other business men he'd dealt with in town were accompanied by a large number of women. A dozen or so young boys and girls stopped running around the yard and plopped down on the porch steps; big grins were on every face.

Welby didn't know what to think, especially with the preacher standing there wearing overalls and a work shirt. But there was no mistaking him. The man stood a head taller than all the other men and, unlike any of the others he sported a long black beard on his skinny face. Welby wasn't any too happy to see the preacher on his porch, but he had enough manners to be polite. He drew to a stop near the sturdy looking porch railing. The group of waiting people clapped and cheered.

"Welcome home, Welby!" The chorus of shouts were hearty and in

119

unison. He'd no sooner taken in the scene when Doctor Rhodes pulled his buggy up beside Welby, a big grin on his face.

Well if that doesn't beat it all, Welby thought. What had he done to deserve such a welcome to his own place? He stepped down from the buggy, using the cane, careful not to put his full weight on his healing leg, and offered a hand to Leoma and Lillian as they stepped down. Kristina didn't wait for help. She jumped down from the other side and ran to join her friend Doris on the porch steps.

George stepped forward, the first to shake Welby's hand. "Welcome home. I invited the Reverend and a few others out to give you a little house warming. I hope you don't mind."

Welby extended his hand to George, then to Reverend Gilroy who shook it warmly. There was no sign of judgment or criticism on his face. Other men and their wives followed, as they made a path for Welby to enter his house. Some folks slapped him on the shoulder, others shook his hand. "Glad you're finally up and around," George said. "As you can see we did a little more work on your house so you wouldn't have to worry about it."

Welby gazed around the porch that faced the west. He nodded and tried to imagine spending evenings there watching the sunset. What more could the men have done beside finish the roof, build the porch, and paint? That was far more than he'd expected, but still, why the big gathering? This was supposed to be no more than a private picnic with Leoma, Lillian, and his children, just to satisfy the gabby, insistent women. Were they the ones behind this entire shindig?

"Go on inside and take a look around," George said.

Welby stepped into the front room as if he were visiting someone else's home, a little hesitant and feeling out of place. The smell of fresh paint was strong. His eyes roamed from one side of the room to the other. Along the wall on one side of the living room stood a couch, not brand new, but it was decent and comfortable looking. A new kerosene lantern sat on the wide fireplace mantel. White curtains were tied back at the sides of both opened windows, allowing fresh air and sunlight to flood into the room. The curtains were plain but fresh and new. Louise would have liked them. There was plenty of room to add more chairs and a side table or two, and plenty of space for the children to play.

"We realize it's not much furniture, but you'll have something to sit on at the end of the day," George said coming up beside Welby.

"I appreciate it. Thanks." Nearly speechless, Welby walked from room to room. He'd built the house with a bedroom for him and each of the children, but he hadn't had time to finish the floors or do any interior work before he'd gone off in a fit of anger and had his accident. He was undeserving of all this and he felt a little foolish now, as he realized a group of men, mostly strangers, had finished what he started. He'd never be able to repay all the kindness and hard work that had gone into finishing his house.

Amazed at what he saw in his bedroom, he shook his head. Everything was finished, from dark green paint on the walls to clean wood floors. A full-sized bed was already made up complete with a comforter and pillows. On the night table was another lantern. The tall chest on the opposite wall was large enough to hold more clothes than he'd ever own. The furniture appeared well used but sturdy and polished.

Welby wasn't much for worrying about what the curtains and bedding looked like, but the bed appeared comfortable. It was covered with a brightly colored patchwork quilt and the mattress didn't sag in the middle. He ought to sleep real sound tonight. Fresh white curtains, like those in the living room, hung on the opened window, and they were drawn back to let a pleasant breeze fill the room.

Across the hallway it was easy to tell which bedroom belonged to Kristina. She ran into the room eyes wide, all smiles. Against white walls Welby found a single bed, a night table, a small dressing table, and a chair. Apparently some woman had done hours and hours of sewing. A pink and white spread covered the bed, and matching ruffled curtains hung on the window. Reclined against the pillow on the bed was a rag doll with yellow hair and wearing a bright flowered dress.

"This is your new bedroom, Kristina," Leoma said as she stepped into the bright, sunny room and hugged the girl.

Welby turned to see his daughter smile. She ran to the bed and picked up the doll, hugging it tightly to her chest. "She doesn't look like my Suzy," Kristina said after examining the cloth doll.

"No, but she's brand new and special just for you," Leoma told her.

Kristina pressed the doll to her shoulder. "Thank you."

Welby couldn't imagine what he'd find in the next room. He opened the door and walked into what was definitely Dyer's room. Blue curtains donned the window, and a full-sized crib was ready for his son with neatly folded blue blankets. A small oak chest of drawers stood against one wall, and a next to it was a good looking rocking chair. And right in the center of a large, oval hooked rug of every imaginable color, was a small wooden wagon which held some brightly painted wooden blocks. The toys appeared to be hand made and finely crafted.

Welby turned to George. "I hardly know what to say. This is—"

"You can thank the good reverend," George said. "He organized the work crews. And all the ladies sewed the curtains and bedding. Everyone at the church pitched in, donating their time, money, and furniture, and the women put the rooms together. Leoma and Lillian made all the bedroom curtains."

He tried to imagine Leoma's prissy mother sewing anything, let alone curtains. The picture didn't develop in his mind. For certain, she'd be the type to buy only the best window coverings at the finest stores in Boston. It seemed a little more likely that Leoma might try her hand at sewing. She did have a knack for fixing up a room real nice and pretty. Her style was just too fancy for his liking, but he appreciated the way they kept everything here simple. "Thank you, all of you. I don't know how I'll ever repay you."

The preacher landed a hand on Welby's shoulder and gave a gentle squeeze. "No repayment is expected, Welby. We only did what the Lord would have his people do. It's out of love that we did this for you, and we hope you and your children will be comfortable."

"But there are so many families that still have damage and need help. Why me?" Welby had never felt so humbled, or so grateful. Maybe these church folks weren't half bad after all.

"We've been a busy flock," the preacher said. But you have lost so much more than most, not just your home, but your wife before that.

And you nearly lost your son, not to mention your own life. We want you to know that we all care, and we will always be here for you. Repairing your home is the least we could do."

How could Welby fault the minister or the people of the church? This was a gift he didn't deserve and far more than he could ever imagine. Still, as much as he appreciated the kindness and work these people had done for him, he hoped they wouldn't expect him to go to the church meetings just because they'd done him a favor.

Anna Jo came up beside Welby and put a hand on his elbow, a barely noticeable touch. "You have more to see," she said. "Come into the kitchen."

The kitchen floor had been almost done when Welby had his accident. George had told him the floor was finished days ago, so what was so important for him to see?

"You'll have to get a cook stove," Anna Jo said, "but we did as much as we could."

"You piped in water?" Welby walked over to the metal sink beneath a curtained window. He pumped the brass handle up and down a few times. Suddenly a burst of cold water splashed into the basin.

Everyone clapped. Not many people had water inside their houses yet, but he'd noticed Leoma was clearly proud of the modern kitchen her husband had built for her. Not only did she have piped in water she had the newest, biggest cook stove Welby had ever seen. Why, she even had one of those iceboxes shipped from the east coast, and even though he hadn't been upstairs in her house, he knew she had one of those new fangled, pull-chain flush toilets up there. Kristina had been excited about using it and explained it to him in great detail. Welby turned his mind back to his kitchen.

A wooden cupboard with doors below and open shelves on the upper half, stood against one wall. It had two large side-by-side drawers as well. Every dish, eating utensil, serving dish, cup, and glass he'd need was there, including two sharp knives, a small paring knife and a large butcher knife. Curious what he'd find behind the two lower cabinet doors, he swung them both open at the same time. A variety of large bowls, pots, skillets and baking tins were neatly arranged on the two shelves. "You all must think I know how to cook." Welby chuckled, wondering what he'd do so many utensils.

"We kind of figure you might need a woman to help you with all those gadgets," the Reverend said, followed by loud laughter.

Welby closed the cupboard doors and turned to examine the rest of the kitchen. The big plank table in the center of the room was long and wide, with a chair at each end. Flanking each side were long sturdy benches. It was more than enough space for a large family, which of course he'd never have, but it was nice the folks provided a spacious table. It would seem a bit strange when he and Kristina sat down to eat, just the two of them, with all this space.

"There's just one more thing." George guided Welby to the other side of the kitchen where he'd built a small pantry for canned foods and staples. Across the front someone had hung curtains that matched the window curtains. "Take a look," George said pulling back the blue fabric.

It looked as if the grocer had emptied his store and filled the shelves. Once again, he shook his head, amazed at what he saw. If Louise were alive she'd be thrilled to see so much food stored up in her kitchen. He'd emptied the cellar and given what remained to Leoma, but this was ten times more than what he'd given away. Welby scanned the items, neatly lined in straight rows on the shelves. He saw home-canned fruits and vegetables, flour, sugar, corn meal, molasses, dried beans and peas, spices, vanilla, coffee and much more. It looked like a six-month supply. Why, there was even a tin of store bought cookies. He and Kristina would enjoy those.

Something wet dripped down Welby's face, and he swiped at it with the sleeve of his shirt. Too overwhelmed to speak, he had to compose himself before turning to face the room full of people. He couldn't let the other men see a grown man shedding tears. Finally, he turned, overwhelmed with gratitude, and thanked everyone in the room for this gift of kindness. He felt as if he'd forever be indebted to these people.

"You're as important to us as anyone in this town, Welby," the preacher said. "God's grace is good, and we just wanted to share his loving kindness with you and your children. We love you and your two little ones, just as God loves you all. He cares about every small detail of your life. Please keep that in mind, and if you're ever inclined to come to church services, you're more than welcome."

A hearty amen filled the room.

Welby's jaw tightened. He knew, sooner or later, the preacher would get around to nagging him about attending church. But at least the man didn't try to make him feel guilty. It seemed everything that had been said and done here was out of genuine love. He supposed if that's what church-going did for folks, well, just maybe it wasn't so foolish a thing to do. Louise had begged him to take her to church for years, and Welby had refused. The memory of his stubbornness with his wife sent a stab of guilt through his chest. Oh, if she were only here now. He'd pack her up come Sunday and head straight for that church building. Well, on second thought maybe—"

"Papa! Papa!" Kristina ran into the kitchen, bright eyed and smiling. "Come outside. We're ready for the picnic. Come see. Come see." As quickly as his daughter ran in to get him, she flew back out the door into the back yard. He hadn't seen her that excited in months; it did his heart good.

"It sounds like the ladies have the food ready." George slapped Welby on the shoulder. "I don't know about you, but I'm mighty hungry. Let's go see what they've set out."

Welby had never seen anything like it. Many of these people were strangers, yet they treated him like a good friend. Someone, he supposed the men, had made three tables of saw horses and planks of wood. Each one was covered with a blanket and filled with food of all kinds. The fried chicken made his mouth water, and he couldn't wait to dive in to one of those cherry pies. He'd never seen so much food, and it wasn't even a holiday or a special occasion.

Ann Jo put a plate into his hand. "Leoma and Lillian will take care of the children. You go dip what you want and eat."

Welby nodded his thanks. He scanned the tables of food wondering what to take first. Besides three platters of fried chicken, there were two plates of ham, and bowls of potatoes made in various ways. There were different kinds of vegetables, salads, and deviled eggs. One table held all manner of desserts, from cherry and apple pies to chocolate cake and cookies. At the end of that table were jugs of lemonade. It was a feast fit for royalty. "I hardly know what to say."

Anna Jo smiled. He'd never noticed what a pretty woman she was, with those kind blue eyes and bouncy red hair. Her face glowed and something special radiated from her smile, just like he'd noticed on Leoma's face lately.

"Let's begin by asking our gracious Lord to bless the food." From the top porch step, Reverend Gilroy shouted in his loud, preacher voice above the chatter and laughter of the crowd.

Feeling a bit awkward, Welby bowed his head like everyone else did. He waited. The preacher said a short, simple prayer, ending with, "Ain't nothing better than a church-going woman's cooking. Bless every tasty bite, Lord!" A rousing chorus of "amen" was mixed with laughter. With that finished, the chatter resumed. Everyone fell into line behind Welby and began filling their plates with food.

Blankets were spread on the ground, and a few people found seats on the ends of wagons. Welby sat down on his back doorstep and watched his daughter go through the food line with Leoma. Leoma dipped a plate of food for Kristina before serving herself, and she made sure his daughter was situated on a blanket with Doris and some other children. A middle-aged lady he didn't recognize held Dyer, cooing and laughing with him, giving him tastes of something on her finger.

George eased down onto the porch step next to Welby, his plate piled high with food. Welby bit into a piece of tasty fried chicken. Across the yard Jason Alder, the young man Welby had met only briefly when he came to Leoma's house, approached Leoma where she sat with another woman on a brightly striped blanket. Welby couldn't hear what Jason said, but Leoma smiled and nodded. The handsome young man sat down beside her and began to eat. Welby couldn't swallow. He couldn't take his eyes off of the couple.

"You worried that young feller might take a liking to Leoma?" George said, and elbowed Welby in the side.

Welby was forced to swallow the mouthful of chicken before he could speak. "What?"

"It looks to me like the young man over there has taken a shine to her."

Welby grunted and bit into the chicken drumstick. It wasn't any of his business what Leoma did, but deep inside a tinge of edginess poked at his gut. He didn't like the feeling.

Chapter 13

WHEN THE LAST OF the people drove off in their wagons and buggies, quiet overcame Welby with a sense of emptiness, even though Kristina was in her bedroom a few steps away. The house was full of new things, and he appreciated that, but something was missing. Louise would never share this home with him. It would be weeks, perhaps months, before his son would occupy his bedroom. The home Welby had built for his family was gone—ripped off the face of the earth. Everything about his life was different now.

After several weeks at Leoma's house, he felt lost in a strange place. Leoma's home was alive with activity, people were coming and going, music filled the air, and the house was filled with warmth and love. It seemed his new home was void of all that. Nothing resembled the home he'd built for Louise, or the house he'd begun to rebuild after the tornado. Even his family was torn apart. Why? If Leoma's god was so kind and loving, why must he endure this shattered, painful life? Immediately, Welby realized he was already forgetting all he'd just been given, and the kindness that had been shown to him and his children. Ashamed, he determined to be more grateful for his neighbors' generosity and kindness, and to remember the good things in his life.

George and his family, along with Leoma and Dyer, were the last to leave after the housewarming. Welby had stood on the front porch for several minutes, watching until George's buggy was out of sight. The sun still lingered in the afternoon sky, leaving Welby plenty of time to explore his new surroundings and get comfortable. He looked around the near-empty living room, listening to the silence. As he peeked into each room

Welby tried to imagine Louise there, cleaning, caring for the children, relaxing with a book like she often did. Not being able to see her clearly disturbed him. Her face was no longer vivid, her voice a distant, fading memory. For a scant moment he envisioned Leoma Fisk there, smiling and singing. He closed his eyes and shook his head, trying to rid his mind of the sight, then, he walked down the hallway.

Welby found Kristina perched on the edge of her bed, her new rag doll clutched against her shoulder, gazing out the window. She didn't move. "Kristina," he said with a lift in his voice. She turned his way, a blank look on her face. "Do you like your bedroom?"

Kristina shrugged and said nothing.

"The ladies fixed it real pretty for you." Unsure what else to say or do, Welby stepped closer to his daughter and reached out his hand. "Let's go outside and sit on the front porch for a few minutes. Papa needs your company."

Kristina jerked up both shoulders again then slipped off the edge of the bed. Her hand was so tiny and fragile in his big, calloused grip. The new screen door opened easily without a squeak. He stepped outside with Kristina next to him and walked across the porch. Together they sat down on the top step. His daughter hadn't spoken a word since Leoma and Lillian had hugged her good bye. Now she stared straight ahead, her new doll clasped tightly against her chest.

It hadn't been easy leaving Leoma's house. Oh, Welby was mighty glad to come home to his farm, away from those two overbearing women, but Kristina had grown fond of Leoma and her new friends in town. First she'd lost her mother, and now she'd been taken away from the only other women to take Louise's place. It was clear the girl wasn't very happy right now.

Just like she'd been after Louise had died, Kristina was withdrawn. Welby's earlier promises of going into town to visit had done little to appease the child. Accustomed to letting his wife care for the house and children, he didn't know what to do. Glancing down at his daughter again, he tried to think of something to say or do to cheer up his little girl. Hopefully, time would take care of her sadness and everything would be fine, but it sure was hard in the meantime, feeling so helpless and all. He let his thoughts move to something else, hoping Kristina would come around soon. For now he had to think about finding someone to take care of his daughter and the house during the daytime, and he had to buy another buckboard and horse so he could return Leoma's rig.

Leoma had generously loaned Welby her horse and buggy, and she'd left them with him today. Feeling out of sorts about using the woman's only means of transportation didn't set well with him. It was an inconvenience for them both, and Welby needed something large enough to haul farm supplies, not a fancy little get-up that held four or five passengers. He'd have to see about buying his own horse and rig real soon—hopefully before the end of the following week. Fall was just around the corner, and one never knew when the first freeze would come. Leoma would need her buggy soon.

A good feeling crept into Welby as he thought about the afternoon, and all the work the people from the church had done for him. It was too bad he hadn't been able to help his neighbors more, and finish his own house. But then he knew it was no one's fault but his own. While he lay in bed healing from his accident, men were helping restore each others' businesses and homes, including his. What a fool he'd been, allowing his anger and craving for alcohol to endanger his life, and putting him down for a month. He was fortunate to have all those people show him so much kindness.

Still, it was difficult to figure out. The church folks were a happy bunch, unlike any group he'd ever seen. They were full of funny stories and laughter, nothing like the staunch, cold people from his grandfather's church. And not once, did anyone here ridicule or condemn him for his actions.

Doc Rhodes was right, though. Welby's fool hearty temper had nearly gotten him killed. Of course, if it hadn't been for Leoma and her mother's nagging about him going church, and their constantly pushing their religion on Kristina, he wouldn't have become angry and stormed off the way he did in the first place.

After pondering on that thought Welby realized he was blaming his stupidity on Leoma and Lillian, who only believed they were doing the right thing. He sucked in a deep breath of air and let out a sigh. Well, maybe it wasn't their fault, but he didn't need their advice or nagging, and once Dyer was old enough to come home permanently, Welby would never have to see Leoma Fisk and her hoity-toity mother again.

He was appreciative that Leoma had nursed his son back to health and saved the child's life, and Welby was grateful she'd given him and his children a place to stay after the tornado destroyed his house, but that was all behind him now, except for her nursing Dyer a little longer. His jaw and lips tightened. Yup, it was fine with him, if after he had his son back home, he never saw the woman again. Then he remembered his promise to Kristina. She'd want to visit Leoma now and then.

Leoma, Leoma. Enough about her.

Welby turned from where he sat on the step, and he surveyed what he could see across the front of the farm house. It was nicer than the old place, and he could have done without that fancy Victorian trim the men had put on the porch, but he had to admit it added a certain charm to the house. Louise would have loved it, but for him it would take some getting used to, and it would add to upkeep. He patted Kristina's back and looked down at her. She was still so tiny, like a fragile doll. He couldn't help but wonder what she was thinking. "Do you like our new house?"

Kristina lowered her head, her chin pressed hard against the rag doll's yellow yarn hair. Welby bent forward to see her tightly shut eyes. No tears. That was good. He didn't deal well with tears from females—especially from his little girl.

"Don't you like the nice curtains Mrs. Fisk and her mother made for your bedroom? They're the prettiest ones in the whole house."

Still the girl didn't move or speak.

Welby stood up, carefully putting his weight on his good leg, and fetched his cane, which he'd leaned against the porch railing. Kristina ignored his outstretched arm. He bent forward and touched her shoulder. "Come on, sweetheart. Papa doesn't want to go into our new house all alone. I need my girl to help me find my room." He reached down and nudged her elbow, tugging lightly, encouraging her to go back inside with him.

Just then a scraggly, brown puppy he'd never seen bounded around the corner of the house. The dog bounced and yapped, and caught

131

Kristina's full attention. His daughter's eyes grew wide. Welby wasn't sure where the young dog had come from, but if it coaxed his daughter off the step and drew her out of her silence, he'd gladly feed the scrawny critter a scrap of food.

"Is he ours?" Kristina said in a low, hopeful voice.

"Well, I'm not sure who he belongs to. He looks a might skinny and lost to me."

"Can we keep him?" Dropping her doll on the porch, Kristina stood up and ran down the steps to the dog.

"I don't know. We'll have to ask around, and see if we can find his owner." Welby patted the dog to settle it down and rubbed behind his ears. "We'll take care of him until someone claims him," he said, hoping that was the very thing to cheer up his daughter.

Kristina wrapped her arms around the dog's neck and after a moment she patted his dusty back. "Hi puppy," she said in a small voice. "You can sleep in my room tonight."

"Well now, don't be too sure he'll stay," Welby warned. He didn't want the child to get her heart too set on the dog staying, only to have her heart broken again if the mutt ran off.

Welby supposed it might take Kristina's mind off of her loneliness and missing her mother if the pup hung around. Actually, he wouldn't mind having a good dog on the farm. It had been over ten years since he'd owned a dog.

Ignoring his words, Kristina ran into the house with the dog bounding close behind her. Welby picked up the forgotten doll, and followed his daughter at half her speed. Kristina's happy chatter at the animal carried from her bedroom all the way through the living room. The girl would be heartbroken if the dog couldn't stay or just decided to run away the next day. Welby couldn't help but hope the animal was from a litter of unwanted pups, and had strayed from its mother. The dog looked old enough to be weaned.

Welby walked into Kristina's room. It was fresh, and much nicer than the bedroom in the old house. The dog sat patiently on the floor letting Kristina stroke his back. Suddenly, the animal plopped down and rolled onto his back, his legs pointing straight into the air, his tail sweeping back and forth against the pine floor. Welby reached down and stroked the dog's belly. "See, he wants you to rub his tummy."

"Is he a boy dog?"

"Yes, he's a boy dog." Welby held his breath for a moment, hoping his young daughter wouldn't ask him to explain why he knew the dog was a male. It was a woman's job to explain such things.

"Can I name him Brownie?" Welby's daughter looked hopeful. How could he say no? Kristina rubbed the dog's stomach and lowered her face close to his nose. "Hi, Brownie. Hi."

"Now, Kristina, don't get your heart set on keeping him, until we know for sure he doesn't belong to someone else. Some other little girl or boy might be looking for him."

Kristina frowned and puckered her lower lip. "I hope no one else wants him. I want him to stay here. "You want to stay here, don't you, Brownie?"

Welby sighed, knowing full well he was going to loose this battle. It was better, he decided, to let the child enjoy the pup.

Still on the foot of Kristina's bed was the small parcel of clothes Leoma had brought that morning. Leoma had packed it and told Kristina there was a new hairbrush in the bundle for her. He wondered if there was a nightgown for Kristina among the items. After the tornado all they had left to wear were the clothes on their backs. So absorbed in his losses, and trying to get back on his feet, Welby hadn't paid much attention to his daughter's needs while they stayed at Leoma's house. Leoma had taken over the care of both his children and he knew someone had donated a few clothes. He didn't know what Kristina had been sleeping in all this time, and he opened the bundle to find out what was there.

When Welby removed the twine and opened the washed flour sack, he discovered two shirts he didn't recognize. They were neatly pressed and folded. He lifted them out and held up the bright blue, long-sleeved shirt to examine it. It was brand new and the workmanship was excellent. Beneath the shirts he found two print dresses.

"Miss Leoma sewed that shirt for you," Kristina said, jumping up from the floor. She grabbed up the print dresses. "And Miss Lillian made these for me."

"Miss Lillian sewed those? That was nice of her." Welby didn't know what to feel. Gratitude? Humility? Amazement? Those women had done so much sewing for his house, and yet, they took time to sew these clothes without a request for compensation. They must have spent a fortune on fabric. Who would have guessed Lillian could sew a girl's dress that looked as perfect as store bought? It was like something right out of that Montgomery Ward catalog Louise had shown him.

"Look, papa." Kristina held up a white cotton nightgown with a pink bow at the neckline.

"Did Miss Lillian sew that too?"

"No. Miss Leoma made it. She said she'd sew me a warmer one for winter, too."

The minister's words at the picnic earlier came to Welby's mind. *We only did what the Lord would have his people do. It's done out of love.*

Out of love. "It's what the church folks do," Reverend Gilroy had said. How could Welby continue to find fault and criticize people who had so much goodness in their hearts? The least he could do is be thankful for all they'd done, especially Leoma, and for their kindness to his family and others in the town with problems. Still, that didn't mean he had to go to church and pretend to be holy— like his grandpa had done.

From the time his grandfather Soderlund had moved in with Welby's father and mother, the old man insisted every one in the family attend church every Sunday. No excuses could get him out of sitting on that hard, front pew. Every Sunday, the preacher pounded on the pulpit and yelled about going to Hell until Welby had a headache. "Good morning, Reverend. Good sermon. God bless you, Reverend," his grandfather would say at the end of the service using his kindest tone as he tipped his hat.

What was good about scaring a young boy half to death?

What was good about going to church and acting holy, then going home and being as mean as the devil? Every single Sunday as soon as the family returned home, the old man would change into a tyrant. Not a day went by that Grandfather Soderlund didn't take out his fiery temper on his own family, especially on Welby. He didn't understand it. He remembered many times, running and hiding when his grandpa was spittin' mad and preaching his own brand of religion. Welby shook his head. No sir, he didn't need that kind of holy hogwash in his life. Welby believed there was a God, but no one had convinced him he was a good and loving God. It seemed to him God was just there to keep people in line and punish them when they were bad. Welby shrugged and clamped his jaws tightly together.

He supposed, as soon as Leoma was done nursing his son she'd be up at the church every Sunday, though she didn't seem the type to put on holier-than-thou airs—like Lillian—or carry on the way his grandpa did. He'd never heard Leoma raise her voice in anger, and she seemed to have something special in her life that gave her peace, even in the midst of her losses and troubles. Regardless, church was just fine for a lady like Leoma, if that's what she wanted. It sure wasn't for him, although, he wouldn't mind having the peace of mind she had. He just wasn't sure her inner joy came from going to church. There had to more to it than that.

"Papa, someone is knocking on our door." Kristina ran from the room before the tapping registered in Welby's brain. The girl's excitement brought him out of his cogitating. It seemed lately, Leoma popped into his mind way too often for his comfort. Cane in hand, he followed his daughter to the front door.

"Hello there," a woman said as soon as his daughter opened the door. Welby stepped closer and saw Mr. and Mrs. Gallager on his porch.

They'd just settled on the land down the road right after Welby moved onto his property. He wondered why he hadn't seen them among the folks who had come for his welcome home gathering, but it didn't matter. Jess Gallager was a friendly sort of guy, but Welby didn't know the family very well. The Gallagers had barely finished building their house when the tornado hit and damaged it. He pulled back the door and invited them inside.

"We thought you could use a pot of stew for this evening, seeing how you just came home," Mrs. Gallager said, as she jerked her head toward a cast iron kettle her husband held. "And here's a fresh loaf of bread." She thrust the towel-wrapped bread in his direction.

"Thank you. Come in, come in." With one hand Welby took the bread from the neighbor woman and suggested her husband follow them to the kitchen. "I don't have a cook stove yet, but I'm sure the stew will still be warm when we sit down to eat our supper. I appreciate your kindness."

Jess Gallager put the cast iron pot on a folded towel near the center of the table and turned to Welby. "We have an old wood stove with a small cooking surface out in the barn. The tornado spared our barn, and the old stove is just out there collecting dust. I hauled it all the way from Missouri and we ain't used it once out here in Oklahoma. The wife convinced me to buy her a four-burner with an oven for the new house, and that thing done survived the tornado. The old stove ain't much good for fixing big meals, but I'd be right happy to haul it over here for ya. You could use it 'til you buy somethin' better."

"Thank you. I'd appreciate that." Welby couldn't cook much, but it would be mighty nice if he could brew a pot of coffee in the mornings.

"Good. Me and my boys will load it up right away and have it over here before dark."

"That's right kind of you," Welby said, as he shook the man's hand. "By the way, do you happen to know who that dog belongs to?"

The pup had followed Kristina to the front door and then trotted into the kitchen, following after the scent of food. The animal eagerly wagged his tale, clearly begging for a handout. His sad brown eyes were hard to resist.

"Nope." Jess reached down to rub the dog's head. "Can't say I do. He's a fine looking animal, a bit skinny, though. I'll ask around."

"Kristina is set on keeping him and she already has a name for him."

"Those people up east of us have a bunch of dogs. I hear them barking all hours of the day and night," Mrs. Gallager said. "It's probably one from their last litter. I doubt they'd even miss him."

Regardless, Welby would ride over as soon as he could and check with the people. As much as his daughter wanted that dog, he didn't feel right about keeping an animal that didn't belong to him.

Shortly after the Gallagers rode away in their wagon, Welby stepped out the back door to survey the farm. His gaze wandered over the scarred land, his destroyed cotton crop. Not much he could do about that until spring except plow it under. With the gang of people at his house earlier he hadn't gone much beyond the back porch except to get his plate of food. He'd admired the new chicken coop from a distance. It was bigger than the original one and it looked sturdy. Welby would have to think about buying a dozen or two new layers and a rooster. And as soon as he could put up a pen he'd buy a pig, but he supposed he'd have to wait until spring on that, too, unless some neighboring farmers had young ones they wanted to part with. Miraculously, his Jersey cow had survived the storm, and George had made sure she'd been milked. She'd need milking again this evening, but he'd see to that after checking out the chicken coop.

As Welby meandered across the back yard he suddenly heard clucking and cackling. He scratched his head, puzzled. Every single one of his chickens had been killed and scattered from here to who-knew-where during the storm. He hadn't heard the cackling when all the folks were milling around his yard and house earlier. It was probably because of all the chatter and laughter during the home coming, but apparently someone had donated a couple of hens to his newly built chicken coop.

Welby opened the sturdy, wood-framed, wire door and stepped inside the coop. He scratched his head again and began to count. There were nine healthy looking hens. Come spring he'd have to buy a few dozen more to fatten up for butchering. A commotion up high in a corner behind him caught his attention. He sensed pair of eyes staring at his back. Slowly he turned, expecting to see a rattle snake.

"Well, I'll be jiggered." Welby laughed and scratched his head. "How can that be? Must be a miracle for sure." Perched on a two-by-four was his old rooster Crank. Where'd he come from? And how'd he get in there? Welby was pretty sure it was the same old feisty critter. Crank, that's what Louise had always called the rooster because the bird was cranky and obstinate. He definitely ruled the roost. Louise had called Welby Crank more than once, too. Smiling at the memory, Welby figured he more than likely deserved it.

Welby checked the straw nests. Sure enough, he found several eggs, most of them nice, large, brown ones. Someone had even thought to hang a basket on a nail near the door. He took it down, and by the time

Welby emptied the nests he had eleven eggs. If he had that stove now he'd scramble up a batch for Brownie. *Brownie?* Now why was he getting all soft and calling that stray dog by name? He chuckled. Anyway, he'd heard eggs were good for a dog's fur. Whether or not it was true didn't matter, the poor dog needed a good meal even if he didn't stay around. The basket of eggs in hand, Welby headed for the house in long strides, his mind wandering back to Leoma. He no sooner opened the door when a wagon rumbled into the yard.

"Howdy, neighbor!" Jess called, as he and two of his sons pulled their wagon up near the back door and stopped.

The Gallagers had made record time getting that stove over to Welby's house. He stood aside as the two stout teen-aged boys carried the cast iron stove into the kitchen. Jess helped Welby hook up the vent pipe and had it ready to use in no time. The boys, both broad-shouldered red haired fellows, carried in a pile of cut firewood they'd brought from home. "We brung a little wood just in case you're short on cut wood," Jess said.

Welby thanked his neighbors, and built a good fire beneath the cooking surface before they left. He'd cook up a batch of those eggs for the dog then set the pot of stew on to heat. There was enough food left from the pot-luck picnic to feed him and Kristina for three days, and he was getting as hungry as that mutt looked. The stew smelled too good to pass up and the fresh bread would be real tasty. He licked his lips just thinking about dipping a thick slice of the bread into the stew's rich brown gravy.

As Welby worked in the kitchen alone he listened to the quiet. No cheerful chatter drifted from other rooms: no singing, no laughter, and no companion to talk with. Scanning the large room, his eyes rested for a moment on the empty table then moved on. This room was nothing like the old kitchen. Louise would like this bigger work space and those ruffled curtains on the window, he was pretty sure. And the indoor water at the sink would have thrilled her. Fresh sorrow, something he hadn't expected to strike again, tugged at his heart. It was as if he'd been ambushed by his emotions and he didn't like the feeling. He knew Louise was gone forever but he still missed her. Only a few hours had passed since his son left with Leoma and he missed the little guy already, too. What he wouldn't give to see Dyer smile right now.

Welby's thoughts shifted as he cracked the eggs into a skillet and began to stir. He found himself wondering what Leoma was attempting to cook on that big fancy stove of hers. The woman still couldn't fix a meal worth eating, so far as he was concerned, but he had to admit, reluctantly, she was giving it a good try. Lately her biscuits and gravy were turning out pretty tasty, but her corn bread needed a lot more work. Now that he thought about it, he couldn't remember the last time she'd burned anything. Maybe in time she'd put together a decent meal. Of course if she ever opened that bookshop she'd talked about she probably wouldn't have time for cooking. She'd probably want a cook and a maid like her mother had in Boston.

He had to admit, Lillian had learned to bake a few things while Welby was there, something she'd apparently never done in Boston, from what he'd overheard. As he recalled, Lillian would be leaving for home the day after tomorrow, probably back to her servants and high society life. He wouldn't miss the bossy old gal, but he was sure Leoma would miss her mother when she was gone. Suddenly he wondered what it would be like for Leoma when she was all alone again, rambling around in that big house by herself. She'd be in the same situation he was in. Maybe it was a good thing Dyer was still with her for a while longer. The child would be good company and keep her busy.

Brownie scampered into the kitchen as if he owned the place and came to a screeching halt beside the stove, his tail waging so hard his entire body shook. Kristina followed close behind. Welby pushed the eggs around in the skillet with a wooden spoon making sure they didn't scorch, not that it would matter to a half-starved dog. He turned to Kristina and smiled. "Do you think Brownie will like scrambled eggs?"

Kristina looked up and nodded. "I like eggs too."

Welby smiled, certain Kristina was hungry. His little girl had blossomed during their stay in town with Leoma. Her cheeks were filled out and rosy pink. Her dark hair gleamed, clean and smooth. And he realized she cried less lately. Except for this afternoon when Leoma and Dyer went home, Kristina had been more outgoing and she appeared much happier. It probably wasn't Louise his daughter was missing so much these days, but Leoma.

Welby had Leoma Fisk to thank for his daughter's change. The woman seemed to take real joy in caring for Kristina and Dyer, reading and singing to them, keeping them bathed, and making sure Kristina's hair was clean and brushed. The woman had not only saved Dyer's life, but she'd given Kristina the motherly attention the girl needed. It sure was too bad Leoma had lost her baby girl. She would have been a good mother. He'd have to do his best to take better care of his daughter and not neglect her, like he'd done after Louise passed away. Thinking back on the past several weeks, it almost seemed that having his house destroyed by the tornado was a blessing. The time Welby had spent at Leoma's, aggravating as it was at times, had helped him and his children heal, and it had given them a new start. It must have been hard for Leoma having them under her feet all that time, but she never complained.

As much as Welby hated to admit it, he was getting all soft in the head about Leoma. And, his attitude about the church folks had changed. He had them to thank for all they'd done. They did a real fine job furnishing his house and making it feel like a home. He felt like a different man.

Welby realized he wasn't hankering for a drink or a cigarette, and he wasn't stewing in anger. He didn't understand what was happening to him, or when the changes came about, but it was a good thing. His own mother would be proud and happy if she could see him now. She'd always said liquor would destroy a man's family and cigarettes would destroy his body. A man that wallowed in both was bent for pain and misery. His mother was right.

Welby set the dish of cooled eggs on the floor and watched Brownie gobble them down in about three loud slurps. They were nearly gone faster than Welby could straighten up. The plate licked clean, the dog wagged his tail and begged for more. But first Kristina needed to be fed. After slicing the bread and dipping two bowls of the rich brown stew Welby poured a ladle full of the stew into the dog's dish making sure it contained a few big chunks of beef.

He sat down next to Kristina on the bench, and folded his hands on his lap, motioning with a nod for the girl to do the same. They'd been made to wait for a blessing before every meal at Leoma's table, and with the wealth that had been heaped on him he figured it was a good idea for him to say thanks. Having never said a prayer at his table Welby didn't know what words to use. Stammering at first and feeling a bit embarrassed, Welby talked to Leoma's God the same as he would a friend, saying a simple thank you for the house and food. Whether God heard him, or not, he felt downright good when he said his amen.

Welby was grateful he'd been given a fresh start all the way around, and he had a good feeling that his life was somehow going to be better from now on. He could feel it in his bones. Oh, the future wouldn't be easy. He figured he'd have a long, tough road ahead, trying to raise two kids and running a farm, but he knew everything would be all right. The sorrow and grief had let up a bunch, and he was sure better days were ahead for him and his children. He dipped into his stew with a hearty appetite. Suddenly he had a strong hankering to plow up the fields and replant his cotton crop.

Chapter 14

Leoma dragged herself out from beneath the warm comforter and
shivered. The floor was cold against her bare feet as she padded into the
bedroom across the hallway. Dyer lay in the crib crying; he'd fussed
throughout the night. Between walking the floor, rocking him, and
nursing him, Leoma had gotten very little sleep. Each time the baby
had dozed off he woke again in less than an hour, wailing a pathetic,
painful cry. What was she to do? The child didn't seem to have a fever
but she couldn't be sure. He always felt warm to her. Leaning into the
crib, she lifted the baby into her arms, and tried to sooth him with gentle
murmurs as she paced around the room.

Welby had promised that after he finished his morning chores, he
would come by to check on her and Dyer. Lately she looked forward to
his visits, but right now, she was just too tired to think about entertaining
the man and his little girl.

Aware that Doctor Rhodes was in town full time now, Leoma
wondered if she should take Dyer to the doctor's office. As she tried
to decide what she should do, she cuddled Dyer and rocked from side
to side. Since Welby had returned her horse and buggy, she could get
to the doctor's office faster than walking, but Dyer might get too cold.
It seemed best to wrap the baby warmly and carry him the few short
blocks. Perhaps the doctor could find the problem and cure what ailed
the child.

Dyer was usually cheerful, and rarely cried, unless he woke up from
a nap wet and hungry. He laughed easily and reacted with smiles to
Leoma's attention. He liked the little games she played with his feet and

hands, and he chortled and cooed when she sang to him. His strength improved each week. Since he'd begun to thrive and grow from her care nearly seven months ago, he'd never been sick, at least not that she recognized. Hoping she hadn't missed something vital, Leoma tried to think of everything Dyer had eaten the last few days, and she recapped in her mind his daily routine and habits. Everything seemed normal up until yesterday evening. No falls, bumps or bruises, no vomiting or diarrhea.

"What's wrong, little man?" Leoma spoke softly. Not two hours had passed since she'd nursed him; he couldn't be hungry. She stroked his cheeks with her fingers and kissed his forehead. "I believe a visit to the doctor is definitely a must. I don't think we should wait until your daddy arrives to ask his permission."

Feeling unsure of her mothering skills and a bit flustered, Leoma said a silent prayer, asking God to touch the child's body and to give her wisdom. Snuggling Dyer to her breast after changing his diaper she carried him to her bedroom. She tucked him into her bed and covered him to his chin with the quilt. Hopefully he would be content long enough for her to dress and brush her hair. The sun wasn't yet shining, but clearly she wasn't going to get any more sleep.

Dyer fussed and fidgeted, freeing his hands and stuffing his chubby fingers into his mouth. He seemed to do that a lot lately. Leoma slipped into a plain, long sleeved cotton dress and quickly buttoned it up the front. Perched on the edge of the bed she tugged on a pair of stockings and shoes. "I'm almost done, sweet boy," Leoma said as she turned around and patted the baby's tummy. "Be patient with me my little love."

For a moment Dyer was quiet and peered at her through watery eyes, then, he puckered up and wailed loud enough to wake all the neighbors. Leoma ran the hairbrush through her hair a few times. With the baby demanding her attention there was no time to braid her hair or pin it up in elaborate curls. She hastily tied it at the back of her neck with a piece of ribbon. Before going out she'd slip on a hat so no one would see her hair anyway. Right now she just needed to pacify Dyer until the sun was fully up. She also needed something in her stomach before she could carry Dyer anywhere. Thankfully she'd baked a batch of muffins yesterday afternoon. They hadn't turned out too bad, although, she doubted Welby would like the plain, heavy concoction. At least it was nourishment. While she ate one of those with a cup of coffee she'd see if she could coax the baby to eat a few bites of applesauce.

Last month the doctor had told Leoma to begin feeding Dyer small amounts of smooth table food, and Anna Jo had given her instructions how to make baby foods, like she'd fed her own children. Leoma fed him only tiny amounts at first. Dyer had taken right to mashed potatoes thinned with butter and milk, and he'd gobbled down the milk gravy she'd allowed him to taste, but the home-canned applesauce Welby had provided from his cellar seemed to be Dyer's favorite. So far, the table foods seemed to agree with him and he was growing chubby. Until yesterday he'd had a hearty appetite.

With Dyer braced on one hip, Leoma went down the stairs, gripping the banister with her free hand to steady her steps. The baby had become quite a load. She placed him in the wooden high chair Welby had provided, and she used an apron to tie him securely in place. He sat up quite well now but she didn't want him to wiggle and slide out of the seat. "There you go sweet boy. Sit tight."

Daylight crept through the kitchen window. Leoma started a fire in the cook stove and put on a pot of coffee. Dyer fussed and whined, but it seemed he was doing his best not to be cranky. He normally had a cheerful disposition but nothing seemed to make him happy today. She kissed the top of head and smiled. What ever was bothering him made the poor little fellow miserable. Attempting to entertain him she put a wooden spoon in his hand. Usually he liked to beat on the tray of the high chair, but this time the spoon went straight to his mouth and he began to chew.

"My goodness, you can't be that hungry," Leoma said, amazed at the way Dyer gnawed on the spoon.

As if she'd suddenly awakened, it occurred to Leoma that Dyer might be cutting a tooth. She didn't know much about these things, but she recalled Anna Jo saying her babies fussed and drooled a lot when they cut new teeth. "Everything went into their mouths that would fit," Anna Jo had said. If Leoma remembered correctly her friend had said Doris was seven months old when her first bottom tooth popped through. Maybe that's why Dyer was fussing constantly and chomping on everything he could put into his mouth.

"Let's see what's going on in that little mouth of yours," Leoma said, as if the child understood. She coaxed the spoon away from him, cajoling the baby as she worked his mouth open with one forefinger. Sure enough, as she rubbed the pad of her finger across his lower gum she felt a hard nub of something just below the surface. The baby bit down on her finger. Thankfully the little tooth wasn't completely through the surface yet and the pressure of his bite didn't hurt. Unsure what she could do to relieve his discomfort, she worked her finger out of his mouth and gave the spoon back to him.

Between bites of her muffin and sips of coffee Leoma attempted to feed Dyer a small amount of applesauce. More of the fruit ended up down his chin and on the tray than in his stomach. Finally she gave up, washed his face, and removed him from the highchair. As she carried him into the parlor, he cried louder. She snuggled him against her shoulder, sat down in her rocking chair, and she rocked. If she could pacify him a few minutes longer perhaps she wouldn't have to disturb the doctor before his office opened. As she rocked back and forth and hummed a lullaby, her head dropped back against the rocking chair, and her eyes fell shut. At last Dyer quieted.

Early mornings like this had become Leoma's favorite time of day, while things were calm and quiet. She was at peace with her losses, at peace with God, and at peace with nurturing another man's child. Her heart swelled with tenderness each time she held the little boy.

Thinking forward to the day in the near future, when Welby would take his son home, brought a lump to her throat. Immense sorrow washed over her. She would no longer nurse Dyer, bathe him, or hear his laughter and see his precious smiles. Her arms would be empty again. Leoma opened her eyes, her vision blurred. With the back of one hand she swiped away a tear. How would she get through her days when she no longer had Dyer to care for? Without realizing it, so much love for this baby had crept into Leoma's heart, and it seemed as if she'd carried him in her womb and given birth to him.

Turning Dyer so she could cradle him in the crook or her arm and see his precious face, Leoma stroked the child's head, touched his fat cheeks, and examined his chubby little arms and hands. He was a handsome boy, looking more like his father each day now that his flaxen hair was growing longer. He responded to Leoma as if she were his mother. His eyes drifted shut. Leoma studied every feature of his face, committing his image to her memory.

She couldn't give him up—she couldn't.

After a minute her own eyes dropped shut again and her rocking slowed. With the warmth of the child cuddled against her she became drowsy. Oh what she wouldn't give to have Dyer sleep in her arms for two or three hours so they could both get some rest. The coffee pot forgotten, she drifted into a dreamy, much-needed sleep.

The early fall days had grown cooler, and Welby was glad he'd insisted Kristina dress warmer this morning. He glanced down at his daughter. She was as cute as she could be and looked especially pretty in the pink sweater Leoma had knit for her. Kristina was doing well about brushing her hair every morning, the way she'd been shown while staying at Leoma's, and she sat straight and proud beside him, her hands folded in her lap. The bonnet she wore wasn't so pretty and it didn't match the sweater, but he was thankful for the things the community had donated to him and his children. If not for friends and those folks at the church his girl wouldn't have much of anything to wear, other than the two dresses and the sweater Lillian and Leoma had made for her. People had given her handed down stockings, shoes, nightgowns, and several dresses. There was even a wool coat that would fit her when winter set in. The brown coat wasn't brand new, just another hand-me-down from George Langley's girl, but after putting out money for the new rig, Welby was thankful he wouldn't have to buy her a coat.

Welby coaxed his new horse into a slow trot, pleased with the young stallion. He was a good strong worker and the two of them got along well. The horse was ready to run and Welby held tight to the reins, keeping steady control of the speed. Since his accident he'd been more cautious. His stay at Leoma's house had given him a lot of time to reflect on his bad habits and his attitude. He'd had time to heal, not only his body, but his heart.

It took some doing, but Welby had to admit, he appreciated everything Leoma had done for him and his children. He didn't hesitate to give her credit for all she continued to do while still caring for Dyer. He especially appreciated the fine shirts she'd sewn for him. Beneath Welby's clean overalls and jacket he wore the darker blue shirt today, pleased with how well it fit. It amazed him that Leoma sewed shirts that fit him perfectly without ever having him try one on, and the workmanship was excellent. For a young city girl she took to living in the new territory pretty well, especially without her husband there to care and provide for her.

Leoma's fancy ways still weren't much to Welby's liking, but he had to admit she was a fine woman—finer than he'd first thought. She was as different from Louise as a winter night was from a summer day, but he liked Leoma's light, fresh appearance, always bright as a sunflower garden. She had a cheerful outlook on life, too, and her warm, pleasant way with his children was something to behold. He couldn't recall Leoma ever sounding angry or upset with his boy or girl. And the way he'd acted at times, he couldn't fault her for being angry at him. He'd been a real moron more times than he cared to admit.

"Papa." Kristina tugged on Welby's jacket sleeve drawing him out of his meandering thoughts. He had no business thinking so much about Leoma, and he was glad for the diversion. His daughter pointed toward town. "What's that?"

Welby had noticed the growing plume of dark smoke, and he wondered what was burning to make such a large amount of smoke. "Something is burning," he said. "It's probably someone's trash pile."

"Oh." Kristina let it go at that, but Welby watched, concerned that a fire that large was more than trash. A fire that big could spread; it could destroy the town.

He snapped the reins and pushed the horse into a gallop. The road was straight and fairly smooth from here on in and he felt comfortable with the increased speed. He might be needed to help fight the flames. It didn't take long to see the fire was near Leoma's house. His heart raced. There weren't but three or four houses in that area and Leoma's was the largest one along that road. "Go like lightning," Welby shouted, prodding the horse as fast as he dare. *Lightning.* That's what he'd call the young un-named stallion. It was fitting. "Go, Lightning!"

Welby tightened his grip on the reins; his heart pounded, and his mind raced with fear. He was less than half a mile away now, and he was certain Leoma's home was burning. Orange flames raged and licked the sky. His heart sank as he drew closer. A group of men and women stood in the road gazing at the blazing structure. A long line of men passed buckets of water, and others beat at the flames with blankets but clearly it was a hopeless battle.

Where was his son? "Please tell me he's safe. And Leoma. Oh, please let her be safe." Welby wasn't sure who he was talking to. Maybe this was how a person prayed? It didn't feel the same as his prayer for supper, but it didn't hurt to give it another try. "God in Heaven please let Dyer and Leoma be safe." Shocked at his own raised voice, Welby spoke a prayer with greater fervency than he'd ever known. If Leoma's God was real, Welby sure hoped he was listening.

As Lightning approached the crowd of men who battled the blaze he hesitated and whinnied. Welby pulled back on the reins and drew to a stop a safe distance away. Bracing his hands firmly on Kristina's shoulders he looked down at her. Terror filled her eyes. It was clear she realized this raging inferno was Leoma's house. He pulled his daughter close to him for a brief moment and held her securely. Drawing back he told her, "Papa needs to help those men, Kristina. I want you to stay right here where it's safe. Do you understand me?" He looked at her sternly until she nodded.

"Yes, papa."

"Do not get down from this wagon!" Kristina nodded and tears filled her eyes. Welby wiped the tears off the child's face with his thumb and kissed her forehead. "Everything will be all right. Just do as I said."

Welby jumped down and tied the horse to a nearby tree. Without the aid of his cane he ran toward the burning house, hoping for some word of Leoma and Dyer, hoping perhaps there was something he could do to help. His heart pounded; he was frantic.

"It's a goner," a stranger said. His face was smeared with soot and sweat. "The blaze is too big."

"Do you know where the woman and child are?" Without waiting for an answer Welby looked for something to beat the flames or a bucket for water but he found nothing. Without hesitating he jerked off his jacket and attempted fight the fire.

"It's no use!" The stranger shook his head, a look of defeat on his face, and walked away.

When Welby had arrived some of the men were still throwing buckets of water on the flames, but clearly they weren't making any headway. Intense heat from the violent fire pushed everyone back. Fearing for his own life, Welby backed away, too. He spotted George. His friend's face was red from being too close to the flames and his hair and clothes were a disheveled mess. He ran to George. "Where are Leoma and my son?" Welby shouted above the crackling and roar, fearing the worst. When he looked into George's eyes he saw tears.

George shook his head. "I haven't seen them. Several of us grabbed buckets and got here as fast as we could. By the time we gathered water from the neighbor's wells it was too late. We couldn't get to Leoma's pump out back; it's too close to the flames." George wiped his shirt sleeve across his face, his eyes red and glazed. "I've been here a while, but she might have made her way out before I arrived. I suppose she could be anywhere in town. I just don't know."

"She isn't with your wife?"

"No, I haven't seen her at all."

"What about her horse and buggy?" Welby said, hoping they were gone. That would mean she'd ridden away from the fire.

"They're out back." George pointed to the rear of the property beyond the carriage house. "I hitched up the horse and moved them as soon as I got here. I was afraid the carriage house would go up in flames, too. The fire was already so bad no one dared to go inside. We hollered and called out her name several times, but there was no answer, nothing."

Tempted to rush into the flaming house, Welby strode closer. The raging blaze nearly singed his beard. Flames shot out of the already broken windows and the front door, licking the side of the house. George grabbed his arm and tugged him away. Just then the roof caved in, sending huge sparks into the sky. Welby and George stumbled backwards, barely escaping large flying embers.

"Leoma! Dyer!" His cries were useless, but he couldn't stop yelling their names. He wanted to believe Leoma had taken Dyer into the storm cellar, or perhaps she'd run into town for help, but why wasn't she somewhere nearby with the other people. He shouted again and again until George grabbed him by the shoulders and dragged him farther away from the fire.

"The house is gone, Welby. There's no point staying here. Maybe they're safe in town. Come on."

"They could be in the storm cellar." Welby started to run toward the back of the house.

George grabbed his upper arm and jerked him back. "There's no way we can get to the cellar door right now. Besides, I don't think she'd go there. Come on, we aren't doing any good here. Let's go ask around town about them."

"My girl's over there in the wagon." Choked with grief, Welby pointed toward his rig as he forced each step toward his waiting daughter. How would he explain to Kristina if her little brother whom she adored had died in that awful inferno? How would he tell her that Leoma, the woman she'd come to love and depend on, was dead? He couldn't bring himself to believe Leoma and Dyer were dead. He couldn't.

"Get on up there with Kristina and make room for me," George said. "I'll take the reins."

Leoma sat in stunned silence holding Dyer tightly as she waiting for information. It seemed almost everyone in town had run toward the fire when news of it billowed through the main street. She didn't know what was burning and feared the fire might spread throughout the town.

Thinking a neighbor's house or perhaps a business was burning, Leoma waited to see the doctor.

Dyer hadn't stayed asleep earlier when she'd dozed with him in the parlor of her home. He'd only rested a few minutes when he'd begun to kick and wail uncontrollably. After changing his diaper and walking the floor failed to quell his crying, she feared something terrible was wrong with him. She had thrown on a sweater, wrapped Dyer in a warm blanket, and walked as fast as she could into town. It was a pleasant enough morning and the short walk did her good. It was easier than harnessing the horse and buggy and driving, especially the way the baby was screaming. It hadn't taken more than ten minutes to arrive at Doctor Rhodes' office and she'd been happy to see he'd turned the sign on the door to OPEN.

The physician was already seeing another patient. Leoma sat down on a cushioned chair in the front section of the office and tried to hush Dyer's crying. She rocked her body back and forth on the stationary chair, hugging him closely and trying to sooth him. She hadn't been there more than a few minutes when a man ran past the door shouting something about a fire.

Immediately Doctor Rhodes came out from the small examining room, Mrs. Connelly right behind him holding a rag to her red nose. The patient excused herself and left the office. The doctor glanced out the door, obviously curious to see what all the commotion was about, then, he closed the door firmly, saying nothing to Leoma about the fire. The way the Soderlund baby was crying the doctor didn't want to waste a minute to get to the bottom of the infant's troubles.

"Let's see what's bothering this little fellow." Doctor Rhodes smiled and motioned for Leoma to bring the baby into the examining room. "What seems to be the problem?"

Doctor Rhodes questioned Leoma and checked the baby from head to foot, prodding around his stomach, listening to his heart and lungs. He looked into Dyer's ears and up his nose. When the doctor forced the baby's mouth open he smiled and nodded. "Ah ha! So that's what hurts, young man," Doctor Rhodes said. "Those teeth are giving you some trouble, but they'll pop through any day now."

Leoma let out a sigh of relief, a bit embarrassed for her panic. But how was she supposed to know what was going on, when the child who never fussed about anything suddenly wailed and kicked repeatedly? Worried about handling the baby properly during these episodes she bit down on her lip and frowned. "What can I do to make him stop crying when he's in pain?"

"There's not much you can do. I'd suggest—"

The door of the doctor's office opened. A man shouted. "Big fire! Fire!"

Leoma couldn't see who the person was but his panic was clear, as the doctor excused himself and left the examining room. Within seconds Leoma heard the front door burst open again and slam closed. Doctor Rhodes rushed into the examining room, a grim look on his face. "Mrs. Fisk, I need to have you stay right here until I know for sure what's happening," the doctor said. He seemed to weigh his words carefully. "You'll be safer here."

"What is it?" What wasn't the doctor telling her? Panic flooded the room and grabbed her at the same time she realized the strong smell of smoke had drifted into the office through the opened door.

The doctor knelt in front of Leoma and placed one hand on her shoulder. "The fire is out toward your place. I don't know whose place it is, but you need to wait here with me. I don't want you and that baby out in the smoke, and we're quite safe here.'"

"But, if it's my house I—"

"That was Reverend Gilroy a moment ago. He's is going to find out whose home it is and see if there's anything he can do. A group of men are already fighting it the best they can."

"Did you tell him I'm here?"

"Yes, I did. But I think it's best if you stay here with me until we know more. Reverend Gilroy will let us know as soon as he can. Meantime, let's talk about Dyer's problem."

Leoma listened, and tried to concentrate on what the doctor was saying, but her mind was in a frenzy wondering if her house was burning to the ground. How was she supposed to sit here and wait? She tried to remember if she'd left anything on the stove with the fire still burning.

She remembered making coffee and that was all she'd fixed. She'd left the pot on the stove when she went into the parlor to rock Dyer. When he'd awakened crying she didn't recall smelling smoke. However, she was exhausted from the sleepless night and she'd rushed out of the house, so concerned about the baby, she hadn't bothered to go back into the kitchen. Surely the coffee pot wouldn't have started a fire.

Suddenly Leoma remembered her horse was in the stall at one end of the carriage house. The horse would have no way to escape if the carriage house caught fire. Pain gripped her chest. Her heart felt as if it would stop beating and she could hardly breathe. She squeezed Dyer closer to her breast, trying hard to keep her fear in check. It was nearly impossible with the horrible vision of her house burning down and her horse struggling, unable to flee from the flames.

Oh, God, my Lord and savior, I pray no one is hurt in that fire. And, please, please, please don't let it be my house. Please keep the fire from spreading through the town and protect those men who are trying to put out the flames. Amen.

As soon as Leoma had silently prayed she realized it was selfish to ask God to spare her house. The neighbors in both houses down the street were delightful, kind, God-fearing people, and they were becoming good friends with her. They didn't deserve to lose their homes any more than she did. No matter whose home was burning, it was a terrible disaster. Still, she waited and prayed that her house would somehow be miraculously spared. Maybe the men had put the fire out before the building was destroyed. She had to believe that God had heard her plea. She must remain calm for Dyer's sake.

Arms wrapped around Dyer's warm little body, she hummed softly, a nameless tune. It was better than fretting when she didn't know the details of the fire. A song always seemed to put her at ease. Dyer was quiet for the moment and she didn't want to upset him.

The doctor handed her a small bottle of liquid and she listened as he instructed her to rub a tiny amount on the baby's lower gums to help numb the pain. She watched as Doctor Rhodes applied the medicine to Dyer's swollen area. When the baby settled against her and quieted

Leoma thanked the doctor and continued to hum and rock her body on the chair. At last, Dyer fell asleep.

Pounding footsteps of what sounded like a herd of cattle came down the wooden sidewalk toward the doctor's office. It sounded as if several men were running. The front door crashed opened startling Leoma. She stood up clutching Dyer to her. Welby and George burst into the examining area, Reverend Gilroy right behind them with Kristina in his arms. Welby cried out his son's name the moment he saw the baby in her arms.

Leoma's heart pounded. Anguish mixed with relief covered Welby's tear-streaked face. Before she could ask whose house had burned Welby threw his arms around her and the baby nearly crushing his son between them. His entire body shook as he sobbed.

No one had to tell her the answer.

Chapter 15

ALL THAT LAY IN front of Leoma were the charred remains of her beautiful home. Her body shook so hard she handed Dyer to his father for fear she'd drop the child. She fell to her knees and sobbed, and covered her face with her hands. Was this her reward for obeying God's every word, for loving him? While her own baby lay in the mean, cold grave, she nursed a starving child and saved his life. Even today she continued to nurture and protect another woman's child. She'd given the Soderlunds a place to live in this very house when their home had been destroyed. She had cared for Welby after his accident and watched over his children as if they were her own. And this was her reward? *Why, God? I don't understand.* She cried without embarrassment, wailing for all her losses, more lost and alone than she'd ever been in her life.

Why are you crying? You are not alone Leoma cupped her tear-soaked hands over her ears. She didn't want to hear those incessant whispers. Not now. *I have not left you dear child. Lean on me and I will give you peace and new joy unlike any you have ever known.*

Someone touched Leoma's shoulder for a second but said nothing. Finally she glanced up. It was Welby close beside her, Dyer secure in his arms. It must have been a great relief to find his son alive, but Leoma sensed there was more to the emotions that distorted Welby's face.

Welby cleared his throat, looked at the ground for a moment, then looked into her eyes. "You're welcome to stay at my house until we get your house rebuilt, unless you decide to go, back to Boston."

Leoma was surprised by the hesitation and crack in Welby's voice. Did he really care whether she left Oklahoma or not? The thought of returning to her home town hadn't crossed her mind in several months. There had been no time to think about tomorrow or the next day. The lovely home Jeremy had built for her and everything she owned was reduced to a heap of ash. At the moment the idea of returning to Boston didn't appeal to her, though it might be the wisest thing to do. At least there she had her family and best friend. She needed time to think, to overcome her shock. Her nerves were too raw to make a rational decision, but she did know she couldn't leave the child she'd grown to love as her own. Besides, Dyer wasn't weaned. Oh, what was she to do? It would be wrong to live with Welby and his children, but she couldn't just leave.

It was considerate of Welby to offer her a place in his home until she could rebuild or decide what to do. Certainly it would be convenient for him, having her there to care for his children, but it just wasn't a fitting thing for her to do, and she certainly wasn't going to live in his barn. "I appreciate your kind offer but I can't accept it. It wouldn't be proper for me to live with you," Leoma said.

The disappointment on Welby's face was clear. "You weren't concerned about having me live in your home after the storm."

Welby's tone made her cringe. Perhaps he was insulted by her refusal. Whatever the case, that situation was completely different, and the living circumstances were not the same. Welby didn't live in the main house; the carriage house where he slept was a separate building all together. "I don't consider you living in the carriage house the same as living inside my home."

Welby's brows lifted in unison. "But what about the month I slept in your parlor? How was that different or proper?"

She huffed, exasperated. He had a point, but again the circumstances were nothing like Welby suggested. When she spoke her tone was sharp; a new burst of tears threatened to fall. "First of all my mother was staying with me, and secondly, I don't know why the doctor brought you to my house after your accident to begin with. Perhaps he felt it was the only place to take you, beings you were already sleeping in the carriage house and I was caring for your children. What was I supposed to do? It was more convenient for everyone to have you there until you recovered."

Leoma had never seen Welby look so crestfallen. "I just want to return the favor," he said. "You could share Dyer's room."

"My carriage house is still intact. I can stay there." Leoma spoke as if the idea had just popped into her head. It was a good idea, actually, and there was plenty of space there for a crib for Dyer. The room at the end of the carriage house where Welby had slept for a time was quite spacious, and it would do very well for a few months. If she stayed there at least she'd be on her property. A new lump formed in her throat and she cupped her hands over her face.

My property. My beautiful home. My horse. Challenger!

Leoma's heart skipped a beat and she could hardly breathe. She hadn't asked about Challenger. Here she was discussing where to live and she hadn't had a chance to check on the well being of her horse. If he wasn't moved away from the house surly he was dead from breathing the thick smoke. Stinging tears welled in her eyes and cascaded down her face. "What about my horse? Where's Challenger?" Her throat constricted and her words came out in choked spurts. "I don't see him."

Welby answered in a reassuring tone. "George moved him out back beyond the carriage house, out of harm's way. I didn't go check on him but I'm sure he's fine."

"I have to go find my horse." Anxious to see for herself, Leoma stood and straightened her skirt. She hurried around the perimeter of the burned house, not caring if Welby and his children followed her or not.

At the far corner of the property Challenger was tied to a fence post, her buggy still attached. He was eating grass at the edge of the field. Running to him she let out a cry of relief that he'd been spared along with her buggy. Both had been gifts from Jeremy right after they moved into their house, and there were none finer in the town. They were all she had left, aside from the carriage house and the land beneath the ashes. She nuzzled the animal's neck with her face, and she stroked his sleek black coat several times before untying his tether. Fearing what lie in store for her Leoma guided the horse through the field, back toward the charred remains of her house. She was homeless, and except for the carriage house and horse and buggy, she had nothing more than the clothes on her back.

You have been given far more than you see. Have you forgotten the blessings from above that will be with you always? Do not be afraid for I am with you. I will supply all your needs.

She stopped in her tracks, ashamed of her lack of faith and her unseemly actions. She had allowed material possessions to gain far too much importance. She'd become more dependent on the things and people in her life than God. All her earthly belongings were temporary, but God's grace and love were eternal, she reminded herself. She had the assurance of God's divine presence and the knowledge that he was in control. Calmer now, Leoma acknowledged the gentle whispers, the loving reprimand. Standing in the middle of the field, she bowed her head in reverence, and she thanked God for the quiet reminders. She thanked him for speaking to her in loving whispers. Tears washed over her face again as she thanked God for her life and the life of little Dyer.

WELBY WATCHED AS LEOMA led Challenger back to the carriage house with her buggy in tow. He wondered why she'd stood in the middle of the field so long, as if she were praying, or perhaps crying. She walked slowly, making her way across the span of an acre. He waited. Dyer fidgeted in one arm and Kristina, solemn and still, stood close beside him. What would it take to convince Leoma to accept his offer?

The thought of proposing marriage, simply for convenience, of course, crossed Welby's mind, but he dismissed it quickly. It was a crazy thought. He still pined for Louise, and he and Leoma were far too different in every way. He'd heard widowed people often married for no other reason than convenience, but he didn't believe he and Leoma Fisk could live peacefully under the same roof as husband and wife. He didn't want the woman bossing him around day and night for the rest of his life. Not only that, she'd be expecting him to go to church every Sunday and he wasn't about to set foot in that church building.

The thought of marriage no more than flashed through his mind, when the preacher walked up beside Welby and slapped a hand on his shoulder. "She's a fine woman, Mr. Soderlund. There's not a nicer lady in this town right now, except perhaps my Mattie."

Welby frowned. "Now why would you be telling me that?"

The preacher smiled. "I figure a man with two little children could benefit by having a good woman in the house."

"Not that one. Least not as a wife."

"Meaning?" Reverend Gilroy looked at Welby, one brow raised, a frown clouding his face.

"Meaning, I offered her a room at my house until she rebuilds. That way she'd have a place to stay until she weans my boy. But she turned me down flat. Besides that, you know my Louise hasn't been gone more than half a year. It ain't right thinking about taking another wife."

The preacher slapped his shoulder again. "My friend, I understand, but you can't expect a fine Christian lady like Leoma Fisk to live under your roof outside of wedlock. Of course she told you no."

"You telling me I ought to marry her."

"It wouldn't hurt to ask her." Welby could see Reverend Gilroy was dead serious.

"You know, Preacher, you have no right meddling into my personal business." Welby turned and walked away, hoping he'd heard the last from that man. What gave him the right to tell Welby who could live in his house, married or not?

Reverend Gilroy followed so close beside him Welby could hear him breathing. He wanted to run. He didn't like the churning in his gut every time the preacher was in his presence. Something about the man's quiet, easy manner, and that feeling in Welby's stomach that the preacher could see right through him, made Welby's blood churn.

Oh, the reverend hadn't pressured him about attending church, and Welby had to admit the fellow seemed like a genuine man of God—if there was such a thing. Still, he had no doubt when the preacher stood in his pulpit the condemnation and shouting would begin. The congregation would weep and wail, repenting of their evil ways, then they'd go home and go right back to their drinking, fighting, and hurting each other. Sunday morning Christians, he'd heard them called. So far as Welby could see that's the way all the Bible-toting church goers were. Just like his grandpa. No thanks!

"I'm sorry if I offended you, my friend," Reverend Gilroy said stepping up shoulder-to-shoulder beside Welby. "You must understand it's my duty to bring the truth and good news to the people of this town."

Welby came to an abrupt stop and turned to face Reverend Gilroy. "The truth is, preacher, what I do in my home is my business, not yours."

"Perhaps that's true, but it is my business to proclaim God's word." The preacher smiled yet spoke humbly. "God tells us the upright should avoid all appearances of evil."

"And how does my offering a room to Leoma Fisk appear evil?" Heat rose to Welby's face. He shifted Dyer to his other arm. The implication that his kindness was misconstrued as evil didn't set well with him.

"Your offer isn't evil, Welby, and I'm sure your intent is pure. But if Leoma lives with you, it creates the appearance of evil, and other people might judge her unfairly. I'm only keeping her best interest in mind."

"Well I'd appreciate it if you would stop being so interested in my affairs." Welby grabbed his daughter's hand and strode to his wagon, causing Kristina run to keep up with him.

He wouldn't argue with the preacher, and he wouldn't hang around and beg Leoma to take the room. If she changed her mind she knew where he lived. She could figure out what she wanted to do without his help. "Get in the wagon, Kristina," Welby said. "We're going home."

"But, papa, we can't take Dyer with us without Miss Leoma."

Welby glared at his daughter for a moment, realizing the girl was right. Dyer wasn't weaned and Welby wouldn't know what to do with the infant. The baby needed Leoma. Welby let out an angry huff. Blast it all. He didn't want to admit it but he needed Leoma, too.

FROM A DISTANCE, LEOMA watched Welby rush up the road to his wagon, Dyer tucked haphazardly beneath one arm like a sack of oats. The man practically dragged Kristina behind him. His stride was long and unyielding. Reverend Gilroy stood in front of her burnt house, hands on his hips, apparently watching Welby storm away. From where she stood it was difficult to tell what had transpired, but clearly Welby was angry. The preacher wasn't one to offend people, but Leoma had seen first hand how easily Welby could be angered. She never knew what might set him off. She had to stop Welby before he drove off with Dyer in the wagon. The man obviously wasn't thinking straight, taking both children with him. How did he think he would feed the baby? Any minute now, Dyer would be fussing and hungry.

With swift ease, Leoma tied Challenger to the post beside the carriage house and raced across the back yard. She tripped on the hem of her skirt and almost tumbled to the ground. Righting herself, she lifted her skirt and ran as fast as she could toward Welby's wagon. Kristina was already perched on the seat. Leoma shouted waving both hands above her head. "Stop!"

Welby held Dyer in one arm and effortlessly climbed into the wagon. Leoma was breathless when she reached Welby's wagon, but she grabbed the harness of his horse. "What do you think are you doing, Welby Soderlund?"

It wasn't her intent to sound harsh, but the shocked look on Welby's face was priceless. His mouth dropped opened, both brows shot up, and deep furrows appeared across his forehead. He plopped down on the seat and Leoma almost grinned. When he regained his usual stern look he spoke resolutely. "I'm taking my children home."

"Dyer will be crying in less than an hour for his next feeding. Just how do you plan to manage that?" Standing firm, Leoma continued to hold the harness with a tight fist and stood her ground. If Welby Soderlund thought he was taking his son home now he was out of his mind.

"I, umm—"

"Just as I thought. You didn't think. You bull-headed—"

"Woman, I offered you a room out at my place. If you want to reconsider, climb on up here and let's go." Welby jerked his head sideways at the space beside Kristina. "Otherwise I guess you're done nursing my son. He's old enough."

"I can't just *stop* feeding your son all of a sudden. It takes time to wean a child." She wanted to scream "you ignorant man," but she clenched her jaws shut. How could he be so stupid?

"Then climb up and let's get going. You can wean him at my house."

Leoma let out an exasperated breath and dropped her skirt to the ground. She pointed toward the carriage house. "I will *not* go with you, Welby. I will live right there in my carriage house until my home is rebuilt."

The small building was bigger than some of the houses people had slapped together in the community, and it would certainly be better than living in a tent again. The weather hadn't turned very cold yet, and if it did, there was a small woodstove that would provide plenty of heat for the space.

"You'll do no such thing!" Anna Jo said as she came up beside her. Leoma's friend was gasping for air and red in the face. "You and Dyer will stay with me and George as long as you need to. My husband and I have already discussed it."

Leoma turned to Anna Jo, her mouth opened to object.

"No arguments and no questions." Anna Jo stood firm. She stared at the burned home and shook her head. She put one arm around Leoma's shoulders and drew her closer. The Langley's house was small, barely adequate for their family. If she moved in there with Dyer it would be awfully crowded. She didn't want to impose on her friends. "I appreciate the offer but I don't want to imp—"

"I said no objections. We won't take no from you. You've done so much for everyone else, now it's time for us to help you. You will use Doris's bedroom, and now that Jody's crib is empty Dyer can sleep in it. I have a box full of my boy's baby things, and I'm sure others in town will be happy to help out with clothes and such."

Clothes? Leoma hadn't thought about clothing. She and Dyer had nothing but the clothes they wore at that moment, not even a dry diaper. For an instant she felt helpless and alone, then, almost immediately she remembered God's gentle whisper, and the warmth of a friend's arm reminded Leoma she really wasn't alone. She needn't worry about such trivial things as clothing. All the fancy clothes in Boston couldn't replace her life or her friends. Accepting Anna Jo's offer was the right thing to do.

George walked up with several curious residents and stood on the other side of Leoma. He put his arm around her shoulders along with his wife's. Minnie from the new lady's clothier in town rushed up, eyes wide, her lace-ruffled hat fluttering in the breeze. "Oh, dear me," said Minnie. "Dear, dear, me! I'm terribly sorry you lost your magnificent home, Leoma. I insist you come to my shop right away and let me provide whatever clothing you need at no charge." Minnie bent closer and said proudly, "I just received several of those brand new Gibson Girl styles. You really must try them on."

"Thank you," Leoma said her eyes glazed over. "What a kind gesture. Perhaps I'll come in tomorrow or the next day."

"Any time my dear, any time," Minnie said. "You'll need a hat or two, and of course," the woman whispered, "you'll need some personal things as well."

Welby cleared his throat, using full volume, and turned everyone's attention back to him. Leoma released the harness and moved away from Anna Jo and George. She stepped close to Welby's side of the wagon and forced a smile. Dyer fussed and wiggled, reaching for her. It was almost time to nurse him. The hardness in her breasts told her she couldn't wait much longer to feed the child. Late morning sun glittered through the leaves of a large oak tree causing shadows to dance across Welby's face. Holding his son securely, posture straight and tall, pride shone on his face. His clear blue eyes questioned her but he said nothing.

"I appreciate your offer, Welby, honestly I do, but I would like to accept the Langley's invitation. It's best that I stay with them." She stretched her arms upward expecting Welby to hand his son down to her. "You know Dyer isn't old enough to be weaned yet. I should continue to care for him until he's closer to a year old. He will be fine with us."

Leoma waited, arms outstretched, trying to understand Welby's feelings. It was generous of him to offer her a room, and she knew his coming into town daily was difficult now that he'd moved back out to his farm. But her genteel upbringing would never allow her to live way out of town with Welby and his children.

"Did the preacher tell you it was wrong to take a room at my house?" The heavy agitation in Welby's voice was loud and clear.

"Absolutely not. I must do what I believe is proper."

"Proper! Proper?" He knew half the people in this town kowtowed to anything the preacher said because they feared being sent to the *so-called* eternal pit of fire when they died. Most of them were too scared to think for themselves.

"You don't want to compromise Leoma's reputation and standards, Welby," George said, his tone stern.

"Compromise? Now you're taking Reverend Gilroy's side, too," Welby shouted.

The muscles in George's jaw tensed. Clearly dismayed with Welby, he shook his head. Leoma didn't know how long the two men had been acquainted but she hated seeing them at odds with each other. She appreciated, however, that George was looking out for her best interests. That's what he'd promised her after Jeremy's death, but this was the first time he'd come forward in such an aggressive manner on her behalf, and she rather liked being looked after by a loyal friend.

George put a hand on Leoma's forearm and patted lightly. "I'm not taking anyone's side. My only concern is for Leoma and your son. After all this woman has done for you, I'd think you'd respect her wishes. Anna Jo and I will make sure Leoma and Dyer are well provided for and comfortable in our home. You and your girl are welcome to come by and visit any time, just like you did at Leoma's house. This young woman is doing what's right by staying with us."

Welby's frown softened and he appeared to take in what George had said. George stepped aside and scratched his head, a grin forming on his face. "*Now,* if you'd marry the woman right quick that would be a different story."

A unified gasp, followed by giggles, rustled through the group of onlookers that had grown to two dozen or more. Leoma gasped as well and heat burned her cheeks. She wanted to slug George with her fist. Instead she glared at him and shook her head. He gave her a half grin and winked. Welby said nothing, but he gave a loud, disapproving grunt.

When Dyer began to wail and kick Leoma was glad for the distraction from the conversation.

"He's probably wet and hungry. May I take him now so I can nurse him?" Leoma kept her voice as kind and patient as possible, not wanting to stir any more ire in the child's father. She wiggled her fingers as she reached even closer and forced a smile. "The only thing that has changed is that I'll be caring for Dyer at the Langley's home for a while. He'll be just fine."

Without hesitation Welby bent forward and put the child into her arms. Leoma had no doubt the man's pride had been trampled, and it wasn't easy for him to give in to her, but she was grateful the confrontation was over and he'd come to his senses.

Nuzzling and swaying with Dyer to shush him, Leoma thanked Welby and handed him the reins. "Will you come into town tomorrow to see him?"

Welby nodded, his lips tightly pursed. "Guess I'll have to." He lifted the reins and guided his horse into a slow walk. A twinge of sadness tugged at Leoma's heart as the back of Welby's wagon disappeared in the distance.

Chapter 16

Six weeks had passed since Leoma moved into George and Anna Jo's home. The Langleys made her feel right at home, as if she were part of the family. The way Anna Jo helped with Dyer and doted on him, one would think he was her own child.

Leoma fed Dyer his breakfast of mush and nursed him. She treasured every moment with the child, for it wouldn't be much longer until she had to send him home with his father. When Dyer finished nursing she put him on her shoulder, gently patting his back. Almost instantly he produced a hearty burp. Then he giggled.

Leoma lowered the baby to the floor, and he crawled lickety-split across the room, turned, and came back. When Jody got down on his knees and crawled after Dyer, barking like a puppy, the race was on. That had become Dyer's favorite game the last few days. While Doris and Jody entertained Dyer on the floor Leoma sat down to write a letter to Glenda. Just yesterday Leoma had received a letter from her friend announcing her planned visit to Oklahoma. Obviously, Glenda hadn't received Leoma's letter her telling about the fire and her temporary living situation. She sat at the kitchen table and began to write.

> *My Dearest Friend, Glenda,*
>
> *Your letter brought me so much happiness in the midst of the turmoil here. I wonder if you didn't receive my last letter telling you about the fire. Perhaps our latest letters crossed in the mail.*

It would be wonderful to have you visit, but after fire destroyed my house I moved in with my neighbors George and Anna Jo Langley. They have been kind enough to allow me and Dyer to stay with them until my house is rebuilt.

The men who are building my new home say it should be done and ready for me to move into by Christmas, but it seems almost every day something goes wrong to delay the building. The bad weather we are having this week could delay it even more. They say the house will be just as nice as the one Jeremy built, but I don't know how that can be without the original plans and Jeremy here to oversee the work. However, I am blessed to have outstanding Christian friends and a community of people who truly care. They have been so good about helping me get reestablished.

Would you believe, the lady who owns the dress shop in town insisted I come in and try on some of the newest Gibson Girl styles? Have you seen them? Oh, I'm sure all the ladies in Boston are wearing them. She gave me two of those beautiful dresses, a hat, and an array of personal under garments. My friend Anna Jo is helping me sew two house dresses, and the preacher's wife gave me a beautiful winter coat that fits perfectly. Several families have provided baby things for Dyer so his father wouldn't have to buy everything new. So in spite of my losses, I remind myself daily, that I am blessed beyond measure.

The Langleys never complain about the added work of having me and Dyer here, and I do all I can to be of help, but Anna Jo is actually a great help to me. She has become a wonderful friend. I'm sure the instant you meet her you will like her as much as I do. Their home is very small and crowded with their two young children plus me and Dyer, but no one seems to mind.

I long to see you and would welcome your visit, but I would hate to see you stay at the hotel. Oh, it's nice enough, but I would much rather have you in my guest room when my house is complete. Perhaps, too, it would be best if you postponed your visit until spring. Travel at this time of year is very difficult with winter drawing near and unpredictable weather.

Springtime is pretty here, and by then I will be settled into my new house. Also, by that time, Dyer will be weaned and living with his father. Just think of the grand visit you and I could have. It will be like old times. Whenever you come, I pray you will be able to stay for a long visit.

I hope you receive this before you make definite travel arrangements. Give my love to your parents. I pray you are well and God will keep you in his care. Please write back to me soon.

Leoma signed the letter and slipped it into the envelope. After addressing it she fixed the two-cent stamp in the corner. Following Dyer's afternoon nap, she would put him into his carriage and stroll into town to mail the letter.

Dyer pulled himself up gripping the edge of Leoma's chair and grinned. He bounced on his wobbly legs before he plunked his bottom down on the floor. Leoma laughed. What would she have done all these months since Elizabeth's death, without Dyer to fill her heart with so much delight? Even the loss of her home didn't over shadow the incredible inner joy she felt each day with this adorable child. He was nearing ten-months-old and he was a cheerful, delightful child. She reached down and smoothed his thick, sandy-blonde hair back from his face, and tickled the soft flesh beneath his chin. Oh how she loved the little guy. Truly, he was a blessing from God. She smiled and lifted him onto her lap. If only she were his real mother and didn't have to give him back to his father.

A week ago Leoma had eliminated Dyer's afternoon feeding, and now she only nursed him in the morning at breakfast time and again before bedtime. With her help, he was doing well sipping from a small cup. Soon he'd be weaned from his morning feeding, but she was in no hurry. How much longer could she convince Welby that Dyer needed the nourishment she provided, and he couldn't yet be completely weaned? How long would she be able to cuddle and rock this adorable child she'd come to love so deeply?

Leoma smiled into Dyer's impish face and kissed the top of his head. The baby patted her forearm as he happily chattered something that sounded like "momma." She sucked in a breath. To avoid upsetting Welby, and to spare her the anguish when she no longer had Dyer in her care, Leoma had been careful not to get too attached to the child—not that it worked. She would never deny the bond they shared, but she hadn't taught Dyer to call her momma. Most likely he'd learned it from Jody and Doris.

"My dear sweet boy," Leoma said softly as she snuggled him close to her. He wiggled and laughed. She turned Dyer and seated him with his back against her stomach and breast, and she held his little hands between hers, clapping them together as she sang. "Jesus loves me this I know, for the Bible tells me so, little ones to him belong, they are weak but he is strong." Dyer sang along, making his own vocabulary and funny melody. Soon, both were raising their voices louder and louder in musical competition. "Someday you will sing beautiful praises to the Lord," Leoma said as she clapped his pudgy little hands together one last time.

How wonderful it would be to see the child grow up, and use his talents and abilities for God's glory. Leoma would continue to pray for Dyer and Kristina, for there was no telling what would become of them in their father's godless, churchless upbringing. She must pray for Welby as well, hard as it was sometimes. But the children's future was important to her and she wanted the best for them. She wanted to see them saved and living for God.

"My, my, what talent we have," came Anna Jo's melodic voice as she entered the kitchen, a smile spread on her lovely round face. Such a dear, sweet person she was; her friendship was immeasurable. Anna Jo was a shining example of Jesus Christ living in her.

"I think Dyer will be an excellent singer," Leoma said. "He loves it when I sing, and as you heard, he joins right in."

"Yes, I heard him." Anna Jo laughed and patted the baby's cheek. She turned to Leoma. "With your lovely, triumphant singing filling the house, I assume you didn't hear that we have a guest.

Surprised, Leoma shook her head. Oh my, she hoped the visitor in the other room didn't hear her raucous singing.

"Jason Alder is here to see you. I suppose he needs to discuss something with you about work at the house. He's waiting in the front room."

Carrying Dyer on one hip, Leoma found Jason warming himself in front of the fireplace. He greeted her with a tentative smile. Jason was one of the many men helping George and Welby build her new house. They'd started clearing the debris and working on it as soon as the embers cooled, but one storm after another had delayed the progress. Now, well into November, they were having a lengthy break in the weather. They worked every day from sunrise to sunset, except Sundays. Welby, of course was willing to work on Sundays, but Leoma had said absolutely not.

Dressed in denim work clothes, a heavy jacket, and a wool cap, Jason appeared more mature than his twenty-six years. Anna Jo had said some time ago that was his age. When he said hello his eyes had a twinkle in them that Leoma hadn't noticed before. His smile broadened, then he shifted his eyes away from her, as if he'd suddenly become uneasy. What could possibly be wrong?

So far as Leoma knew the men had all the building materials they needed for now. Other than dreadful weather there hadn't been any serious problems that George couldn't handle. The walls of the house were complete and the wood was on the roof. It was just a matter of weeks until the inside would be ready for paint and floor coverings. "Is something wrong at the house?"

Jason shifted from where he stood and leaned an elbow on the fireplace mantle. "No. Everything's going fine. I suppose I shouldn't be here, but in an hour or so we'll be quitting for today, since it gets dark so early these days, and I couldn't wait until later to come and talk to you. I wonder if perhaps you'd join me for dinner tonight."

Surprised by Jason's invitation it took Leoma a moment to answer. She'd noticed him looking at her lately whenever she went to see how her house was coming along, but she hadn't thought anything about it. She assumed Jason was aware that she was a widow and had lost a baby. Having worked with George and Welby, Jason must also know the child she held in her arms was Welby's son. She sucked in a quick breath and shrugged one shoulder. "Well, goodness, I—"

To Leoma's dismay, she knew almost nothing about Jason, except that he was a skilled carpenter, according to George. He'd built the nice front porch on Welby's house, and she was told he was doing an excellent job on her house. Prior to the day he came by her home with the preacher, before going out to Welby's farm a few months back, she didn't recall seeing him around town much. So far as she knew he wasn't working in the area when Jeremy was alive, however, it didn't seem to be the appropriate time to ask if he'd known her husband, not that it would help her make a decision. If Jason had a wife and family Leoma wasn't aware of it, and she assumed he was single or he wouldn't be asking her to join him for dinner. Since she'd been staying at the Langleys she'd taken Dyer to church every week and she had seen Jason leave the church building alone. He always appeared to be in rush, as if he didn't want to be seen, but he seemed to be a nice enough man.

Ten months had passed since Jeremy's death and Leoma found each day a little easier. Oh, she still missed Jeremy something awful, but it wasn't nearly as difficult lately. After this much, time it seemed acceptable to enjoy the company of another man, yet it was awkward just thinking about it. Jeremy was the only man who had courted her, the only man she'd kissed, the only man she'd loved. She chided herself for jumping to ridiculous assumptions. Jason was waiting patiently for an answer to a simple dinner invitation. "I'm sorry to keep you waiting. I just don't know. What would I do with Dyer?"

Jason seemed to mull her response over in his mind.

Leoma realized it was foolish to use Dyer as an excuse to say no. In fact, the more she pondered the thought, the more she realized a nice dinner in the company of a gentleman might be rather pleasant. Before either she or Jason could speak again, Anna Jo rushed in from the kitchen, a dishtowel swinging in the air. "You can leave Dyer with me. I've been telling you for weeks it's high time you get out of this house and have some fun for a change."

Leoma chuckled. She should have known her friend would be listening and quick to volunteer her help with Dyer. She even wondered briefly if Anna Jo had put Jason up to this idea. Anna Jo wiped her hands on the towel she'd carried into the front room, a big grin across her face, her bright blue eyes filled with mischief.

"Are you sure?" Leoma said. Then she bit her lip and frowned. "What will Welby think if he comes by and I'm not here taking care of Dyer?"

Anna Jo swished the stained rag through the air as if shooing away a fly. "You've taken care of his son morning, noon, and night for all these months. Welby doesn't have any say in what you do, as long as you feed that boy. Judging by those fat little legs and pudgy cheeks, and his clean face and clothes, I'd say you've done an excellent job. You've done far more than necessary. It's time you do something for yourself."

Anna Jo had been gracious, cheerful, and giving, never complaining about the added work of having two extra people taking up space and eating her food. She'd gone out of her way to make Leoma feel at home. Still, Leoma hated dumping another burden on her neighbor. "Are you sure you don't mind watching him for a short time?"

"You know better than that. I would love to watch this little fellow and give you a break, as long as you're home before he's squalling for his bedtime feeding." Anna Jo chuckled. She jiggled Dyer's chin with her forefinger and clucked her tongue. "He's such a good boy, what could possibly go wrong?"

"Well then, that settles it," Jason said. He smiled at Leoma, an expectant glimmer in his eyes. He winked sending heat to her face. "That is, if you say yes."

Without further pause Leoma nodded. "Yes. Okay. If you're sure we won't be out late."

"I promise. I wouldn't want to interfere with the boy's schedule. Five o'clock, then?"

Leoma agreed on an early dinner, giving her plenty of time to return before Dyer's bedtime.

"I hope you don't mind a little walk this evening," Jason said. "My buggy is being repaired but the restaurant is just a few blocks away."

"Not at all. I would enjoy the walk."

Jason promised he'd arrive promptly at five o'clock. "Until then," he said as he turned to leave.

Leoma tried to stifle the fluttering in her stomach. Still worried about how Welby would react to her leaving Dyer, she constantly buffeted against doubts, and she had second thoughts about going with Jason. After a moment she took a deep, calming breath, and determined to stop being silly. Anna Jo was absolutely right, everything would be fine. She left Anna Jo in charge of Dyer and rushed into the bedroom. There wasn't much time to change her clothes and fix her hair. Jason had mentioned the new restaurant in town, so she'd wear the dark blue Gibson Girl dress Minnie had given her. Leoma's fingers shook as she buttoned the multitude of tiny covered buttons up the front, taking much longer than it should.

Catching her reflection in Anna Jo's cheval mirror diverted Leoma's mind from the worries and doubts. She turned one way and then another; she was pleased with what she saw. Her waist looked tiny, and the silky fabric flowed nicely over her hips and to the floor. For the first time since before she'd been hugely pregnant with Elizabeth, she felt attractive and shapely.

Jason would arrive in less than ten minutes. Instead of working her hair into a chignon like she'd worn so often in Boston, she brushed it down over her shoulders. It seemed that was more the style these days in the West and it was certainly easier. With every brush stroke Anna Jo's words echoed through Leoma's mind.

What could possibly go wrong?

"I KNEW THAT MAN had something up his sleeve. I knew it!" Welby wanted to spit nails. The heat under his collar grew more intense. "I can't believe Leoma went off with Jason and left my son here."

When Welby and Kristina stepped into George's front room Welby was anxious to see his son, but perhaps the boy wasn't the only one he looked forward to seeing. For the past several weeks Welby had enjoyed his evening visits at George and Anna Jo Langley's house. It was the only time he was able to interact with Kristina and Dyer, but lately, he'd found that he looked forward to seeing Leoma as well. As fast as his boy was growing it wouldn't be much longer until he'd take his son home with him. Leoma had promised a few days earlier he'd be weaned soon.

Leoma. Pretty Leoma. Every time she came over to see the progress on her house, Welby couldn't help but notice how attractive she looked. She had become healthier and shapelier, no more sunken cheeks and bony shoulders. Everything about her seemed to have changed since she'd been nursing Dyer. It was almost as if she'd blossomed into a full-blown woman. He'd noticed, too, lately she had a special glow about her. Right now, he wasn't just confused about these strange thoughts and feelings, he was downright mad that she'd gone out to dinner with Jason. A sharp poke to his chest jolted Welby out of his revelry.

Anna Jo squared her shoulders and puffed up her chest as if she were ready to do battle. Her stout finger jabbed him again. "There is absolutely no reason why Leoma shouldn't enjoy a pleasant meal out in the company of a nice gentleman." Showing no fear even though Welby stood a good foot taller, the stout little woman now pointed her finger right in his face. He almost wanted to laugh but clamped his mouth tightly shut. "Dyer is perfectly safe and happy in my care," Anna Jo said.

The woman had a lot of guts. He glanced across the room wishing George were there to side with him. Or did Anna Jo put George in his place just as easily?

Nearby in the center of a big rug, Kristina and the Langley children played contentedly with Dyer. Dressed in fresh clothes, his son's face was scrubbed clean, and his hair was neatly combed with a part on one side. What a handsome little man he was. The boy stacked two wooden blocks then clapped his hands together several times and laughed. The older children cheered.

For a moment, the sight made Welby forget his anger.

George and Anna Jo were good people. They had happy, well behaved children. Welby didn't want to admit his anger had nothing to do with Dyer being left in Anna Jo's care. The fact that Leoma was having dinner in that fancy, new restaurant in town with another man just didn't set right with Welby. Was this jealousy eating at him? Whatever caused the gnawing in his gut, it was foreign to Welby; he didn't like it. As new heat rose in his chest, he stepped back and took a deep breath, shoving both hands into his pant pockets. The last thing he wanted to do was cause a ruckus in George's home. Leoma was a grown woman. She could do what she wanted. His shoulders relaxed and he smiled down at the children, and then he looked at Anna Jo.

"I'm sorry I raised my voice. I know my boy is fine." In a lower tone he said, "When will Leoma be back?" It couldn't take that long to eat a meal.

"Before seven o'clock. She promised she'd be here long before Dyer's bedtime feeding." Anna Jo glanced at the small clock on the fireplace mantle. "About an hour I suppose."

"That long? It shouldn't take them that long to eat." The heat was rising again in Welby's chest.

A door beyond the kitchen closed with a thud and George walked into the front room, a puzzled look on his face. Then he smiled and held out a hand. "Hello, Welby. Glad you came to visit your boy. Won't be long before you'll be taking him home, huh?"

"I'd take him right now if he was weaned," Welby said. It looks like Leoma is more interested in going out courting with Jason Alder."

George laughed. "Well, my man, someone is going to snatch that beautiful woman up before long. Her husband's been dead nearly a year and she's a mighty fine woman, and a good Christian too."

"What do you know about Jason? How do you know she's safe with him?"

"Well, I do know that he comes to church on Sunday mornings."

"So that makes him better than me?"

"Now, Welby you know that's not what I mean. I simply believe that he is a good man and wouldn't do anything to harm Leoma."

Welby grunted. He knew what George said was true. The trouble was, his feelings for Leoma were all jumbled up in his head and making him a little crazy. The *Christian* part still troubled him, and he had a hard time erasing his view of her as a hoity-toity Bostonian. She wasn't his type. And, no doubt, Leoma saw him as a dumb farmer that couldn't give her all the frills and fancy things she wanted. So why couldn't he stop thinking about her lately? And why was he so worked up about her being out with that Jason fellow?

While working on Leoma's house this week, more than once, Welby had visualized her going from room to room her hips swaying, her long, dark hair flowing down her back. On several occasions he'd imagined her in the kitchen fretting over burnt biscuits, and he wondered with a smile, if her cooking had improved any more lately. He'd shamefully fantasized about her wearing a pretty, flowing nightgown, and slipping into bed in that huge bedroom, where he'd nailed down the floors and helped install the two big windows. Able to hear Leoma's angelic, pure voice, Welby sometimes visualized her in the parlor reading and singing to Kristina and Dyer. More and more lately, regardless of her different background, it was Leoma he thought about rather than Louise.

When George slapped a heavy hand on his shoulder Welby jolted, realizing he was lost in thoughts he shouldn't be thinking. He was beginning to like Leoma more than he should and he didn't even understand why. There was one thing he did understand; he didn't like the idea of her being out alone with that young, slick, handsome Jason.

"Have a seat," George said releasing the grip on Welby's shoulder. George motioned to a cushioned chair near the fireplace. Anna Jo had gone into the kitchen. "Have you and your girl had dinner?"

"We ate some soup before we drove in." Sweet smells drifted from the kitchen and filled the front room with mouthwatering aromas. Welby's stomach acted as if he hadn't eaten a bit of food all day.

"You're welcome to eat more." George grinned and rubbed his round stomach. "Anna Jo makes the best blackberry cobbler in town. Smells like she just took one out of the oven. Why don't you and Kristina join us at the table and we can talk some more?"

Welby nodded his acceptance. "Thank you. We'd be happy to." He'd barely eased into the comfortable chair when Anna Jo called her family to the table, inviting Welby and Kristina to join them. She picked up Dyer off the floor like he was one of her own, and settled him in a wooden highchair, tying a clean dish towel around his neck to protect his shirt from spills. Welby walked over and ruffled his son's hair then smoothed it back into place before taking a seat at the table.

George took his wife's hand and offered his other hand to Doris. They waited until everyone joined hands including Dyer. The boy was quiet, clearly accustomed to the routine. Welby was the last to bow his head. The blessing George said was filled with thanks for everything God had provided their family, including the food. He prayed for friends and family, those who were sick, and the lost. What did he mean by lost? He hadn't heard about anyone being lost or missing. Welby listened and waited until George said amen. It was followed by a quiet amen from Anna Jo and the children as well. Then, in a hearty voice Dyer said, "Men!"

Everyone laughed except Welby. It seemed everyone was determined to force their religion onto his children, whether he liked it or not. However, since he truly appreciated the generosity and kindness of the Langleys, he held his tongue and accepted the platter of roast beef from George.

The table was laden with more food than he'd seen since his housewarming. Thick slices of bread, churned butter, and a dish of jam sat within Welby's reach. He helped himself to each then passed them to Anna Jo. He dipped small amounts of each item onto his plate and allowed Kristina to take what she wanted. She was a good eater and wasn't fussy about what was put before her. She even spooned a small serving of sliced beets onto her plate.

"Papa," Kristina said nearly bouncing off her chair with excitement. "I want to be an angel."

"You are my little angel," Welby said. "Now settle down and eat your food."

"But I want to be an angel in the Christmas play at church. Anna Jo and Leoma both said I would be a good angel."

Welby directed his attention to Anna Jo. "What's all this about my girl being in a Christmas play at the church? No one asked me about that."

Anna Jo stopped short, coffee pot in hand. She smiled. "We need another angel to sing in the little Christmas cantata in two weeks. Kristina has a lovely voice and she would be perfect for the role. She wants to take part. I'd be happy to make her costume."

"Please, papa. I know the song. Do you want to hear me sing it?"

"Not now," Welby said to his daughter. And to Anna Jo he said as calmly as he could, "You know how I feel about putting church ideas in my daughter's head."

George held up a hand bringing immediate silence, a stern look on his face, but when he spoke his tone was kind and gentle. The man never seemed to get upset. Welby kept silent. "You know, Welby, this is a perfect opportunity for Kristina to take part in something special with friends her age. What's it going to hurt to let her wear an angel costume and sing a couple of Christmas songs? You do believe in Christmas, don't you?"

Welby sighed and grumbled trying to find an answer. "Of course I believe in Christmas. I just don't know about, it's just that—"

Anna Jo piped in, not quite as gently as her husband. "Just what? The Christmas play is *just* what she needs to help her get through this tough time after losing her mother and all. You should allow her to use her talents and do things with other children."

"Please papa. Oh, please. I really want to be one of the angels."

Perhaps George and Anna Jo were both right. Welby couldn't think of a good argument against what either of them said. And how was he to deny his daughter's sweet smile and heartfelt plea? He could see he was never going to win the battles with his little girl.

"You'd be mighty proud of her," Anna Jo said patting Kristina on one shoulder. "You will let her do it, won't you?"

Welby knew he was outnumbered. No doubt Leoma would also insist he say yes. "All right, but don't expect it to be a regular thing."

"Christmas only comes once a year, Welby." George reached for the big bowl of potatoes and spooned some onto his plate. "Certainly you'll be there to watch her sing, right?"

"You have to come see me sing, papa."

That was pushing him a little too far. But thinking about his little girl all dressed up like an angel, and singing her heart out in that sweet voice, was something he couldn't miss. He didn't dare. Louise would come right up out of her grave and clobber him on the head if he didn't go watch Kristina sing. He still didn't like the idea of sitting in the church with all those Bible toting folks, but he'd go. "Yes, sweetheart, I'll go to see you sing."

Kristina cheered. Anna Jo offered a big smile and held up the coffee pot. "Would you like a cup of coffee?"

Welby watched her, wondering if she always smiled like that. The woman looked as if she had a belly full of smiles and she might burst any minute. "Yes, thank you."

Welby's mind went back to George's prayer. In spite of not wanting to hear about God, he was impressed by George's ease and his open conversation with God. He couldn't help but wonder if that's what made him want to listen to the man who had become his friend in recent months. There was something in George's tone, his confidence, and his demeanor that Welby admired. Welby realized he wasn't put off by the mention of God so much when George was praying over dinner. Something about the Langleys and their apparent happiness, created a curiosity Welby had never felt until recently. The older children chattered among themselves as they ate, and Dyer was content for the moment with a crust of buttered bread and a few green beans. Welby turned to George. "What did you mean when you prayed for the lost?"

Leoma took a small bite of pork roast and chewed thoughtfully. The tender meat was tasty and better than anything she'd eaten in months. Across from her Jason sat quietly, the candle light reflecting in his dark eyes. She'd never seen eyes so stunning on a man and it was difficult not to stare. She'd seen him in work clothes, and lately in church clothes on Sundays, but tonight he was more handsome than she'd realized. Jason was well dressed and possessed impeccable manners, but he seemed a bit fidgety. So far, all the conversation had been about Leoma's house and how it was coming along.

"If the weather cooperates you should be able to move in before Christmas," Jason said before he glanced away. He'd only made eye contact with her briefly two or three times.

Leoma was thrilled to know her house would be finished by Christmas. "That's wonderful. I won't have much furniture, but I can manage with what I've bought. The few things my parents shipped should be here by then, too."

Leoma had ordered a feather bed with four posters, a living room sofa, and a writing desk for her parlor. Those pieces were already stored in the carriage house. Anna Jo and Minnie had given her a few linens, too, and she had no doubt that when the house was done, the community would come together with more things, like they'd done for Welby. They were a helping, giving group of folks. She wasn't the least bit worried about filling her house with furnishings right away. That was the least of her concerns. God was generous and caring and Leoma knew he would provide all she needed.

"What will you do with all that space by yourself?" Jason said.

Leoma scrunched her lips together and pondered the question. In the warmth of the Langley home she'd grown accustomed to having a family around her, and she wondered how she would feel in the spacious house with only Dyer to keep her company. And what about after he went home with Welby? It wasn't something she'd given much thought until now. "I will simply try to enjoy it. When Jeremy and I came here, I had dreams of opening a bookshop, something special and different from the typical shops back home. I have wondered if later perhaps, the downstairs rooms of my house might make a lovely place for such a store."

The new house was very similar to the one Jeremy had built with a spacious living room, flanked by the east parlor for small gatherings such as ladies teas, and the west parlor for her personal desk and library. In addition, the dining room was large enough to accommodate a large group comfortably. She'd decided to place all of the four bedrooms upstairs. Several windows flanked one side of the big kitchen, and the indoor water closet had the latest type flush toilet. There was also an enclosed back porch for her wash tubs and a wide front porch. It was indeed a large place for one woman. Having a bookshop occupy most of the downstairs would certainly provide plenty of activity to keep her busy, but that was all a dream, a what-if.

Leoma had also considered rebuilding a much smaller house, but she still had hopes of someday having a family and she couldn't imagine anything smaller. Money wasn't an issue, so why not build the house of her dreams, and let the future take care of itself. Accustomed to living in a large house, she couldn't imagine living permanently in something little like Anna Jo's cottage.

Jason smiled and nodded. "With the town growing in every direction, your home will soon be in the center of everything. I think your house could easily accommodate a bookshop downstairs."

This was the first time since before Jeremy died that she'd discussed her plans to this extent. For so long it seemed as if her dream had died with her husband. After all, he was the one with good business sense, and he'd encouraged her from the first time she mentioned the idea. By Jason's interest, Leoma assumed he also had a passion for books. "Do you really think it would work?"

"I do. Your living room and parlors alone would give you plenty of space. If you incorporated the dining room as well, it would be quite an impressive shop."

Leoma appreciated Jason's encouragement. New enthusiasm billowed within her. Perhaps she should think seriously about using her home for such a bookshop, rather than building a separate store like she and Jeremy had planned. Talking about it lifted her spirits. Ideas flitted through her mind giving her new hope for her future. God had not forsaken her, and she realized more each day how blessed she was. She had dear friends and two beautiful children to care for, even though they weren't her own. Dyer and Kristina brought her great joy and filled her heart with laughter.

She wiped her mouth and folded her hands in her lap. Leoma wanted to know more about Jason, his family, his background, and where he was from. Interested in knowing everything about him she said, "Tell me all about you."

Suddenly a thick vale of darkness fell across Jason's face. His narrow smile was clearly forced, and he hesitated. "There isn't much to tell," Jason finally murmured, looking across the room as if seeking an escape.

"You must have family, a mother and father. Where are you from?" Leoma didn't want this to be a one-sided conversation about her. She was curious and truly interested in hearing about Jason's life. Even though she'd sensed some uneasiness in the beginning, the conversation had flowed fairly easily. His demeanor had been lively and open until now. Suddenly, he was edgy, clearly uncomfortable.

"My parents died in a row-house fire three years ago in New York."

"I'm so sorry. What a horrible loss and shock that must have been for you." Leoma's heart went out to him. "I'm terribly sorry."

"Don't be." His words were blunt, almost a warning.

A chill seeped into dining room. Leoma bit her tongue, unsure what to say. Dishes and silverware clattered around them yet seemed far away. Voices from other tables were muffled by her concern. So far as

Leoma knew Jason didn't have a wife. What about brothers or sisters? She couldn't help but wonder what was going on behind the wall he'd suddenly thrown up between them. For a moment she thought she saw fear in Jason's eyes. He shifted in his chair and fiddled with his napkin and fork. She wasn't sure what to say, but she didn't like the sudden silence between them. "I didn't mean to pry, but everything doesn't have to be about me. I'm interested in your life."

"There's nothing of interest, nothing worth talking about," Jason said. "My past is dead—a sealed tomb."

What a morbid thought. Leoma couldn't imagine her life without pleasant memories from the past, all the good times she had in her childhood, holidays with her parents. So many things came to mind. Even with all her recent losses she had reason to celebrate life and move on.

Jason gazed around the room his eyes darting away from her. The moment he received the dinner check he pulled a few bills from his pocket and paid the waiter. "Are you ready to leave?" he said rising to his feet.

"I guess I am." Her meal was half eaten, but clearly this dinner engagement was over. What had she said or done to shut Jason down? Had she said something wrong? Still puzzled, she pulled on her coat and followed Jason to the door.

The night air was brisk and a light wind had begun to blow. She pulled her coat collar more snugly around her neck. Jason's hands were stuffed in his jacket pockets as he walked silently beside her, back to the Langley's house. When she glanced up at him his eyes were focused dead ahead on the walkway. Totally confounded by Jason's actions Leoma walked fast attempting to outrun the questions that raced through her mind.

Nearing the end of the sidewalk Jason slowed and grasped her elbow to assist her down onto the dirt path. It was dark, the moon hidden by clouds, and only a dim glow from nearby shop windows gave off faint light. At least he wasn't oblivious to her presence she mused. He did use his manners. "Thank you," she said after finding her footing on the bumpy walkway.

"You're welcome."

The remainder of the walk to George and Anna Jo's house was a short jaunt. The small cabin style home sat close to the road and had a small, unfenced yard of dirt. Light glowed from the front room window illuminating the area. Beside one corner of the porch, the yellow rose bush Leoma had given Anna Jo that spring, was dormant now and hadn't been pruned. As Leoma stepped up onto the narrow covered porch, she was careful not to snag the hem of her cloak on the thorn-covered branches.

Jason took a deep, audible breath, clearly nervous. Before she reached for the door knob, he clasped both her hands in his. His voice quivered when he spoke. "I would like to see you again."

"Are you sure?" Leoma didn't know how to read this man. She supposed she should at least give him another chance. After all, she had felt awkward tonight, and maybe he was just extremely shy. Perhaps if they became better acquainted, Jason might be more comfortable with her and feel free to talk about himself.

"I'm sure," Jason said looking at his feet. "That is, unless you'd rather not see me again."

"Oh, no, that's not the case at all." Uncertainty made it difficult to think straight. "Maybe next week, if you wish, you can call on me."

Jason glanced up and smiled briefly. "All right. Well, good night."

"Good night." Leoma stepped inside the front room and briskly rubbed a chill from her arms, but she couldn't dispel the hoary shadow of doubt that clouded her mind. Perhaps she should reconsider seeing Jason again.

Chapter 17

KRISTINA WAS SOUND ASLEEP in her bed and Welby tossed two large pieces of wood into the fireplace. He rubbed his hands together and shivered. Before nightfall the gray sky had threatened snow. One never knew what early December winds would bring. He just hoped bad weather would hold off another week or two. He needed several more days to finish the wall-to-wall bookcases he'd built in the parlor of Leoma's new house.

The two-story Victorian house was nearly ready for Leoma to occupy, and he wanted everything to be perfect. Last week, when she'd stopped by with Dyer and Kristina to see how the work was progressing, Welby had asked her to stay out of the house for the remainder of the time, while the men finished the final interior work. He'd insisted the paint fumes and dust wouldn't be good for her or the children. It was the only way he could keep the bookcases a surprise. All that remained was another light sanding and a final coat of varnish. In this cold weather it would take at least twenty-four hours to dry.

Some of the town ladies had already made kitchen curtains for Leoma's house, and Welby had heard they'd also collected a few knick-knacks and dishes for the housewarming. Reverend Gilroy and the Gallager boys had promised as soon as the painting on the wall was dry, they'd move in the new bedroom and dining room furniture that had been stored in the carriage house. The Gallagers had hauled in a wagon load of fire wood just yesterday morning and piled it near the back door. It wouldn't be long before Leoma would once again warm herself and Dyer in front of the fireplace in her own home.

Welby was more excited about Leoma's house, than he'd been when he moved back into his own place. He'd been a bit perturbed when Leoma went off for the evening with Jason, but after his conversation with George he settled down. Now all he could think about was seeing the look on Leoma's beautiful face when she walked through the front door of her home. He looked around his front room and listened to the wind whistle outside the house. Inside everything was quiet and he wondered what it would be like filled with children.

Before he'd tucked Kristina into bed, she'd been so excited about the Christmas play tomorrow night it took her awhile to fall asleep. Now in the silence Welby's thoughts returned to the recent conversation over supper at George and Anna Jo's house.

Since George had explained to him what the Bible meant about lost souls, Welby couldn't get that conversation out of his mind. A persistent curiosity and hunger made him eager to find out more. He turned up the new hurricane lamps in the living room as bright as they would go and sat down on the couch, Louise's Bible in hand.

The Bible had suffered some damage during the tornado last spring, but he smoothed the rumpled pages and looked through the ones that hadn't been torn or muddied. For a man his age, his reading was poor, and he wished he'd had a better education. Fortunately, his mother had been strict about using proper grammar, and she'd taught him more than he'd learned in school. Still, he struggled with the strange way some of the words in the Bible were written. They seemed totally foreign. He thumbed through the damaged pages and glanced at different parts. He'd never read much in the Bible and words like hast, didst, and foresaketh made no sense to him. He scratched his head, as he tried to figure out what the blazes all that talk about beasts and angels and vials in the last book was about. Then there were a lot of complicated names that he couldn't pronounce at all, such as Ab-sa-lom and Ca-per-na-um, what ever they were. He shrugged, positive he'd never figure out what the Bible was all about.

Who could sit and read such a long, complicated book, anyway? And why? Discouraged and frustrated, he was ready to close the book and forget about trying to read it, when his eyes fell upon some words that were underlined in pencil. Apparently they'd meant something to Louise. He held the book closer to the light and read the marked words. *For God so loved the world, that he gave his only begotten Son, that whosoever believeth in him should not perish but have everlasting life.*

George Langley had said those very words. Welby read the verse again, working his way slowly through begotten, whosoever, and believeth, and tried to recall exactly what George had told him when he explained it. He remembered hearing the verse as a child but he never understood it. The way George explained it God had a son named Jesus who was sent as a baby to be born on Earth to a young virgin girl. That certainly seemed a bit far-fetched, yet, something in his gut told him this was true even if he couldn't understand it. George said God sent Jesus to tell the world about his father's love, and then Jesus was crucified and died on a cross to save all the sinners on Earth. All you had to do was accept Jesus as your savior and do as Jesus taught his disciples to do.

The whole idea still puzzled Welby and he wasn't sure he was ready to buy that teaching. In Welby's mind the idea that God would let his own son be tortured and killed seemed all wrong. And moreover, it still didn't make since to him why this God, who supposedly loved everyone so much, would allow babies and young mothers to suffer and die. And why did he allow tragedies, like destroying homes with tornados or fires?

The picture of Leoma falling to her knees in front of the charred remains of her home haunted him. Welby's mind wandered back to that moment time after time. Yet, it puzzled him the way Leoma was suddenly at peace. It was as if some magical force just took away her anguish and replaced it with calm acceptance. What gave her that power? Was it God? George had said God was all powerful and could do anything. Anything?

Yesterday George had suggested Welby try to read the New Testament, and he showed him where to begin. It was Matthew, he recalled. Also, somewhere near the middle of the Bible, was another book called Proverbs which George showed Welby. He'd read a few of those verses without too much trouble. They were pretty straight forward and easy to understand. Verse five in the first chapter of Proverbs seemed important. It nagged at his subconscious. He flipped back through the

187

tattered pages until he found the place and read it. *Let the wise listen and add to their learning.* He read it again letting the words sink in.

For the first time in his life Welby wanted to understand; he wanted to learn. George made a lot of sense, and the way he explained the Bible made Welby want to hear more. What George told him wasn't anything like his grandfather's condemning religion. And certainly George didn't act anything like Welby's grandfather.

Welby slowly closed the book, holding it on his lap. His mind churned with questions and thoughts about what he'd read in Louise's tattered Bible, and he wondered what he was missing in the damaged pages. Leoma inched into his mind. He squeezed shut his tired eyes and tried to stop thinking about her; it was impossible.

Would Leoma continue to go out with Jason? The man seemed like a nice enough fellow, but there was something Welby couldn't pinpoint, something he was hiding. Jason was a hard worker and had decent manners. It didn't appear he smoked, cussed, or drank hard liquor, nor did he have a nasty temper that he'd ever displayed around Welby. But there seemed to be a thick barrier around him to keep folks at a distance. Nope, something about Jason just didn't seem right. Welby wondered if the guy was guarded and closed when he was with Leoma. The two of them had been to that fancy restaurant for dinner twice that he knew of. Twice! Not that it mattered to him. Why, then, was he fretting again about something that was none of his business? Welby didn't want to see a sweet woman like Leoma get hurt, but who was he to say anything about the men she spent time with? What she did was her business. And he had no proof that Jason was hiding some dark secret. It was just a bad feeling in Welby's gut.

The charred remains of the last log in the fireplace fell sending up a spray of sparks. In a few minutes the fire would burn itself out. Welby shuddered, remembering the blaze that had destroyed Leoma's home.

Welby set the Bible on the table beside the couch and pulled himself up, feeling stiffer and older than usual. He shivered and rubbed his hands together vigorously to warm them. Outside, the wind was kicking up much harder than before. Cold air penetrated the walls of the house. The night was still early, barely past eight-thirty, but before the temperature dropped any more, he figured he best get ready for bed and crawl under the warm quilts.

There were plenty of chores to do at sun up before he drove into town. Anna Jo had agreed to let Kristina stay with her and Leoma again while he and George completed the final work on Leoma's new house, and he wanted to get an early start. Only three days remained until Christmas, and everyone in town was helping in one way or another, to make sure Leoma moved into the house on Christmas Eve day. He'd best get a good nights sleep.

As Welby walked toward his bedroom, he thought about the bookcases he'd built in Leoma's parlor and he smiled. They were larger and more beautiful than the ones in her original house, and the sturdy oak would hold up well under the load of books that he was sure would eventually fill them. He'd already decided to give Leoma the trunk of Louise's books. That would at least give her something to put on the shelves right away. He was thankful that those books had been stored in the barn, and hadn't been destroyed by the tornado. Maybe, though, he'd take a look through the books first to make sure they were still in good condition. Louise had always taken good care of her books, but he'd be mighty embarrassed if mice or rats had gotten into the trunk and chewed on the pages.

Just thinking about Louise and her books made him smile. Not a day had gone by when Louise was alive, that he didn't see her with her nose in a book. Sometimes she read silently, and other times he listened as she read a children's story out loud to Kristina. He could still hear the sound of her gentle, expressive voice when she read to their daughter.

Maybe reading was a female thing, but then again, maybe not. George seemed to be the type of man who knew an awful lot. He had to get all that knowledge from somewhere. Welby had noticed several books on a small shelf in the Langley's living room, but he'd never looked close enough to read the titles. He recalled a small shelf of books in his parents' house, too, and his mother had said a person has to read to know what the world is all about. But his father and grandfather had scoffed at her words and didn't allow Welby and his brother enough spare time to open a book. Except for Louise's storm-damaged Bible he hadn't turned the pages of any book since he finished eighth grade, well, other than the monthly farm magazine.

Wouldn't it be something to sit and read a story to his children someday? He kind of liked the idea.

Then, hmmm, Welby had another idea. Maybe—he rubbed his beard between his thumb and forefinger. The more he thought about the idea the more he liked it. His heart raced. Wouldn't Leoma be surprised? But first, he would keep his promise to his daughter. He had to attend the Christmas play tomorrow at the church.

LEOMA ADJUSTED THE GARLAND of silver tinsel on Kristina's head while Anna Jo helped Doris into the white robe with wings attached behind the shoulders. All the angels flitted around the room, hardly able to stand still for a single minute. It was the first time Leoma had helped with a children's Christmas play instead of being in one, and she enjoyed it more than anything she'd done in many years. "You're the most beautiful angel I have ever seen," Leoma said to Kristina. "Your papa is going to be so proud of you."

"Will you be proud of me, too?"

"Oh, yes. I am already very proud of you." Leoma gave Kristina a reassuring hug.

Kristina's smile spread wide, new excitement radiating on the child's beautiful round face. She had been scrubbed clean and Leoma had brushed her hair until it glistened. The halo was secured atop Kristina's head and she was ready for the play. "Now remember, Kristina, when you stand up front, smile real big and sing nice and loud, the way you did when you practiced." It probably wasn't necessary to remind Kristina to sing out, for she had the best pitch and loudest voice of all the children. It was just that she tended to be shy amidst the hubbub and crowd of people.

"Okay." The big smile on Kristina's face lit her eyes.

"I sing loud," Doris said bobbing her head repeatedly.

"Yes you do." Leoma patted Doris's back and smiled. "And you are absolutely beautiful."

Doris bobbed her head up and down again, causing her halo of white fabric and tinsel to come unpinned and slip sideways. Leoma gave her a quick hug and fixed the halo in place with extra hair pins. "There we go. Now be careful so it will stay on your head during the play. It's almost time to begin."

A few minutes later, Leoma sat on the front pew next to Anna Jo, with Dyer on her lap. He was wide-eyed and curious about the colorful decorations and all the activity. She looked over her shoulder, wondering if Welby was already seated somewhere in the church. When he'd dropped off Kristina earlier so she could get into her costume, he'd promised he would be there to see his daughter sing.

The church filled quickly and it was difficult to see through the people still milling about. One thing she was pretty sure of, Welby wouldn't march down front and sit on the pew with her, even though George was there next to Anna Jo. That was all right. As long as he showed up she'd be happy. Kristina needed to see her father in the audience. And Welby needed to hear the message.

Leoma thought back to some of the recitals and plays she'd been in during her youth, and nothing was more important than seeing her father and mother smiling up at her and applauding her performances. She'd almost forgotten how dear those memories were.

The organ began to pump out strains of *Joy to the World*, and the congregation quieted. Leoma took one last glance over her shoulder. A happy sigh escaped. Right next to the aisle in a pew a few rows back, she spotted Welby. Leoma caught his eye and smiled, and Welby acknowledged her with a broad smile. Satisfied, she could now enjoy the Christmas presentation, without worrying that Kristina's heart would be broken. The little girl would sing her heart out for her papa.

Chapter 18

AFTERNOON SUNSHINE STREAMED THROUGH the wide living room window, filling the crowded room with warmth against the brisk winter day. George lifted a hand high in the air, and whistled to silence the chatter of some thirty or forty people who had come to welcome Leoma to her new home. "We tried to follow the original layout but we didn't have the blueprints," George said to Leoma, his hand upon her shoulder in a friendly gesture.

Leoma gazed around the room once again, and her eyes glazed with tears of joy. She dabbed at her face and eyes with a clean white handkerchief. The house was beautiful, and the craftsmanship was as excellent as the home Jeremy had built. The few minor differences she could see didn't matter, in fact, if anything, this house was more elegant. The newel posts on the stairway and all the doorways were trimmed with fancy scroll work. The bookcases in her parlor were beautifully finished and accented with Victorian trim across the top. But what mattered most at this moment, beyond having her health, was having her own home again, a place where she could begin afresh. "You've done a wonderful job," she said directing her comment to George. "Everything is beautiful."

A fire crackled in the living room hearth and in one corner stood a Christmas tree decorated with shiny red balls, handmade silver stars and gold bells, and a garland of red paper roses. Someone had spent many hours making those delicate flowers and all the pretty decorations. All around the tree were piles of gifts. Some were wrapped in colorful paper with bows, some were in brown paper, and others weren't wrapped at all, like the deep mixing bowl that held an egg beater, and a blue blanket tied with a wide white ribbon and bow. The generosity and love of the people in the community was overwhelming, filling her heart so full of joy she feared it would burst.

Leoma glanced through the large group of friends that were gathered around her, and searched for Jason and Welby. Neither was present. How odd it was, especially for Welby to be missing, for along with George, he was the person driving the crew to get the house finished before Christmas. How odd, too, was the disappointment that churned in her stomach at not seeing Welby. Not a day had passed that he wasn't there working on her house until sunset. Two young men who had worked on buildings in town with Jeremy, had also helped frame and roof the house, and they were present with their pregnant wives.

Leoma knew Welby was in town today because Kristina had been with her at the Langleys all day. She'd walked here to the house before Dyer's morning naptime, and Welby had been there then, although she wasn't allowed to go inside. It was no secret that a big surprise was being planned for her, and it appeared Welby was behind it all. She couldn't imagine where he was now, why he wasn't among the group to share this special time. She shifted Dyer to her other hip, and peered around corners and through doorways to see if perhaps Welby was lingering in the background. That would be like him. From where she stood she could see all of the living room, dining room, and a portion of the parlors. She tried to avert her attention back to George and the others who were excitedly leading her from room to room.

The kitchen was superb, with wide counter tops to work on and plenty of built in cabinets. A new sink and water pump was in the same location as before with a wide window above to let in morning sunshine. The stove she'd purchased only days earlier was installed and ready to use. She could hardly wait to try her hand at baking berry cobbler from the recipe Anna Jo had given her.

Upstairs the house looked much the same as before, except for the lack of furniture. There were four large bedrooms and at the end of the hallway was a spacious lavatory with a flush toilet, a claw foot bathtub, and running water.

Leoma stepped into the master bedroom, the only bedroom fully furnished. Along with a chorus of other women she expressed her delight. The new four-poster bed she'd stored in the carriage house had been brought up, and it was already dressed with linens and a fluffy hand sewn comforter. A big oval rug with a floral design in pinks and blues was spread beside the bed. She could imagine her bare feet sinking into the rug. The soft colors on the comforter were her favorite shades of blue and beige. Cream colored lace curtains with deep ruffles graced the windows that flanked each side of the bed. On the mirrored dresser was a large, white bowl and pitcher. Clearly, Anna Jo had a hand in the décor, for they had talked often about the colors and furnishings they liked.

Leoma led a group of ladies from the bedroom to the wide upper landing of the stairway, where several husbands stood chatting about the fine wood trim around the doors and windows. As usual, the women were chattering all about the fabrics and colors, and the men were discussing the construction. She began her way down the steps with Dyer securely braced on one hip, careful to hold the banister with her free hand. The sturdy oak was smooth and polished to a gleaming shimmer. Half way down the stairs Leoma came to a sudden halt. A man she'd never seen before stood at the bottom of the stairs gazing up at her. A half grin worked its way across his very handsome face, as if he knew her. Should she know who he was? Baffled, she studied the masculine features, wondering why he looked strangely familiar, yet—no, it couldn't be.

The man was tall and broad shouldered like Welby, with sandy-blonde hair the same color as Welby's. But this man was clean shaven and sported a well-groomed head of short, wavy hair. Unlike Welby's usual denim overalls and work shirt, this man wore tailored, dark gray slacks and a nice, blue pull-over sweater exposing a white shirt collar. On the man's feet were fine leather dress boots that had been polished to a gleaming shine.

The stranger flashed another broad smile. The dazzling smile, strangely familiar, took her breath away. She gasped along with a chorus of others behind her. Her hand went to her mouth when she realized it *was* Welby. *Oh my.* His new look was deliciously agreeable. She paused for a moment; she had to catch her breath and still her heart.

Suddenly Dyer flapped his arms up and down and jumped on Leoma's hip as if riding a pony. "Dada, dada," he squealed.

Her head dipped, an attempt to hide the heat she was sure had blushed her cheeks. She proceeded carefully down the remainder of the steps, until she was almost nose to nose with Welby. She examined his handsome face; she couldn't take her eyes off of him. Without the wooly beard his slightly squared jaw gave his face the appearance of strength, but it wasn't rugged. His smooth skin and full mouth made his nose more aristocratic than she'd noticed before. Humor sparkled in his pale blue eyes—or was it amusement she saw there? Leoma sucked in a quick breath and tried to still her racing heart. "My goodness. You look like a completely different man. I didn't recognize you at first."

Welby rubbed his chin between his fingers and thumb and grinned. "I suppose I should have kept the beard for winter, but I've noticed you seem to like the clean shaved type of man."

He must have been referring to Jason Alder, almost too handsome to be a man. Somewhat embarrassed her words came out in a whisper. "You did this to impress me?"

"Did it work?" Welby's eye sparkled.

Leoma didn't know what to say. She'd never had a hint that Welby might be interested in her, although he'd toned down his temper lately, and she hadn't seen him smoke a cigarette in several weeks. Come to think of it she hadn't noticed the smell of liquor on his breath, either. He'd been acting nicer all the way around, but if he'd done all that for her, she was completely unaware of it. "Yes, I must say it did," she finally said, completely baffled.

Leoma was simply the wet nurse Welby had hired for his son; she'd nursed the child to save his life. The decision hadn't come easily in the midst of her grief, but she had to obey the gentle coaxing of God's whispers. Oh how happy she was that she'd obeyed. The boy had filled her heart with so much love and joy in recent months. He'd helped take her mind off her house after it burned, and made her realize the value of both their lives. In a way she had begun to feel like Dyer was her own child and she loved him as such. But this surprise from Welby stopped her on the spot. "Would you like to hold your son for a while? He's becoming quite a heavy little guy." She leaned toward Welby encouraging the toddler to go to his father.

Until now, so fixed on the change—and Welby's very handsome face—she hadn't noticed that he held a gift in one hand. He motioned for her to take the wrapped present before he took his son. In one swift move, he hoisted Dyer onto a pair of very broad shoulders and gripped his son's fat little hands tightly, before turning from the base of the stairs and walking into the living room. She followed, all but forgetting the group of people who witnessed the exchange. All she could see directly in front of her was a strong, tall body with a powerful back and shoulders, narrow hips, and a pair of straight, long legs. And to think that all this time he'd been hiding that stunning creature beneath a scraggly beard and dirty, baggy overalls. My, oh, my.

Leoma stilled her heart and chided herself for her thoughts. Since Jeremy had died, she'd had no interest in looking romantically at another man. Her casual dinner dates with Jason, though pleasant, hadn't stirred an ounce desire within her. It took a few moments to collect her wits and calm this sudden rush of emotions. And though she was still puzzled as to Jason's whereabouts, she was glad he was nowhere in sight.

She stepped in front of Welby and turned to face him. She examined the neatly wrapped gift and wondered if he had done the tidy wrapping job himself. The man was full of surprises. "Shall I put this beneath the Christmas tree with the others?"

"No. Please open it now," Welby said. With Dyer still perched on his shoulders, Welby waited and watched, anticipation filling his eyes.

Leoma untied the red satin ribbon. She could press it and use it in Kristina's hair. When she removed the green paper she found a used copy of the popular story, *A Christmas Carol*, by Charles Dickens. It was one of her favorite stories. "Oh, thank you. It's lovely."

"I thought you might like to start a new collection for your parlor. All those shelves are bare."

"Thank you. But where did you find this copy? There isn't a single bookshop in town."

"It belonged to Louise." Welby lowered his head for a moment then looked up again. For a moment sadness clouded his eyes then he smiled. "I would like you to have it now."

"I'm grateful, Welby. And I will cherish it. Thank you." Leoma pressed the book to her bosom knowing what a sacrifice it must have been for Welby to part with it.

Many of Leoma's books that had been destroyed in the fire were gifts from Jeremy, her parents, and her dear friend Glenda. The loss was heartbreaking. Her books were like cherished friends. There was something special about being surrounded by them, knowing that each character had a unique personality, and that she'd been a part of every life and adventures. She'd shared their joy and their sorrows, gasped at their tragedies, and cheered their triumphs. Few things were more cherished than Leoma's books.

Very few people in town knew of her desire to open a bookshop, and she wondered if that dream would ever come to fruition. Even after discussing it briefly with Jason it seemed impossible, but who could know what the future held. God seemed to work in mysterious and wonderful ways, and Leoma had no doubt he was in control of her life. How well she understood, that material things of this earth were transitory—gone without warning. Even books were temporary, but their stories remain in the minds of the readers. Unlike her life, however, books could be replaced. New adventures would be written, and new characters would come to life on fresh pages. They would bring new laughter and tears, awaken the imagination, and teach new lessons.

"Well now," Anna Jo said as she came to Leoma's side. "Since you have opened one gift, why don't you go over to the Christmas tree, and open the gifts all your friends and the people of this community have given you?"

A bit overwhelmed with the extreme generosity of the people, Leoma sat down on the floor beside the tree, even though she been taught ladies should never sit on the floor. With both legs bent to one side, she spread her long skirt over them. She inhaled the fresh pine scent of the tree. This was, without a doubt, the most meaningful Christmas in all her life. "I don't know where to begin," she said. "My heart is overflowing with gratitude for all of this. Having the house rebuilt so quickly would have been more than enough."

"You'll need things to get started again, especially in the kitchen." It was Mattie Gilroy's sweet comment. Mattie had no idea what a lousy cook Leoma was.

A short snort came from Welby, followed by playful laughter. "She'll need a lot more than a few gadgets if she's going to learn how to cook a meal."

Laughter filled the spacious front room and dining room. Even Leoma laughed, knowing that this time Welby's comment was said in jest, and she knew he was right.

Leoma ripped the butcher paper off of a rolling pin, and wielded the wooden utensil in Welby's direction. "I may not be a good cook, Welby Soderlund, but I'm a pretty good aim with one of these." That brought a roar of laughter from the women and several warnings for Welby from the men.

Welby laughed, clearly delighted by her quick wit. It took Leoma a moment to take her eyes off of him and refocus on the piles of gifts. When he laughed his whole face lit up and his eyes gleamed. She'd never seen him look this happy. A ravishing smile combined with his clean-shaved face, haircut, and nice clothing, altered his entire appearance and character. Something else was different, too, something she couldn't quite put her finger on. For a moment Leoma lowered her face, hoping the heat on her cheeks didn't show.

Leoma went back to opening gifts, careful as she went to acknowledge and thank each person for their kindness. In addition to the rolling pin, she'd been given pots, skillets, hand embroidered dishtowels and aprons, bowls, and every necessary piece of cutlery and dinnerware she could possibly need. Two hand-hemmed sets of bed sheets, along with embroidered pillow cases, were in one package and a thick wool blanket in another. George and Anna Jo gave her a beautiful comforter and two down-filled pillows.

The next gift brought a big smile and another comment from Welby. "She'll need that cookbook to figure out how to use the rolling pin,"

Welby said, drawing new laughter, even from Leoma. She had to admit, he was right again.

From Reverend Gilroy and his wife, Leoma received a new leather bound bible. And still there was more. Kristina nudged her way through the crowd of grown ups and knelt at Leoma's side. She held out a small square box. "I have a present for you, too."

Leoma removed the narrow ribbon and lifted the lid. Inside was a pink paper rose. "Anna Jo helped me make it," the girl said. "It's pretty, like you."

Fighting back a well of tears, Leoma pulled Kristina into her arms and hugged her. What a precious child this was. Leoma had grown to love Kristina as much as she loved Dyer, and since Kristina and Welby had returned to their rebuilt home, she missed seeing the girl every day. How wonderful it would be if Dyer and Kristina were her children. "Thank you, sweetheart. This is the loveliest gift of all; I will keep it forever."

Leoma gave Kristina another long hug and kissed her cheek. With one arm around the girl, Leoma reached for another gift to unwrap.

When there were only three gifts remaining Leoma picked up a small, flat box. It had no tag. Curious, she shook it lightly, hearing only a soft shuffle inside. The white paper came off easily without tearing. On the lid of the box was a large silver F scrolled in fancy script. Inside she found elegant stationery, trimmed around the edges with silver, and F inscribed at the top and center. Neatly folded into quarters on top of the writing paper was a hand written note. She unfolded it and glanced at the signature. Jason. Perhaps this note would explain why he wasn't present, but now wasn't the time to read a personal letter meant only for her. She simply told the guests the stationery was from Jason Alder, and she refolded the note and placed it in the box. She would read it later when she was alone.

Several comments passed through the room about Jason's whereabouts. No one had seen him today. His horse and buggy were gone before sunup, someone informed the group. It seemed he'd left town during the night. No one knew where he'd gone, or if he'd return any time soon. Leoma didn't understand why Jason would go away without saying good bye to his friends, but she wasn't terribly surprised or disappointed, just puzzled. Her two dinner dates with Jason had been pleasant enough, but lacked communication and connection. As long as their conversation was about Jason's work or Leoma's life he was fine, but his past and his family, seemed to be a taboo subject that caused his guard to immediately go up. She shrugged up a shoulder and set the box aside.

Welby looked as if he'd overcome a huge obstacle. A pleased look was plastered on his face. Fascinating. *What is going on in that man's mind?*

Later, after everyone had gone home, nightfall brought a quietness Leoma hadn't experienced in months. Without the chatter, and pitter-patter of little feet, and noises she'd become accustomed to while staying at George and Anna Jo's house, the silence was almost deafening. Dyer was tucked into the crib George had carried over from his house and placed upstairs. The baby was down for the night and probably wouldn't wake up until six o'clock in the morning.

Still feeling the afterglow of the housewarming party, Leoma fixed a cup of tea and settled into the new Queen Anne style chair in her parlor. Curious, and hoping to learn of Jason's whereabouts, or perhaps to see a cheerful Christmas greeting from him, she lifted the lid off the box of elegant stationery and set it aside. She unfolded the letter. The lanterns cast a cheery glow that matched her lingering happiness. She scanned the page and the neat penmanship. Before beginning to read she took a deep breath, expecting words of good news.

Dear Leoma,

I sincerely apologize for leaving town without first saying goodbye. I cannot explain right now my reason for going away or disclose any information. I can only say it was necessary to return to New York to settle some unfinished business regarding my parents. Please understand, this was a difficult decision for me, but it seemed best this way.

I do hope by now you are enjoying the comforts of your new home and you find it to your liking. Perhaps, if I am able to return to Oklahoma in the future, you would allow me to explain my sudden departure in person, and if I might be so fortunate, I would like to continue courting you. Until then . . .

Kind regards,

Jason Alder

Bewildered by the vagueness and stiffness of Jason's letter, Leoma dropped the sheet of paper on her lap. What could be so important or secretive that he couldn't explain his departure in person, or at least in this letter? The brief note left nothing but suspicion and doubt. He'd not even left an address in New York, where she could reply to his note to thank him for the gift. Granted, they hadn't known each other long, so perhaps Jason didn't feel safe confiding in her.

Leoma lifted the letter and re-read the end of the last paragraph. *If I am able to return to Oklahoma . . . If?* What could possibly prevent him from traveling back to Oklahoma, unless he was in some kind of trouble with the law? Her mind reeled with possible scenarios. Had he deliberately started the fire that killed his parents? Or perhaps it was accidental, but he'd fled and left them to die. Had he murdered his parents? Was some one else involved? A comment he'd made during their first dinner seemed odd and she mulled it over again in her mind. When she'd told Jason how sorry she was about his parents' awful death, he'd curtly responded, "Don't be." It seemed such a cold, bitter response. What was she to think? The letter gave no indication when Jason might return, *if* he intended to return at all. In the future, it said. One month, six months, a year? Lips pursed, she shook her head. Even though she had no intention of allowing him to court her, if he did return, his sudden departure left her wondering and wishing for some solid information. It also gave her a sense of distrust.

Whatever Jason was hiding, she was convinced now more than ever, it had to be bad. She should give him the benefit of the doubt, of course, but after further thought, the best thing she could do was put Jason Alder completely out of her mind for good. She had no desire to see him again.

Chapter 19

WHEN LEOMA AWOKE, SHE forced her swollen eyes to open as she pushed her body up from the bed. She'd slept little, feeling weepy off and on throughout the night. Perched on the edge of the bed, she contemplated how she would face this day. She listened for Dyer's voice in the next room, but not a peep came from him. It wouldn't be long before he woke up hungry and soaked, and she could hardly wait to pick him up and tend to his needs.

This would be Dyer's last morning with her, and she wanted to spend as much time with him as possible. Before slipping into her robe and building a fire to warm the house, she knelt on the thick rug beside the bed and prayed.

Lord, you've blessed me by placing Dyer in my care all these months, and I thank you for that. You helped me overcome my grief and sorrow, and you've given me strength to nourish this little boy and help him grow strong and healthy. I'm happy I had this opportunity. You also put special love in my heart for him. Please give me the courage to gracefully return Dyer to his father today as we agreed, and take away this terrible ache within me.

The New Year had brought weeks of frigid wind and snow that chilled the bones, but this morning the sun shone brightly and the air was still. Leoma welcomed the sunshine beaming through her bedroom window, and she drew in a long, deep breath, hoping to capture a bit of the warmth. Since the Christmas program at church Leoma hadn't missed a Sunday service, nor had she seen Welby set foot in the church since he came to see his daughter in the Christmas cantata. Leoma had hoped wholeheartedly that Dyer's father would have a change of heart by now, especially since this would be the last Sunday she'd have Dyer in her care. She'd prayed every day that God would touch Welby's heart and draw him to the Lord.

This afternoon, Welby and Kristina would arrive at Leoma's house at two o'clock to pick up Dyer and his clothing. Leoma had nursed Dyer the final time two nights ago. Weaning him had gone smoothly without the boy crying or fussing, though she herself felt tears form in her eyes more than once. Oh how she already missed the closeness of his little body snuggled contentedly next to her. Soon she wouldn't see Dyer at all. There would be no more lullabies at bedtime, no more little games with his pudgy hands and feet.

At last, that sweet, good-natured chatter from across the hallway alerted Leoma that Dyer was awake. The sound of his baby talk sent Leoma rushing into his room, tying her robe more snugly as she went. He stood in the new crib clinging to the side rail, one hand slapping the wood, his smile flashing two bright rows of little teeth across the front of his mouth. Leoma's heart ached with heaviness as she lifted him into her arms and held his warm little body tightly for a moment. She nuzzled her nose against his neck and savored the sweet baby smell and the softness of his skin as she kissed his chubby cheeks. "I'm going to miss you, my little man," Leoma said. "This house is going to be very lonely without you."

Dyer jabbered gleeful baby noises she couldn't begin to interpret. A short time later they were both dressed, fed, and ready for church. Dyer was bundled snugly in layers of warm clothes, his wool cap tied securely beneath his double chin. Leoma adjusted her hat and slipped into her coat and gloves. She was ready for their walk to the church.

Dyer did a little jig in her arms on the way out the back door. "I know, I know, you're ready to go aren't you?" she said, giggling. "Let's get you to the carriage house and into your baby buggy."

The child was quite an armful when he wiggled, and Leoma was glad to set him into the fancy, little buggy his father had bought two months earlier so she could take Dyer on outings. It was quite a contraption, with a hood to shade the baby on sunny days, and big springs to make the ride smooth. Dyer bounced on his bottom several times gripping the sides as Leoma tried to tuck a heavy blanket over his lap. By now she knew Dyer's bouncing, was his way of showing her he was ready to roll. "Be patient little man. We're on our way."

Thank goodness Welby had shoveled a wide path through the recent snow from the carriage house to the street. Leoma could have taken the horse and buggy to make the trip faster, but she didn't want the hassle of hitching up the horse. On such a pleasant morning she didn't mind the walk. It was a good day for a stroll through town to the church, and for their final outing, the last walk with Dyer to church. This would also be the last time she would hold him on her lap or hip and sing songs with him. Dyer settled obediently into his spot in the buggy. Leoma left the top down so he could look around as she pushed him across the yard and onto the street.

Up ahead, George and Anna Jo came out of their house with Doris and Jody, all of them bundled in warm winter coats and hats. Leoma called out and waved so they would wait for her to join them. This Sunday morning ritual of walking to church with the Langleys was one Leoma had come to enjoy. It was a good time to chat and see what new things were happening in town. George seemed to know what each new building was going to be, and Leoma liked the excitement of carpenters sawing and hammering away. Of course on Sunday the tools were quiet. Building, selling, and buying ceased for the Lord's Day. When Leoma joined the Langleys they greeted each other with hugs and fell into place, walking leisurely along the main street. After greeting Dyer, Jody and Doris skipped ahead.

Anna Jo pointed to a partially built structure in the next block. "I can't believe how rapidly they're building another department store. I sure hope they sell women's and children's readymade clothes."

"Wouldn't that be a dream come true," Leoma said. She missed shopping with her mother and Glenda in the fine department stores in Boston. Ordering from a mail order catalog just wasn't the same. You never knew if the clothing would fit, and it seemed nothing was ever as pretty or nice as the pictures showed.

"As soon as the weather begins to warm up, some big company is going to build a hotel over on that corner," George said as he continued to walk and pointed across the street. "Three or four stories tall I'm told.

I hope to get some work on that job. By the way, Leoma, have you heard from Jason Alder since he left?"

Leoma almost stumbled. The question caught her off guard. "No."

She hadn't received a single letter from Jason since he'd left. A lot of good the fancy box of stationery was, since he didn't even leave her an address where she could write to him and thank him. Supposedly, he'd gone back to New York. Rumors floated around town that Jason had been summoned by the court in New York for being an accessory to the deaths of his parents. But no one seemed to know the truth, and Leoma had no idea where the information had come from. She'd given up on hearing from Jason long ago, and she didn't much care if he came back or not. When dining with him she'd enjoyed his well-mannered and gracious demeanor, but she hadn't felt anything special or desirable toward him. Besides, she was far from ready to consider a serious relationship with another man. However, she must admit, she certainly liked the changes in Welby. He was awfully nice lately, too. Leoma kept her smile in check.

"It's mighty strange the way Jason disappeared," Anna Jo said. "I wonder if any of those rumors are true. I thought he was a very nice young man—too nice to be involved in his parents' deaths."

Leoma shrugged. She still didn't understand why Jason was so secretive and kept everything inside, unless perhaps he really was hiding something terrible. She just didn't know what to think. "I felt bad for him at first, but he didn't want sympathy. He refused to talk about his family or his past, either. Maybe the rumors are true."

"Well, he was a mighty fine carpenter," George said. "This town could use him."

Leoma eased the buggy across a rut in the road and into the churchyard. George lifted one end of the carriage, and helped her move it close to the porch steps. She would leave it there until the end of the service. She lifted Dyer into her arms and kissed his rosy, cold cheek. "Let's hurry inside where it's warm."

Leoma scurried up the steps and through the white double doors to get Dyer inside. The church was almost full to capacity, fifty or perhaps sixty people she guessed. Leoma enjoyed the fellowship and the love that flowed among the congregation. As she made her way forward with the Langleys, to their favorite pew near the front, she greeted several worshipers.

GOOD. EVERYONE WAS INSIDE. Welby was rarely late for any appointment or meeting, but he didn't want to arrive at the church early. He wanted to avoid a bunch of staring eyes and gaping mouths, especially Leoma's. He figured it would be a whole lot easier, and more comfortable, to slip into the back of the church unnoticed if the service had already started. Surprised to see so many carriages and buckboards, Welby eased the rig into an area far away from the door. Leoma's horse and carriage was nowhere in sight. He climbed down and helped Kristina down, careful to avoid a puddle of melting snow.

"We need to be real quiet," Welby said to Kristina, putting a finger to his lips. He took her hand and they walked together. As he rounded the buckboard and headed for the church entrance, he spotted the baby buggy he'd bought for his son.

"Can we sit with Miss Leoma and Dyer?" Kristina spoke in a near whisper.

Welby shook his head and touched his finger to his mouth again. His legs were a little shaky as he climbed the five steps to the door. He paused, his gloved hand on the metal door handle. If not for Kristina, he'd turn around and leave before anyone saw him.

No, he couldn't high tail it back home like a sissy. George Langley's words and those Bible verses he'd read had been eating at him night and day lately. Welby knew full well it was time to turn his life around once and for all. It didn't matter what anyone else thought. His foolish pride was a thing of the past. He was ready to face his future, and his children's future. The more he thought about what George had been sharing with him, the more he realized why George's family was happy and content. Welby had some serious changing to do in his own life. He wanted that kind of peace in his home; he was ready to do whatever it took to have that. Even if it meant opening the doors and walking into the church service right this minute.

Inside the pump organ spewed out loud chords of a faintly familiar hymn his mother used to play on her piano. The congregation began to sing. Kristina tugged at his hand, prompting Welby to draw open the door. He pulled slowly and peered inside, hoping no one would hear the low squeak from the cold hinges. No one turned. Nudging his daughter inside first, Welby stepped in beside her and closed the door without a sound.

The church appeared to be full, and on first glance he didn't see an empty place to sit in the back. He sure wasn't going to march down the center aisle to the front pew the way his grandfather made him do. "There are always empty seats up front," the old man had said. Then he'd parade the family right to the front row, no matter how many other seats were available. Well his grandpa wasn't there to make Welby sit up front today.

Welby craned his neck left and right. Finally he spotted an empty space big enough for the two of them in the third row from the back, near the center aisle. His hand firmly guided Kristina as they slipped into the vacant place while everyone stood singing. He avoided eye contact with those around him until a man offered a handshake. Welby shook the man's hand and nodded.

Still standing, Welby glanced to one side and toward the front. From the back and side profiles of people in the rows just ahead of him he, recognized Bernard and his wife from the feed store, and there was Ben Schmidt and a few other familiar faces. He was certain it was George Langley's head he glimpsed, standing several rows up near the front. It seemed half the town's folks were in church, and he was quite sure Leoma would be standing with his son near the front. He searched that area but he couldn't see her through the throng of standing men and women. Not that it mattered; he just wanted a glimpse of his boy. Leoma wasn't expecting to see him, until he and Kristina arrived at her house at two o'clock to take Dyer home with him. Wouldn't she be surprised when she saw him in church? Welby grinned. Then his gut tensed.

The singing ended and he sat down quickly when others around him began to sit. The wooden pews creaked, shoes shuffled on the bare wooden floor, and song books thumped into the racks on the back of the pews. The noises, all welcoming sounds, snuffed out the loud beating of Welby's heart. Anticipating that the preacher would begin his tirade and pulpit pounding momentarily, Welby's jaw tightened.

Instead, a hush fell over the room. Welby waited. Reverend Gilroy bowed his head and all the people followed. Silence seemed to stretch for hours before the minister began to pray out loud. He addressed God the Almighty Creator and Father of all mankind, as if he were talking to a best friend. In plain straight forward words the preacher thanked God for a long list of things, then, he asked God to help those in need and to heal those who were sick. He even said the names of several who were ill with one disease or another.

"Bless this congregation of believers and those who do not yet believe," Reverend Gilroy said. "And I pray Father, you will open the hearts and ears of those who need to confess their sins and come to you this very day. Give me the words as I bring forth your divine message for these, my dear friends, to hear. Amen."

The Reverend smiled, scanning the congregation as if to greet each person. He opened his Bible. *Now, here we go. Here comes the shouting and condemning for sure.* Welby was prepared. Wrong again. Firm, but gentle words addressed the people: words about love and forgiveness, words about peace and inner joy, words that seemed to be aimed directly at him. Welby's body trembled from the inside out. His mind reeled with sudden questions. He wanted to understand the message he was hearing. He longed to have the peace and happiness other church folks here seemed to have.

Suddenly a quiet voice Welby didn't recognize spoke within him, filling his head with unusual thoughts. *Forgive your grandfather and stop allowing that to hinder your walk with God.* What walk with God? God wouldn't be seen on the same road with him!

Not only would I be seen on the same road with you, my son, I will hold your hand. I will guide you every step of the way. I'll even carry you through the bumpy spots in your life if you let me.

What had come over him? Was he losing his mind? First of all,

Welby argued, where was God when Louise died, when his son was near death, when his farm was destroyed? Where was God when Leoma's baby died, when her house burned to the ground? The voice in his head didn't answer those questions.

I am with you. Are you ready to hear me? Are you ready to follow me? This time Welby almost jumped out of his skin. Was that the same voice that sometimes guided George? Hadn't Leoma also mentioned hearing the voice of God? Welby tried to shake the thoughts out of his mind and concentrate on the preacher's sermon. Reverend Gilroy still hadn't begun to pound the polished, oak pulpit, and his tone, though firm and expressive, was gentle. He looked directly at different people and spoke to them as if they were dear friends. As Welby absorbed the message about the peace of God in one's soul, something akin to fire began to stir inside him, and he thought about the voice that prompted him. The preacher paused. The organ began to play softly.

"If any among you have not turned your life over to God, now is the time," the Reverend said.

The urge was strong to obey the minister's call, to walk up the aisle, and give his life to God. Even though Welby's decision to answer set his insides to quaking, he sensed calmness in his soul unlike anything he'd ever known.

Everyone stood and began to sing another familiar song. He'd heard it almost every Sunday as a child. Welby clinched the back of the bench in front of him, his legs like rubber. The minister issued his invitation again, telling the importance of taking this step forward. There wasn't a harsh word, not an ounce of condemnation. No yelling or pounding.

Go, son. Now is your time. I will walk with you. Welby's heart thumped out of rhythm with the music, as the gentle voice nudged him right out of his place. His feet felt like size eighteens as he put one weighted foot in front of the other. The pulpit seemed to be a mile away.

HEARING FOOTSTEPS COMING UP the aisle from the rear of the church, Leoma opened her eyes and lifted her head slightly. She gazed down at

Dyer sleeping soundly in her arms. She'd been deep in prayer for the child and his sister and father. Intense love for the children filled her heart. The thought of sending this precious child she cradled against her bosom home with Welby later in the day, tore at Leoma's heart. Dyer and his sister needed a home with a daddy who was sober, who would bring them to church, and teach them about God. They needed a father with a gentle hand, patience, and a kind heart, yet one who would be a strong head of their household.

The footsteps slowed on the wooden floor as they neared Leoma's pew. She glanced sideways. A man, tall and broad-shouldered, stepped into view. Leoma gasped, unable to hold back the tears that sprang to her eyes. Another few steps and Welby stood before Reverend Gilroy. The two men shook hands.

Welby wore dark slacks and a white shirt like he'd worn the night of her house warming, but this time, he had on a dark necktie and a black wool jacket. His hair was freshly cut and neatly combed, and his face cleanly shaved.

As the preacher continued to shake Welby's hand the cleric laid his left hand on Welby's shoulder. Leoma couldn't hear what they were saying but clearly, the Reverend's smiles and nods indicated he was pleased. The two men talked quietly for a minute then bowed their heads. The congregation lowered their heads but Leoma couldn't close her eyes. She wanted to see Welby's face when he turned around.

Leoma's heart filled with surprising joy, racing so hard she feared she would have to sit down before her knees buckled. Perhaps her reaction was simply caused by her happiness, and seeing Kristina and Dyer's father take this step of faith that would truly change his life. Not a doubt came to mind that Welby had made the decision to follow Jesus; she could feel it in her soul. Her prayers for the children had been answered. They would be cared for by a godly, caring father.

Oh Lord, my God, I thank you for answering my prayers. Thank you for bringing Welby here, and for speaking to his heart. Help me be a kind and helpful friend as he enters this new life with you. Please help him to be an excellent father to Kristina and Dyer, and help him lead them in a righteous and godly manner as they grow up.

After a moment the men shook hands again, and Welby turned around to walk back to his seat. As Welby passed by Leoma's row, his eyes met hers. He smiled—a broad, stunning smile. Peace radiated from Welby's face. It glowed like nothing Leoma had ever seen. Suddenly, she understood what had been evading her earlier, that niggling little difference in Welby she couldn't pin point; change had already begun to take place in his heart. God had been working on his soul, preparing him for this very moment, when he would make this life-altering decision.

Anna Jo nudged Leoma's elbow, a barely perceptible touch. Leoma glanced sideways to see both Anna Jo and George smiling, their eyes glazed with tears of joy. Satisfaction was written all over George's face. With her heart full of love, Leoma smiled down at the sleeping child in her arms. This was the moment she'd been praying for. Why, then, did heaviness suddenly weigh her down like a wagon load of bricks?

Chapter 20

AT THE END OF the service Leoma walked slowly as she moved down the aisle of the church, shaking hands and chatting with newfound friends. It was the only way to delay the pain of handing Dyer over to his father, and watching them leave. Now that Welby was here, there would be no waiting until two o'clock as they'd agreed.

Dyer was wide awake now, and eager to gaze around them. She held the child upright against her shoulder to give him that freedom. He was heavy, nearly twenty pounds she'd guess, but she wanted to hold him forever. Her hand rested on the back of his head, the silky hair between her fingers. She drew him close and rested her cheek against his head, as she hummed a soft tune until the preacher's young wife approached.

Mattie Gilroy cooed and tickled Dyer's neck, drawing big smiles and giggles from the baby. Everyone in the church knew Mrs. Gilroy was anxious to have children, but so far, she hadn't been blessed with any. "I think it's wonderful the way you've taken care of this little boy," Mattie said. "He surely would have died if you hadn't nursed him and loved him. I'm sure God will bless you in return."

"Thank you, Mattie. I just don't know how I can send him home with Welby today, but I promised." Leoma's words came out in choppy syllables. "I know it's time."

Anna Jo stepped next to Leoma and put a hand on her shoulder. "This isn't an easy day for you, is it?"

The kind gesture from her friend, thickened the lump in Leoma's throat, and her eyes blurred. "No."

"At least Welby is changing," said Mattie, all smiles. "Wasn't it exciting to see him come forward today? Praise God for answered prayers I think he will be a good father."

"Yes." Leoma agreed, but that didn't make giving up Dyer any easier.

Welby stood several feet away talking to a small group of men, shaking hands, looking surprisingly at ease. Handsome and confident, he turned her way and smiled. He wasn't supposed to come to her house for another two hours, and Leoma wanted that time alone with Dyer. But she couldn't ignore Welby. She couldn't make him wait on the front steps until she was ready to turn his son over to him. Her heart twisted. She turned away and hugged Dyer closer. He squirmed and squealed playfully, impatient to be set free with the other children.

Anna Jo put an arm around Leoma's waist in a sisterly hug. "Why don't you come to our house for dinner? The children can play while we visit. I've already invited Welby."

"I don't want to impose," Leoma said, wanting to take Dyer home to be alone with him. She wanted to keep him to herself as long as possible.

"You won't be imposing at all. I have a big pot of beef stew on the stove; it's more than enough."

Leoma appreciated Anna Jo's invitation and she didn't want to hurt her friend's feelings. What would it hurt to have dinner with the Langleys? Even though Welby would be there, Leoma could still be close to Dyer. Dyer was almost ready to walk on his own, and Leoma didn't want to miss a single thing in his development, especially his first steps. She'd been coaxing him, and his legs were growing strong and steady. But so far, when he let go of her fingers he'd plop down on his bottom. Most times he laughed and clapped his hands and Leoma clapped with him. She was sure he would take those steps any time, maybe today.

Anna Jo continued. "I know how difficult this is for you. I thought if you and Welby both came to dinner, it might ease things for you. By the time we're all done eating and visiting it'll be two o'clock. We could make it a special send off."

"That's what I'm dreading. I can't bear to let him go." Leoma swiped the wetness that dribbled down her cheek.

"But you must," Anna Jo said. "You knew this day would come. Let us help you through it."

Thinking it over, Leoma nodded. Perhaps with her friends surrounding her it would be easier. "All right."

Shortly after two o'clock Leoma parked the baby buggy at the base of her front steps. She allowed Welby to lift Dyer out and carry him into the house. Welby put his son on the thick rug in the center of the front room and told Kristina to keep her brother company for a few minutes.

"Okay." Kristina joined Dyer on the rug and entertained him with hand games and funny faces.

"I'll get his things," Leoma said. "It will only take a minute." She headed for the stairs, each step heavy and slow.

Welby followed her to the base of the stairway. "May I go up with you? I'll help you carry everything down."

She hesitated for a second then sighed. "Yes, thank you." Leoma feared her legs would collapse before she reached Dyer's bedroom. Nearly faint from the pressure within her chest, her heart was ready to burst when she stepped into the boy's room. There on the big bed were the bundles of Dyer's belongings she'd prepared earlier. She stopped just inside the bedroom door, forcing herself to move forward. A gentle hand touched her shoulder.

"Leoma," Welby said his voice soft and full of compassion. She turned her head, looking over her shoulder into a kind face. "I know this is difficult."

Fresh tears threatened to overflow as she forced a nod. She swallowed hard. How could Welby possibly understand her feelings? She'd been a devoted mother, a giver a life to Dyer for nearly a year, and now the baby was being taken away from her, leaving her alone again, with empty arms.

"You must know how much I appreciate you." Welby looked into her eyes, his own eyes pools of shimmering water.

"Thank you." However, Welby's appreciation could never be enough to take away the burning pain and replace the joy of having a child in the house.

Welby put both hands on her shoulders turning her to face him, and though his smile was closed and narrow, gentleness filled his eyes. "I've come to admire you more than you know," he said, "and I don't want this to be good-bye for any of us."

"But—"

"No buts about that. I'm not taking my son away from you, as if he'll never be part of your life again. Surely you must know that."

"Are you sure?"

"Yes, I'm sure. I want you to be in my life forever. Both of my children love you and they need you in their lives. They also need to be with each other, in their own home with me."

What did Welby mean—about being in his life forever? Her heart sped into double time. She turned her gaze to the window for a few seconds, absorbing what Welby had said. If he was suggesting they enter into a personal romantic relationship, she wasn't sure she was ready for that yet, even though Welby had changed—very much to her liking.

Earlier, during dinner at George and Anna Jo's, she'd watched Welby's every movement, listened to each word and the tone of his voice. His conversion appeared to be genuine; his eagerness to learn about God was proof of a major change in his life. He was learning to be the kind of father his children needed. Leoma no longer doubted that Kristina and Dyer would be well cared for, but she was quite sure she didn't fit into their household.

"I've hired a girl to help me with the children during the daytime," Welby said. "I want you to visit us as often as you wish. And if you wouldn't mind, we'll visit you whenever possible. I can't imagine not having you in our lives." Welby's comment surprised her.

"Thank you. That's very kind of you." Leoma wasn't sure where Welby was going with this conversation, but she was happy that today wouldn't be the final goodbye to Dyer and Kristina—or Welby.

"You're more important to me, Leoma, than you'll ever know; you saved my son's life."

"I did what God told me to do," Leoma said.

"God *told* you to wet nurse Dyer?" Welby's brows lifted. He appeared puzzled.

"Yes." Leoma wondered how Welby would react if she told him about God's whispers. Cautiously, she explained, hoping he wouldn't think her crazy. "When I fled the cemetery that horrible afternoon, I was tormented by my grief. But I was selfish, not wanting to help you. That night I didn't sleep a wink. Between sobbing, fretting, and feeling sorry for myself, God whispered to me so clearly it startled me. He reminded me of his love for us all, and he made me realize I had lost my compassion for others. He made it clear that I must nurse Dyer; I had no choice but to obey. At the same time, I felt good about doing what was right. God assured me he would give me strength and help me through the difficult times."

Welby's eyes were filled with curiosity. "How do you know it was God speaking to you?"

"I knew in my heart. It was so powerful I couldn't deny it. So, I promised to do everything in my power to give your son life. If I'd known where you lived, I would have come to your house right then, in the middle of the night, to tell you I would care for your son."

Welby's smile spread across his face and gleamed from his eyes. It seemed, perhaps, he'd heard from God as well. "Thank you," he said. "I fear I'll never be able to repay you."

"You've already repaid me, by allowing me to be part of Dyer and Kristina's lives, when my own life was desolate and empty. And God promised me I would be greatly rewarded. He never breaks his promise to those who love him."

"Still, I will always be indebted to you, and grateful for what you've done." Welby's hands kneaded her shoulders affectionately and he drew her into a hug.

Leoma hadn't felt the warmth of a man's arms since Jeremy's death. It was awkward, but she allowed herself to sink into Welby's embrace, to drink in the closeness and strength of his body. She breathed slowly and deliberately, willing her heart to slow to its normal pace. They pulled apart, smiling, neither of them speaking as they gathered up Dyer's belongings.

HE'D ONLY HAD DYER home a few days, and once again Welby found himself on his hands and knees, beneath the kitchen table, sopping up milk with a dishtowel. He grumbled beneath his breath with each swipe. What he wouldn't give to have the boy's mother here now to take care of these disasters. Had Leoma gone through this very thing with his son? If so he'd never heard a complaint. He wished Angie could stay later, until the children were both in bed, but she had to go home to help her family as soon as she finished preparing supper for Welby and his youngsters.

The 17-year-old girl he'd hired to help during the day with Kristina and Dyer was finished with school, but hadn't yet married. It seemed she was a little slow when it came to her speech, and he wasn't sure what grade she'd completed. It didn't matter. Angie had come highly recommended by Doctor Rhodes. When Welby had offered her the job, she'd jumped at the opportunity to earn a few dollars a month. The oldest of eight children in her family, she was very good with younger children, and she did an outstanding job keeping the house tidy. However, it seemed the minute Angie went home, chaos began: spilled milk, nasty diapers, crying spells. Even Brownie acted up, chewing on shoes and demanding that he come in the house at all hours of the day and night.

"Bring me another towel, Kristina." Crouched on the floor, Welby waited until his daughter handed him another dry dishtowel. Pretty soon there wouldn't be a clean towel left in the house. Near his head Dyer's feet swung to and fro playfully, banging the back of his feet against the front of the wooden high chair, then nudging the edge of the table. The boy chattered and pounded on the tray with a wooden spoon making a terrible commotion.

Welby bit his tongue to hold his temper; it wasn't easy. He was finding out real fast that taking care of an infant took a lot of patience. This was a new experience for him; it shouldn't be this difficult. He suddenly visualized God under the table with him, sopping up milk, and Welby chuckled to himself.

Still standing nearby, Kristina tossed him another towel. She bent to pick up the empty tin cup that Dyer had gleefully tossed to the floor after dumping the milk. "Miss Leoma said you should only put a little tiny bit of milk in Dyer's cup."

"Oh, Miss Leoma said that, did she?" Welby's words came out in a growl.

"Miss Leoma said that way, if Dyer drops the cup, there won't be so much spilled. She said if you help him hold the cup he won't throw it on the floor. And—"

"Okay, okay! Enough about Miss Leoma." Welby grunted. Leoma, Leoma, Leoma!

Every time he turned around Kristina was spouting something about the woman. Miss Leoma said this, Miss Leoma said that. *Miss Leoma* wasn't here to take care of his children. He would manage just fine without her advice, he just had to figure out how to do it.

Welby let out a puff of air through pursed lips, and tried to calm down as he wiped up more milk. Things would get easier. They had to. It had been only four days since he'd brought Dyer home. Angie was a good worker during the day, so Welby was able to get his chores done and take care of business around the farm. He'd even ventured into town earlier today to buy a few staples, and Angie had managed fine while he was away. It was during the evenings, when Welby was alone with the children that were difficult. How had Louise managed? How did Leoma do it?

How had Leoma managed to care for his son with so much ease and grace? All those times he'd been in her home, he never saw her flustered or upset with either of his children. He'd never seen her angry, except when he showed up at her dinner table drunk, and he realized now that she had every right to show her anger and indignation with him.

Welby didn't want to admit it, but Leoma was on his mind more than ever since he brought Dyer home. He wouldn't see her again until Sunday, when he'd promised to have dinner at her house after church along with the Langleys. Dyer would turn one-year-old on Sunday, and Leoma wanted to have a birthday party for him at her house. Considering all she'd done for the boy, it seemed only fair to allow her that pleasure. Besides, the children were more at home at Leoma's house than here, and what did he know about having a birthday party?

"Papa!" Kristina cried. "Aren't you done yet? Come up here. Come quick!"

The alarm in his daughter's voice startled Welby. He jumped up, banging his head on the edge of the heavy oak table, nearly toppling it over. He grabbed the table and settled it then rubbed his head, sniffing and grimacing as he stood to his feet. What *was* that nasty smell?

"What are you yelling about?" He frowned at Kristina.

Kristina held her nose and pointed at Dyer's seat. Welby looked and backed away, nearly vomiting up his dinner. Brownish-green mush oozed from his son's diaper and filled the highchair seat. Dyer grunted; his face turned bright red. Another loud gush let loose and the mushy mess ran over the edge of the seat and on to the floor. Before Welby knew what was happening, the boy reached his hands down and patted the stinky stuff, then swiped his fingers across his face and through his hair.

Welby gasped. "No!"

His experiences changing Dyer's diapers hadn't been pleasant, but this was the first time he'd been faced with such a disgusting mess.

"Well, Kristina, what would Miss Leoma do about this predicament?" Welby glared at his daughter, totally exasperated. Right now he wished Leoma was there to help.

Kristina shrugged up both shoulders, still holding her nose. "What's pre-dic-a—?"

"Never mind." What ever made Welby think motherhood was an easy job? Raising two children, especially young ones, was a lot harder than he would have ever imagined.

Dyer laughed, clapping his hands and kicking his feet, splattering the runny poop through the air and onto the floor. At the same time, Brownie barked several times in the front yard. His barking continued, unusual for the mutt. Then Welby heard the rumble of wagon wheels in the yard. That's just what he needed now—company!

Welby didn't know whether to grab his son and head for the bedroom, or go to the front door and see who was coming. Before he could move one way or the other, there was a loud knock at the door. "Go see who that is, Kristina," Welby said, as he reluctantly approached Dyer in the highchair.

Kristina darted from the kitchen. A second later Welby heard voices that sounded like Mr. and Mrs. Gallager. When the neighbors walked into the kitchen, Welby was still standing dumbfounded, trying to figure out how to go about handling Dyer, and trying not to gag.

"Oh, dear, dear me! What have we here?" Mrs. Gallager burst out laughing, her shrill cackle vibrating the air throughout the house. Mr. Gallager backed up several feet beside Kristina, both of them holding their noses and grimacing.

At a loss for words Welby shook his head repeatedly. He didn't know where to begin. This was the most embarrassing thing he'd ever faced. As if surrendering, he threw up both hands. He was grateful when Mrs. Gallager stepped in and took over. "Get a big pot of water on to heat, and bring in the wash tub," she instructed Welby. "Do you have any old rags?"

"A few out in the shop."

Mrs. Gallager didn't waste time. She grabbed up the teapot and began filling it. "I'll get the water going. You go fetch those rags—bring a big bunch—and bring me a bar of soap. This child needs a scrubbing from head to foot." The neighbor cackled again as she set the pot of water on the fire.

Dyer clapped his messy hands and squealed in delight, then, he mimicked the woman's cackle.

Immediately upon stepping out the back door, Welby sucked in a huge breath of fresh air. When he heard Dyer mimic Mrs. Gallager's laugh, Welby couldn't restrain his own laughter. It would have been even funnier, if he didn't have to go back into the house. All the way to the barn he could swear he still smelled the nasty muck in his kitchen. He gathered up all the rags he could find and reluctantly headed back to the house, not at all ready to deal with the stench. A swig of brandy sure would be good right now to dull the senses. Something in his conscience immediately admonished him. He hadn't thought about having a drink in months. "I know, I know, God. It was just a thought."

The desire was strong but Welby knew better. Those days were behind him. Besides, there wasn't a drop of liquor anywhere on the property. He'd made sure of that. Two months had passed since he poured out every last drop of brandy he had left. There were times like now that he desperately wanted to have a drink, but just as God promised, he was there to help Welby overcome the temptation, and keep him on the straight and narrow. Sometimes, though, it sure was hard. He wondered if Leoma could see the difference in him now that he'd tossed out the cigarettes and liquor. Welby hoped so. It seemed like Sunday would never come around again; he could hardly wait to see her. Thinking about Leoma made him smile. Just as quickly, he scolded himself for thinking about her so often.

Welby pushed open the back door to the kitchen, carrying in the washtub along with the rags he'd gathered. His mind turned to getting his son and everything in his kitchen cleaned up. Mrs. Gallager grinned as if she'd been through this before. With all those sons she most likely had. He plopped the galvanized tub down at one end of the table and handed the rags to the woman.

"It's a good thing we came to visit," the rotund neighbor lady said. "You still look like you're in shock, young man."

"I never imagined taking care of an infant would be this much trouble. I've shoveled out cow barns and chicken coops all my life, but nothing ever gagged me like this." It wasn't an easy confession but it was the truth. Welby had been raised on a farm and cleaned up plenty of foul manure, but this was the worst. How could such a little boy produce so much stinky dung?

"It'll be a story to laugh about when the boy is older," Mr. Gallager said chuckling. "This is just the beginning of the fun surprises you can look forward to. Pour a few inches of cold water into the tub," Mrs. Gallager said to her husband.

Mr. Gallager tiptoed around the other side of the table, cautious every step of the way. The woman proceeded to get the water ready, swishing her hand through it several times to test the temperature. Finally, she removed Dyer from his chair without flinching or grimacing.

In no time Welby's son was scrubbed clean and dressed in a fresh diaper and night clothes. A new batch of water was in the tub for the soiled clothes and towels. The high chair, table, and floor were scrubbed clean with soap and water and dried.

When the job was finished Mrs. Gallager swiped her hand together with hearty slapping noises and said, "Well, now young man, if you don't want this to happen again you need to learn how to secure that boy's diaper more snugly around his legs. The rag was practically falling off of the little guy. And keep his long dungarees on him until you put him into his night clothes for bedtime."

Mr. Gallager piped in, grinning from ear to ear. "If you don't want to deal with this kind of mess, I'd suggest you get busy and marry that Fisk woman, quick as you can."

Welby gulped. "I doubt a city woman like her would be interested in marrying a farmer with two youngsters and a crazy dog."

"Hogwash!" Mrs. Gallager said. "The way she loves those two babies of yours, why I bet anything she'd jump at the chance. Why, you'd think that little boy was conceived in her own womb, the way she dotes on him. Everybody in town knows how she loves your boy. I bet she's pining away this very minute over missing that child. You can mark my word on it, young man."

Mr. Gallager slapped Welby on the back as he spoke. "You best snap her up before some other young feller comes along and snatches her right out from under your nose."

"Like that handsome Jason fellow if he comes rambling back to town," the woman warned, wagging her finger in front of his face.

Welby cringed. He hadn't thought about Jason coming back and courting Leoma, but now that it was mentioned he gritted his teeth, heat rising beneath his collar. The scoundrel wouldn't dare show his pretty face at Leoma's door after the way he disappeared. Would he?

One thing Welby did know for sure. Mrs. Gallager didn't have to tell him how much Leoma loved Kristina and Dyer. It was clear every time he saw Leoma with them, the way her smile brightened. Few mothers were as devoted and loving toward their own children as Leoma was with his. They loved her, too. Kristina had asked about Leoma at least two dozen times in the last four days, and it was clear by the way Dyer searched his surroundings nearly every waking hour, that he missed Leoma and wondered where she was. One time he could swear the boy said "momma."

Welby thought about the gentle way Leoma had with his children, and how well they minded her every word. She was good at mothering.

Admittedly, he'd grown fond of her over the last eleven months, more so, since he'd moved back into his own house, but courting her was the last thing on his mind.

Or was it?

Why else had he cut his hair and shaved off his beard, dressed in slacks and a dress shirt, and got all slicked up for Leoma's housewarming? Some would say that was a form of courting. If he wasn't interested in Leoma, why else did he get hot under the collar at the mention of Jason Adler possibly returning to town? Okay, okay, so maybe he was more interested in Leoma than he let on. But marriage? No, that was just plain out of the question.

On the other hand, Welby pondered long and hard, rubbing his chin. It would be mighty nice to have a woman like Leoma around the house to watch over the children, come spring when he had to spend long days outdoors tending the farm. It wasn't unusual for widowers to marry for convenience. Most likely it was more common for widowed women to do the same. But those weren't good enough reasons for him to take another wife. Not only that, he just couldn't imagine Leoma giving up her big fancy house and moving to his farm, and he certainly couldn't pack up and move to town. What on earth would he do there? He was a farmer through and through. No, the idea of proposing marriage to Leoma was all wrong. It would never work.

Hours after the Gallagers said goodnight and went home and the children were asleep, Welby sat in his front room, the lanterns shedding a soft glow on the pages of his Bible. The problem was he couldn't keep his mind on what he was reading for ten seconds. He wished his neighbors hadn't planted the idea of marrying Leoma in his head. It wasn't that he hadn't had a single romantic thought about her, but now he couldn't stop thinking about her at all. His mind went in every direction: what would it be like to wake up with Leoma every morning? Would he mind if his children called her momma? What if she never learned to cook a decent meal? Would she be content living on a farm? What if she expected fancy clothes and do-dads all over the house that he couldn't afford? He had to stop this senseless confusion.

Still attempting to put thoughts of Leoma out of his mind, Welby crawled into bed; it was long after midnight. He punched his pillow into a comfortable cushion for his head and closed his eyes. They shot opened. Through the darkness he gazed at the empty pillow next to him, and envisioned Leoma asleep there, her shimmering, long, wavy hair spread across her pillow like black silk, her pretty face so close he could kiss her mouth. He reached out and touched the cold pillow. His groan echoed in the room as he rolled over and faced the wall, eyes squeezed shut.

Hey, God. I'm not much good at praying yet but my friend George said you'd hear me if I talk to you, and I've been trying. He talks to you all the time and he said you give him answers. I read in your book you'd help me and guide me through tough times. This is pretty tough, God. I'd appreciate it if you'd either take that woman out of my thoughts or show me what to do. I need your help here.

Eventually Welby dozed off and slept soundly, until old Crank crowed several times. When Welby opened his eyes Kristina stood beside the bed gazing at him. "Good morning early bird. It there something you want?" he said.

Kristina smiled. "When are we going to visit Miss Leoma?"

"I don't know, sweetheart, but we can't go today."

"Okay. Kristina's shoulders slumped as she turned and walked out of the room.

Welby felt he'd let his little girl down. How could he explain his feelings to his daughter? She wouldn't understand. He still didn't know the answer to his dilemma about Leoma, or whether he should attempt to court her. Thankfully, he was more at peace now than when he'd fallen asleep. Angie would arrive soon, and a new day with his children and the outside chores, would keep his mind busy on things other than Leoma. For now he was content with that. Some how, he was pretty sure God would give him an answer to his prayer, one way or another.

Chapter 21

LEOMA PACED FROM ROOM to room, listless and wondering if Dyer was all right. Sleep hadn't come easily the past few nights, and several times Leoma found herself listening for the baby in the next bedroom. Five long, lonely, days had passed. She longed to hold Dyer in her arms, to hear his sweet laughter. The same emptiness she'd felt after Elizabeth's death inundated her. She tried to reason with her emotions, knowing she would see Dyer again Sunday, but that didn't remove the hollow feeling she experienced right now.

Had Jeremy not been killed, her house would eventually be filled with the joyful noises of children, running and playing through the rooms. If not for the horrible grief and strain after Jeremy's death, Elizabeth might have been born full term, and they would soon celebrate her first birthday. Perhaps Leoma would already be expecting their second child. Why had everything in her life turned upside down and backwards?

Why, Lord? What is your plan for my life? Expecting to hear a gentle whisper, Leoma waited, head bowed, her heart lamenting.

A long silence followed.

No answer came.

Suppertime had come and gone, and darkness closed around the house. In the past, this was the time of evening Leoma had enjoyed the most. She'd curl up in a chair with Dyer on her lap and read him a story before bath time, then after bathing him she'd nurse him and tuck him into his crib for the night.

Did her sweet little guy wonder where she was?

Would his father read him a story?

Leoma's eyes blurred with unexpected moisture. Would the tears ever end? As Leoma wandered into the front room, the pain in her chest was almost unbearable, as if it would crush her to death. The cavernous house was cold, hollow. Empty spaces glared at her. The fireplace mantle, where a wedding photograph of her and Jeremy should stand, was bare now. The corner where the phonograph player should be was empty, and her organ was gone. So many things had been lost in the fire that hadn't yet been replaced. Some things, like the portraits, would never be replaced. If she could fill the house with music, perhaps her surroundings wouldn't feel so empty and lonely, but she had no instruments now. She stooped in front of the hearth, and added two pieces of wood to the fire, moving them into position with the iron poker.

After warming her hands Leoma walked into the parlor and gazed around. The bookcases were empty, except for the book Welby had given her and the new Bible she'd received from Reverend and Mattie. It would take years to fill the empty shelves. The beautiful gilt-framed portrait of her mother and father that had hung in the original parlor could never be replaced. The bare wall cried out for something cheerful to fill the space.

Leoma took the book by Charles Dickens from the shelf. She sat down in the wooden rocking chair Anna Jo had given her, attempting to read but it didn't hold her interest. She closed the small book and dropped it onto her lap. Nothing filled the huge gap that was left when Dyer went home with his father. She imagined the baby on her lap, feeling the sweetness of his little head against her bosom as she told him a story. Without realizing it at first she rocked, back and forth, back and forth, her mind wandering in several different directions until she began to pray again.

Leoma's requests were unselfish these days, as she earnestly thanked God for all of the rich blessings he'd bestowed upon her, never forgetting how thankful she was to be alive. She sought peace that she knew only God could provide, just as it was promised in Psalm 29. Reciting the verse from memory Leoma spoke the words aloud. "The Lord gives strength to his people; the Lord blesses his people with peace."

After pondering the verse for several moments a sweet calmness overcame her and she continued to pray.

Lord, thank you for the months I had with Dyer, for giving me the strength to nourish him and love him. Thank you that he is healthy and beautiful, that you spared both our lives from the fire. Please watch over Dyer and Kristina, and make the new responsibility of caring for them easy for Welby. Give him patience, God, and help him be a godly, loving father. Keep him close to you and bless him. Let your love fill this loneliness within me and show me what you have in store for me and my future. Show me how I may serve you. And please, Lord, continue to settle my heart with your everlasting peace.

Restored and believing better days awaited her Leoma slipped the book back onto the shelf. With a lighter step, she went up stairs to prepare for bed. After brushing out her hair she slipped into a nightgown and hugged it close to her body, relishing the comfort and warmth of the flannel. When she crawled into the soft bed and snuggled beneath the fluffy comforter, she finally slept. For the first time in over a year, Leoma had pleasant dreams.

On waking she replayed the dreams in her mine. Girls and boys played in a field of wildflowers, singing and dancing. She dreamed of being surrounded by laughing children, and then she walked through a meadow, wearing a filmy spring dress and a wide-brimmed hat adorned with delicate flowers and ribbons. A dark-haired little girl held her hand and skipped along beside her.

It wasn't clear to her what that meant, but Leoma remembered waking once or twice with very happy feelings, and she was thankful for the sweet rest and pleasant dreams. If only she could capture those dreams and keep the joy they brought throughout each day.

Thanks to Anna Jo's timely morning visit, Leoma remained in a happy mood. Her friend knew just what was needed to keep Leoma from falling back into the doldrums. "George picked up mail for us first thing this morning. He thought he'd save you the trouble of going to the postmaster's office." Anna Jo pulled an envelope from her coat pocket and handed it to Leoma. Leoma recognized Glenda's handwriting before looking at the return address. "Thank you. I'll read it later."

"Is that your friend in Boston you've spoken of on several occasions?"

"Yes, it's from my life-long friend Glenda. We grew up together. I'm hoping she'll be able to come for a visit later this spring. I'm sure you'll love her when you meet her."

"If she's anything like you, I'm sure I will. I look forward to meeting her."

Leoma put the letter aside and sat with Anna Jo at the kitchen table, sunlight streaming through the window promising a lovely day. While Doris and Jody played on the floor with the wooden toys they'd brought from home, Leoma and Anna Jo drank coffee and munched on the delicious applesauce muffins Anna Jo had brought. They talked about recipes and cooking disasters, and when Leoma retold the story of Welby's first visit, when she'd allowed the coffee to boil over and burn smelling up the entire house, they both laughed long and hard. Leoma was grateful for all she'd learned from Anna Jo, and she looked forward to showing off her cooking skills when her dear friend Glenda came to visit.

Anna Jo took a sip of coffee and carefully set the china cup in the saucer. She patted Leoma's hand. "Have you begun to plan Dyer's birthday party?"

Leoma swallowed the bite of muffin and shook her head, her throat suddenly blocked with a lump that grew painful. Her eyes misted. "I've wandered around this empty house missing Dyer and worrying about him—until last night that is. I think God heard my prayers; the most wonderful peace came over me. Then I had the sweetest dreams."

"How wonderful. Tell me all about the dreams." Anna Jo settled in to listen, both elbows on the table and her chin propped on her hands.

Leoma told Anna Jo, describing the most delicate details.

Anna Jo rose from her chair at the kitchen table and threw her arms around Leoma's shoulders. Isn't it wonderful the way God comforts us in times of need?

"Yes, but I still miss Dyer, something awful."

"Well of course you do. That baby was like your own. But just think," Anna Jo said beaming with smiles. She sat down in her chair again.

"Sunday will be such a happy day with him. You'll have a house full of friends here to celebrate his first birthday."

"True. But that seems so far away. I yearn to hold him and hear his laughter, now. I missed him yesterday and I'll miss him tomorrow."

"You said Welby gave you a standing invitation to visit them any time. Why don't you hitch up Challenger and drive out to his place this afternoon. I'm sure Kristina and Dyer would be thrilled to see you."

Leoma gave the idea serious thought. The weather was fine. It might do her good. But would Welby welcome her so soon? "Do you think it will upset the children if I'm there for a while, then I leave? It might make it easier for Welby if I hold off visiting until next week after they've settled in."

Anna Jo scrunched her nose. "I don't know. I suppose they might be trying to adjust to the new house and new routine."

As much as Leoma wanted to follow Anna Jo's suggestion, she wasn't yet comfortable with the thought of visiting Welby in his home. It would be best if she waited until after he and the children had made a visit or two to her house, or at least, until after Sunday. She certainly didn't want to look overly anxious or forward, and she didn't want to give the neighbors anything to gossip about. In a small town such as this surely it wouldn't take much to set the tongues wagging. "I think I better wait a few more days, perhaps next week if it seems appropriate."

"Well then," Anna Jo said slapping her hands together. "Get out that new cookbook of yours and let's look at the cake recipes. It's time you get that birthday party planned. We have a lot to do in only two days."

"I want to bake a chocolate cake." Leoma retrieved the thin book of recipes from the nearby counter top and sat back down, flipping through the pages. "It should be a two-layer cake with chocolate frosting."

In no time at all the cake recipe was selected, plans were underway and soon Leoma was bustling with things to do: make a list, go to the new market, dust and polish the furniture, find a special gift. What would a one-year-old boy like? Leoma thought long and hard after Anna Jo went home. Having no little brothers when she was young, she didn't know what boys played with. Then she remembered a small wooden rocking horse in the corner of Jody's little bedroom. That's it!

Before Anna Jo and her children went home, Anna Jo had told Leoma about a carpenter at the other end of town, south about a mile past the bank. His reputation was growing as a talented, fine woodworker, the only carpenter in the area who made sturdy tables, chairs, and toys, and sold them at reasonable prices. Leoma believed it was there that Welby had purchased the wooden high chair which still sat in her kitchen. The more Leoma thought about it, the more she considered driving her buggy down there right away to see what kind of toys he had to sell. Her mind was set on a rocking horse.

First she would sit down and read Glenda's letter. In all her excitement about the party she'd almost forgotten about it. She pulled a chair near the kitchen window, where the sun streamed in, and tore open the letter. She began to read.

> *My dear Leoma,*
>
> *I hope this finds you well and settled happily in your new house. I was so glad I hadn't made travel plans before your letter arrived. I agree it will be much nicer to travel later in the spring or early summer so I've made all the travel arrangements and I will arrive at your house on June 1. By then I'm sure travel will be safe and comfortable, and it will be a most pleasant time for us to spend long hours visiting, walking, and catching up on all that we've missed. I hope it won't be an inconvenience for me to stay three weeks. That's the amount of time my boss will allow me to take off. I can hardly wait.*

Three full weeks! Leoma jumped up like a child, and clapped her hands several times. She waltzed into the parlor, the letter in hand, and finished the last short paragraph of Glenda's letter before marking the dates on the small calendar she kept on the desk.

The remainder of the day was filled with excitement. As Leoma planned every detail of Dyer's party, her list grew long: buy rocking horse, ingredients for birthday cake, use best lace tablecloth, good china and silverware, tapered candles on dining room table. The dark green Gibson girl dress would be perfect, and she'd fix her hair in a chignon, using her pearl-trimmed hair pins. It would be a wonderful party, like the ones her mother had given for her when she was a young girl. Leoma hadn't been this giddy with excitement since her wedding day.

Saturday evening after Leoma had dusted, polished, cleaned, and checked off everything on her list, she rushed around the kitchen, hoping Anna Jo would show up soon to help with Dyer's birthday cake. This was the first time Leoma had baked a two-layer cake; she wanted it to be perfect. Anna Jo had promised that as soon as the children were in bed, she would come help make the frosting and put the cake layers together. The party was set for tomorrow afternoon, following church and Sunday dinner, and she wanted everything ready tonight. She didn't want to leave anything until the last minute.

Again, Leoma double checked her list. Everything was crossed off except the cake, and that would be done before she retired for the night. She walked into the parlor where Dyer's gift was hidden, and for at least the tenth time, she stooped to adjust the red bow she'd tied around the neck of the sturdy rocking horse. She ran her fingers through the tail made of thin leather strips and smoothed the mane of thick yarn. Excited to see the look on Dyer's face when he first saw the horse, she nudged the steed to set it rocking.

It was clear Leoma had put lot of effort into making this dinner and birthday party very special for Dyer's first birthday. Welby stepped into the wide foyer and removed his coat, hanging it on a hall tree beside the door. The house was cheery and warm, with small homey touches that were new since he'd taken Dyer home. A round oak table and fancy glass hurricane lamp now stood in front of the window. The table was flanked by two fancy armchairs; it looked very nice. The dining room table appeared to be set for royalty, with burning candles and fine dishes. The delicious aroma coming from the kitchen reminded him of his mother's Sunday dinners when he was a youngster. But what really held his attention was Leoma.

Welby could hardly take his eyes off her. What a beautiful sight she was in that dark green dress, her ebony hair drawn back in a fancy twist of some sort, and little swirls of hair framing her face and neck. Not in a million years would he have thought he'd be attracted to a woman like Leoma, but the tingling pang that made him catch his breath convinced him he still had feelings, and it didn't seem to matter about status or class. His notion about Leoma being too persnickety and citified for him had definitely changed. What man in his right mind wouldn't be attracted to a fine looking, well-bred woman like Leoma Fisk?

Of course Welby had no way of knowing if Leoma had the same feelings for him. Probably not. She'd given no such indication, other than the admiring look on her face when he'd appeared at her house warming on Christmas eve, all shaved and slicked up.

"Can't take your eyes off her, huh?" It took a moment for George's quiet remark to sink in.

Welby turned his attention to his friend and tried to hide his grin. "I have to admit, she's a fine looking lady."

"The finest. Too bad she rambles around in this big house all by herself." George's whispered tone hinted at something Welby wasn't sure he wanted to question. He needed time to digest this new feeling that had his legs wobbling and his stomach churning, and there was a whole lot more to consider than just her beauty.

"She wanted this house rebuilt just like the one that burned," he reminded George. "I suppose she thinks a large house is important." The woman was accustomed to a fancy lifestyle, so who was Welby to question the size of her house? "I figure if she could afford to build it she can afford to live in it, and that's her business."

The truth was the size of one's house had nothing to do with being lonely. Loneliness was no stranger to Welby in his small place. He supposed without a partner a person could be lonely anywhere.

"When Leoma's husband built their original home, they had planned to have a large family to fill the rooms." George spoke quietly. "Maybe she still hopes for that someday."

"Could be, I suppose."

"She's been good with your two children," George said, that underlying hint in his voice again. "Treats them like her own. I think she especially misses your boy."

Welby couldn't deny George's comments, but it seemed there was more than met the ear behind his words. "What are you getting at?"

"Seems to me you should be able to figure that out on your own, my friend. The way you look at the woman is a pretty good sign you like her." George laughed and slapped a hand on Welby's shoulder. "Maybe it's time you do something about it."

Welby's thoughts were interrupted by someone else entering the house. Leoma came rushing from the kitchen and greeted the preacher and his wife. She took their coats and hung them beside Welby's on the coat tree.

The men shook hands and right away Leoma called them to the dining room. She and Anna Jo had already settled the children at the kitchen table with plates of food. Dyer sat in the high chair with bits of bread and some green peas on the tray and he seemed content.

Leoma said to Reverend Gilroy when everyone was seated, "Would you ask God's blessing on our meal?"

The prayer was simple and short. "I don't believe in long drawn out mealtime blessings," the minister said. "God blessed this good hot meal and I want to dig in while the food is still steaming."

Mattie Gilroy giggled.

George said a hearty, "Amen."

From the kitchen came another loud "amen" from Dyer.

Everyone laughed, putting Welby at ease. This was the first time he'd eaten dinner with a preacher, and the man clearly appreciated Dyer's response from the kitchen.

"Please serve your selves," Leoma said, offering the meat platter to the minister.

Welby picked up the bowl of mashed potatoes from directly in front of him. After he dipped a reasonable portion onto his plate he passed it to Mattie. It wasn't long before conversation flowed easily and he forgot his discomfort with dining at the same table with Reverend Gilroy. The minister wasn't like any other preacher Welby had ever met and he admired him. It didn't appear there was a hypocritical bone in either Reverend Gilroy or his pretty young wife. They were humble, modest, sincere, and both possessed a keen sense of humor. Nothing about their conversation set them higher than the others at the table or smacked of false pretenses. It was interesting to hear them talk about normal things, such as the growth of the town and the building of a new school and more churches. They seemed like ordinary folks.

Mattie dipped tiny servings of food onto her plate, hardly enough to feed a child, and Welby wondered if she felt sick. She appeared to be healthy and certainly wasn't a skinny girl, nor was she too heavy. Maybe she feared losing her youthful figure.

"Well," Reverend Gilroy said with gusto. "Now that we've all filled our plates Mattie and I have an announcement to make."

All eyes turned to the preacher, then to the cleric's wife. Mattie looked shy at first then suddenly radiated with smiles. "We're going to have a baby."

That explained the lack of food on Mattie's plate. As Welby recalled, there were times early in Louise's pregnancies, when she felt like everything she ate would come up. In the beginning she was sick a lot, mostly in the mornings, but after a couple of months she got over that and soon she had a big appetite. He wondered if every woman went through the same thing when they were expecting. It sure didn't sound like much fun to him, but it must not be too bad if what George had said was true about Leoma wanting a large family.

Applause accompanied spoken congratulations. "You'll need to eat more food than that if you want a healthy baby," Anna Jo said in a kind motherly tone.

Mattie smiled and dipped her head. "All of the food looks wonderful, but my stomach is rebelling against the smell of the meat," she said.

"That will pass," Anna Jo said the voice of motherly experience clear. "Just be sure you eat well and stay healthy."

Welby noticed Leoma's mood grow solemn. She didn't join in the conversation. No doubt this was a difficult reminder of her loss. His heart ached with compassion like none he'd ever felt, and he wanted to hold her and promise her she would have other children, but who was he to make such a promise. She may never want to marry again after all the heartache she'd endured. He cut a piece of pot roast and popped it into his mouth chewing thoughtfully, and he wondered what he could say to lighten Leoma's spirits. The meat was tender and moist and the gravy was rich and dark. Very tasty. He swallowed, wiping his mouth before talking. "Your roast is delicious, Leoma. I haven't tasted a piece of beef this good in a long time."

"Thank you." Leoma's smile held his until she looked away, a fresh tinge of pink on her cheeks.

"I guess that new cookbook is coming in handy." He grinned, hoping to bring a bit of laughter to the table.

"Just wait until you taste the chocolate birthday cake she baked," Anna Jo said.

Anna Jo and Mattie helped Leoma clear the empty plates and serving dishes off the dinner table. With little delay Leoma carried the cake into the dining room, and she let the other women bring dessert plates and coffee cups.

"Would you bring Dyer into the dining room," Leoma said to Welby. "We'll have the children join us at the big table now."

Leoma served coffee to the adults and watched as Welby picked up his son, highchair and all, as effortlessly as if the chair were empty. He nudged the boy up to the edge of the table. Dyer, smashed peas between his chubby fingers, clapped and wiggled up and down in his seat. Anna Jo helped the other three children up to the table while

Leoma served each guest an ample piece of cake. After wiping the peas and bread crumbs off the highchair tray, she placed a small wedge of the cake in front of Dyer. Though she'd started teaching him to use a spoon while he was still in her care, she was sure his fingers would serve him best today. And, of course, she didn't want to take a chance of having a good china plate ending up in pieces on the floor.

"Happy birthday, sweet boy," Leoma said bending to plant a kiss on Dyer's round, warm face. She pinched off a tiny piece of the cake and held it to his mouth. The baby opened wide and accepted the rich dessert. "I think he likes it."

Welby forked a large bite of the cake and put it into his own mouth.

Leoma held her breath and waited for Welby's response, not realizing at first how much importance she placed on his approval. He immediately took another bite.

"Mmmm. That's excellent cake." Welby finally said rubbing his belly. "Delicious."

"Thank you," she said, pleased beyond words. Leoma wanted to cheer, but instead she took a bite to decide for herself. Inwardly proud of her accomplishment, she took another bite. Not even her mother's cook of twenty-five years had produced a better cake.

Dyer seemed to enjoy his birthday cake, too, though little of it went into his mouth. Chocolate frosting oozed between his fingers and decorated his face like brown war paint. Everyone at the table ate heartily which filled Leoma with immense satisfaction. Even Mattie managed to eat her entire piece of cake, but instead of coffee, at Leoma's insistence, she had a glass of milk. When all the plates were scraped clean, Leoma quieted everyone and made her announcement. "I have a surprise for Dyer; let's all retire to the front room."

After the children's hands and faces were wiped, and Dyer was taken out of his highchair, Leoma excused herself for a moment. She went into the parlor to retrieve the gift she'd bought. As she carried it into the front room her heart swelled with love for Dyer. She could hardly wait to see him astride the rocking horse. When she entered the room Welby's eyes grew wide. She set the wooden horse on the floor in the center of the room, and without hesitation, Welby picked up his son and set him atop the shiny brown animal. He placed the baby's hands securely on the little pegs at each side of the head and stood back.

Doing his little jig, like Dyer often did in the high chair and baby buggy, he set the horse in motion. Leoma's heart melted with joy, thrilled to see how he enjoyed rocking back and forth. Everyone clapped and the other children gathered around to encourage him and cheer him on.

"Look at that," Welby said beaming. "My boy is riding a horse before he can walk. All he needs is a cowboy hat and some chaps."

Secretly Leoma was happy to hear Dyer hadn't taken his first steps yet. She placed her hand on his back, gently keeping with the rocking motion. Inwardly she lamented, saddened that she would never experience all those things with her daughter. And now she would miss so many of Dyer's first experiences, too. She wanted to be there when he began to walk. That was such an important milestone in a toddler's life, an exciting event she wanted to witness first hand. Leoma looked at Welby. "Have you stood him up and tried to help him take a step?"

"No." The man looked dumbfounded, as if the child was just going to take off walking on his own.

Perhaps some babies did that, but half the joy was in being part of that big experience. Maybe fathers didn't think of those things, especially men who worked in the fields on their farms from sunrise till sunset. Leoma didn't know what Welby did with his children at home. It didn't seem this time of year he'd be all that busy outside. Surely the man would enjoy spending time playing with his children and encouraging the boy to walk.

After a few minutes Dyer attempted to slide sideways off the rocking horse. Leoma lifted him into her arms and hugged him. Moving a few feet away from Welby she bent and lowered Dyer to the floor in a standing position. She held his hands securely at first then loosened her grip. He wrapped his fingers around her forefingers and bounced up and down. She walked forward two steps prompting the baby to do the same. After a few tries she smiled at Welby, his arms outstretched and ready to catch his son.

"Walk to Daddy," she said letting go of Dyer's hands. Welby clapped his hands together urging his son to come to him.

Dyer plopped down on his bottom.

Again, Leoma stood the baby to his feet and went through the same routine. This time when she let loose Dyer took one step before sitting down. Everyone clapped and cheered. Dyer patted his hands together and chattered several baby words. After another try Dyer took three steps toward his father, and Welby caught the boy up into his arms for a big hug. Another loud cheer and applause filled the room. Welby put his son on the floor coaxing him to walk back to Leoma. He took four steps this time and Leoma lifted him into her arms. She hugged Dyer to her and covered his face with kisses. Her heart was merry, her soul rejoicing. "Good boy, Dyer," she praised. "What a big boy you are!"

Welby gazed at her and for a moment, something glistened in his eyes that Leoma hadn't seen before. Pride? Attraction? Admiration? She wasn't sure, but for a split second there was a hint of something intimate that passed between them. It took her a moment to compose herself and turn her thoughts to the other guests. "I think there are more birthday presents for Dyer," Leoma said. She sucked in a deep breath and focused her attention back on the birthday boy.

A firm knock at the door drew everyone's attention. No one else had been invited to celebrate Dyer's first birthday this afternoon. Puzzled, still holding the child on her hip, Leoma excused herself and hurried to the door to see who was there.

"Hello, Leoma." Jason Alder stood on the porch, hat in hand, as exquisitely dressed and as handsome as she remembered. "I hope I'm not intruding. It appears you have company, so if you'd prefer, I can return another time."

Dumbfounded and speechless, Leoma stared until she forced her gaping mouth shut. Behind her the chatter in the front room ceased. Finally, she gathered her wits. "No, no, come in. We're celebrating Dyer's first birthday, and as a matter of fact he just took his first steps." She kissed Dyer's cheek and shifted him to her other hip as she spoke to the baby. "Didn't you sweetheart?"

Ignoring the baby as if he were invisible, Jason stepped into the front room and briefly touched Leoma's shoulder as he moved past her. As if he'd never gone missing, Jason shook Reverend Gilroy's hand and greeted everyone in the room. Leoma closed the door wondering what had brought Jason back to town, and specifically, why was he here at her house? As she turned to her friends she caught a most unpleasant glare on Welby's face.

Chapter 22

EVENING NEARED AS WELBY loaded his children and birthday gifts into the buckboard. They were the last to depart from Leoma's home, and he found himself dilly-dallying with every little thing; he wanted to stay longer. Actually, he didn't want to say goodbye to Leoma at all. The afternoon had opened his eyes, giving him a deeper insight into the woman Leoma had become in the last year. There were so many things he wanted to explore further, questions about her family, things he appreciated, things he wished to say, but didn't know how. She was everything he was not: educated, well-bred, interesting, accustomed to fine living. Yet she didn't flaunt her status, and she was the most caring, giving woman he knew.

Leoma had given his son something neither of his children had ever had—a real birthday party. Kristina had received equal attention and love today, even though it was Dyer's birthday. Not only that, Loma had made the day special, not only for all the children, but for the adults as well. Welby felt at home, comfortable, and he enjoyed Leoma's warm hospitality.

The meal she'd prepared was outstanding, the cake the best he'd ever tasted. It was something he'd never have believed possible, but Leoma had done an excellent job with every detail, and she'd been a gracious hostesses. If she had a stuffy, big-city bone in her body he sure didn't see it.

It was also clear to see how much Leoma loved Dyer by the way she celebrated his first steps with so much joy. It seemed to be important for her to share that special moment, and Welby was happy his son had given her that pleasure. In fact, as he thought about it, he realized that being able to share that event with Leoma had given him a great deal of pleasure as well.

Yes, the day had been flawless, perfect—until Jason Alder arrived. It had taken a while for the heat beneath Welby's collar to cool, and he was relieved and glad when the young man excused himself after a very short stay. Jason had remained at Leoma's only long enough to let everyone know he was back in town and looking for work. It appeared he wanted to talk privately with Leoma, but he'd had the decency and manners to realize it wasn't the proper time. Welby noticed more than once, however, that Jason could hardly keep his eyes off of her. He'd accepted a piece of birthday cake and a cup of coffee, and wasted no time cleaning the plate and draining the cup. He left shortly after finishing the dessert, with barely a glance and a nod in Welby's direction.

Welby didn't have a single doubt, that before he and his children were back at the farm, Jason would be knocking on Leoma's door. He didn't like the idea one bit, but what was he to do about it? He had no claims on Leoma. She had every right to see whomever she wished. And after all, she'd had dinner out with Jason at least twice that Welby recalled. Maybe Leoma had feelings for the man. Welby tried to brush his unpleasant thoughts of Jason from his mind. He secured the rocking horse in the back of the buckboard so it wouldn't get damaged on the drive home, then he turned to say goodbye to Leoma.

Leoma stood on the front porch of her house, having already hugged and kissed Kristina and Dyer goodbye numerous times. She wore a broad smile and clutched a shawl around her shoulders. Welby had never seen her look more radiant or beautiful. She'd regained a healthy glow to her complexion, and though she was still very thin, she wasn't lacking curves in all the right places. He smiled and walked back to the steps.

"Thank you for allowing me to have Dyer's first birthday party here," Leoma said.

He owed Leoma his thanks. "You're more than welcome. Thank you for the wonderful meal, and for doing so much to make my son's birthday special."

"You're very welcome." Leoma's smile was radiant. He was glad to see her appear so happy.

Welby took a few steps backward and gave a timid wave before he climbed into the seat beside the children and lifted the reins. Leoma waved and smiled sending them on their way. The vision of Leoma standing there stuck in Welby's mind. As he steered Lightning toward home, he sure wished he'd said something to her about his feelings after the others were gone. It had been the perfect opportunity to at least drop a hint, but he wasn't any good at this type of thing. Still, maybe if he'd let Leoma know he was growing fond of her she wouldn't let Jason court her again.

What a senseless fool he was. If the sun wasn't already disappearing, and he didn't have evening chores to do and two tired children to care for, he'd turn around this minute and go back to Leoma's house. Angry at himself for his ignorance about such matters with women, Welby snapped the reins and kept going toward his farm. It was best to get on home and let whatever happened happen.

What the preacher had said weeks ago, and George's prodding him to marry Leoma, played on Welby's mind over and over. He tried to imagine her living in his farm house and working in the garden, but he just couldn't picture it. He groaned. Leoma wanted to own a bookstore and live in her big house in town. Could he possibly leave the farm and live in the city? That idea was even more far fetched. How would he make a living? Farming was the only thing he knew. He'd gone over this a dozen times before, and still he had no answer, but he couldn't dash the strong emotions that continually tormented him. The woman had somehow managed to get in his blood, and he didn't even know how or when.

"Papa! Papa!" Kristina shouted and tugged at his sleeve. "You're going too fast!"

Startled, Welby pulled back on the reins to slow the horse. His mind had been racing in every direction except on his driving, and without realizing it he was flying along at a reckless pace. Suddenly recalling the night he'd crashed and nearly killed himself, he took several deep breaths to calm down. "Are you two all right?"

Kristina nodded and snuggled against his side. Dyer was all grins in his little traveling box. There was no point in trying to explain his carelessness to his daughter, but Welby apologized. The rest of the way home he plodded along, attempting to keep his mind on the road, but thoughts of Leoma were far from being left in town. Welby's mind rambled along with the clip-clop, clip-clop of Lightning's hooves. There was no denying that he cared deeply for Leoma. New feelings he'd never experienced filled him. He was falling in love with her, but there was something more he didn't understand. Two thoughts kept plaguing him. Welby knew nothing about courting a lady of Leoma's standing, and he had nothing in common with her.

Louise was the only woman Welby had courted, and it wasn't much of a courtship. Like Welby, Louise had come from a simple farm family. When he was growing up no one had taught him how to treat a female. Certainly, his grandfather wasn't the example he wanted to follow. As he recalled, his mother and father's marriage had been arranged, and he was quite sure his mother was secretly happy when his father died. Welby had been on his own to figure things out.

His courtship with Louise had been short, spent mostly at one family's home or the other. The first time he'd kissed her was the night he'd awkwardly asked her to marry him. Unpracticed and scared witless, he'd kissed her again, lips tight, his hands shoved deep into his trouser pockets. Right or wrong, Louise didn't complain or run the other direction, and without hesitating she'd accepted his blunder-headed proposal.

On their wedding night Welby had been shy and clumsy. He and Louise bungled their way through the early months of marriage, acting on instinct, allowing passion to guide them. So different from Louise, Leoma was a genteel lady, a woman used to being treated in ways Welby couldn't even imagine. Why, for goodness sake, he'd never even eaten in one of those fancy restaurants in town like the one Jason had taken Leoma to and, he'd never worn a proper dress suit; he didn't even own one.

Welby glanced down at Kristina and his drowsy-eyed son and considered how much they needed a woman to mother them, especially

Kristina. Maybe it wasn't too late for him to learn a few new tricks. He grinned, and wondered if he was just plain loco to think he could win Leoma's heart and hand.

Welby guided Lightning to the front door of his farm house and eased back on the reins until he came to a stop. He sat quietly for a moment facing the dark house. The thought that no one awaited his return filled him with a sense of emptiness, unlike anything he'd felt after Louise had died. For the first time that he could recall, Welby hated going into his home without a mate, and it wasn't because he missed his deceased wife. Oh, he missed her still, at times, but this was different.

During the next two days Welby continued to spend his free time settling problems for Angie, trying to pay attention to both children, and adjusting to the new responsibilities of being the sole parent of two youngsters. He'd been tempted to rush right back to Leoma's first thing Monday morning, for fear Jason would persuade her to resume their courtship, but Welby realized he was foolish to let jealousy rule his thoughts. He'd spent some time praying and waiting. If it was God's will for Leoma to be in Welby's future, nothing Jason could say or do would change that. Or at least that's what he hoped. Besides, he didn't have a clue what Leoma felt for Jason.

God, if you hear me, I sure would like you to help me calm down and get my head cleared out. I don't want to go and do anything crazy. Could you give me a little guidance here?

During the following days, with Dyer walking now, Kristina and Dyer kept Welby so busy, even with Angie there to watch over them, he didn't have time during the daytime to dwell on his growing feelings for Leoma. Yet, it seemed she was always right at the edge of his thoughts. Once the two children were in bed asleep each night, however, thoughts of Leoma followed him everywhere and filled every minute.

Picking up the Bible late Tuesday night, Welby settled into the couch and searched for words to help him. There had to be something to calm his mind or give him direction. Maybe he'd find something in the Psalms. He knew how to locate that part of the Bible. Feeling clumsy, he opened the tattered book, but before finding the Psalms the pages fell opened to some of Louise's underlined verses. Welby worked at pronouncing

Corinthians and tried to figure out why it said First Corinthians. Was there a second Corinthians? There was so much to learn. He put his finger on the underlined words in the thirteenth chapter.

Welby looked closer, some of the writing difficult to make out from wear and damage. But he began to read slowly, following his forefinger to keep his place. *Love is patient, love is kind. It does not envy, it does not boast, it is not proud. It is not rude, it is not self-seeking, it is not easily angered, it keeps no record of wrongs. Love does not delight in evil but rejoices with the truth. It always protects, always trusts, always hopes, always perseveres. Love never fails.*

Welby read the underlined words again, this time with more ease. He didn't recall ever hearing those words before. Why hadn't his grandfather taught him this when he was a boy? Did Grandfather understand this kind of love? It didn't appear so. But surely Louise must have, and Welby was pretty sure Leoma did, too. Pondering long and hard, Welby realized this was exactly what he needed. Again, he read out loud, the entire portion of scripture.

"Love never fails . . . never fails!" He'd been told recently God's love never fails, but what about love between a man and woman? Different as he and Leoma were, could he ever share that kind of never-failing love with her?

Suddenly it seemed the room brightened and he saw his surroundings for the first time. Lightness he'd never felt filled his chest and made his heart stutter; it almost frightened him. Then, a familiar voice filled his head with whispers, much like what he'd heard in church that Sunday when he decided to follow Jesus.

Why do you fret? Do you not realize you and Leoma have the greatest thing of all in common? Consider your faith in me and the love you both share with your Heavenly Father. In Christ all things are possible if you trust in Him.

All things? Welby shuddered. For some time he sat in silence, stunned, bathing in the warmth of such an encounter. To think God would talk to him overwhelmed Welby with awe.

After darkening the house he undressed and crawled into bed. Peace filled his heart and settled his mind. He no longer had doubts, or needed to hash everything over and over in his mind. He said another short prayer thanking God for directing him in such a powerful way.

"That's that," Welby muttered as he pulled the comforter up to his chin. He felt like shouting and hooting like a young school boy. If he wished to take Leoma as his wife, he had God's assurance that their faith was the strong common ground he sought. The Lord would help him work out the earthly details. Worries about their differences had already faded into the darkness. His decision was made; he'd go a courtin'.

Relaxed and at peace, Welby wondered what Leoma was doing—sleeping no doubt. He thought about her smile, and visualized what it might be like to hold her in his arms and never let go. With his eyes closed he tried to imagine such pleasure and smiled into the darkness. After a few seconds he rolled onto his side, and at last began drifting into a pleasant sleep. It was midnight and old Crank would start crowing in a few short hours.

Chapter 23

"Good morning, Leoma." Jason removed his hat and smiled. "I hope I'm not calling too early."

Surprised and momentarily stunned to see Jason Alder on her front porch at six-thirty in the morning, Leoma hesitated. What could he possibly want at this time of day? She'd barely had time to dress and put a pot of coffee on the stove. "It is rather early, but what can I do for you?"

"I haven't slept a wink since Sunday, because of fussing and fretting about what I need to say to you. May I come in for a few minutes?" Jason fiddled with the brim of his hat. Something certainly had the man in a nervous tizzy.

Leoma pushed the door back and nodded. "Come in. Please be seated in the front room. Would you like a cup of coffee?"

"Yes, thank you. Black, please." Jason stepped inside and sat down in the chair nearest the fireplace. Perched rather stiffly toward the edge of the chair, he hung his hat on one knee.

Loma's curiosity ran rampant as she walked to the kitchen. She poured two cups of coffee and placed them on a serving tray. Perhaps Jason had come to ask if he could resume courting her. Why else would he be so nervous? A chill sent bumps up her arms and she tried to rub them away before picking up the serving tray. Her hands shook as she carried the tray into the living room. After serving Jason his coffee, she took her cup and sat down in the wing-backed chair across the room. She waited several moments, hoping Jason would speak up. An awkward silence lingered in the air. After a sip of the hot coffee soothed her throat she spoke. "What is it you wish to talk to me about, Jason?"

Jason cleared his throat, took another drink and pursed his lips. "First, I need to apologize for lying to you."

"Lying?" She couldn't imagine what Jason was talking about. Now he had her full attention.

"Yes. I told you both of my parents died in a house fire. That wasn't true." Jason paused and looked around the room, then took a deep breath and continued. "You see, my father died in the fire, but my mother jumped from the second story window; her clothes were on fire. A fireman saved her life, but her burns and injuries left her crippled and disfigured."

"I'm so sorry. That's awful." Having seen the destruction of her own home, Leoma could only imagine what Jason's mother had endured.

Jason set his coffee on the side table and began to fiddle with the brim of his hat again. It was several long moments before he went on. "I was blamed for the fire, and my mother never forgave me for my father's death or for her injuries."

"Were you responsible for the fire?" Leoma thought about her own house burning down, and the anguish she'd experienced trying to figure out if she'd caused it. She couldn't imagine the guilt and horror Jason must live with, after what happened to his parents.

"I don't know. One night I came home drunk and I was smoking. Both were prohibited in our home. My parents and I argued violently until they went to bed and I flew out in a rage. I guess I left a lit cigarette behind and that started the fire, but I honestly couldn't remember."

"So you ran away and came to Oklahoma?"

"Not until after the court said there was no proof and I was found not guilty for the fire. They called it an accident." Jason shrugged a shoulder and looked away.

"What happened to your mother?"

"My sister took Mother into her home and cared for her, but I was dead to them. My sister blamed me for everything, too. That's why I left home. I wasn't welcome there, so figured if I went far away I could put it all behind me and make a clean start."

Leoma's heart ached for Jason. What a tragedy it must have been to lose his father, and then be blamed and shunned by his mother and sister. Still, that didn't explain why Jason had disappeared from Oklahoma City two months earlier without telling a soul. And why had he really come back? "Why did you leave here without a word to anyone on Christmas Eve?"

Jason looked at her now, sorrow in his eyes. His voice was choppy and he cleared his throat. "The day before your housewarming, I received word from my sister that Mother was dying and she wanted to see me. To forgive me, she'd said. All I could think of was getting home as fast as possible."

"Did you arrive in time?"

Jason hung his head and slowly moved it from side to side. "Mother died one hour before I arrived, she told Amelia, my sister, she forgave me. She made Amelia promise to tell me."

Sensing Jason's shaky emotions, Leoma remained silent. Jason straightened and picked up his coffee cup. After a long drink he went on. "I helped Amelia with burial arrangements and took care of some unsettled family business. She still hates me and blames me for both deaths, so there was no reason to stay there. I need to get on with my life. So here I am. I hope you can forgive me for lying, and for fleeing without explaining the situation."

"Yes, of course I forgive you. If your mother was able to forgive you, certainly others should as well. I hope in time your sister will also."

Great relief flooded Jason's face and he sighed deeply as he stood. "Thank you, I hope others here will be as understanding as you have been."

Jason stepped to where Leoma was seated and stretched his hand toward her. She accepted his hand and stood as he spoke again. "I know you and I got off to a bad start, but would you consider allowing me to call on you. I would like to court you if you'll have me."

Leoma pulled back slightly and smiled. "I'm sorry, but no."

It was almost heartbreaking to see the immediate disappointment on Jason's face, but things had changed in the two months he'd been away. "It has nothing to do with what you've told me," she said. She freed her hand from Jason's grip and looked up at him. "While you were away a lot happened, and I have special feelings for someone else."

After explaining, Leoma smiled and walked Jason to the door indicating the visit was over.

Chapter 24

BY THE TIME ANGIE arrived Wednesday morning to care for the children, Welby was counting the minutes until he could hit the road into town. The children had become comfortable with Angie, and he'd decided she could handle anything that might arise while he was gone. It would be for only a short time—perhaps two or three hours.

He'd slept off and on throughout the night, his mind going over what he wanted to say to Leoma. He'd gotten out of bed before Crank crowed at the first hint of dawn. The sun had barely peeked over the snowy horizon before he'd finished milking the cows and feeding the chickens. The eggs were gathered and Angie had the children fed and dressed in warm clothing.

Welby was raring to go.

The buckboard was loaded with the heavy trunk of Louise's books from the barn, thanks to the help of the oldest Gallager boy. Welby estimated there were over one-hundred books, some of them quite thick. The books wouldn't come close to filling the wall of shelves he'd built in Leoma's parlor, but it would be a decent beginning.

It was time to give the books to someone who would appreciate and enjoy them. Leoma was that person. One of these days he'd give Kristina new books so she'd have her own collection. And who knew, maybe someday he'd buy his children books in that book shop Leoma wanted to own. Ready to leave, Welby gave Angie and the children last minute instructions, and carried a small basket containing a dozen eggs to the buckboard. He supposed eggs weren't very romantic, but he was pretty sure Leoma would appreciate them almost as much as the books.

Scattered white clouds floated on a light breeze, and crisp air filled Welby's lungs as he rode along the frozen bumpy road. He couldn't remember ever seeing the sky so blue or feeling this lighthearted. It was nearly enough to make him break into a song—that would be a shock to his own ears. Lightning clopped along at a gentle pace matching Welby's rambling thoughts. How would Leoma accept his gesture? He hoped she wouldn't think it strange, for him to give her a trunk of used books that had belonged to his deceased wife. Welby didn't have a clue what type of books Leoma was interested in reading. From what he'd seen during his brief glimpse in the trunk, there was a variety of subjects such as novels, autobiographies, poetry, and religious books. None of them looked familiar or interesting to him. It seemed books were kind of a personal thing, so he hoped Leoma would like the ones in the back of the buckboard.

Welby thought Leoma seemed the type of woman who'd read poetry, but since he knew very little about her taste in literature, there was no way to know for sure. He hoped, however, this would give them something to talk about, and a way for him to learn more about her interests. It was one way to find out if they had anything else in common, other than their faith.

Surely there had to be something they both liked, something that would give Welby a chance to win Leoma's heart. "I guess I should be talking to you about this, huh, God? I heard you loud and clear last night. You know what's on my mind and in my heart, and according to George and Reverend Gilroy you care about every part of our lives here on Earth. The preacher said you like to see us believers happy, that you take pleasure in blessing us. Now that I'm one of yours, God, I sure would be happy if you would bless me by helping me figure out what to say to Leoma when I get to her house, and I'd like it if you could help me and Leoma build a solid friendship. She brings me a whole bunch of pleasure, God, and I surely do like her."

Welby's chest filled with overwhelming desire. At the same time he worried he might make a fool of himself, like he was right now talking to God out loud. His shoulders and neck were tense, his jaw tight. If he put his heart in Leoma's hands and told her how he felt and she rejected him, he wasn't sure what he would do. It would break his heart, for sure. If he'd only made a move before Jason showed up in town he might have had a better chance. He shook his head at his doubts, wondering if God was doing the same. Or, more than likely, God was looking down at him right now and chuckling.

Leoma's house was no more than a quarter mile away and he could see smoke rising from the chimney. At least he knew she was up and about. He continued to talk to God, speaking out loud again. This was all so new to Welby and he felt a little foolish talking to the sky, yet he found comfort knowing he could turn to a great God who cared about him and ask him anything. It would be a lot easier if he could see God face-to-face and talk to him like he talked to George, but George said that's where faith came in.

George was a good friend now and he seemed to have a lot of wisdom, so Welby trusted the man's words. But George couldn't answer Welby's desperate pleas, or his prayers about his desires and feelings for Leoma.

The front of Leoma's house came into clear view and Welby tightened his grip on the reins. His palms grew sticky with sweat even though the air was frigid. He slowed Lightning and tried to do the same with his racing heart. Not even his first date with Louise had caused him to feel this young and excited. He drew in a long, deep breath. What had come over him?

"Lord, God in Heaven, it's me again. Don't let me pass out on Leoma's door step. Please keep my heart beating properly and my breath flowing. Help me keep my body upright and my steps straight. Make me speak clearly, too. And, please Lord, let Leoma accept my gift without thinking I'm crazy or foolish."

Welby came to a stop just beyond the fence in front of Leoma's house and took several slow breaths, hoping he wasn't calling too early in the morning. He hadn't given a thought to what time Leoma might rise, considering she wasn't a farm girl. A faint light glowed through the lace curtains on the front window so that was a good sign. He sat back on the wooden seat and paused to calm his nerves and collect his thoughts. Again, he sucked in a long, slow breath conjuring up his courage.

Just then the front door of Leoma's house opened. Curious, Welby sat forward. Then, the last person on Earth he wanted to see, stepped onto the porch—Jason. Leoma stepped to the door smiling, clearly happy as she spoke to Jason. Welby's body froze but his mind went wild. *What was I thinking, coming here all worked up and thinking I could court such a woman? I should have known better.*

Welby snapped the reins and nudged Lightning out of Leoma's yard, going lickety-split, without a care about the rough road. The buckboard rattled and bumped through several holes, tossing half of the eggs out of the basket. Slimy whites and yolks oozed around his boots.

"Welby?" He barely heard Leoma's voice shouting his name. "Welby, come back here. Welby!"

Without looking back he continued toward home, slapping the reins wildly against Lightning's hide. Welby's lower lip suffered the hard chewing he gave it as he bumped down the road. He should have known the minute Jason Alder came slithering back into town he'd be knocking on Leoma's door. "I should have high tailed it right back over there first thing Monday morning. Now it's too late," he said to Lightning.

A mile down the road Welby slowed the buckboard. The sound of horse's hooves coming up from behind drew him out of his angry tirade, until he saw Jason ride up next to him. Jason waved and shouted. "Pull up."

"Now why should I do that?" He had nothing to say to the young scoundrel.

"Because Leoma sent me! She insisted I catch up to you and talk some sense into your head!"

Welby slowed slightly, not sure he believed Jason. Why should he?

"Come on, Welby, stop! I have better things to do than chase you all over the country."

Reluctant to listen to anything Jason had to say, Welby pulled back on the reins and brought Lightning to a stop. He glared at the younger man. "All right, I'm stopped. Now what?"

"Leoma wants you to return. She wants to talk to you."

"And what about you? I suppose you had a good reason to be calling on her so early in the morning. Are you courting her again?"

Jason grinned and shook his head. "Nope. She turned me down flat."

Welby grunted. "Why's that?"

"Said she has special feelings for someone else. I suppose she meant you, although I can't imagine why she'd be interested in a turnip diggin' farmer like you."

Welby grunted again, but cautiously his spirits lifted a little. Why would she want him to come back to her house, unless maybe he really was that someone she had feelings for? Could it be? Well, by jiminy, he was going to find out.

After a long hesitation Welby stepped down from the buckboard. When his feet hit the ground his knees almost collapsed like a newborn calf. Once steady he looped the reins around a fence post and walked up the porch steps, the half-full egg basket in hand. He knocked on the front door. Waiting was unnerving especially after his encounter with Jason. Everything he'd rehearsed to say had changed. All the way back to Leoma's house he'd worried about what to say.

The door opened. There stood Leoma, prettier than ever, a smile on her face.

He took a deep breath attempting to calm his heart.

"Good morning, Welby," Leoma said her voice cheerful, surprise twinkling in her eyes. Was she actually as happy to see him as she appeared? He sure hoped so.

Welby jerked off his hat and whacked it against his thigh. "Good morning."

"What brings you to town so early this morning?"

"Am I too early to call? Seems to me you're mighty busy already." That didn't come out quite right and he lowered his eyes for a moment. What if she turned him down like she did Jason?

"You're not too early and I'm definitely not too busy. I was worried you wouldn't come back, and I'm very glad you did."

"You are?"

"Yes, I sure am." Leoma wore a pink printed dress with a ruffled collar and her hair flowed freely over her shoulders in dark, silky waves.

Her skin was creamy smooth, her eyes lively. The grief she'd worn so heavily for months was gone.

Welby forced himself to breath calmly. Should he question Leoma about Jason or keep his mouth shut and let her explain? He bit his already suffering lip.

"Please, come in. Tell me what brings you here this morning."

"I have a big trunk full of books I want to give you, and I, well, I wonder if we could talk for a few minutes." Welby inwardly kicked himself for stammering instead of spitting the words right out.

"Books?" A look of excitement came over Leoma's face.

"I've been meaning to give them to you for some time. I know how much you like books, and since you lost all of yours in the fire, I thought you'd like to have the ones my wife had stored in the barn. They're all there in the buckboard. Well, that is, all except the ones that were in the house and were destroyed by the tornado."

Leoma's hand went to her throat, her eyes filled with joy. Suddenly Welby knew he'd done the right thing by coming back. His nerves settled and he relaxed exhaling a long breath.

"How wonderful. Are you sure you want to part with them?"

"Absolutely. May I bring them inside?" Welby's heart raced. He'd never been inside Leoma's home alone with her. There had always been the children, her mother, the preacher, or other neighbors like George and Anna Jo present. He hoped visiting Leoma wouldn't start a whirlwind of gossip that would cause her embarrassment. After thinking about it, though, it would probably cause happy rumors, after the way George and the preacher had prompted him to pursue Leoma.

"Oh, yes. And thank you for the eggs."

"You're welcome." He wouldn't mention the slimy mess of broken eggs that coated the floor board of his wagon. He glanced down at his boots hoping they were clean. They'd pass.

Leoma stepped out onto the porch and took the basket of eggs from him. The morning sun cast golden light against her hair and highlighted her pink cheeks. His breath caught. Oh how he wanted to kiss her lovely lips right then. But of course he shouldn't be thinking such improper thoughts—not yet—and certainly not outdoors for the whole town to see. Welby turned and nearly ran to the buckboard to fetch the large trunk of books, not sure he could carry them without help.

It was easier to get the trunk off the buckboard and drag it than it had been to lift it up with his helper at home. Still, it took every ounce of strength to get the load up the walkway and up the porch steps. Leoma held the door back while he carried it into the house, working with all his might to keep his grunts and groans silent. He sure didn't want to look like a weakling in front of Leoma. Careful not to scratch the polished oak floor of the parlor, he eased down the heavy container one end at a time and let out a long sigh of relief.

Leoma tore into the trunk like a hungry bear cub. Then she lifted each book as if it were made of fine crystal or china, reading titles and running her hand over the covers. One at a time she placed them on the shelves, arranging and rearranging them like a puzzle. With one shelf full she paused and looked at him, her eyes liquid pools of rich brown. "Oh, Welby, this is a priceless gift. Thank you. And thank you for building these beautiful book cases."

"You're welcome. I'm happy you're pleased with both."

"Pleased? I'm thrilled. We've both lost so much; I'm more grateful than ever for such blessings." Leoma paused, looking at the book in her hand. "Anna Karenina! I've been dying to find a copy of this!"

With what appeared to be reverence, Leoma placed the book on the shelf next to one titled *Little Women*. He'd seen Louise read that one at least twice. Leoma stepped closer to him, holding his gaze. Her hands outstretched she smiled, searching deep into his eyes. Welby took both her hands in his. He shuddered at Leoma's closeness causing his heart to race. With a gentle squeeze of his fingers, Welby drew her to him. Leoma came into his embrace without hesitation.

Unable to move or think straight, he simply held her, breathing in her sweet fragrance. Unlike the time he'd hugged her on Christmas Eve, this time he sensed from Leoma tenderness and desire—definitely something more than gratitude for giving her a few old books. The perfume of her skin was like a fresh spring morning. The softness of her body could make him forget his manners if he didn't draw back. When he pulled away Leoma's eyes met his. Something in her gaze connected with his soul. He drew in a jagged breath.

"Do you have time to sit down at the kitchen table and have a cup of coffee now?" Leoma's invitation was exactly what Welby had hoped for all the way into town. He had so many questions to ask her. There was so much about Leoma he wanted to learn.

Welby didn't hesitate. "Yes. That sounds good."

HAVING WELBY AT HER kitchen table gave Leoma a new, unexpected sense of happiness that she'd believed, until recently, she would never feel again. The inner changes in him over the last few weeks had been so marked it could only have come from God. It wasn't just that he'd stopped drinking liquor and puffing on those nasty cigarettes, but more than that, it was his acceptance of Jesus into his life.

There was something else she noticed. Since he'd shaved off the scraggly beard and began wearing his hair in a shorter cut, it seemed to change not only Welby's appearance, but his demeanor as well. Now that she thought about it, Leoma hadn't seen him in overalls on his many trips into town in quite some time. Today he wore a pair of clean denim jeans and a wool plaid shirt that emphasized his broad shoulders. He was quite handsome, with that strong jaw and thick hair the color of golden wheat ready for harvest.

Leoma poured steaming coffee into a large brown mug, like the one Welby had used during his convalescence in the original house and, remembering that Welby drank it black, she set it before him. Then she filled a smaller china cup for herself. "Would you like a slice of gingerbread?" she asked before sitting down. "I baked it myself."

Welby tilted his head as if skeptical, then after a long grimacing frown, he graced her with a broad teasing smile. "Yes, I would enjoy a piece, especially since you baked it."

Relieved that she didn't have to swat the man with her dishtowel, Leoma cut two slices of the spicy brown loaf and placed them on small plates. She put a fork on each dish, set them both on the table, and sat down in the chair across from Welby.

Silence.

Leoma picked up her fork and paused. She didn't want to appear anxious and speak too quickly. After all, it was Welby who'd come to see her with something clearly on his mind besides the books.

"That was quite a surprise to see Jason Alder coming out your front door." Leoma heard a hint of jealousy in Welby's voice.

"Yes, I suppose it was." What more could she say? She had no feelings for Jason, and until this morning when he'd come to apologize, she only knew bits and pieces of information that she'd heard from the neighbors since his return.

"He said you turned down his offer to court you. You're not interested in him being your beau?"

Leoma almost laughed at the puzzled look on Welby's face. "Goodness no! I realized that long before he left on Christmas Eve. This morning he came to apologize for the lie he had told me when we dined together. I'll explain that later if you'd like."

"Fine. But he did ask you if he could court you?"

"Yes he did." Leoma took a bite of the spicy gingerbread and chewed a moment before going on. "And I said no."

Noticeably more relaxed, Welby also took a bite of the dessert, his face slowly brightening. "This is very good." Leoma could see he studied the taste for a moment. "A dash of extra ginger and cinnamon, right?"

What man would have detected that? "Yes. How did you know?"

"My mother made it often. When I was young—believe it or not—I liked to hang out in the kitchen when she baked. She told me that was the secret to the best gingerbread. "At Christmas time when she made gingerbread men, she always let me help put the frosting faces and buttons on them."

"What a nice memory. So, you must like gingerbread."

How interesting that Welby liked being in the kitchen with his mother. Leoma tried to imagine him putting eyes, a nose, and a mouth on gingerbread cookies. The picture certainly didn't match the image of the brawny man sitting before her. Yet it was a pleasant image.

"It's my favorite dessert," Welby said almost in reverence.

"Mine too! But I didn't know how to bake it until Anna Jo wrote down her recipe for me."

"I guess I owe Anna Jo my gratitude. Now you and I have something in common." The satisfied look on Welby's face pleased her. Now that he was a Christian she felt a strong bond with him.

"We have more than gingerbread in common." Leoma took a moment to chew another bite and swallow. "I think it's wonderful that we both share our faith in God now," she said, hoping it didn't make Welby uncomfortable talking so boldly about God and all. It was more important than anything else they could share.

He nodded and took a drink of coffee. "Yes, there is that. But I have so much to learn."

"We all do. No one is perfect and God is patient. I was thrilled when you came forward and made the decision to follow the Lord. And I'm glad you are attending church with Kristina and Dyer. May I be so bold as to ask if you're reading the Bible?"

Welby nodded. "I suppose it's the only way to learn. Only problem is, all I have is the little Bible Louise had, and it got pretty messed up in the tornado."

"I imagine Reverend Gilroy would have an extra one he would give you if you ask."

"I reckon so. Maybe I'll ask him Sunday."

Leoma's heart soared. This was what Leoma had prayed for day and night while she'd still had Dyer. She loved both of Welby's children deeply, and she couldn't bear the thought of them being in his care when he was drinking, and especially before he decided to turn his life around. God was good to answer her prayers. "Well I sure am glad to see you turn your life over to God."

"It wasn't easy. When my grandfather lived with us he had a different idea about religion. I'm afraid he soured me on the whole thing."

"Why?" This was the first time Welby had talked with her about his personal experiences, especially concerning his family and religion, and she was happy to see him open his heart to her.

"When my grandpa came to live with us, he dragged me and my

brothers and sisters down to the front pew every Sunday morning, and he twisted our ears if we so much as sneezed. He sang with his hands raised high in the air and shouted "amen" and "hallelujah" for all the church to hear. Afterward he'd go home and yell hateful things at our mother and us, and drink his hard liquor until he got so mean we'd hide from him. Not a day went by that he didn't tell me I'd burn in the fiery pit of hell if I didn't behave myself. When I married Louise and left home I wasn't yet eighteen, and I swore I'd never set foot in another church."

"Goodness. I don't blame you. What changed your mind?"

"George, Reverend Gilroy, Doc, and you."

It took a moment for Leoma to speak. "Me?"

"I'm sure you know I had a very wrong opinion of you in the beginning."

"Well, that was mutual." Leoma laughed.

"After a while I began to see how genuine you are." Welby gave the sincerest smile Leoma had ever seen. "I mean, George is a great man and I respect him. Same with the preacher and Doc. But I watched you live your faith every day after all your losses and sorrow. Instead of turning bitter against God or putting on an act in the church building on Sunday morning, and cuttin' loose like the devil the rest of the time, you are a perfect example of what a real believer should be like every day. You're patient, gentle, kind and loving."

"I make an effort, but certainly, I'm not perfect." Leoma knew she was far from perfect.

"But you are genuine. Sometimes your face just glows like nothing I've ever seen."

Leoma simply smiled her response, too modest to speak.

Absorbed in conversation, time swept Leoma away. As she shared stories and life experiences with Welby, his deep laughter filled her with joy. He was full of funny stories, and he seemed happy to share his feelings with her. She told him about Glenda's upcoming visit in the spring, and she was thrilled that he looked forward to meeting her friend.

Suddenly she couldn't imagine any other man drinking coffee at her kitchen table, or eating and discussing gingerbread. For the first time since Jeremy's death Leoma wanted to share her life, her home, and her bed with a man. She wanted more than anything to live a life pleasing to God, but she also desired a companion to spend the rest of her life with—a new companion God would choose for her. Was Welby to be that mate? She smiled, pretty sure he was. For the first time since Elizabeth's death Leoma longed to carry another child in her womb, to give birth again, and hold a newborn baby to her breast.

Owning a bookshop could wait.

Leoma was ready to love again and to be loved. She was ready to accept all that God had in store for her. She was even willing to change where she lived if necessary. *Did I not tell you your reward would be great and your blessings would be many if you obeyed me? Though you have suffered much, you have given much. Because of your faith, much will be given to you. I know the desires of your heart.* Leoma recognized the voice that whispered to her soul. Her heart swelled; it took a moment to catch her breath.

Something new and glorious shone on Welby's face when she gazed across the table. Once gray, forlorn, and filled with anguish, his eyes were as beautiful and clear as an aquamarine gemstone. They were filled with compassion, gentleness, and joy.

Smiling Welby extended a hand toward her. She slid her hand across the table until her fingers touched his, then, slowly became entwined. Her insides burst with new love—love she saw clearly reflected in Welby's eyes.

"I'd like to court you, Leoma," Welby said without hesitation. "And I'm wondering, when the time is right, if you might like to be Kristina and Dyer's mommy."

Surprised at the suddenness of Welby's round-about proposal, Leoma gasped then almost giggled. She suddenly thought of Glenda's visit. What a perfect time for a wedding. Her heart filled with so much new excitement she could hardly speak. "I'd love nothing better," she finally said.

Abundant blessings will fill your life with great joy.

Leoma acknowledged the whispered promise with a full heart and great joy. The blessings had already begun.